BALLAD of SWORD & WINE

QIANG JIN JIU

1

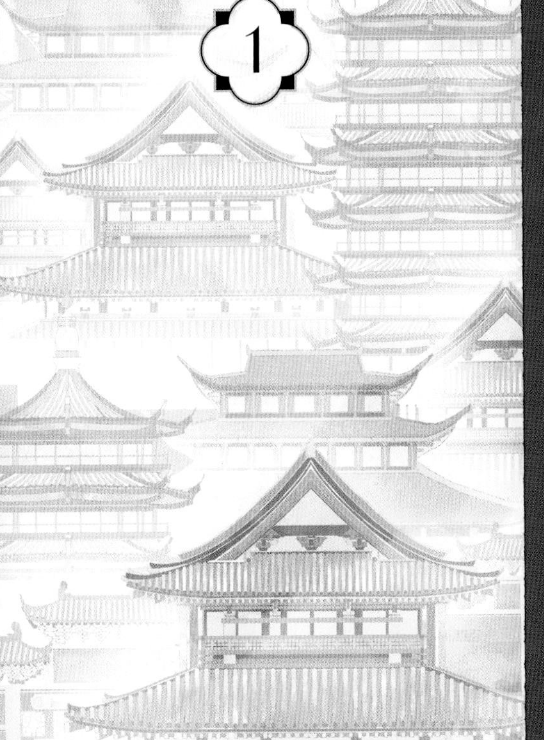

Luoxia Pass
Glacial River
Huaizhou
Quancheng
Chuncheng
Dancheng
Qudu
Cuocheng
Mount Feng
Nanlin Hunting Grounds
Wucheng
Jincheng
Dicheng
Chuancheng
Kailing River
Sea
Juexi

Hongyan Mountains
Libei
Hongjiang River
Chashi Sinkhole
Duanzhou
Dunzhou
Zhongbo
Fanzhou
Dengzhou
Chashi River
Tianfei Watchtower
Cangjun
Bianjun
Qidong
Chijun
Suotian Pass

BALLAD of SWORD & WINE

QIANG JIN JIU

WRITTEN BY
Tang Jiu Qing

ILLUSTRATED BY
St

TRANSLATED BY
XiA, Jia, amixy

Seven Seas Entertainment

Ballad of Sword and Wine: Qiang Jin Jiu (Novel) Vol. 1

Published originally under the title of《将进酒》(Qiang Jin Jiu)
Author©唐酒卿(Tang Jiu Qing)
English edition rights under license granted by 北京晋江原创网络科技有限公司
(Beijing Jinjiang Original Network Technology Co., Ltd.)

Cover & Interior Illustrations: St

Seven Seas press and purchase enquiries can be sent
to Marketing Manager Lauren Hill at press@gomanga.com.
Information regarding the distribution and purchase of digital editions is available
from Digital Manager CK Russell at digital@gomanga.com.

Follow Seven Seas Entertainment online at
sevenseasentertainment.com.

TRANSLATION: XiA, Jia, amixy
ADAPTATION: Dara
COVER & MAP DESIGN: M. A. Lewife
INTERIOR DESIGN & LAYOUT: Clay Gardner
COPY EDITOR: Jehanne Bell
PROOFREADER: Kate Kishi, Hnä
EDITOR: Kelly Quinn Chiu
PREPRESS TECHNICIAN: Melanie Ujimori, Jules Valera
MANAGING EDITOR: Alyssa Scavetta
EDITOR-IN-CHIEF: Julie Davis
PUBLISHER: Lianne Sentar
VICE PRESIDENT: Adam Arnold
PRESIDENT: Jason DeAngelis

ISBN: 979-8-88843-258-7
Printed in Canada
First Printing: June 2024
10 9 8 7 6 5 4 3 2 1

TABLE OF CONTENTS

APPENDIXES

FRIGID WIND

"SHEN WEI, the Prince of Jianxing, suffered a crushing defeat at Chashi River in the northeast. The prefecture of Dunzhou's front line fell into enemy hands, and thirty thousand soldiers were buried alive in the Chashi Sinkhole. You were among them—so how is it that you're the only one left alive?"

Shen Zechuan's eyes were glazed and unfocused. He didn't answer.

The interrogator slammed his hands on the table and leaned in, a vicious glint in his eyes. "Shen Wei had long been in secret communication with the Twelve Tribes of Biansha. He intended to hand the six prefectures of Zhongbo to our enemies on a silver platter. Together with your Biansha allies, you planned to breach the defenses of Qudu from within and without. This is why the Biansha Horsemen spared your life, is it not?"

Shen Zechuan's dry, chapped lips parted as he struggled to understand the interrogator's words. The jut of his throat bobbed as he answered with difficulty, "N-no."

"Shen Wei immolated himself to escape judgment. The Embroidered Uniform Guard has already presented correspondence proving his secret liaisons with the Biansha tribes to the emperor. And yet, boy, you still deny it. Your stubbornness borders on stupidity!" the interrogator snapped.

Shen Zechuan's head felt heavy, his mind dazed. He had no idea how long it'd been since he'd last slept. He felt as though he was hanging from a single thread thousands of feet in the air. If he negligently let go for so much as an instant, he would plummet to the ground and be smashed to pieces.

The interrogator opened Shen Zechuan's written statement and gave it a cursory glance. "You said last night you were able to climb out of the Chashi Sinkhole alive because your elder brother protected you—is that so?"

The scene swam hazily before Shen Zechuan's eyes. The sinkhole was so deep, countless soldiers packed together within. But even as the pile of corpses grew higher and higher beneath their feet, still they could not reach the edge. No matter how they struggled, they couldn't climb out. The Biansha Horsemen surrounded the sinkhole, and the whistle of arrows mingled with the frigid night wind. The blood rose up to his calves as the anguished wails and final gasps of the dying crowded close to his ears.

Shen Zechuan's breaths came fast and shallow, and he shivered in his seat. He clutched at his hair despite himself, unable to prevent a strangled sob from escaping his throat. "You're lying."

The interrogator held up the statement and flicked it with a finger. "Your brother is Shen Zhouji, the eldest lawful son of the Prince of Jianxing. This brother of yours abandoned thirty thousand soldiers before the Chashi Sinkhole and attempted to stealthily flee with his own private guards. The Biansha Horsemen lassoed him with a rope and dragged him to death on the public road along the Chashi River. He was dead by the time the Twelve Tribes of Biansha slaughtered those soldiers in the sinkhole. It's impossible for him to have saved you."

Shen Zechuan's mind was awhirl. The interrogator's voice sounded so far away; all he could hear were the unending wails.

Which way out? Where are the reinforcements?

The dead crowded against the dead. Putrid, decaying flesh pressed down on his hands. Mu-ge[1] shielded him from above, sprawled over the bloodied corpses. Shen Zechuan listened to Mu-ge's ragged breaths, and the cries that escaped his throat were those of despair.

"Your brother is invincible." Ji Mu struggled to squeeze out a smile, but tears were streaming down his face and his voice hitched as he continued, "I'm an impregnable fortress! Hang on just a bit longer; it'll be fine. Reinforcements will arrive soon. When they come, we'll go home and get our parents, and I need to find your sister-in-law..."

"Come clean with it!" the interrogator barked, banging on the table.

Shen Zechuan began to struggle as if to break free of invisible shackles, but the Embroidered Uniform Guard swarmed over and pinned him to the table.

"Since you arrived in our Imperial Prison, I've taken your youth into account and haven't meted out severe punishment. But it seems you don't know what's good for you—don't blame us if we're ruthless. Men, carry out his punishment!"

Shen Zechuan's arms were bound with rope; they dragged him to an open space in the chamber. Someone set down a bench with a clatter and tied his legs to it. The burly man beside him lifted his broad wooden staff, hefted it briefly in his hands, and swung it down.

"I'll ask you one more time." The interrogator brushed at the foam on his tea with the lid of his cup and took a few unhurried sips. "Did Shen Wei collude with our enemies and commit treason?"

---

1 *Ge, a term of address for one's older brother. When added as a suffix, it can be an affectionate address for any older male.*

Shen Zechuan gritted his teeth and refused to yield. He shouted between strikes of the heavy staff, "N-no!"

The interrogator set his cup aside. "The Shen Clan wouldn't be in this position today if you'd shown such fortitude on the battlefield. Continue!"

"Shen Wei didn't collude with the enemy..." Shen Zechuan rasped, his head hanging and his voice hoarse. He was crumbling, bit by bit.

"We suffered a crushing defeat at the Battle of Chashi River all because Shen Wei recklessly met the enemy head-on. After that loss, he had a chance to turn the tide at the Dunzhou front line—yet despite his great advantage in strength over the enemy troops, he withdrew his forces. Because of this, the three cities of Duanzhou Prefecture fell into enemy hands. Ten of thousands of common citizens lost their lives on the edge of Biansha scimitars."

The interrogator heaved a lengthy sigh and continued with rueful disdain, "All six prefectures of Zhongbo were bathed in blood. Shen Wei took his troops and retreated south once again. But the battle he fought in Dengzhou Prefecture was the most suspect of all. The Chijun Commandery Garrison from Qidong had already crossed Tianfei Watchtower to provide assistance—yet he abandoned this pincer attack. Instead, he mobilized thousands of cavalry to escort his own family to the city of Dancheng. The entire front line at Dengzhou Prefecture collapsed without these troops. Was this not intentional sabotage? If it weren't for the Libei Armored Cavalry racing three days and nights to cross the Glacial River, the Biansha Horsemen would even now be at the gates of Qudu!"

Shen Zechuan was drenched in cold sweat, his consciousness fading. The interrogator flung the statement at him in contempt, and it slapped against the back of his head.

"Rather a dog than a man of Zhongbo, eh? Shen Wei is a sinner before Great Zhou. Do you yet deny it? You have no choice but to accept your guilt!"

Shen Zechuan was in agony, half of his body numb. He lay collapsed on the bench, the paper fluttering before his eyes. The ink strokes on it were clear, every character like the humiliating lash of a whip on his face, announcing to the world:

Shen Wei betrayed his country. He's less than a dog.

They had left the six prefectures of Zhongbo piled high with bodies. To date, the corpses at the bottom of the Chashi Sinkhole remained uncollected. Everyone in the cities of Dunzhou who might have collected them had been massacred.

Shen Wei had burned himself to his death, it was true—but this debt of blood must be borne by a living person. Shen Wei had a harem of wives and concubines who bore him a bounty of sons, but every one of them had perished when the Biansha Horsemen entered Dunzhou. Only because Shen Zechuan was of low birth, raised far from the family, had he managed to escape with his life.

They dragged Shen Zechuan back to his cell, his heels leaving twin trails of blood in their wake. He faced the wall and gazed at the small, narrow window. Outside, the frigid wind howled, and the snow came pelting down. The night, black as pitch, stretched without end.

In his head was primal chaos. Amid the cries of the wind, his mind wandered back to the sinkhole.

Ji Mu was dying. His breathing had grown labored. Blood dripped down his armor onto the back of Shen Zechuan's neck, where it quickly turned cold. The wails around him had quieted, leaving only the groans of unendurable pain and the bellows of the biting wind.

Shen Zechuan lay nose-to-nose with a dead man whose features were no longer recognizable. His legs were pinned under the weight of human bodies; a shield dug painfully into his ribs. All he could smell as he gasped for air was the thick stench of blood. He gritted his teeth, tears streaming down his face, but he couldn't afford to cry aloud. In despair, he stared down at the face trampled beyond recognition, yet could not tell if this was a soldier he knew.

"Ge," Shen Zechuan sobbed softly, "I...I'm scared..."

Ji Mu's throat bobbed. He gently patted Shen Zechuan's head. "It's all right... We'll be okay."

Shen Zechuan heard the singing of the soldiers at death's door. The gale tore apart the sound of their songs and sent tattered pieces fluttering away into the frigid night.

"Battle in the city south... Death within the city north...

Graveless, left exposed to rot... May the crows feed."[2]

"Ge," Shen Zechuan whispered beneath him. "I'll carry you on my back... Ge."

Ji Mu's body was like a bent and broken shield. He smiled and said in a hoarse voice, "I can walk on my own."

"Were you struck by an arrow?"

"No." Ji Mu's tears had dried up. He said breezily, "Those Biansha baldies have no aim."

Shen Zechuan's fingers were soaked in flesh and blood. He wiped his face with some difficulty. "Shiniang[3] made dumplings. Once we get home, we can eat as many as we like."

Ji Mu sighed. "I'm a slow eater. Don't...snatch."

Shen Zechuan gave a firm nod beneath him.

---

2 *"The Eighteen Cymbal Songs: Battle in the City South" is a yuefu poem, or folk song, from the Han dynasty about those who have perished on the battlefield. It describes the cruelty of war and expresses the poet's opposition to it, asserting that the common folks are only a sacrifice of war.*

3 *Shiniang, a term of address for the wife of one's shifu, or martial master.*

The snow gradually blanketed Ji Mu's body. He seemed very tired, so quiet was his voice, and he hadn't even the strength to move his fingers. The song was sung achingly slow, and when it reached the line, "*the valiant rider died in the fray*," Ji Mu closed his eyes.

"I...I'll give Ge my money too, to get married..." said Shen Zechuan.

"Ge."

"Ge."

Ji Mu remained silent. As if he were weary of listening to Shen Zechuan speak and couldn't help but drift off.

Shen Zechuan trembled all over. He didn't remember when the Biansha Horsemen left or how he had clawed his way out. When he finally pushed himself up and pulled himself out, it was to dead silence amid the heavy snow. The stacked corpses cushioning his knees had the look of discarded burlap sacks.

Shen Zechuan turned to glance down and choked with sobs.

Ji Mu's back had been pierced with such a dense cluster of arrows that his body was like a curled hedgehog. All his blood had trickled down onto Shen Zechuan's back, but Shen Zechuan hadn't realized it. The thunder of horses' hooves came swiftly toward him like the looming storm.

Shen Zechuan shivered and jolted violently awake.

He felt like retching. But then he realized—his wrists had been firmly bound, and a burlap sack filled with soil was pressing down on his body.

The sack became heavier and heavier as it crushed his chest. He couldn't make a sound. This was an old prison trick habitually inflicted on prisoners whose jailers would rather see them dead than alive. By smothering them with an earth-filled sack, they would leave no trace of injury. Had Shen Zechuan not woken when he did, by daybreak, he would've been but a corpse gone cold.

Someone was trying to kill him.

DEATH BY FLOGGING

IN THE GLOOM of the Imperial Prison, Shen Zechuan desperately twisted his wrists, but his hands were cold, his lungs were beginning to ache, and the rope was so tight it was futile. The sack of earth pressed down on his chest. He felt as if he'd been thrown into a deep pond—his ears rang and his breath came in frantic bursts, like he was drowning.

Shen Zechuan shifted his gaze to the candlelight beyond the bars.

In the hall, several members of the Embroidered Uniform Guard were drinking and shouting as they played a finger-guessing game, too preoccupied to spare Shen Zechuan a glance. The sack of earth nailed him to the crude straw mat, and suffocating nausea engulfed him like floodwater. His vision swam. Shen Zechuan raised his head and gritted his teeth to move his legs. They had been flogged numb; he felt nothing when he raised them. He placed his foot against the left corner of the wooden bed where vermin had eaten away its sturdiness; on his first day, he'd damaged it just by sitting down. He struggled to gather a breath.

Shen Zechuan braced himself and kicked at that rotten corner with all his strength. His legs were so weak the bed didn't even groan; the planks hadn't moved an inch. Cold sweat streamed down his back, soaking his shirt.

He yearned to live. Shen Zechuan whimpered frantically; he bit his tongue until it bled and kicked the planks again. Ji Mu's mangled, barely recognizable body was the horsewhip at his back, spurring him on. His brother's voice echoed in his ears.

He *must* live.

Shen Zechuan struck the plank furiously until he finally heard a dull *thud*. Half the slats collapsed, and he slid off to one side, the heavy sack tumbling down beside him. He hit the ground and gasped as if breaking through the water's surface.

The ground of his cell was icy. Shen Zechuan's injured legs were useless, so he propped himself up with his elbows. Sweat trickled down the bridge of his nose. Despite the cold of the prison, his body burned as if his insides were coming to a boil. At last, he put his head down to dry heave.

Shen Wei deserved to die.

There were one hundred and twenty thousand troops in Zhongbo, divided among the six prefectures to form a defensive perimeter. After the defeat at Chashi River, the Biansha Horsemen had invaded Dunzhou. It was as the interrogator said: at that point, there had still been a chance to turn things around. Not only did Shen Wei have a well-trained and powerful army, he had ample provisions and the authority to deploy the garrison troops in the three cities of Duanzhou. Yet, to everyone's surprise, he had abandoned the prefecture and cowered back into the Dunzhou Prince's Manor.

This retreat was prelude to the fall of Zhongbo. The Biansha Horsemen slaughtered Duanzhou's three cities, after which the garrison, their morale shattered, fled south in a panic. Everyone had thought Shen Wei would make his stand against the Twelve Tribes of Biansha in Dunzhou—yet he had taken to the road again at first news of their arrival.

Time and time again the Zhongbo army had retreated in defeat while the Biansha Horsemen cut through the six prefectures' territories like a steel blade. They traveled light, feeding on the spoils of war as they advanced, until they were within eight hundred li[4] of Qudu, the capital of the Zhou empire.

Had Shen Wei implemented a scorched-earth policy during his retreat and burned the granaries in the cities he left behind, there would have been nothing left for the enemy, and no way for the Biansha Horsemen to advance so far. The invaders carried no supplies and relied solely on the cities they conquered to replenish their provisions. If the grain had been ash, the Biansha Horsemen would have starved.

A starving soldier could not fight. The Libei Armored Cavalry could have seized the chance, crossed the Glacial River, and intercepted the Biansha Tribes' retreat while the garrison troops from Qidong's five commanderies sealed off their escape route from Tianfei Watchtower. The Biansha scimitars would've been trapped like turtles in a tub; they wouldn't have survived the winter.

But Shen Wei had done none of that.

Not only did he abandon any resistance, he abandoned the city granaries, still intact. The enemy fed on Zhou grain as they razed Zhou lands. Thanks to Shen Wei, the Biansha horses were well-fed enough to herd Zhongbo's common folk and captured soldiers all the way to Chashi River, where the Horsemen butchered them all in a single night.

Shen Zechuan had escaped by the skin of his teeth. Now that Qudu wanted to settle accounts, it was obvious that Shen Wei's deployment orders had been unusually sloppy. All signs pointed to his collusion with Biansha. Yet to escape justice, Shen Wei had

---

4 里, *li*, *an ancient measure of length. One li is approximately five hundred meters.*

not only immolated himself but destroyed any relevant documents along with him. Even the Embroidered Uniform Guard, notoriously effective and efficient in their investigations, were at their wits' end. If the emperor wanted the truth, his only recourse was to get answers, at any cost, from the only remaining individual who might know: Shen Zechuan.

However, the son of a dancer in Duanzhou—Shen Wei's eighth son of common birth—had no place in the clan, whether in rank or age; the man had too many sons. Shen Zechuan had been sent away to Duanzhou long ago to fend for himself, and Shen Wei had likely forgotten this son's existence.

And yet, someone wanted to kill him.

It was no secret that many wanted him dead. He had been brought to Qudu as a scapegoat for his father. As the last member of the Shen Clan in Zhongbo, he was obligated to pay his father's debts. Once his interrogation in the Imperial Prison was over, the emperor would no doubt offer Shen Zechuan's death as appeasement to the souls of the thirty thousand soldiers who lost their lives at Chashi River.

Even so, it shouldn't happen through an assassination in the dead of night.

Shen Zechuan spat blood and wiped his lips with his thumb. If Shen Wei had indeed conspired with the enemy, then Shen Zechuan's death was only a matter of time. Why bother to assassinate an insignificant common son? Someone in the capital was worried about the interrogation—and if that was the case, then there must be more to the defeat of Shen Wei's troops than met the eye.

But Shen Zechuan knew nothing.

He had a shifu[5] in Duanzhou. His brother, Ji Mu, had been his shifu's only son. To Shen Zechuan, Shen Wei was merely the Prince

5 *Shifu, a term of address for one's martial master or teacher.*

of Jianxing. Shen Zechuan had nothing to do with him, and absolutely no idea whether Shen Wei had committed treason.

Nevertheless, he had to deny it. Sprawled on the frigid ground of his cell, he felt even more alert than during the day. He knew he was a felon held by the Embroidered Uniform Guard under imperial edict. All arrest warrants, summons, and official documents came directly from the top, consigning him straight from the hands of Xiao Jiming, the Heir of Libei, to the Imperial Prison. They had bypassed even the Joint Tribunal of the Three Judicial Offices: the Ministry of Justice, the Court of Judicial Review, and the Chief Surveillance Bureau. It was clear that the emperor was determined to get to the bottom of this. Who had the guts to risk silencing him before the emperor could complete his interrogation?

The bitter wind howled at the window. In the darkness, Shen Zechuan stared at the wall; he dared not close his eyes again.

Dawn had scarcely broken when Shen Zechuan was escorted back to the hall. A snowstorm raged outside. Ji Lei, the interrogator, had been nothing but grim these past few days. Yet now, he was all smiles as he waited deferentially beside a wooden armchair and served tea with both hands.

A fair-faced, beardless old eunuch sat in the chair, resting his eyes. He wore the official hat of a eunuch in velvet for the wintry weather, with an ornately embroidered mandarin square on his robe—a gourd at its center to mark the season. His overcoat was draped over his shoulders, and he held an exquisite plum blossom hand warmer of gold and jade. Sensing movement, he opened his eyes and looked at Shen Zechuan.

"Godfather," Ji Lei bent to say, "Here is the filthy descendant of the Prince of Jianxing."

Pan Rugui eyed Shen Zechuan. "What happened here?" Pan Rugui was not asking how Shen Zechuan had ended up dirty and stinking, but why Ji Lei hadn't yet pried the hows and wherefores from him.

Ji Lei's forehead ran with sweat, but he didn't dare wipe it. Still hunched, he responded, "The boy is ignorant. He's been delirious since they brought him back from Zhongbo. Who knows who put him up to it, but he refuses to confess."

"A felon, by His Majesty's own decree." Pan Rugui did not accept the tea. "A child no older than sixteen sent to the famed Imperial Prison to be personally interrogated by your esteemed self, and you can't get a confession out of him."

Still holding the teacup, Ji Lei smiled sheepishly. "His importance is precisely why I didn't dare use harsher methods without authorization. He was already ill when he arrived. If he dies in our hands, the case against Shen Wei will go cold."

Pan Rugui scrutinized Shen Zechuan for a moment. "We are all our master's dogs. There's no point keeping a dog whose fangs have dulled. I know you have your own challenges, but this is part of your duty. His Majesty wishes to see him now; this is his way of showing consideration for the Embroidered Uniform Guard. What do you have to complain about?"

Ji Lei hurriedly prostrated himself. "It is as Godfather says. This son has been duly castigated."

Pan Rugui snorted. "Clean him up. He can't appear before His Majesty covered in filth."

An attendant led Shen Zechuan away to wash and bandage his injured legs, then gave him a set of clean cotton clothes. He allowed himself to be shuffled about; he was in such pain he could barely walk, and it took quite an effort even to step up into the carriage.

As Shen Zechuan departed, Pan Rugui finally accepted the cup from Ji Lei. Staring after the carriage, he asked, "Is he truly the last of the Shen Clan?"

"Yes. The sole survivor of the Chashi Sinkhole. The Heir of Libei captured him personally. He was detained in the Libei Armored Cavalry's prisoner wagon the whole way and had no contact with anyone else."

Pan Rugui sipped his cold tea. After a long time, he gave Ji Lei a smile that didn't reach his eyes. "The Heir of Libei certainly is discreet."

Shen Zechuan stepped down from the carriage and let the guards hustle him down a long path. The heavy snow blew into his face, and the eunuch leading the way hurried along without any unnecessary chatter.

When Pan Rugui arrived before Mingli Hall, his arrival had already been announced. The junior eunuch waiting under the eaves stepped forward and took Pan Rugui's overcoat, helped him shrug on his outer robe, and took over the hand warmer. Pan Rugui kowtowed by the door and said, "Your Majesty, this lowly servant has brought the boy."

There was a pause. A low, unhurried voice rang out. "Bring him in."

Shen Zechuan's breath hitched, but they were already dragging him inside. Though there was incense burning, it wasn't stifling. He heard intermittent coughs and caught a glimpse of feet lined up on both sides of the hall.

The Xiande Emperor was dressed in a deep blue day robe that couldn't hide his frailty; illness had constantly plagued him in the three years since he had ascended the throne. His pallid complexion made his oblong face look all the more gentle and delicate.

"Ji Lei has been trying him for several days now." The Xiande Emperor glanced at Ji Lei, who was kneeling at the back of the hall. "Have you discovered the truth?"

Ji Lei kowtowed. "To answer Your Majesty, this boy's words are incoherent and his story is full of holes. Nothing he's said can be believed; all of his words are contradictory."

"Present his testimony," the emperor commanded.

Ji Lei produced a written statement from within his robe and handed it respectfully to Pan Rugui, who in turn hurried forward to present it to the emperor with all due reverence.

The Xiande Emperor read it through. When he reached the part about the Chashi Sinkhole, he covered his mouth and began to cough. He refused to let Pan Rugui help him; instead, he wiped the blood from his lips himself with a handkerchief. "Thirty thousand soldiers lost their lives in that sinkhole," he said solemnly. "Had Shen Wei lived, he would have suffered the wrath of all!"

Shen Zechuan closed his eyes as his heart began to pound; he already knew what was coming.

"Raise your head!"

His breathing quickened. His palms braced against the floor were numb. Shen Zechuan raised his head slowly, his eyes carefully landing on the Xiande Emperor's boots.

The emperor looked down at him. "As Shen Wei's son and the sole survivor of the Chashi Sinkhole, what do you have to say?"

Shen Zechuan's eyes grew red at the rims. He shivered with wordless sobs.

The emperor's expression never changed. "Speak!"

As Shen Zechuan raised his head, tears rolled down his cheeks. He glanced up for a fleeting moment, then kowtowed hard again, his shoulders shaking as the sobs rose in his throat. "Your Majesty,

Your Majesty! My father was devoted to the nation and his countrymen in Zhongbo. He was too ashamed to face them after his losses on the battlefield. That's why he set himself on fire—to atone!"

"What nonsense!" the emperor barked. "If he was devoted to the nation, why did he retreat time and time again?"

Shen Zechuan's voice was hoarse from weeping. "My father sent all his sons into the field. My eldest brother, Shen Zhouji, was tortured to death by the Biansha rider who dragged him behind his horse along the Chashi public road! If it were not for undivided loyalty, why risk his own heir?"

"You dare bring up Chashi! Shen Zhouji fled from the front lines. His crime is unpardonable!"

Shen Zechuan looked up at the emperor, tears leaving tracks down his cheeks. "The battle at Chashi was a bloodbath," he rasped. "My eldest brother might be incompetent, but he defended Chashi for three days. In those three days, vital intelligence was able to reach Qidong and Libei. If it weren't for those three days..." He was so choked with emotion he couldn't go on.

The emperor reread the statement in his hand. The hall was quiet save for the sound of Shen Zechuan's sobs. In the interminable silence, Shen Zechuan dug his fingernails into flesh.

Abruptly, the emperor let out a long sigh. "Did Shen Wei collude with the enemy?"

"Never." Shen Zechuan's voice was resolute.

The emperor set down the statement and declared in a voice that had gone frigid: "This cunning boy attempts to deceive his sovereign. He must not be allowed to live. Pan Rugui—have him flogged to death at Duancheng Gate!"

"Yes, Your Majesty!" Pan Rugui immediately bowed and retreated.

Shen Zechuan went cold, as if doused with a basin of icy water. Struggle as he might, it was useless; the guards clamped his mouth shut as they dragged him out of Mingli Hall.

RAPTOR

PAN RUGUI STRODE toward Duancheng Gate. The Embroidered Uniform Guard flanked the path, silent as cicadas in winter. The instant Pan Rugui announced the emperor's edict, the guards began their work. They gagged Shen Zechuan and swiftly wrapped him in a thick cotton-padded garment, forcing him face down on the ground.

In the freezing wind, Pan Rugui leaned over to observe Shen Zechuan's predicament. He raised his fingers to delicately cover his lips and coughed a few times before murmuring, "You're a mere child, yet you had the gall to put on such a mawkish display before His Majesty. If you had truthfully confessed Shen Wei's treason, you might have stood a chance."

Shen Zechuan shut his eyes tightly. Cold sweat soaked his clothes.

Pan Rugui straightened. "Begin."

The guards shouted in unison, "Begin!"

A thunderous roar followed: "Strike!"

Before the word was out, the iron-wrapped staff with its hooked barbs whistled down onto Shen Zechuan's back.

After three strikes, another shout: "Harder!" The searing pain of the blows built into a fire, until he couldn't move except to bite desperately on the gag between his teeth. The blood in his throat pooled faster than he could swallow, and the coppery taste of it coated his mouth. Shen Zechuan clung to his last breaths as dripping sweat stung his wide-open eyes.

The sky was overcast, and the heavy snow fell like catkins.

Flogging was not a task assigned to just anyone. As the saying went, "faint at twenty, lame at fifty"—to do it well required skill. It was handed down the generations, a family trade. Moreover, this job required not just physical prowess, but also a discerning eye. The experienced flogger needed only glance at the expressions of the high-ranking eunuchs from the Directorate of Ceremonial to determine who should receive superficial wounds but serious internal injuries and vice versa.

The emperor's decree was death by flogging, and Pan Rugui seemed to show no sympathy. There was no chance of an about-face; this person had to die. Thus the Embroidered Uniform Guard held nothing back—they would make certain Shen Zechuan was dead within fifty strikes.

Pan Rugui, minding the time, noticed Shen Zechuan had already gone motionless, his head lolling. Placing a hand on the hand warmer, he was about to give further instruction when he saw an umbrella drifting toward them on the path, hiding a beauty in royal garb.

The dark clouds on Pan Rugui's face were instantly dispersed and replaced by a smile. Though he did not personally step out to receive her, the quick-witted junior eunuch beside him rushed over to offer his arm.

"My sincere respects to the third lady. It's such a cold day. If Her Majesty the Empress Dowager has any instruction, surely someone else would do to carry the message," Pan Rugui said, coming forward.

Hua Xiangyi raised her hand lightly to stay the Embroidered Uniform Guard. Delicate and beautiful, she had been raised at the empress dowager's side since childhood and was said to bear quite a resemblance to her aunt in her youth. Although she was addressed as the third lady of the Dicheng Hua Clan here in Qudu, everyone knew she was a distinguished lady of the palace. Even the emperor doted on her as if she were truly his younger sister.

"Gonggong,[6] is this the boy from Zhongbo's Shen Clan, Shen Zechuan?" Hua Xiangyi said in a soft, measured voice.

"The very same," Pan Rugui replied, keeping pace with Hua Xiangyi's steps. "His Majesty has issued the decree to flog him to death."

"His Majesty spoke in anger earlier," Hua Xiangyi said. "If Shen Zechuan dies, we'll never get to the bottom of Shen Wei's treason. Her Majesty the Empress Dowager arrived at Mingli Hall a little while ago. His Majesty heeded her advice, and he has calmed himself."

"Oh, my," Pan Rugui exclaimed. "His Majesty always listens to the empress dowager's counsel. He was in such a terrible rage earlier, I dared not say a word."

"His Majesty's decree was 'flogging.' Haven't you done so?" Hua Xiangyi said, smiling at Pan Rugui.

Pan Rugui took a few more steps and smiled in return. "Of course. I was in such a rush earlier. As soon as I heard the word *flog*, I made sure to give him a good beating. How should we deal with him now?"

"Keep him in the Imperial Prison until His Majesty wishes to question him again. Preserving the boy's life is of utmost importance. I'm counting on Gonggong to inform Lord Ji to take good care of him," Hua Xiangyi said, her gaze sweeping over Shen Zechuan.

"Say no more," Pan Rugui replied. "Ji Lei wouldn't think of turning a deaf ear to the third lady's wishes. The weather is cold, and the ground is slippery. Xiaofuzi, be sure to hold the third lady steady."

---

6 *Gonggong, a term of address for a eunuch.*

The moment Hua Xiangyi had gone, Pan Rugui turned to the two rows of guards. "His Majesty gave the order to flog, and we've done what's required. Drag him back. You heard the third lady; it is the empress dowager's wish. Tell Ji Lei: everyone with a hand in this case is leagues above his level. If something happens to the boy on his watch..." Pan Rugui coughed once. "Even the Jade Emperor himself couldn't save him."

Xiaofuzi returned to support Pan Rugui by the arm. The long stretch of road was empty, but still he furtively whispered, "Lao-zuzong,[7] if we let him go like this, will His Majesty not blame us later?"

"His Majesty knows in his heart that the blame does not lie with us," Pan Rugui said, pacing through the snow. Snowflakes squeezed their way under his fur collar. "A promise is worth a thousand gold; a sovereign reneging on his word does not bode well. His Majesty has suffered another bout of illness from the stress of the Biansha invasion. He will accede to anything the empress dowager asks these days. To please her, the emperor is even considering elevating the third lady to a princess—never mind sparing one man's life." Pan Rugui looked over at Xiaofuzi. "And when have you ever seen the empress dowager change *her* orders?"

In every case, the real master was the one who stood by their word.

Shen Zechuan was delirious with fever. One moment, he saw Ji Mu dying before him, the next, he saw himself still living in Duanzhou.

The wind brushed the banners. His shiniang lifted the curtain and stepped out carrying a white porcelain bowl of plump dumplings

---

7 *Lao-zuzong, literally "old ancestor." An intimate and respectful term of address from a junior eunuch to a more senior eunuch.*

with thin skins. "Go tell your brother to come home!" she called. "He can't sit still for a second. Tell him to hurry back and eat!"

Climbing over the veranda railing, Shen Zechuan bounded over to his shiniang and bit the dumpling right off the chopsticks before running off. It was so hot it scalded his tongue. As he went out the door, huffing to cool his mouth, he spotted his shifu, Ji Gang, on the stairs and squatted down beside him.

Ji Gang looked up with a grunt from the rock he was grinding in his hands. "Silly boy, a dumpling is worth hardly anything. You treat it like some kind of treasure! Go get your brother, and the three of us will go to Yuanyang Tavern for a proper meal."

Before Shen Zechuan could answer, his shiniang was pulling Ji Gang's ear. "Turning your nose up at my dumplings, huh? Good for you. If you're so rich, what are you doing with a wife? Take these silly boys and go live on your own!"

Shen Zechuan laughed as he leapt down the stairs, waving to his shifu and shiniang before racing out of the alley to find Ji Mu. But it was snowing heavily; Shen Zechuan couldn't find any trace of him. The longer he walked, the colder he became.

"Ge!" Shen Zechuan called into the storm. "Ji Mu! It's time to come home!"

The sound of hoofbeats rose around him; snow obstructed his vision. Shen Zechuan was trapped in the thunder of hooves, but he couldn't see anyone. The sound of slaughter exploded in his ears and warm blood splattered his face. Shen Zechuan felt stabs of pain in both legs as an overwhelming force pinned him down. He saw the dead man's face inches away from his. The deluge of arrows whistled in the wind. The man on his back was heavy, and something warm and sticky trickled down his neck and across his cheeks.

This time, he knew what it was.

Shen Zechuan woke trembling, drenched in sweat yet shivering uncontrollably with cold. He sprawled over the wooden slats of the cot as his eyes struggled to adjust to the darkness. He wasn't alone in the cell. An attendant had been cleaning up, and now lit the oil lamp.

Shen Zechuan's throat was painful with thirst. The attendant seemed to anticipate this and set a bowl of cold water on the bed. Waves of sweat and chills washed over him as he slowly nudged the bowl toward himself, spilling half the contents in the process. Neither spoke. The attendant withdrew and left Shen Zechuan in the cell.

He slipped in and out of consciousness. The night dragged on without end; no matter how long he waited, dawn never came.

When the attendant again came to change Shen Zechuan's bandages, his mind was clearer. Ji Lei looked at him through the bars and said coldly, "You're one lucky bastard. A scourge truly never dies. The empress dowager spared your life; I suppose you don't know why."

Shen Zechuan lowered his head and kept still.

"I know your shifu is Ji Gang, the outcast of the land," Ji Lei said. "We were fellow disciples twenty years ago and served together in the Embroidered Uniform Guard here in Qudu. You probably don't know, but he was once a vice commander of the Guard and a third-rank official. I'm trained in the same Ji-Style Boxing he practiced."

Shen Zechuan raised his head and looked at Ji Lei, who opened the door of the cell and waited for the attendant to leave. Once they were alone, Ji Lei sat at the edge of Shen Zechuan's bed.

"Later, he got into trouble bad enough to warrant losing his head. But the late emperor was benevolent and spared his life—just banished him beyond the pass." Ji Lei propped his elbows on his knees and grinned at Shen Zechuan from the shadows. "Your shifu is no talented man; he's just a worthless wretch with good luck. You know how he survived? Just like you did—because of your shiniang. You probably don't even know who she really is. Her name is Hua Pingting, from the same Hua Clan of Dicheng that produced the current empress dowager. It was for your shiniang's sake that the empress dowager spared your life today."

Ji Lei leaned in and whispered, "But who'd have known your shiniang already met her end in the chaos of the attack? Ji Gang really is a worthless wretch. To lose his father twenty years ago, then lose his wife and son now. Do you know who's to blame? You must know better than anyone—the culprit is Shen Wei!"

Shen Zechuan's breath hitched.

"Shen Wei abandoned the defensive line at Chashi River; he allowed the Biansha Horsemen in. A scimitar slit your shiniang's throat, but what she suffered before her last breath would make Ji Gang wish he'd died instead."

He continued mercilessly, "Duanzhou fell into enemy hands. You said your brother saved you." Ji Lei sat up and studied the back of his hand. "Ji Mu, huh? Ji Gang raised you, and Ji Mu was your older brother: Ji Gang's only son, the only continuation of Ji Gang's bloodline, and the Ji Clan's only descendant. But because of Shen Wei—because of *you*—he's dead too. Pierced by a thousand arrows, his remains forgotten in the sinkhole, humiliated and trampled under the hooves of Biansha horses. If Ji Gang's still alive, I wonder how he felt as he collected his son's body."

Shen Zechuan surged up, but Ji Lei easily shoved him back down and held him there.

"Shen Wei colluded with the enemy and betrayed his country. That is a debt you must shoulder. When you plead for your life today, know that countless ghosts of Zhongbo are wailing for justice.

When you dream tonight, seek your shiniang and your shifu among the dead. You might be alive, but it's a life more agonizing than death. Can you forgive Shen Wei for all this? If you exonerate him, then you'll be letting your shifu and his entire family down. Ji Gang raised and nurtured you. How could you disgrace him with such a disloyal and unfilial act?

"Besides, even if you drag out a feeble existence, not a soul in this world will pity you. Now that you're in Qudu, you've become Shen Wei. The rage of the common folk cannot be quelled; countless people hate you to the core. Your death is a foregone conclusion. Rather than dying for nothing, why not speak frankly to His Majesty and come clean about Shen Wei's crimes? It would comfort your shifu's departed spirit."

He suddenly stopped. Shen Zechuan, still pinned to the wooden bed, smiled up at him, his deathly pallor gone frostier still.

"Shen Wei did not collude with the enemy." Shen Zechuan bit each word out through clenched teeth. "Shen Wei *never* colluded with the enemy!"

Ji Lei lifted Shen Zechuan from the bed and slammed him against the wall. Bits of earth and dust rained down, and the impact was enough to set Shen Zechuan coughing.

"There are so many ways to kill you," Ji Lei said. "Unappreciative little bastard. You managed to escape death by the skin of your teeth. Do you think you can survive past today?" He kicked the cell door open and dragged Shen Zechuan into the hall.

"I'm impartial in my duties and serve at the pleasure of the empress dowager. But there are plenty in Great Zhou who can do as they please without consequence. If you're so hopelessly foolish, I'll honor your wishes. You want to die so badly? Well, someone's here to kill you!"

The city gates of Qudu opened wide, and a line of pitch-black armored cavalry stormed through like rolling thunder. Ji Lei dragged Shen Zechuan along the main road to meet them. The Embroidered Uniform Guard scattered, and the packed crowd parted to make way for the horses.

A Libei gyrfalcon circled overhead as the clang of armor reverberated in Shen Zechuan's chest. The rumble of hooves drew nearer. He opened his eyes and saw the horse in the lead charging straight for him. The steed beneath the heavy armor was a ferocious beast, huffing out hot clouds of air. It skidded to a stop just as it threatened to crash into them and reared back dangerously. Before its front hooves hit the ground, its rider had already leapt off.

Ji Lei stepped forward, calling, "Welcome, Xiao—"

The rider didn't spare Ji Lei a glance. He marched straight up to Shen Zechuan, who barely had time to shift his shackles before the rider kicked him square in the chest, swift as lightning. The kick was so powerful he had no chance to steel himself; the impact sent him tumbling. Shen Zechuan opened his mouth and vomited until nothing was left but blood.

LAST DESCENDANT

SHEN ZECHUAN WATCHED a pair of soldier's boots crush snow underfoot as the stranger approached. When he was close enough, he nudged Shen Zechuan's face up with a toe, tainting the leather with blood.

"Shen Wei is your old man?" The voice was muffled beneath the helmet.

Crimson seeped through Shen Zechuan's clenched teeth despite his best effort to keep it in; even when he pressed his hands over his mouth, he couldn't hide it. He didn't answer.

The stranger looked down at him. "I asked you a question."

Shen Zechuan lowered his head with a muttered affirmative, mouth filled with blood.

"He's the eighth son of Shen Wei," Ji Lei offered, seeing an opening. "His name is Shen..."

The stranger removed his helmet, revealing a youthful face. The gyrfalcon wheeling overhead came to land on his shoulder, its wings scattering a puff of fine snow. He looked at Shen Zechuan as if looking at a pair of worn-out shoes. It was hard to tell if his gaze contained disdain or loathing, but it was as frigid and cutting as a blade.

Shen Zechuan didn't know him—but he recognized the Libei Armored Cavalry.

When Shen Wei had fled pathetically westward, Cizhou became Zhongbo's last line of defense. The Libei Armored Cavalry had sped south, and the Heir of Libei, Shizi[8] Xiao Jiming, led his troops through heavy snow for three days without rest, crossing the Glacial River straight toward Cizhou. To the astonishment of all, Shen Wei failed to defend Cizhou, and Libei's troops had found themselves besieged. If Xiao Jiming hadn't had reinforcements on the way, it would have ended in another bloodbath.

Libei had loathed the Shen Clan of Zhongbo since that day. This youth was not Xiao Jiming—but he had a gyrfalcon on his shoulder and rode freely in Qudu. He could only be the Prince of Libei's youngest son and Xiao Jiming's brother: Xiao Chiye.

Ji Lei had a mind to fan the flames, but seeing Deputy General Zhao Hui looming behind Xiao Chiye, he kept his mouth shut.

Xiao Chiye tossed his helmet to Zhao Hui. His lips curled into a smile, and that razor-sharp gaze dissolved like melting ice. A frivolous temperament settled over him like a cloak; under it, his armor suddenly seemed out of place. "Your Excellency." The young man threw his arm around Ji Lei's shoulders. "I've kept you waiting."

"It's been two years since we last met—you've become so distant, Er-gongzi!"[9] Ji Lei met Xiao Chiye's eyes, and they both laughed.

"I'm carrying a blade, see. I'm pretty much half a soldier now," Xiao Chiye said, pointing down to the scabbard at his belt.

Ji Lei seemed to notice it for the first time. "An excellent blade!" He chuckled along with Xiao Chiye. "It must have been a rough journey, coming all this way to the royal rescue. Let's have a drink tonight after you report to His Majesty!"

---

8 *Shizi, a title for the heir apparent of a feudal prince.*

9 *Gongzi, a respectful term of address for a young man from an affluent household. With the prefix "er" (two), it means "second young master."*

Xiao Chiye gestured regretfully toward the deputy general behind him. "My elder brother sent a minder; how could we drink to our hearts' content? How about in a few days once I've time to breathe. It'll be my treat."

Zhao Hui bowed expressionlessly to Ji Lei. Ji Lei only smiled in response; to Xiao Chiye he said, "Let's head to the palace, then. The ceremonial guards are expecting you."

The pair turned toward the palace, chatting and laughing. Zhao Hui followed, casting a long look at Shen Zechuan as he went. The Embroidered Uniform Guard nearby caught the hint; they hauled Shen Zechuan back to the prison.

Ji Lei watched Xiao Chiye all the way until he entered the palace. The moment he was alone with his men, he spat indignantly at the ground. The genial smile dropped, leaving only a sneer.

This ruffian was usually so impudent and rash. It would be no surprise if he killed a man. Who would have expected this numbskull was crafty enough to handle the situation with such care? One kick, and he'd let Shen Zechuan go.

Zhao Hui handed Xiao Chiye a handkerchief as they entered the palace. He wiped his hands as he walked.

"That kick was too risky," Zhao Hui murmured. "If the last descendant of that Shen dog up and died, the empress dowager would be awfully displeased."

Xiao Chiye's smile sank into gloom. He had come fresh from the battlefield, and his murderous aura was so hostile the eunuch leading them didn't dare eavesdrop.

"That was exactly my intent." Xiao Chiye spoke with cold detachment. "That old dog Shen Wei made a cemetery of Zhongbo. They've been burying soldiers from the Chashi Sinkhole for half a month with no end in sight. And now the Hua Clan wants to protect that dog's last descendant because of some personal connections? How could they expect everything to work out in their favor? Besides, my brother rode thousands of miles to come to the capital's aid; there are no greater honors left to bestow on him. Libei is at the peak of its glory; it has become a very long thorn in the empress dowager's side."

"As my master the shizi often says, the moon waxes only to wane," Zhao Hui said. "The reward from Qudu this time is most likely a Hongmen banquet[10]—every dancer secretly brandishing a sword. Our main forces are camped thirty miles from here, but the eyes and ears of noble families are around every corner in the city. Now is not the time to be impulsive, Gongzi."

Xiao Chiye tossed the handkerchief back to Zhao Hui. "Got it."

"Is A-Ye here?"

The Xiande Emperor was feeding his parrot. The creature had been spoiled rotten and was wily as anything; the instant the emperor spoke, it opened its beak and screeched, "A-Ye is here! A-Ye is here! A-Ye pays his obeisance to Your Majesty! Your Majesty! Your Majesty! Long live! Long live! Long live Your Majesty!"

"He should be here now," answered Xiao Jiming, the Heir of Libei, his hands full of bird feed.

"It's been two years, has it not?" The Xiande Emperor prodded at the parrot. "We haven't seen him for two years. The boy takes after your father; he grows so fast. We fear he'll be even taller than you someday."

"He's taller to be sure, but he's still a child at heart," Xiao Jiming said. "Spends all his time at home stirring up trouble."

---

10 *A banquet set up with the aim of murdering the guest. Refers to a famous episode in 206 BC when future Han emperor Liu Bang escaped an attempted murder by his rival, Xiang Yu, during a sword dance at a feast held in his honor.*

The emperor was about to say more when the coughing took him again; Pan Rugui held out a cup of tea, and the emperor took a sip to soothe his throat. Before he could continue, a eunuch announced Xiao Chiye's arrival.

"Come in." The Xiande Emperor lowered himself into his chair and leaned against an armrest. "Come in, let us have a look at you."

The palace eunuch drew aside the curtain, and Xiao Chiye strode across the threshold, bringing the winter chill with him as he kowtowed before the emperor.

"A fine lad you are, all mighty in your armor," the emperor said with a smile. "We heard that when the Biansha troops raided our roads and relay stations at the frontier, you showed your prowess and captured several alive. Isn't that so?"

Xiao Chiye laughed. "Your Majesty flatters me. I did catch a few, but they were all small fry."

The year before last, the Twelve Tribes of Biansha had launched a raid on the food supply route north of the pass. It had been Xiao Chiye's first time leading troops in battle, and he'd received a thrashing from those Biansha baldies. Xiao Jiming had to clean up the mess for him. News of it spread, and the incident became a punchline that undermined Xiao Chiye's reputation; he was now widely known as an infamous good-for-nothing.

Seeing him so dismissive, the Xiande Emperor's tone softened. "You are young. Just to ride a horse while brandishing a spear is no small skill in itself. Your elder brother is one of our nation's Four Great Generals; surely he regularly instructs you on military tactics. Jiming, we can see that A-Ye is motivated. You mustn't be too hard on him."

Xiao Jiming solemnly promised.

"The Libei Armored Cavalry distinguished itself in coming to our rescue this time," the emperor added. "In addition to yesterday's major reward, today, we wish to give A-Ye some small consideration."

Xiao Jiming rose to his feet and bowed. "It will be my brother's honor to receive His Majesty's favor. However, he has no merits nor contributions to speak of. How could he receive such a lofty reward?"

The emperor paused. "You crossed thousands of miles and the Glacial River to come to our aid; your merits are immeasurable. Even your wife, Lu Yizhi, shall be rewarded, let alone A-Ye." Turning to Xiao Chiye, he said, "Libei is a frontier of great strategic importance. You are young, A-Ye; surely you will find Libei dreary if you remain there long. We wish for you to come to Qudu and take up a post as the carefree commander of the Imperial Regalia. What say you?"

Xiao Chiye had knelt motionless all this while. Now he raised his head. "If it's a reward bestowed by Your Majesty, of course I accept. My whole family is made up of uncouth and burly warriors—I can't even find a place to sit and enjoy a song. If I stay in Qudu, I'll doubtless find life here so agreeable I'll never want to go back."

The Xiande Emperor laughed aloud. "What a lad! We've asked you to take up an official post, but you just want to have fun! If your father heard, we're afraid you wouldn't escape a beating."

The atmosphere in the hall was relaxed; the emperor even kept the brothers behind for a meal together. When it was time for them to go, the emperor remarked, "We heard Qidong sent someone as well. Who is it?"

"Lu Guangbai from the Bianjun Commandery," Xiao Jiming replied.

The emperor leaned back in his chair with an air of fatigue. "Tell him to return tomorrow," he said as he waved them off.

Xiao Chiye followed Xiao Jiming out. They hadn't gone far when they spied a man kneeling on the veranda outside. Pan Rugui approached first, leaning over with a smile. "General Lu, General Lu!"

"Pan-gonggong," Lu Guangbai answered wearily, opening his eyes.

"You should get up, General," Pan Rugui advised him. "His Majesty has retired for the day. You won't be able to see him till tomorrow."

Lu Guangbai was a reticent man. He nodded without another word and rose to his feet to walk out with the Xiao brothers. Only once they stepped out of the palace gates and mounted their horses did Xiao Jiming ask, "Why were you kneeling?"

"His Majesty doesn't want to see me," Lu Guangbai said.

The two men shared a silence. Both knew full well the reason for the emperor's reluctance. But Lu Guangbai didn't appear bitter. He turned to Xiao Chiye. "Did His Majesty reward you?"

"He's keeping me on a leash," Xiao Chiye replied, taking up the reins.

Lu Guangbai reached over to pat Xiao Chiye's shoulder. "Not you; that leash is on your father and brother."

They rode a while. Amid the sound of hooves, Xiao Chiye said, "When His Majesty mentioned my sister-in-law, I almost broke out in a cold sweat."

Lu Guangbai and Xiao Jiming burst out laughing. Lu Guangbai asked, "Are your father and Yizhi well?"

Xiao Jiming nodded. Armorless and with a coat draped over his court attire, he didn't cut as young and valiant a figure as Xiao Chiye, yet his presence commanded attention. "They are both well," he answered. "My father is still concerned about the old general's leg injury, so he specially instructed me to bring you the medicinal plaster he uses. Yizhi is well, too. She's missed you all very much since being with child and wrote many letters that I've brought along. You can read them when you come over to my manor later."

"All we have back home are unrefined men," Lu Guangbai said uneasily, pulling on the reins. "There's not even a female relative we could send to keep her company. The Libei winters are freezing. I got the news while leading the troops out of Bianjun Commandery, and I've been worrying the whole way."

"Yeah." Xiao Chiye turned to them. "When my brother was trapped in Cizhou and the situation was dire, he told me not to write home in case it made my sister-in-law anxious. The conflict broke out so abruptly; they didn't find out about her condition until after he'd left."

Xiao Jiming, ever a man of restraint, merely said, "Our father stayed behind to guard the home front and watch over Yizhi. Don't worry. Once I return home after New Year's, I'm not going anywhere."

Lu Guangbai sighed. "Libei has been caught in the heart of the storm these recent years. You have to think twice every time you dispatch troops. This time, we have only Shen Wei to blame for turning tail without a fight and leaving that rotten mess. When my troops rode past the Chashi Sinkhole, the blood on the ground lapped at the horses' hooves. He knew he couldn't escape capital punishment, so he burned himself to death. Still, there's something off about the whole business. Jiming, you captured his son and brought him to the capital. Did you notice anything amiss?"

"Shen Wei always attached great importance to the distinction between lawful and common birth," Xiao Jiming said, drawing his overcoat shut against the wind. "The boy was his eighth common son born to a mother whose family had no connections; he was abandoned to be raised in Duanzhou. It's obvious that he had no access to inside information. Yet there must be a reason why His Majesty places such importance on the boy."

"Public wrath is hard to quell," Xiao Chiye said, putting on his helmet. "His Majesty personally handed command of the Zhongbo garrisons to Shen Wei. After this debacle, someone's head needs to roll as proof of his impartiality."

However, the one with real executive power in the Zhou empire was not the emperor but the empress dowager, who held her own court behind painted screens. With the situation at a stalemate, the eyes of the nation were on Shen Zechuan. If he pled guilty and died swiftly, all would be well; if not, he was doomed to become a thorn in the emperor's side.

The Xiao Clan of Libei was at the peak of their prestige. Even the Qi Clan, who led the Qidong territories, had to give way to them, and Lu Guangbai—the leader of Qidong's Bianjun Commandery—was Xiao Jiming's brother-in-law. Xiao Jiming, lauded as the "Iron Horse on River Ice," one of the Four Great Generals, could mobilize the Libei Armored Cavalry at any time and count on his wife's family to deploy the Bianjun Garrison Troops. How could the emperor in Qudu not be wary of him?

"The empress dowager insists on preserving his life." Lu Guangbai pursed his thin lips. "She's gunning to raise a jackal who can rightfully reclaim Zhongbo, yet is submissive enough to eat from her hand. When the time comes, he could help her consolidate power from within while keeping Libei in check from without—a dangerous liability. Jiming, this boy must not live!"

As they rode into the gale, snow sliced across their cheeks like knives. They lapsed into silence.

Zhao Hui, who'd been quiet behind them, urged his horse forward. "Gongzi kicked him right in the chest, almost as hard as he could. I saw how shallow his breathing was, and how his wounds bled when he fell." Zhao Hui mulled it over. "Yet he did not die."

"After days of the trial and a flogging, his life was already hanging by a thread," said Xiao Chiye, riding crop in hand. "My kick was meant to kill. If he doesn't die tonight, I'll acknowledge his tenacity, at least."

But Zhao Hui frowned. "He was frail to begin with and suffered a cold on the journey here. By all rights, he should be dead. Yet he's still hanging on. There's something fishy about it. Master—"

Xiao Jiming swept them a sidelong glance, and both shut their mouths. Bracing himself against the fierce wind, he gazed out at the road ahead. After a moment's silence, he said, "Dead or alive, only fate will tell."

The wind howled, sending the metal windchimes under the eaves along the street rattling. The sound seemed to chase away the specter of doom that had closed in around them. Sitting steady atop his horse, Xiao Jiming calmly spurred his mount onward. Zhao Hui leaned forward and hurried to catch up.

Beneath his helmet, Xiao Chiye's expression was inscrutable. Lu Guangbai punched him on the shoulder. "Gotta hand it to your brother."

Xiao Chiye gave him the ghost of a smile. "Fate, huh?"

FRONT LINE

MEDICINE LEAKED from the corners of Shen Zechuan's lips and soaked the front of his robe. The physician was so anxious he couldn't mop the sweat from his brow fast enough. "If he can't swallow the medicine, he's not going to make it!"

Ge Qingqing watched Shen Zechuan with a hand on his scabbard. "Is there nothing else you can do?"

The physician's hands trembled around the medicine bowl, the spoon clattering against the rim. He kowtowed, knocking his head against the ground. "It can't be done! He won't make it! My lord should prepare a straw mat for his burial with all haste."

Ge Qingqing frowned. "Keep trying," he said and turned to step out the door.

Just outside, Ji Lei stood by. Ge Qingqing bowed. "Your Excellency, the physician says he's a goner."

Ji Lei crushed a peanut shell in his hands and blew the dust away. "Has he breathed his last?"

"Still hanging on," Ge Qingqing replied.

Ji Lei folded his hands behind his back. "Keep an eye on him. Make sure he signs the written confession before he croaks."

Ge Qingqing nodded and watched Ji Lei leave. He stood in the courtyard for a moment, then turned to a subordinate beside him. "Call the footman over."

A short while later, a hunch-backed footman wrapped in coarse linen pushed a cart into the courtyard. Night had fallen, and the Imperial Prison was under tight security. Ge Qingqing held the lantern up to scrutinize his face, then motioned for the man to follow him in.

The physician had left some time ago. A single oil lamp cast its glow over the room where Shen Zechuan lay on a cot, his face drained of color and his limbs cold as a corpse. Ge Qingqing stepped aside and said to the footman, "Ji-shu[11]...he's here."

Slowly, the man stripped away the linen bundled around his head to reveal a face disfigured by fire. He stared at Shen Zechuan, took two steps forward, and stretched out a trembling hand to stroke Shen Zechuan's hair. When he saw how thin and bloodied the young man was, he began to weep, tears shining on his scarred cheeks.

"Chuan-er," Ji Gang whispered hoarsely, "Shifu is here!"

Ge Qingqing blew out the lamp. "Don't worry, Ji-shu. Ever since the men from the prison learned he was your disciple, they've kept close watch. The interrogations looked harsh, but they didn't inflict serious injury. For your sake, our brothers were careful with him during the flogging. Even twenty of those strikes wouldn't have maimed him. But the eunuchs overseeing the punishment have sharp eyes; we didn't dare make it obvious. Third Lady Hua came just in time; otherwise, Pan-gonggong would have gotten suspicious."

"I will surely repay this kindness!" Tears streamed down Ji Gang's careworn face. The years had been hard on him; his hair was already half-white.

"Ji-shu! How can you say that?" Ge Qingqing exclaimed. "What our brothers have repaid is the kindness of your guidance and the debt we owe you for saving our lives." He sighed again. "Who

---

11 *Shu, a suffix meaning "uncle." Can be used to address unrelated older men.*

could've expected a wild card to storm in out of the blue? That Second Young Master Xiao was aiming to kill with that kick. Ji-shu, can he be saved?"

Ji Gang felt Shen Zechuan's pulse and forced a smile. "Good lad. He's made the most of the techniques A-Mu taught him. He hasn't reached the point of no return. Don't be afraid, my child. Shifu is here!"

At the tender age of seven, Shen Zechuan had joined Ji Mu in learning martial arts from Ji Gang. Each strike in Ji-Style Boxing was aggressive; it had to be complemented with the Ji Clan's mental cultivation techniques and could only be practiced by those with an indomitable will. Ji Gang had been a heavy drinker most of his life; after teaching the older son, he often forgot about the younger. But Ji Mu took his position as eldest seriously: every stance he learned, he taught his younger brother. Shen Zechuan had unexpectedly mastered the style over the years.

Ge Qingqing bent to take a look. "He's still so young. I'm afraid his body will be permanently damaged after this ordeal. I've sent someone to brew another bowl of the physician's prescription. See if you can get him to drink some, Ji-shu."

Shen Zechuan's throat was parched from fever.

His body ached all over, as if he was lying on the main thoroughfare of Qudu, crushed by every carriage that came and went. The pain was an inferno consuming his body. Lost in the darkness, he dreamed of snow fluttering in the air. He dreamed of Ji Mu's blood, the freezing sinkhole, and the brutal kick from Xiao Chiye.

Ji Lei was right; he was better off dead. He had received this life from his father, Shen Wei, so now he had to receive his father's death sentence. He took the fall in Shen Wei's stead, the target of contempt from all the loyal souls who had perished. Having taken on these shackles, he was bound to drag their weight forever.

But he couldn't take it lying down.

Someone pried his teeth apart and warmth rushed into his throat; the bitterness of the medicine made Shen Zechuan's eyes water. He heard a familiar voice and struggled to open his eyes.

Ji Gang wiped the young man's tears with callused fingers. "Chuan-er, it's Shifu!"

A sob caught in Shen Zechuan's throat; he choked out the medicine alongside his tears. He hooked his finger on the hem of Ji Gang's robe and gritted his teeth, fearing it was a fever dream.

Ji Gang turned his scarred face away from the light of the lamp. "You have to live, Chuan-er! You're all I have left in this ignoble life."

Tears poured from Shen Zechuan's eyes and streamed down his cheeks. He looked up at the pitch-black ceiling and murmured, "Shifu..." The wind outside was howling. Shen Zechuan's gaze gradually focused, and a ferocious glint appeared. "I won't die," he said hoarsely. "Shifu, I won't die."

The next day, the Xiande Emperor rewarded the troops with a feast. Besides providing for the Libei Armored Cavalry and Qidong Garrison Troops encamped outside the capital, the palace hosted a formal banquet for the commanders and generals, with court officials in attendance.

Arrayed in his court attire, Xiao Chiye overshadowed the delicate scholars around him as he took his seat. He, like the embroidered beasts clawing at the clouds on his robe, radiated intensity. Yet that careless persona reared its head again the moment he sat down.

The civil officials enjoying the wine couldn't help stealing glances at Xiao Chiye. A tiger would not beget a dog; how was it that the Heir of Libei took after his father, but the younger son turned out like *this*?

Sharing an unspoken understanding, these officials began to pick apart Xiao Chiye's every move. The air of wild frivolity emanating from him practically struck them across the face. In contrast, Xiao Jiming, sitting straight-backed in the seat of honor, might have come from a whole other world.

"Don't think this doesn't involve you," Lu Guangbai remarked from his seat beside Xiao Chiye. "Since His Majesty rewarded you, he's sure to call on you later."

Xiao Chiye rotated some walnuts listlessly in his palm.

Lu Guangbai turned to look at him. "You went out drinking last night."

"Just making merry before this Hongmen banquet." Xiao Chiye sank shapelessly into his seat. "Now I'm ready. If anyone takes a swipe during the sword dance, I can enact a drunken rescue. Wouldn't that be great?"

"Very well." Lu Guangbai poured himself another cup, "but drinking is bad for your health. If you want to make your mark as a general, best give up this vice."

Xiao Chiye sighed and tossed a walnut to Lu Guangbai. "I was born at the wrong time. With the Four Generals taking their places around the nation, there's no room for me to play hero. If you ever find yourself unable to go on, let me know in advance—it won't be too late for me to kick the habit then."

"In that case, I'm afraid you'll have to wait," said Lu Guangbai, and they laughed together.

As the banquet went on, conversation turned to the Shen Clan of Zhongbo.

"Didn't they say last night that the kid wouldn't make it?" Lu Guangbai asked. He was listening attentively, the walnut still held in his hand.

Behind them, Zhao Hui answered in a hushed tone, "That's right. Didn't Gongzi say the kick was meant to send him to his grave?"

"Did I say that?" Xiao Chiye denied it, but the other two looked back at him in silence. "What?"

"He didn't die," Lu Guangbai pointed out.

"He didn't die," Zhao Hui repeated.

Xiao Chiye held their gazes. "So he's tough. What does it have to do with me? Not like the King of Hell is *my* old man."

"Let's see what His Majesty has in store for him. The boy really is a fighter." Lu Guangbai looked toward the front of the hall.

Kneeling behind them, Zhao Hui ducked his head and applied himself to his meal. "Someone must be helping him in secret," he said offhandedly.

"Even if he doesn't die, he's got to be broken beyond repair." Xiao Chiye glanced coldly at the Hua Clan's tables nearby. "The empress dowager is old. The most she can do now is devote herself to grooming a stray dog."

"What a farce." Zhao Hui somberly stuffed a spare rib into his mouth.

After a few rounds of toasts, when the atmosphere was relaxed and convivial, the Xiande Emperor spoke: "Jiming."

Xiao Jiming rose to his feet and bowed, awaiting the emperor's pronouncement.

The emperor slumped in his throne as if he'd had one cup too many. "On the matter of Shen Wei's failure—there is no conclusive evidence he colluded with the enemy. That Shen..."

"It's Shen Zechuan, Your Majesty," Pan Rugui bent over and whispered.

The emperor paused, but instead of continuing, he turned to the empress dowager and asked, "What does Imperial Mother think?"

A solemn silence descended over the hall as the entire court of civil and military officials lowered their heads to listen.

The empress dowager wore a wide band of fine black silk around her head, embroidered with cloud-dwelling dragons and dripping with strings of pearls. Pearl ropes hung from her ears on golden hooks, embellished with emerald leaves and capped with pearls as big as chestnuts. She was the picture of poise on her high seat, the streaks of frost in her glossy hair the final touch of dignity. Not a soul in the banquet hall dared raise their head to look at her.

"Our morale suffered a serious blow during the attack on Zhongbo because Shen Wei lost his nerve," the empress dowager said. "But his fear of judgment led him to self-immolate, and his descendants have all died in the battle. Only this singular son of common birth is left. It goes against grace and righteousness to eradicate his entire clan. Why shouldn't we preserve his life and teach him gratitude?"

The banquet hall was silent.

"This subject finds it inappropriate." Lu Guangbai suddenly raised his voice. He took three steps forward and knelt in the middle of the hall. "Her Majesty is merciful, but Zhongbo is unlike battles past. Perhaps there is no evidence that Shen Wei colluded with the enemy, but the suspicion remains. This young man is Shen Wei's last descendant. If he is allowed to survive, he may well live to become a serpent under our own roof."

The empress dowager studied Lu Guangbai. "Your father, the Earl of Biansha, has guarded the desert for decades. Yet even he has not emerged victorious from every battle."

"My father is not invincible," Lu Guangbai replied. "Nevertheless, in the decades of his command, no enemy has penetrated so deep past the borders of the Bianjun Commandery."

The pearls hanging from the empress dowager's ears swayed gently. "It's precisely for this reason that we must teach the child etiquette and virtue, so he may understand the disastrous consequences of this war. How easy it is to kill a man. The Biansha Horsemen trampled the fields of Zhongbo and slew tens of thousands of our people. We have yet to seek redress from them for the humiliation of our nation. What guilt could a castoff child have?"

"This subject finds it inappropriate as well." The Deputy Grand Secretary of the Grand Secretariat, Hai Liangyi, had remained quiet all this while. Now he braced himself on the table to stand, then knelt before the throne. "Her Majesty is gracious and merciful, but this is no trivial matter. Even if Shen Wei did not conspire with the enemy, he still deserved a beheading after such a defeat. Moreover, this boy has been tried and interrogated thrice, and his statements are contradictory and illogical. He insists Shen Wei had no congress with the enemy. But as a son of common birth raised far from the manor, how would he know what Shen Wei did or did not do? The boy is cunning by nature and not to be trusted. General Lu is right: if we keep the last remnant of the Shen Clan alive, he will one day be a scourge under this very roof!"

The empress dowager was unruffled. "Please rise, Secretariat Elder Hai."

Pan Rugui helped Hai Liangyi to his feet, and the empress dowager continued. "It is as my dear ministers have said. It seems that my views have been colored by my feelings. I will leave the decision on this matter to His Majesty."

Under the watchful eyes of the hall, the Xiande Emperor gave a sharp, feeble cough. He accepted the handkerchief Pan Rugui passed him and covered his mouth; only after a long silence did he speak. "What Imperial Mother says is not without merit. The boy himself is innocent. However, the fact remains that Shen Wei's troops failed in their duty and abandoned their cities. This child carries the weight of his family's guilt; as the sole living member of his clan, we will give him a chance to redeem himself. Ji Lei."

"Yes, Your Majesty."

"Confine the boy at the Temple of Guilt. Without our order, he is not to cross the threshold!"

Xiao Chiye tossed the crushed pieces of walnut onto his plate.

"Is Gongzi not eating that?" Zhao Hui asked.

"Broken and wasted," Xiao Chiye said. "Who would want it?"

"Have not all sides been satisfied?" Zhao Hui said in a low voice, his eyes on Xiao Chiye's plate. "We didn't get what we wanted, but neither did they."

"Caging him is preferable to freeing him, at least." Lu Guangbai returned to his table.

"Not necessarily." Xiao Chiye pointed to himself. "Am I not caged as well?"

"And thank goodness for that," Lu Guangbai and Zhao Hui chimed in unison.

IMPRISONMENT

SHEN ZECHUAN ENTERED the Temple of Guilt on a rare sunny day in Qudu. White snow blanketed the tiles of the palace roofs, the green plum blossoms of late winter set against vermilion walls. Sunlight shone on the eaves of the prison building, casting a stark border between light and shadow on the ground before his feet.

He had scarcely recovered from his illness and was practically skin and bone. When he opened his eyes in the sunlight, any dreams of his first fifteen years scattered like ashes in the freezing wind.

Ge Qingqing preceded him down the stairs, then turned back and said, "It's getting late."

Supporting himself against the pillars, Shen Zechuan made his way slowly down to the wagon. He'd grown unaccustomed to being exposed under the sun, but it didn't scare him. Any lingering childishness in his features had been crushed by the pallor of illness; his face was studiously blank.

Over at the temple, Ji Lei waited at the entrance with Xiaofuzi hovering at his side. As he looked up at the ancient architecture, Xiaofuzi marveled, "What a curious place. It doesn't seem like a prison at all."

"I see you don't know its history," said Ji Lei. "The Temple of Guilt was originally a place for the royal family to offer incense. It used to house an imperial decree penned in the Guangcheng Emperor's own hand. In its heyday, eminent monks from all over the country assembled here. Those great meetings of minds were the talk of their time."

"Why has there been no mention of it in recent years?" Xiaofuzi eyed the magnificent entrance. "It's rather run down. Repairs haven't been done for years, have they?"

Ji Lei thought a moment. "Twenty at least. At the time, the condemned crown prince instigated the Eight Great Battalions to stage a coup. After their defeat, he retreated to this temple and fought like a cornered beast, eventually slitting his own throat and spilling his blood across the Buddha statues. The late emperor never set foot here again. He stripped the temple of its original name and redubbed it the Temple of Guilt."

"Twenty years!" Xiaofuzi clutched his throat in exaggerated surprise. "I wasn't even born! Your Excellency had just joined the Embroidered Uniform Guard then, hadn't you?"

Rather than answer, Ji Lei snapped, "Why is he not here yet?" as he peered down the road behind them.

The stone tablet at the temple's entrance was engraved with the word *Zhaozui*—Revelation of Guilt. Xiaofuzi approached it, still curious. "But how have I never heard of anyone being locked inside it?"

Ji Lei's irritation was plain. "Only court officials with ties to the condemned crown prince were imprisoned here. Most of them saw their entire clans executed before being beheaded themselves; survivors of the incident were few and far between. It's been twenty years; who would remember?!"

The prison wagon rolled up to the entrance.

"He's here, Your Excellency." Ge Qingqing bowed to Ji Lei.

"Send him in." Ji Lei turned to Shen Zechuan as he passed. "After this farewell, I doubt we'll meet again. His Majesty has been generous. Spend the rest of your sorry life reflecting on the grace extended to you."

Shen Zechuan acted as if he hadn't heard. He stepped forward and over the threshold. As the peeling vermilion doors ground closed behind him, the young man stood in the gloom of the temple and looked placidly back at Ji Lei.

Profoundly irked, Ji Lei was ready to lose his temper when he saw a serene smile spread across Shen Zechuan's face.

He's gone mad. The thought came to Ji Lei unbidden, even before he heard Shen Zechuan call out, "Lord Ji." His voice was very calm. "We *will* meet again."

The doors shut with a heavy *thud*, stirring up a cloud of dust. Xiaofuzi covered his nose and coughed as he stepped back. Ji Lei, however, stood frozen in place.

When he finally returned to his senses, it seemed Xiaofuzi had already called to him several times. He swiftly mounted his horse and turned so his back was warmed by the sun.

"Good riddance!" he managed, too late.

Xiao Chiye was riding through the city streets when he crossed paths with Ji Lei. Reining his horse to a halt, he laughed boisterously. "Lao-Ji, aren't you on duty in the palace?"

"I had to oversee that dirty bastard's imprisonment at the temple, so I'm only now rushing to the palace." Ji Lei cast a covetous glance at Xiao Chiye's battle steed. "What an excellent horse, Er-gongzi! I hear you train them yourself?"

"I had some free time." Xiao Chiye cracked the riding crop in the air, and his circling gyrfalcon swooped down to his shoulder. "Falconry and playing with horses are all the talents I have."

"Once you've assumed your duties in the new year, you'll have more than enough on your plate," Ji Lei said. "The rising star of Qudu! I'm not on duty tomorrow—how about we go for a drink to celebrate?"

"Count me out unless it's fine wine," said Xiao Chiye.

Ji Lei laughed aloud. "Of course it's fine wine! Who would presume to invite the second young master without it? I'll call at your manor later to invite you. Would the Heir of Libei join the fun?"

"My elder brother doesn't think much of that kind of fun," Xiao Chiye said, rubbing his thumb ring. "Why? Is my company not enough?"

"I certainly didn't say that!" Ji Lei said in a rush. "That settles it then, Er-gongzi."

Nodding in agreement, Xiao Chiye spurred his horse to leave. But at the last minute, he seemed to recall something. "How did that little bastard look? Can he walk?"

"He can walk," Ji Lei replied, "but from what I saw, the kid's never going to be nimble. How many survive a flogging like that without lasting injuries? He's lucky he can even stand."

Xiao Chiye rode away without asking more.

When evening fell, the temple attendant brought Shen Zechuan his meal. He left the food untouched. With an oil lamp in hand, he made a round along the small corridors at the sides of the main hall.

Dust had long settled on every surface, and several of the side rooms had fallen into complete disrepair, doors and windows crumbling from rot. After sighting several skeletons that looked like they might topple at the slightest breeze, he returned to the main hall, having found no other living creature.

The Buddha statue at the center of the hall had collapsed, but the incense altar was durable despite its age. The space beneath it was just right. Shen Zechuan draped a tattered curtain over its surface and lay down under the altar table fully clothed. The cold from the floor made his legs ache. Gritting his teeth against the pain, he closed his eyes and counted out the hours.

Fine snow started to fall in the latter half of the night. Shen Zechuan heard an owl hoot twice and sat up, lifting aside the fabric just in time to see Ji Gang step through the door.

"Eat first." Ji Gang opened the cloth bundle he had brought. "Then we'll train. This place is too drafty; it's freezing in here. I'm worried you'll catch a cold if you fall asleep."

Shen Zechuan looked down at the roasted chicken wrapped in oil paper. "One should abstain from meat when recovering from injuries. You have it, Shifu."

"Bullshit! This is the time to fill your stomach," Ji Gang said as he tore off pieces of chicken for him. "Shifu likes the chicken butt; even at home it was my favorite. Save that part for me."

"I'll follow your lead," Shen Zechuan said, "and eat whatever you eat."

Ji Gang glanced at him and laughed. "Brat."

In the end, master and disciple split the roast chicken between them. Ji Gang seemed to have grown a mouth of iron teeth; he chewed even the bones to pieces. Handing his drinking gourd to Shen Zechuan, he said, "Drink some wine if the cold becomes too bitter to bear, but not too much; sip in moderation, like your brother did."

Over these last days, they had never mentioned Zhongbo, Duanzhou, or even the Chashi Sinkhole. Hua Pingting and Ji Mu were the unspoken wounds shared by both master and disciple. Each thought they had hidden their grief, not realizing the blood had already soaked through their bandages, and that their pain was mutual.

Shen Zechuan took a sip and handed it back.

Ji Gang didn't take it. "I quit. Shifu doesn't drink anymore."

Silence filled the hall. Without the barrier of the long-rotted door, powdery snow fell before their eyes, the only scenery in the endless night.

"What are you thinking about, spacing out like that?" Ji Gang asked.

"Shifu," Shen Zechuan began.

"Spit it out."

"I'm sorry."

After a long silence, Ji Gang said, "It's not your fault."

Shen Zechuan curled his hand into a fist. He stared fixedly at the snow, as if tears would fall if he so much as blinked. "Did you look for us at Chashi?" he asked, his voice tight.

Ji Gang slowly leaned back against the altar, submerging his body in shadow. He seemed to be searching for his own voice. After an interval, he answered. "I did. I found him."

He found him.

In that deep pit of snow, Ji Gang had found his son covered in arrows. He had jumped into the sinkhole, stepping over thick piles of corpses, and dug out Ji Mu's body.

Ji Mu was only twenty-three, freshly promoted to squad leader in the Duanzhou Garrison Troops. His armor was new. The day he put it on, Hua Pingting had tucked a protective talisman beneath the chainmail. When Ji Gang found him, he was frozen purple, packed in the mud with his fellow soldiers.

Shen Zechuan raised his head slightly. "I'm sorry, Shifu."

Ji Gang was old. He scratched his white hair and said, "He's the elder brother, isn't he? It's what he should have done. None of it was your fault."

The snow piled in drifts outside the hall.

Ji Gang drew his limbs in, hugging himself. "No one could have known those Biansha bastards would come. He's a soldier; charging to the front lines is his job. I taught him to fight, and knowing his temperament, he would rather die than run. He never could bear to see others suffer, so how...how could he run away? It's neither your fault nor his, Chuan-er. Shifu is the one to blame. I drank too much. Your shiniang scolded me all those years, but I never quit. When the horsemen came, I couldn't even put up a fight. I'm old and ruined, and became useless long ago."

Tears dripped onto the drinking gourd. Shen Zechuan gripped it tight and said nothing.

"Old and ruined." A grinning head suddenly poked out from behind the Buddha statue. "Old and ruined!"

"Who's there?!" Ji Gang bellowed, springing up like a leopard.

The unkempt man slowly emerged from his hiding spot as he parroted Ji Gang. "Who, who!"

That voice was distinctive; Ji Gang pushed Shen Zechuan back down and rasped in astonishment, "Grand Mentor Qi!"

The man shrank back immediately. Kicking the Buddha, he yelled, "No! I'm not the grand mentor!"

Ji Gang ran behind the statue in pursuit, Shen Zechuan right behind him. When Ji Gang saw the man about to crawl through a hole in the wall, he pounced and grabbed him by the ankle. The old man squealed like a stuck pig.

"Your Highness!" he screamed. "Run, Your Highness!"

Shen Zechuan covered the man's mouth and helped Ji Gang carry him back. "Shifu, who is this?"

"You're too young to have known of him." Ji Gang's voice was unsteady as he held the man down. "This is wonderful, Grand Mentor Qi! You're alive! And Lord Zhou? Is Lord Zhou here too?"

Grand Mentor Qi was short in stature and thin as a rail. Too frail to land a proper kick, he resorted to glaring at them as he hissed, "He's dead, dead! I'm dead. His Highness is dead. Everyone is dead!"

"Grand Mentor, it's me, Ji Gang," Ji Gang said, voice heavy. "The vice commander of the Embroidered Uniform Guard. Ji Gang!"

Still badly shaken, Grand Mentor Qi hesitantly craned his neck to examine Ji Gang. "You're not Ji Gang. You're an evil spirit!"

"Grand Mentor!" Ji Gang cried sorrowfully. "In the twenty-third year of Yongyi, I escorted you into the capital. This very temple is where His Highness the Crown Prince met and welcomed you. Have you forgotten this too?"

Grand Mentor Qi's eyes glistened. "They killed the crown prince—His Highness!" He sobbed, "Ji Gang, Lord Ji! Take His Highness away! The Eastern Palace has become a target of all. What crime has His Highness committed?!"

Ji Gang dejectedly loosened his grip. "Grand Mentor...in the twenty-ninth year, Ji Lei sold his soul to the enemy, and I was cast out of Qudu. These twenty years, I've wandered the world. I took a wife and fathered a child in Zhongbo's Duanzhou."

"Even if His Highness is gone, the imperial grandson still lives!" The grand mentor stared at him blankly. "Take him away. You, take him away!"

Ji Gang closed his eyes. "In the thirtieth year of Yongyi, the crown prince slit his own throat in this very hall. No one from the Eastern Palace survived."

The grand mentor leaned back and muttered, "Yes, that's right." He began to sob like a child. "How did it come to this?"

"A parting like clouds adrift, ten years like flowing water passed.[12] Who would guess that we should meet again, in this life, under such circumstances?" Ji Gang said. The events of the night had exhausted him.

Grand Mentor Qi turned and covered his face. "Did they lock you up too? Let us all be locked up! Let them slaughter all men of learning in the world."

"My disciple is being punished on his father's behalf," Ji Gang said.

"On his father's behalf... Well, good," Grand Mentor Qi said. "Who is his father? Did he also anger His Majesty?"

"Last year, Shen Wei's troops were routed in battle," Ji Gang sighed.

To his surprise, the grand mentor whipped his head around at the name *Shen Wei*. He scrambled like a beast toward Shen Zechuan. "This...is Shen Wei's son?"

Ji Gang sensed something was amiss. But before he could move, Grand Mentor Qi lunged at Shen Zechuan, clawing at him with wizened fingers as he howled, "Shen Wei! Shen Wei killed His Highness!"

Sharp-eyed and agile even after illness, Shen Zechuan caught Grand Mentor Qi's wrists before he could do any damage. Ji Gang sprang up to restrain the old man once again. "Grand Mentor! Do you want my disciple to die today for the same reason as the imperial grandson? No matter what crimes Shen Wei committed, what does it have to do with my disciple?!"

"If he's the son of Shen Wei..." There was a quiver in the grand mentor's voice; he panted heavily, "Shen Wei..."

---

12 *From the Tang poem "A Greeting on River Huai to my Old Friends from Liangchuan," by Wei Yingwu.*

Without releasing the grand mentor from his grasp, Ji Gang dropped to his knees in a kowtow. "He was born the son of Shen Wei, but he became the son of Ji Gang. If I've uttered a word of falsehood tonight, may I die a terrible death! Grand Mentor, do you intend to kill my son?"

GRAND MENTOR

DUMBSTRUCK, Grand Mentor Qi pulled his hands out of Ji Gang's grip. He turned his face away, refusing to look at Shen Zechuan. This man had been mad for twenty years, imprisoned in this hall and despising everyone outside it. Yet, all of a sudden, he had to convince himself not to hate the son of his enemy.

"Who..." Grand Mentor Qi's voice was woeful. "Then whom should I kill?"

The snow fell in silence; the crows in the courtyard abandoned their branch. The tattered drapes in the main hall fluttered in the blowing wind. Grand Mentor Qi staggered to his feet and raised his arms high, the picture of utter devastation.

"The die is cast! He who triumphs is redeemed, and he who fails is damned. His Highness's virtuous name has been blackened, and you and I will be condemned to posterity as traitors! Whom should I kill? I should turn my blade on the ignorant and foolish heavens! Twenty years ago, His Highness's blood spilled on these floors. What crime did we commit, that the emperor in his ruthlessness deemed we must die?"

Tears and snot poured down the grand mentor's face. He dropped to his knees, trembling, at the entrance of the hall and banged his head on the floor again and again. "Kill *me* as well!"

The snowy night was miserable and cold; in the desolate old temple, no one answered his cries. Slumped on his knees, Grand Mentor Qi resembled the decrepit Buddha statue, buried under a shroud of cottony snow in the brilliantly illuminated Qudu night.

An hour later, Ji Gang supported a calmer Grand Mentor Qi by the arm as the three of them sat in a circle before the altar.

"Much of what we speak of tonight happened because of me. Allow me to explain everything." Ji Gang rolled up his sleeves. "Grand Mentor, Chuan-er was born of the Shen Clan. He is Shen Wei's eighth son of common birth. Eight years ago, the conflict between the lawful and common branches in the Prince of Jianxing's manor was as volatile as fire and oil. Shen Zhouji, the Heir of Jianxing, won his father's favor and sent his brothers of common birth out of the manor. Chuan-er was only seven years old; he wasn't fit to join the army in Duanzhou, so he lived in an auxiliary courtyard, raised by his late mother's handmaid. However, the woman was greedy and often skimmed the child's rations for herself. Pingting had known the boy's mother when she was alive. When she learned of this, she bade me take Chuan-er home so we could look after him."

"Shen Wei himself was of common birth and suffered his share of injustice in his childhood, yet he ended up putting his own sons through the same." Grand Mentor Qi sneered. "How ludicrous, to favor his children of lawful birth when it was his own lechery that led him to beget so many children. What a disgrace!"

"We sent several letters to the Prince's Manor, but not once did Shen Wei reply. Among the Eight Great Clans of Qudu, even for sons of common birth, such blatant neglect is unheard of." Ji Gang furrowed his brows. "This is how Chuan-er came to be raised by us. Mu-er was fifteen then, and he was delighted to have a little brother.

Our family of four settled down in Duanzhou. It took a lot of effort just to get our names into the military register."

Grand Mentor Qi was silent for a moment. "You left the capital bearing the mark of a criminal," he said. "It would naturally be difficult for you to register your household. Back then, His Highness strictly enforced the Yellow Register system that recorded all households to suppress bandits and prevent civilian unrest."

"I understood his reasons," Ji Gang said. "But Grand Mentor, what happened in Qudu after I left? How did His Highness the Crown Prince meet such an end?"

Grand Mentor Qi dragged over a tattered curtain and wrapped it around his shoulders. "After you left," he began gloomily, "Ji Wufan fell out of favor with the emperor. At the same time, Pan Rugui became a favorite of the empress and rose to the post of Director of Writ at the Directorate of Ceremonial Affairs. The Embroidered Uniform Guard fell into decline, and its Twelve Offices existed only in name. After Ji Wufan's death, Ji Lei took up the mantle. From then on, the eunuchs in the Eastern Depot[13] lorded over the Embroidered Uniform Guard, who ceased working with the Eastern Palace.

"Later on, when the emperor fell ill and was confined to his bed, the daily affairs of the court were to be jointly managed by the Grand Secretariat and the Eastern Palace. But the Hua Clan exploited the empress's sway over the emperor to install numerous incompetent officials in the court. The Six Ministries became riddled with corruption. At that point, the threat posed by the empress's kin could no longer be ignored. His Highness the Crown Prince submitted many appeals to His Majesty, but he didn't anticipate that Pan Rugui would leverage the authority of his office and join forces with the

---

13 *The emperor's secret service run by the eunuchs, tasked with spying on state officials.*

empress to seize control of the court—none of the prince's written appeals reached the eyes of the emperor. On top of that, after His Majesty fell ill, the empress turned away all visitors from the Grand Secretariat and the Eastern Palace whenever they sought after the emperor's health."

"Those castrated dogs are a blight on the empire." Ji Gang sighed deeply. "If I'd known Pan Rugui harbored such ambitions, I never would have urged Father to spare him!"

"Kill a Pan Rugui, and there will be some Pan Ruxi or Pan Ruyi to take his place! The inner palace meddles in state affairs while their kinsmen accumulate power. You don't understand, Ji Gang. These are deep-rooted maladies of the Eight Great Clans. As long as the clans in Qudu are allowed to do as they please, history will repeat itself! How can the empress so deftly manipulate court affairs when she has lived for so long in the inner palace? Because of the long-amassed influence of the Hua Clan! Even if the empress wasn't a Hua, if she hailed from one of the other eight clans, this consolidation of power would still be inevitable."

Shen Zechuan couldn't help but cut in. "But wasn't the crown prince born of the empress herself?"

"No." Grand Mentor Qi bowed his head. "His Highness's birth mother was an imperial concubine. The empress has no children of her own. His Highness was taken into the inner palace at a young age and raised by the empress. Even a tiger will not eat its young, but there is no such kinship in the imperial clan."

The hall fell silent again.

Ji Gang huffed in the cold air and croaked, "It was because of my excessive drinking that my father fell out of favor with the emperor. If not for that, His Highness would never have found himself in such a predicament."

"I didn't anticipate that Ji Lei would turn on us, for the sake of you and Ji Wufan if nothing else." The grand mentor clutched the tattered curtain tighter. The memory left a bitter taste in his mouth. "Who would've thought that he..."

"Grand Mentor, there's something you don't know." Ji Gang looked at Shen Zechuan. "And neither does Chuan-er. My father, Ji Wufan, was the chief commander of the Embroidered Uniform Guard and had weathered life-and-death situations with the late emperor. They were very close. His first wife died young, and he had no intention to remarry, so he adopted three sons. Our eldest brother couldn't stand to participate in the heinous cruelty of the Imperial Prison. He left the capital in his youth for Tianfei Watchtower to be a common soldier. Ji Lei and I served in the Embroidered Uniform Guard and remained by our father's side, where he taught us Ji-Style Boxing and Ji-Style Blade. Later, my father came to believe that Ji Lei harbored some ill intent. He suspected he had political ambitions, so I was the only one to whom he taught the Ji Clan's techniques of mental cultivation. But this only deepened the rift between us. After Father's death, Ji Lei performed a thorough cleansing of those under his command; many veteran guards were sent from the capital and stationed elsewhere. From then on, the Embroidered Uniform Guard was no longer what it once was."

"Such is fate," Grand Mentor Qi murmured. "The Eastern Palace's subordinates did everything in our power, yet still failed to save His Highness. His Majesty suspected the crown prince of plotting a coup with the Eight Great Battalions, even though the reins of these forces were ever in the hands of the Eight Great Clans. Under Ji Lei, the Embroidered Uniform Guard discovered incriminating documents; they insisted these were connected to His Highness. Our men were taken into the Imperial Prison, and many of them died there. Some who couldn't withstand the torture finally crumbled, admitting to a crime they'd never committed. The emperor, still on his sickbed, flew into a rage. With Pan Rugui whispering slander in his ears, His Highness was trapped with no way out."

Tears streamed down the grand mentor's face, and the madness seemed to overtake him again. "His Highness was right here, with no way out! Why didn't they kill me? Why am I left here to drag out this wretched existence? A life like this is worse than death, yet I still can't speed my steps to the grave."

He fixed his gaze on Shen Zechuan, his tone turning frenzied. "I won't take this lying down! Years of strategy and planning, down the drain! Countless compatriots serving the Eastern Palace are dead, and the injustice His Highness suffered is yet to be redressed. I won't accept it!" He grabbed Shen Zechuan's arm again. "You are so young—you still have a chance!"

"Grand Mentor..." Ji Gang rose to stop him.

"You can protect him now. But can you protect him forever?" Grand Mentor Qi tightened his grip on Shen Zechuan. "Today I set aside my grudge out of respect for your fatherly affection, but will everyone in this world do the same? As long as his surname is Shen, there will be those who seek his life! Is prowess in martial arts enough to give him peace of mind? Your father was a master of these arts, Ji Gang, yet did he not die ill and alone? In Qudu, where the tides of power ebb and flow, it is the invisible hand that kills. Will you throw him naked to the wolves?"

Ji Gang clenched his fists but said nothing. Grand Mentor Qi went to his knees. Tugging at Shen Zechuan, he said in a quavering voice, breaking with sobs, "I am Qi Huilian of Yuzhou! You don't know who I am, but I will tell you. I-I was the top scholar in all three levels of the civil exams in the fifteenth year of Yongyi. Since the founding of Great Zhou, only five have emerged first in all three levels of the examination. I was a subordinate of the Eastern Palace, and at the same time the Minister of Personnel and the Deputy Grand Secretary of the Grand Secretariat. I taught the crown prince, and now...now I will teach you! I will impart my lifetime of knowledge, all of it, to you—what do you say?"

Shen Zechuan stared into Grand Mentor Qi's eyes, unnaturally calm. After a brief silence, he dropped heavily to his knees and kowtowed thrice to Grand Mentor Qi.

"If Xiansheng[14] will be my scroll, I will be his sword."

Just before dawn, Ge Qingqing headed off to the Temple of Guilt. The wind was brisk, and the snow still drifted down in flurries. He huffed into his hands and looked for a steamed bun stall as he walked.

He was surprised to hear someone call him from afar. A red silk umbrella floated through the snow, swaying as the person under it stumbled toward him. In Qudu, only those of the fifth rank and above were permitted to carry red silk umbrellas. This was someone of considerable wealth and power.

Ge Qingqing stepped to the side of the road, bringing his hand to his scabbard to pay his respects. The stink of alcohol hit him as the stranger staggered closer.

"The Scarlet Cavalry." The man stopped and reached out to pluck off the authority token hanging at Ge Qingqing's waist. Studying it for a moment, he said, "And where is Company Commander Ge going in this freezing cold?"

Ge Qingqing fixed his eyes on the man's black boots. "Your Excellency, this humble subordinate is on duty at the office today and heading for the palace."

---

14 *Xiansheng, a term of address for a teacher of academics.*

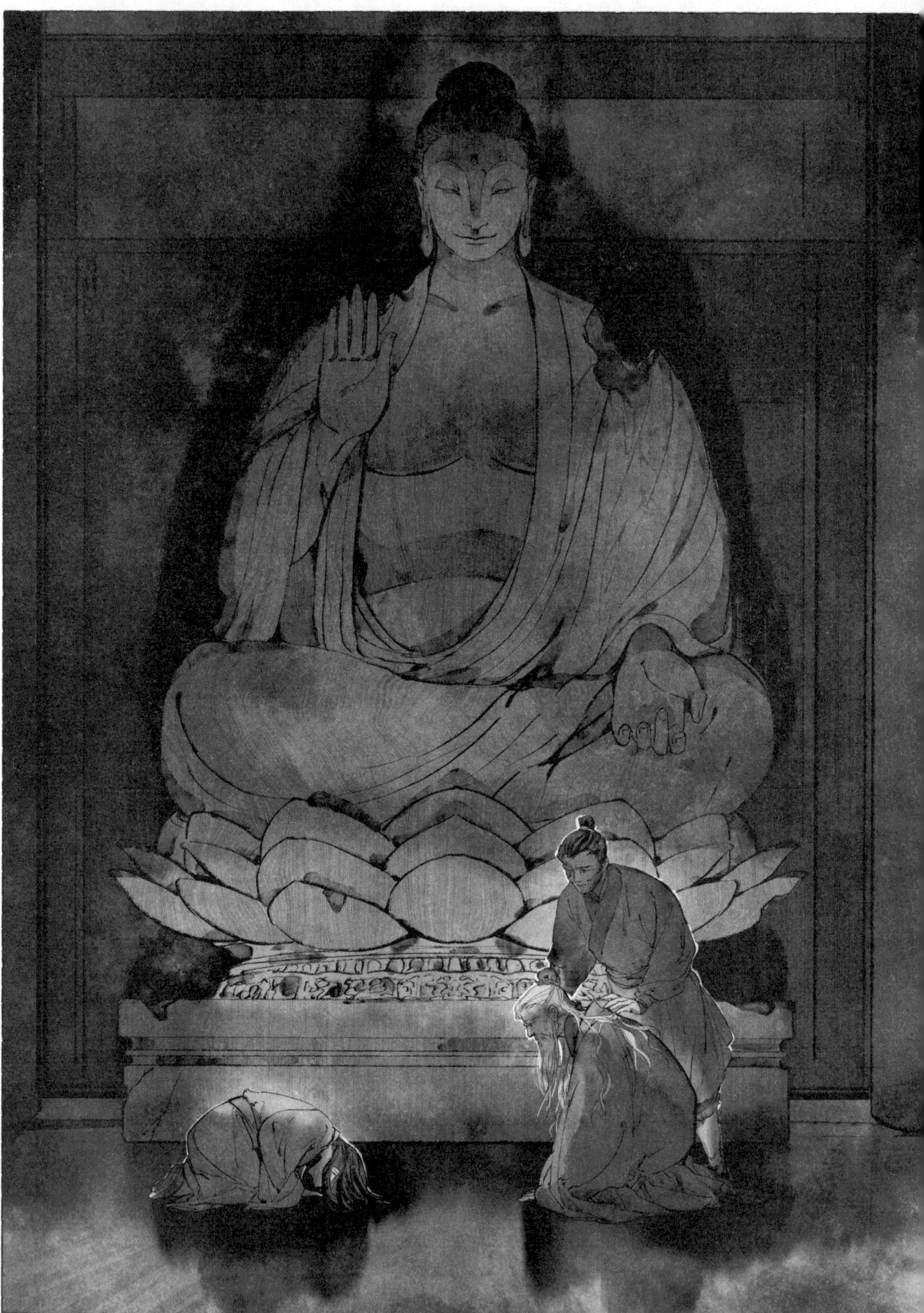

Xiao Chiye had been drinking all night. His clothes were in disarray. He lifted the token and said, "This doesn't seem to be the way to the palace."

Ge Qingqing lifted his head with a sheepish smile. "Er-gongzi leads a privileged life and knows not how the messy common alleys snake around. From here, you need only make a few turns and you'll emerge onto Shenwu Street, which will take you straight to the palace gates."

"You know me?" Xiao Chiye smiled and tossed the token back to him.

Ge Qingqing caught it and said fawningly, "The Armored Cavalry of Libei are brave and skillful warriors. Both the Heir of Libei and the second young master have rendered meritorious service in coming to His Majesty's aid. How could anyone in Qudu not recognize you? Are you heading to your manor, Er-gongzi? The road is slippery. May this subordinate be so bold as to ask if you require an escort?"

Xiao Chiye raised an eyebrow. "Do I look drunk? You may go."

Ge Qingqing bowed again and left.

When Zhao Hui arrived, Xiao Chiye was tapping the red silk umbrella against the ground and nagging the steamed bun stall-keeper to hurry.

"Breakfast is prepared at the manor. Why is Er-gongzi standing around here for it?"

"Too hungry to walk back," Xiao Chiye replied.

Zhao Hui shook open an overcoat. "Wine and lust will lead you astray. Let's go back, Gongzi."

Xiao Chiye draped the cloak over himself but stayed where he was. He took ravenous bites of the steamed bun, paying no heed to the looks of those around them. "Can one reach Shenwu Street from here?" he asked Zhao Hui.

"Theoretically, but it's not an easy path. Common alleys follow the routes of the public sewers. The narrower the alley, the more wastewater and excrement back up in it. The public sewers in Qudu haven't been properly maintained for years, and this area is rotten beyond recognition. Once the weather warms up, with snowmelt and rainfall, wastewater will flood the streets. What do you think, is such a path smooth?"

"I only asked you one question," Xiao Chiye said. "What's with the speech?"

"I only mean you must be sure to take the proper path," said Zhao Hui. "Drinking can wait, Gongzi. You will get there faster in the end if you take the long way around."

"How very strange. Go ask around and see if someone named Ge Qingqing is on duty in the Twelve Offices today." Xiao Chiye wiped his hands and motioned for Zhao Hui to pay. "Hey old man, better find a new line of work; your buns taste horrible."

8

SUSPICION

IT WAS JUST BEFORE shift change for the Imperial Army, and the soldiers were freezing, huddled into themselves where they stood.

The Imperial Army of Qudu had once been the Imperial Guards of the eight cities, the impregnable fortress of the imperial palace in Qudu. Trivialities such as guarding and escorting convicts were, by all rights, beneath them. After the Eight Great Battalions' rise to power, however, their duties had steadily eroded until the Imperial Army became no more than a burden on Qudu. All military drills were abolished, and they became the capital's footmen in every sense; these days the Imperial Army was filled with the sons of old military households who had never seen real combat, there to kill time and twiddle their thumbs.

As a company commander of the Embroidered Uniform Guard, Ge Qingqing was not a particularly high-ranking official in Qudu, but he was perfect for the Imperial Army officers assigned guard duty at the temple: high enough to be worth flattering and low enough to share a friendly chat. Patrolling the same streets of Qudu every day, after all, they had to look out for each other. Were he of slightly higher rank, these guards would not dare to pay "respects" so easily. But Ge Qingqing was affable and exceedingly generous with them, so when he brought Ji Gang, the Imperial Army turned a blind eye and let the man take over the job of the original attendant at the temple.

Ge Qingqing greeted the officers on duty and distributed the hot steamed buns he had stopped for on the way. Ji Gang had yet to come out. Seeing his pensive expression, the squad leader said, "If Qing-ge is in a hurry, feel free to go in and take a look on our behalf."

"Isn't that against the rules?"

The squad leader motioned for the Imperial Army officers guarding the back door to make way. "Qing-ge's one of us," he said through a bite of steamed bun. "Besides, we have this temple completely surrounded; not even a drop of water could trickle through. He's not going anywhere."

Ge Qingqing didn't decline twice; he stepped into the temple.

Ji Gang was sitting outside under the eaves. When he saw Ge Qingqing, he stood and asked, "Is it time already?"

"The sun isn't yet up; Ji-shu can stay a little longer." Ge Qingqing surveyed the temple courtyard. "This place is barely habitable, especially in winter. I'll have some quilts sent over today."

Ji Gang could see he was distracted. "What's the matter?"

"It's nothing." Ge Qingqing hesitated. "I just ran into Second Young Master Xiao on the way here."

Shen Zechuan looked up. "This Xiao..."

"Xiao Chiye," Ge Qingqing said. "He's the younger son of the Prince of Libei. The one who kicked you. He was practically falling over, and he reeked of wine. I'd wager he went drinking last night."

"As long as it wasn't Xiao Jiming." Ji Gang turned back to Grand Mentor Qi. "Grand Mentor hasn't left this place for twenty years, so you probably don't know the current Four Great Generals of our nation. The Prince of Libei begat himself quite an heir. That Xiao Jiming is a remarkable talent!"

Shen Zechuan turned back to Ge Qingqing. "Qing-ge, did he ask you anything?"

Ge Qingqing thought carefully. "He asked me where I was going, and I said I was taking a shortcut to the command office. He remarked that the road didn't seem to lead to Shenwu Street, so I made up an excuse. I figured the son of a prince wouldn't personally investigate the common alleys."

"With anything involving the Xiao Clan, it pays to be cautious. Make sure you go to the palace later and place a mark on the duty roster." Ji Gang rubbed his hands in the snow to clean them. "Chuan-er, it's time to train."

"Wait." Shen Zechuan's gaze was dark and deep. "You say it was a common alley in a residential district; what was a noble son like him doing there so early in the morning?"

Ge Qingqing was stupefied. "Now that you mention it, the entertainment houses are all on Donglong Street, some distance away from that alley. It's freezing out, and he was nursing a hangover. What was he doing there?"

"Lying in wait, probably." With the tattered curtain wrapped around him, Grand Mentor Qi turned over so his rump was facing outward. "Shen Wei's case is of great concern to the Xiao Clan. I heard Xiao Chiye aimed to kill this boy with the kick he dealt him. Yet the boy's still alive and well—how could the young master not be suspicious?"

"If he was truly oblivious, he wouldn't have asked a second question." Shen Zechuan still shivered when he recalled that kick.

"Shit." Ge Qingqing paled. "It's my fault for being negligent. What should we do? He's probably on the way here now!"

Shen Zechuan turned to Grand Mentor Qi. "It's all right. Since Xiansheng has already guessed this much, he must have a countermeasure in mind."

Zhao Hui arrived alone at the command office of the Embroidered Uniform Guard. Although the assistant commander on duty was his equal in rank, he didn't dare put on airs before the Heir of Libei's right-hand man. He led Zhao Hui to the registry. "What does General Zhao wish to see? Here are today's duty rosters for the Twelves Offices."

Zhao Hui wasn't one for small talk; he flipped through the records in silence. "I appreciate the hard work of our brothers from the Embroidered Uniform Guard in patrolling the palace grounds. A few days ago, I received assistance from a company commander by the name of Ge Qingqing. I've come to thank him. Is he on duty?"

"There are quite a few company commanders from the Twelves Offices; they're all listed here," the assistant commander said, moving to the wall where the duty rosters of the Twelve Offices hung, clearly labeled.

Zhao Hui eyed them. These records were off limits to those who worked outside the palace; they weren't for him to touch.

"Perhaps the general knows which office he belongs to?" the assistant commander prompted.

"I heard he works the morning shift, so perhaps the Carriage Office, Umbrella Office, or the Elephant-Training Office," said Zhao Hui.

The assistant commander carefully checked the list of names for each office. After a moment, he turned to Zhao Hui. "General, there's no such person on duty today. Shall I look elsewhere for you?"

Zhao Hui gently closed the book in his hands. "There's no need. I'll find him on my own."

The sky was beginning to lighten as Zhao Hui left the registry. He walked back along the road and out of the palace. The snow that had fallen on Shenwu Street was freshly swept, but the road was slippery. The sedan bearers who carried bigwigs to and fro took every step with care, not daring to move too quickly.

As Zhao Hui passed a particular sedan, he caught a glimpse of the bearer's sidearm blade. That fleeting glance was enough to make him furrow his brow.

"Please hold." Zhao Hui stopped the sedan chair. "Is this chair carrying the chief commander?"

Sure enough, the sedan bearers were members of the Embroidered Uniform Guard. The one in the lead gave a sharp nod. "If you know who's inside, why do you block the way? Move!"

Zhao Hui flashed his own Libei authority token.

The guard bowed his head. "Please excuse the offense, General!"

A slender hand lifted the window's curtain, revealing a lovely face. The woman glanced lazily at Zhao Hui before pouting coquettishly at someone deeper within. "A man looking for you, Your Excellency!"

Ji Lei had been drinking all night. Lounging comfortably in the sedan with his legs spread wide, he called, "General Zhao! Is anything the matter?"

Zhao Hui fixed his gaze on the guard leading the sedan as he answered, "It's nothing. I heard our young master went drinking with Your Excellency last night. Are you just returning?"

Ji Lei laughed. "So you're worried about the second young master! Your young master had scampered off home by the time I opened my eyes this morning. Is the Heir of Libei looking for him?"

"The one who can't help worrying is me." Zhao Hui bowed. "My apologies for the disturbance, Your Excellency."

"It's fine! I'm just now coming back myself." Ji Lei gestured. "Who talked back to the general earlier? Apologize."

The guard in the lead went down on one knee. "This humble servant, Ge Qingqing, was blind to not have recognized the general. For my offense, I'm willing to accept my punishment!"

Zhao Hui was not mistaken. The name carved on the authority token hanging beside the guard's scabbard was indeed *Ge Qingqing*.

Zhao Hui delivered his report as Xiao Chiye sprawled with his leg propped up, reading a play.

"So, it seems he wasn't lying," Zhao Hui said. "He was just assigned to pick up Ji Lei before entering the palace this morning."

"Yeah," Xiao Chiye responded absentmindedly. "Qingjun Pavilion is so close, of course he could make it in time."

"Something still feels off." Zhao Hui rubbed his thumb on the hilt of his blade.

"Can't figure it out?" Xiao Chiye turned the page.

"I can't."

"Then I'll tell you." Xiao Chiye sat up, crossed his legs, and propped a hand on one knee. "You entered the capital at my brother's side, to a personal reception from His Majesty. All Twelve Offices of the Embroidered Uniform Guard were following close behind in ceremonial procession. How could he not recognize you?"

"Hard to say," Zhao Hui said. "Maybe he doesn't remember me."

"You're wearing the same robe and carrying your blade. Even if he didn't recognize you, if he used his brain a little, he'd have guessed your importance and wouldn't risk reproaching you in such a condescending way in the middle of the street," Xiao Chiye said. "Besides, I don't think he has a bad memory at all. He recognized me just fine."

"I did think it was rather too much of a coincidence to run into him just then," Zhao Hui mused.

"Yes, a well-staged coincidence." Xiao Chiye cast aside the play he was reading. "This Shen..."

"Shen Zechuan," Zhao Hui said.

Xiao Chiye's gaze was pensive. "Letting him enter the Temple of Guilt feels like a losing move now."

Ge Qingqing removed his fur collar and wiped sweat from his neck. Wu Caiquan came running sheepishly inside. "Thank you, thank you! Qing-ge, thank goodness for you!"

"Don't mention it," Ge Qingqing replied. "We are all brothers here."

Wu Caiquan grinned and turned to yell toward the person in the registry office, "Lao-Xu! Put Qing-ge's name on the record. He stood in for me to carry the sedan this morning. I caught a cold last night and woke up dizzy. Thank goodness Qing-ge was there to help."

"Since you've caught a cold, let's go to the Xu family's stall for mutton soup later," Ge Qingqing said, wiping his brow.

Wu Caiquan hastened to agree. "Sure! It's Qing-ge's treat! Did you hear that, Lao-Xu? Let's all go together later!"

"Don't rush it." Ge Qingqing patted Wu Caiquan on the back. "Get some rest. Next time you feel unwell, don't hold back like you did this time. Just let me know."

Wu Caiquan bobbed his head like a puppy. So powerful was his craving for mutton soup that he would have agreed to practically anything.

That night, Grand Mentor Qi at long last had a thick quilt to warm his old bones. He sat bundled up across from Shen Zechuan and said, "In half a month, it'll be the Spring Festival. Qudu will host the Court Officials' Feast. At that time, officials from all the provinces and prefectures will travel to the capital to offer New Year's greetings. I've no knowledge of the present state of affairs, so you'll have to fill me in."

Shen Zechuan stood in the snow dressed only in thin layers, holding the starting stance of Ji-Style Boxing. Despite the cold, his brow was sheened with sweat.

"The Prince of Libei has been in poor health for many years," he began, "and the Heir of Libei, Xiao Jiming, has taken charge of all their military affairs. The prince himself is unlikely to attend this year. The five commanderies of Qidong also distinguished themselves by coming to Qudu's rescue. The first of their people to arrive and receive his bestowed title was one of the Four Generals, Lu Guangbai. Marshal Qi should also arrive in the next few days. So two of the major military powers of Great Zhou will temporarily reside—"

"Hold it." Grand Mentor Qi fished out a disciplinary ruler from within his quilt. "Who are these 'four generals'?"

Shen Zechuan obediently intoned:

"Iron horse on river ice, Xiao Jiming;
Beacon-smoke and rising sand, Lu Guangbai;
Windstorm through the scorching plains, Qi Zhuyin;
Thunder on jade terraces, Zuo Qianqiu."

Grand Mentor Qi considered a moment. "I have only heard of Zuo Qianqiu, but this Lu Guangbai must be the son of the Earl of Biansha, Lu Pingyan. Although Lu Pingyan later went to guard the deserts of the Bianjun Commandery, he came up in Libei and is the sworn brother of their prince, Xiao Fangxu. If Lu Guangbai has a sister, she will surely have married into the Xiao Clan, am I right?"

"Yes." Shen Zechuan dripped with sweat. "Lu Guangbai's younger sister is the wife of Xiao Jiming."

"If that's so, why would you call them *two* major military powers?" Grand Mentor Qi asked. "The Lu Clan might as well be a seed Libei planted in Qidong. These branches are more tangled than they seem. Furthermore, Qudu still has the Eight Great Battalions, and under them the Imperial Army. The Eight Great Battalions haven't the numbers of the armies of Libei and Qidong, nor their valiant reputation—but you must remember that Qudu is the beating heart of Great Zhou. These forces hold the empire's life in their hands."

The grand mentor weighed the ruler in his hand, then lifted the gourd and warmed himself with a few sips of wine. "You must also remember this: although the Embroidered Uniform Guard are not technically 'soldiers,' they are much more efficient than any common troops. When the emperor commands his armies, he must be assisted by capable generals. What's more, a general in the field must be resourceful; at times, he may act against the orders of his sovereign. Keep too tight a rein, and you may hinder their progress. Hold on too loosely, and you risk raising a wild beast. It's a difficult balance and requires a ruler to adapt to the situation as it changes. The Embroidered Uniform Guard, however, is a different matter. They are vicious hounds at the foot of the throne, and their chain is held by the emperor alone. Whether to tighten or loosen his grip, whether to pamper or discard them, depends wholly on the emperor's moods. Such a blade, such a pack of dogs—if it were you, would you not prefer them?"

Shen Zechuan struggled to hold his stance for a moment before answering. "I would—so I would spoil them! But such excessive favor and trust will surely breed trouble."

"Your brother taught you well," said the grand mentor. "That's right. Remember that, commit it to memory! An excess of favor and trust breeds trouble. Keeping the virtuous close and the flatterers at a distance is sound in theory. But when you're in the thick of it, when darkness intersects with light, can you distinguish with certainty the virtuous talents from the crafty sycophants? Besides, there are many things a virtuous man cannot do that a crafty and despicable one can. The emperor resides in the depths of the imperial palace. He must understand checks and balances and pay heed to the varied voices of the officials and ministers. Nothing is so neatly divided—with Libei comes Qidong, and likewise, with the Embroidered Uniform Guard comes the Eastern Depot."

Grand Mentor Qi paused. "Water that brims must overflow, and every waxing moon must wane. Why does the Xiao Clan hate Shen Wei so fiercely? Do you see—no greater honor can possibly be bestowed on them after Zhongbo. Even if the Xiao Clan fights another battle, every defeat will be a loss, and every victory will also be a loss. They have come to a dead end."

"A victory is also a loss?"

"Their victory is also a loss! Did Xiao Jiming not lose his younger brother to Qudu immediately after his battlefield triumph? With each battle he wins in the future, the danger will only grow. This time he traded in his brother. Next time, it might be his wife, his father—even himself."

PROMOTION

TOWARD THE END OF THE YEAR, the streets of Qudu teemed with people in their finest nao'e headdresses, cut from silk or gold paper into the flowers and insects of the new season. As the Spring Festival that marked the new year approached, the common folk prepared pastries and cooked meat at home in anticipation. The palace, of course, had started procuring ingredients for the Court Officials' Feast a fortnight in advance. The entirety of the Court of Imperial Entertainments was scrambling like mad to get everything done, yet only the eunuchs managed to line their pockets in the process—through skimming off the top.

As Xiao Jiming dressed, Xiao Chiye riffled noisily through a book of accounts. "When these local officials enter the capital, they'll doubtless have to offer up ice respects[15] to the capital officials. But Pan Rugui is truly impressive in this regard; he's drawn up such a well-organized list. Only after they shell out are they allowed to proceed."

"And this is merely small change at the start of the year." Lu Guangbai brushed aside the foam on his tea. "Let me give you an account: the money a junior eunuch pockets in one year under Pan Rugui far exceeds the funds allocated for a thousand-man battalion

---

15 *In the Qing dynasty, ice respects were one of the "three respects," along with coal respects and departure respects, used to bribe capital officials.*

stationed at the frontier for two years. Meanwhile, year after year when our Great Zhou deploys troops, the Ministry of Revenue grovels and pleads with us like a child to his father each time they ask us to fight. Yet when the battle is over, we're treated like bastards coming to collect a debt."

"The ones with the money are the real masters," Xiao Chiye said with a smile.

"When we came to the emperor's rescue this year, our Libei troops marched through ice and snow," said Zhao Hui. "The men and horses are tired, and repairs on the armored cavalry's equipment must be completed before spring. The payments we owe the workshops are long overdue. Everything requires money." He carefully did the calculations in his mind. "Before we entered Qudu, the Libei Garrison Troops worked the land where we were stationed and sold the surplus harvest to supplement our funds. We have to count every cent and make every cent count. Our heir's consort can't splurge on fine clothing for the household even for the New Year holiday. The money a palace eunuch like Pan Rugui rakes in exceeds what the entire prefecture of Duanzhou collects in tax. Those investigating censors throw their weight around when they're sent to audit the local governments, but they don't dare utter a word about this corruption when they're at home in Qudu!"

"But what can we do? We're broke," Lu Guangbai lamented. "We worry over money year after year. At least with Jiming in the capital this year the Ministry of Revenue can't drag their feet; they submitted the request for funds to the Grand Secretariat long ago. Pan Rugui has also behaved himself and signed his approval. Libei will likely see the money before he leaves the capital."

Xiao Chiye set aside the accounts and turned to Lu Guangbai.

"We have my brother, but what are *you* going to do?"

"His Majesty won't see me," Lu Guangbai admitted. "The Lu Clan is unpopular in Qudu. The Eight Great Clans have always regarded us as uncouth desert dwellers. The Hua Clan especially can hardly bear to look us in the eye. Even if you advised me to pay every kind of 'respect' to Pan Rugui, I don't have the money to do it; as it is, we've barely enough to put food on the table. Other garrisons can work their land to tide them over the bad times, but Bianjun Commandery is yellow sand for miles. No farmland at all.

"This time, we mustered the troops in a hurry, but all the provisions for the men and horses during the journey were paid for out of Grand Marshal Qi's personal savings. To put it bluntly, if it wasn't for Marshal Qi's generosity, my troops would have never made it past Tianfei Watchtower. But how much money does Marshal Qi have? She's dipping into the dowry given to her by the old consort mother. Her private troops are on the verge of selling their own pants! The Ministry of Revenue passes the buck every day—I've gone round in circles with them till I'm dizzy. Dereliction of duty is what it is: they keep refusing to release the funds, figuring a country bumpkin like me can't do anything about it."

It was rare that Lu Guangbai showed his temper, but he couldn't help it. The Bianjun Commandery defended the empire's desert frontier; aside from Libei, they were the garrison troops who clashed most often with the Biansha Horsemen. They ran themselves ragged sprinting from one place to another year-round, eking out a living under the sharp edges of scimitars. They barely slept and never ate their fill. Yet Qudu snubbed the Earl of Biansha so pointedly that he had become an infamous pauper among princes. His clan kept nothing of the rewards bestowed upon them; every bit had been sold and the money used to replenish military provisions.

When Xiao Jiming had finished dressing, the maidservants filed out, leaving only the four of them in the room. Xiao Jiming took a sip of tea and remarked languidly, "It's good timing this year—the Spring Court Officials' Feast. Qi Zhuyin should be arriving any day, right?"

"That's right," Lu Guangbai answered. "I was worried at first, but on second thought, let them drag this matter out as they please. If they delay until the grand marshal enters the capital—well then, good luck to them."

"They all love her in Qudu right now," Xiao Jiming said. "Even the local thugs and loan sharks in Qudu respect her. Maybe these current accounts can be settled, but you can't keep relying on her. The Bianjun Commandery is of great strategic importance. I heard yesterday that the Ministry of Revenue will be asking you to recruit again this year."

Lu Guangbai stroked the rim of the teacup. "Recruitment? Don't even think about it. Everyone's petrified after what happened in Zhongbo. The Ministry is concerned about Bianjun getting skewered by the Biansha; they worry my twenty thousand troops and horses can't hold them. But if we recruit more soldiers, will they grant us the money to pay them? I certainly can't afford it. Even if they hold a blade to my throat this year, I won't do it."

"That's right." Xiao Chiye straightened up. "In the past, however slow they were to provide for other regions, the Ministry of Revenue was always quick to grant funds and rations to the garrisons in Zhongbo. Now that they're all dead, forget the money—what about the grain? There's no way the Biansha Horsemen could carry it all as they fled."

The other three looked at him.

"Silly boy, you can forget about that," Lu Guangbai said. "All the recovered grain was used to pay salary arrears in the thirteen cities of Juexi this year. Do you see why the Ministry of Revenue keeps dodging the issue? The Eight Clans have spent the better part of the last decade building up the Eight Great Battalions, and their equipment and budgets are the best in our Great Zhou. But all the money came straight from tax funds—over two million taels. Anyone could tell you how insane these numbers are! But if both the empress dowager and Secretariat Elder Hua turn a blind eye, who in the Ministry of Revenue would be brave enough to bring the matter up? The thirteen cities were hit with a plague of locusts last year—not a single grain was harvested. With this bite taken out of the state treasury, where would the Ministry of Revenue find the funds to carry Juexi through the hardship?

"They've only scraped by thanks to the Provincial Administration Commissioner, Jiang Qingshan," Lu Guangbai continued. "He forced the prefectural officials of every rank to open their private granaries and distribute food to the affected commoners. Jiang Qingshan saved hundreds of thousands of people, yet he's loathed by every one of Juexi's officials. Before the new year, I heard debt collectors were banging down his door trying to get their money. The man's a provincial official of the second rank, yet his eighty-year-old mother still has to weave to pay off their debt! They'd be forced to their deaths if Qudu didn't pay up. In the end, it was Secretariat Elder Hai who submitted a report and fought the Grand Secretariat and Pan Rugui for a fortnight, and they still barely managed to make up the shortfall."

Zhao Hui couldn't help but chime in. "These capital officials claim to be poor, but the bribes come in such large figures while the ones doing the real work must tighten their belts. We're walking on eggshells here; we might as well not have made this trip to Qudu.

It's disheartening."

Outside, snow was falling, but there was no festive atmosphere within. Messes piled up one after another, and the bright sights of Qudu were like gauze skimming the surface of an open wound, hiding the injury even as pus dirtied the ground. The snow came at a perfect time: concealing everything so beautifully one could pretend not to see the filth beneath, allowing all to keep living like drunkards in this fool's paradise.

In the middle of the night, Pan Rugui sat on the settee with his eyes closed. A paper napkin folded in the shape of a flower sat beside him so he could wipe his hands after meditation. Xiaofuzi didn't dare even breathe too loudly as he waited on the footrest, a brush case in his hands.

After an hour, Pan Rugui exhaled and opened his eyes. Xiaofuzi immediately presented the brush. Frowning in concentration, Pan Rugui wrote a few words in Xiaofuzi's palm.

Xiaofuzi wasted no time buttering him up. "Thanks to His Majesty's recent teachings, Lao-zuzong is becoming more ethereal by the day. Earlier, this little one even saw a wisp of purple smoke rising from your head—how auspicious!"

Pan Rugui wiped his hands and asked, "Do you know why you couldn't get into the Directorate of Ceremonial Affairs?"

"Because you dote on me," Xiaofuzi replied.

"My doting on you is one thing." Pan Rugui tossed the paper flower into Xiaofuzi's waiting hands. "You not being able to read the room is another. His Majesty has been enlightened for two years, yet even he still doesn't give off a purple aura. I'm a mere servant. How can I ascend first? Is that not overstepping my bounds?"

Xiaofuzi handed a cup of hot tea to Pan Rugui with an ingratiating smile. "*You* are my master, my heaven. Seeing Lao-zuzong meditate is like seeing Taishang Laojun[16] himself! Why on earth would I think more of it?"

"Mm." Pan Rugui rinsed his mouth. "This filial piety of yours is about the only worthy skill you have."

Xiaofuzi snickered as he leaned close to Pan Rugui's leg. "The Spring Festival is almost upon us; it's only right I show my filial respect toward Lao-zuzong. While I was making New Year's preparations earlier, I spied a breathtaking beauty in Prince Chu's manor! I made some inquiries and thought, if His Majesty has no use for her, she really ought to be offered to you instead."

"How breathtaking could she be?" Pan Rugui wondered. "Can she compare to Third Lady Hua? Besides, isn't she in Prince Chu's possession? The prince has an obstinate temper; I'm afraid he won't let her go without a fight."

"No matter how noble Prince Chu is, he can't very well be nobler than His Majesty, can he? His Majesty didn't speak against it, so why shouldn't I present her to you? No need to worry; all the proper arrangements will be made before the start of spring. By the time you lay eyes on her, only her good or ill fortune will determine whether or not you accept your gift."

Pan Rugui set the teacup aside. "There's no hurry. I'm not an avaricious or lecherous man. But speaking of the obstinate Prince Chu, how is Second Young Master Xiao faring in the capital?"

Xiaofuzi kneaded Pan Rugui's legs. "Ha! That Second Young Master Xiao is really something. He's been carousing every night since the moment he entered the capital! Aside from eat, drink, and make merry, he hasn't done a single thing. Prince Chu and his

---

16 *Taishang Laojun, or the Grand Supreme Elderly Lord, is a deity in Daoism. It was believed that Laozi, who authored the classic Tao Te Ching, was the incarnation of Taishang Laojun.*

ilk have readily adopted him into their company; birds of a feather really do flock together!"

"That's all well and good, but he's still a member of the Xiao Clan. His Majesty placed him in the Imperial Regalia Service, but it feels too close for comfort—the idea makes me uneasy." Pan Rugui considered for a moment, then broke into a smile. "I've just thought of the perfect spot for him. Put on my shoes. I'm going to Mingli Hall to serve His Majesty!"

The next day was the Court Officials' Feast of the Spring Festival. After several uneventful hours, the feast had begun to wind down when the Xiande Emperor raised his voice. "A-Ye, have you been comfortable in Qudu?"

Xiao Chiye stopped peeling a tangerine to answer. "Yes, Your Majesty, I have."

The Xiande Emperor turned to Xiao Jiming. "We've been thinking. Assigning A-Ye to the Imperial Regalia Service is a waste of his skills. He's a talented lad who has served on the battlefield. Keeping him so close at our side is too restrictive. How about this: let A-Ye go to the Imperial Army. Xi Gu'an used to command the Imperial Army, but now he's overseeing the Eight Great Battalions. He's up to his neck in work, so A-Ye can take his place as supreme commander."

Lu Guangbai immediately frowned. At the very least, the Imperial Regalia Service worked under the nose of the emperor. If anything should happen, His Majesty couldn't ignore it. What good was the Imperial Army? These days, they might as well be the errand boys of Qudu. Was this a reward? How could it be considered one?!

But before Lu Guangbai could rise to his feet in protest, Xiao Chiye was already bowing his gratitude.

"*Supreme commander* sounds awfully impressive, almost like

a marshal." Xiao Chiye flashed a careless grin. "Thank you, Your Majesty!"

Secretariat Elder Hua laughed boisterously. "His Majesty is wise! Now here's a young hero in the making, Shizi."

The sounds of congratulations rose and fell through the banquet hall like the tide. Xiao Jiming smiled but said nothing as he gazed at Xiao Chiye.

"This arrangement may as well be a knife at Jiming's heart," Lu Guangbai murmured to Zhao Hui as he put his head down to drink.

When the banquet ended, Xiao Chiye disappeared without a trace. His rowdy friends had clamored to congratulate him on his promotion, and he'd happily obliged. When they finally emerged from taverns and pleasure houses long after midnight, it was with unsteady steps.

Prince Chu, Li Jianheng, was a few years older than Xiao Chiye and a true scoundrel. Even as he stepped up to his sedan, he was tugging at Xiao Chiye's sleeve, slurring, "Mighty impressive of you! In the Imperial Army, you won't have to bother with patrols or defenses. It's an idle job with a decent salary. No need to put your life on the line, yet you still get the money. All the best things in the world have fallen into your lap! I bet you'll be laughing in your sleep!"

Xiao Chiye also grinned, sharp and wicked. "That's right. Isn't that why I brought you out for drinks first thing? From now on, we'll storm the streets of Qudu together!"

"Yes, yes!" Li Jianheng sighed blearily and clapped Xiao Chiye on the shoulder. "That's the spirit! Come to my manor in a few days, and I'll...toast you again..."

Xiao Chiye watched the sedan dwindle into the distance before mounting his own horse. He had personally bred this steed from a line of wild horses he'd tamed at the foot of the Hongyan

Mountains. It was swift and fierce, with a coat that was pure black save for a snow-white patch on its chest. As Xiao Chiye urged it forward, the shops that lined the street moved to light their lanterns to illuminate his way. He raised a hand. "Put them out."

The shop attendants exchanged glances, but none dared disobey. The lanterns winked out one by one until only the dim glow of the frosty moonlight remained, reflected on the icy road. Xiao Chiye whistled, and his gyrfalcon swooped down from the darkness of night, echoing his call. He spurred his horse forward, and the battle steed snorted a cloud of hot steam and broke into a gallop.

The strong wind battered Xiao Chiye, dissipating the flush from the alcohol. In the dark, he was like a cornered beast trying to break free, the hoofbeats the sound of him crashing against his prison walls. He sped through the deserted streets. The smile on his face dropped away under the cover of darkness until all that remained was a cold, lonely silence.

Who knew how long the horse had been running when Xiao Chiye tumbled off. He crashed heavily into a large snowdrift and remained there, head down. The horse trotted around him, lowering its head to nudge his. The gyrfalcon, perched on his saddle, tilted its head to look quizzically at him.

Xiao Chiye heaved, trying to keep it together, but soon gave up—he propped himself up and vomited into the snow. After several minutes, he finally lurched to his feet and leaned against the wall. The bone ring he wore on his thumb was a little loose, and now he realized it had fallen off during his tumble. He had just bent to search for it in the snow when he heard a low voice from a short distance away.

"Who goes there?"

Xiao Chiye ignored it.

A squad leader of the Imperial Army held out his lantern to light the way. "How dare—ah, Your Excellency?"

Xiao Chiye turned. "You know me?"

The squad leader shook his head honestly. "I'm afraid I don't recognize Your Excellency..."

"I'm your big brother." Xiao Chiye cast away his soiled cloak and dropped his eyes back to the snow, hunting for his thumb ring. He cursed under his breath. "Lantern—here. You—elsewhere."

The squad leader cautiously drew closer. "You're Er-gongzi, aren't you? We just received the decree. It's a little early for an inspection—it's still dark out. Maybe if you come again tomorrow..."

Xiao Chiye held out his hand, and the squad leader handed over the lantern.

"What is this place?" Xiao Chiye asked.

"The wall marks the perimeter of Qudu; this is the Temple of Guilt," the squad leader respectfully replied.

"That'll be all."

The squad leader knew a dismissal when he heard one; he was about to back away when he heard Xiao Chiye's voice ring out once more. "Is Shen Zechuan here? Inside the temple?"

"Yes." The squad leader grew apprehensive. "He's detained in—"

"Bring him out."

For a moment the squad leader was stunned. Then he blurted, "That won't do! Not even if you're the supreme commander! His Majesty strictly forbade—"

"In the Imperial Army, I have final say." Xiao Chiye lifted the lantern.

The squad leader stuttered nervously, "Even so, don't k-kill..."

"I want him to fucking come out here and sing a little song for my pleasure!" Xiao Chiye flung the lantern aside, and the light went out. He stood in the dark, his eyes filling with cruelty.

DRUNK

XIAO JIMING GATHERED HIS CLOAK around him as he waited under the hanging lanterns. Zhao Hui, standing guard behind him, spoke up. "He should have returned by now. The man who went to pick him up said the young master left by himself on his horse. How is he still not back?"

Xiao Jiming huffed into the cold air and turned his face to the sky. "Whenever he was unhappy at home, he would always take his horse for a gallop at the foot of the Hongyan Mountains," he said. "Old habits die hard."

"At the very least, the Imperial Army is a real post," Zhao Hui said.

Xiao Jiming shifted his gaze to him. "Do you know my father's biggest regret?"

Zhao Hui shook his head.

"It's that A-Ye was born too late," Xiao Jiming said. "Three years ago, we were ambushed at the foot of the Hongyan Mountains. Before our father's reinforcements arrived, A-Ye led twenty cavalry who were supposed to be his personal guards and crossed the Hongjiang River in the dark. He trudged around in a muddy bog for half the night setting fire to the Biansha provisions. When I saw him, he was filthy, and the wounds on his legs had festered. He was only fourteen at the time. I asked if he was scared. He said he had a blast.

"Our father often said the Lu Clan are the eagles of the desert, while the Xiao Clan became the dogs of Libei. I don't like this saying. But in recent years, the Xiao Clan has gone into battle like chained dogs; it's never as satisfying as it was in the old days. These long years of fighting have drained the ferocity out of me. The Xiao Clan are not dogs, but A-Ye is the only one of us who still possesses the heart of a wolf. He dreams of the mountains of Libei, yet now he must stay in Qudu and forget the freedom of galloping across the plain. Both Father and I have let him down."

After a moment's silence, Zhao Hui looked at Xiao Jiming. "Don't be so hard on yourself, Shizi. The young master is naturally impetuous; he was never the best choice to continue your father's legacy. Whether he was born earlier or later doesn't matter; the reins of Libei would never be his. The commander in chief must have the iron tenacity of a hammer forged by experience, and willpower as steady as an anvil. The young master is not up to the task."

Xiao Jiming was quiet.

The night wind set the lanterns swinging. Master and subordinate waited in the dark another hour before they spied someone riding toward them in the distance.

"Heir Xiao!" The man tumbled off his horse in his hurry to report. "Something has happened to the young master!"

Zhao Hui's hand went instantly to his blade. "Where?"

An hour earlier.

The squad leader shoved a shackled Shen Zechuan down the steps. "Sing." The squad leader prodded him from behind. "Quick, sing a few lines for the supreme commander!"

Shen Zechuan didn't utter a note as he looked at the man squatting in the shadow of the wall. As soon as he saw the gyrfalcon, his chest tightened. Without thought, he pressed his lips into a thin line and stood unmoving.

"Get over here," Xiao Chiye ordered.

Shen Zechuan exhaled, his breath white in the frigid air. He slowly shuffled forward to stand a short distance from Xiao Chiye.

Xiao Chiye rose to his feet. "Who was your mother?"

"A dancer from Duanzhou," Shen Zechuan replied.

"Then you know how to sing, don't you?" Xiao Chiye's gaze could chill a man to his bones. "That old dog Shen might not have taught you, but with a mother like that, you must have learned *something*."

"...I don't know." Shen Zechuan looked at the ground to escape his gaze, as if intimidated.

"Raise your head." Xiao Chiye nudged the lantern aside with his foot. "Are you afraid of me?"

Shen Zechuan had no choice but to do so. He smelled alcohol.

"Fine," Xiao Chiye said. "If you don't want to sing, get down and look for something for me."

Spreading his hands, Shen Zechuan showed him the shackles he wore.

Xiao Chiye frowned. "Those can stay on."

So Shen Zechuan squatted down and grabbed halfheartedly at a few handfuls of snow.

"Stand up again," Xiao Chiye ordered, staring coldly at the top of his head.

Shen Zechuan braced his bound hands on his knees and stood up.

"Your legs seem fine, if you can bend and stand so easily," Xiao Chiye observed. "Was the Embroidered Uniform Guard too gentle with their flogging, or is a worthless life easier to sustain?"

"Naturally, it's because a worthless life is easier to sustain," Shen Zechuan answered quietly. "I was lucky."

"That makes no sense." Xiao Chiye pressed the tip of his riding crop to Shen Zechuan's chest. "That kick was meant to end this life. Your martial arts foundation must be pretty good."

At the touch of the riding crop, Shen Zechuan shuddered. Cowering back, he pleaded, "I'm just...hanging onto my last breath is all. Er-gongzi is a righteous man—why make life difficult for a nobody like me? I've gotten what I deserve. Please spare me."

"Do you really mean that?"

Shen Zechuan sniffled with soft sobs. He nodded his head vigorously.

Xiao Chiye retracted his riding crop. "Words are easy. Who knows if they're true. How about this: bark for me, and once I'm satisfied, I'll spare you."

Shen Zechuan kept silent.

The look in Xiao Chiye's eyes terrified the squad leader. He urged Shen Zechuan with a few anxious shoves. Face drained of color, Shen Zechuan said timidly, "At least let me do it where no one else can see."

Xiao Chiye didn't waste words. "Move. Get rolling."

The squad leader relaxed immediately, saying happily to Shen Zechuan, "Get rolling! Yes sir, we'll roll right away..."

Xiao Chiye's cutting gaze fell on the squad leader's face. The captain went weak at the knees. Pointing to himself, he said, "Just m-me? Sure—sure thing!" Gritting his teeth, he curled himself into a ball and rolled a few times in the snow before standing up a short distance away.

Shen Zechuan coyly shifted closer. He leaned in and whispered into Xiao Chiye's ear: "Even if you spare me, do you think I will spare you?"

Snow scattered into the air as Xiao Chiye gripped Shen Zechuan's bound hands, his expression scathing. "So, the fox shows its tail. I was wondering about that pitiful act of yours!"

The two tumbled into the snow. Hands still trapped in handcuffs, Shen Zechuan landed a boot in Xiao Chiye's stomach and scrambled to brace himself. "The emperor ordered me confined, yet the Xiao Clan dares defy the throne and take my life. After tonight—" Xiao Chiye dragged Shen Zechuan toward him by the shackles. Shen Zechuan crashed to the ground, snarling through clenched teeth, "—every one of you are accomplices to the Xiao Clan's rebellion! My death means little, but when I go to the grave, the whole Imperial Army will be buried with me!"

Xiao Chiye grabbed Shen Zechuan in a chokehold from behind, forcing his head up, and barked a laugh. "You sure think highly of yourself. You imagine you're a precious treasure worth being buried with? Killing you is like pulling weeds!"

Struggling for breath, Shen Zechuan swiftly reached up and looped his shackles over the back of Xiao Chiye's neck, summoning all his strength to wrench him to the ground. Xiao Chiye was caught off guard, and as he scrambled, Shen Zechuan kicked him square in the chest. In an instant, their positions were reversed.

"Like pulling weeds?" Shen Zechuan leaned down, finally meeting Xiao Chiye eye to eye amid the tumult. "You squandered your opportunity," he spat hoarsely. "From here on out, we'll see who will be the hound and who the quarry!"

Xiao Chiye seethed with murderous rage. "Who is bold enough to help you in secret?! If I find them, I'll kill them!"

The squad leader, horrified at this sudden turn of events, rushed over. "Your Excellency! Your Excellency, you mustn't kill him!"

"That's right!" Shen Zechuan cried. "The second young master means to kill me tonight!"

"Shut up!" Xiao Chiye attempted to smother him with a hand. To his shock, Shen Zechuan bit down mercilessly. He pinned Xiao Chiye to the ground as his teeth tore through the fleshy web between Xiao Chiye's thumb and forefinger.

"You think you can hide behind a tantrum?" Xiao Chiye's voice was frosty. "No way are these the moves of someone on his last breath!"

When his exhortations had no effect, the squad leader cried out, "Pull them apart—quick!"

Blood oozed from between Shen Zechuan's teeth, but he refused to let go. Xiao Chiye was perfectly sober now. He grabbed Shen Zechuan by the back of his collar and tried to drag him off. The pain in his hand felt like it would pierce straight through to his heart, yet it was Shen Zechuan's eyes that seared themselves into Xiao Chiye's memory.

"Gongzi!" Zhao Hui called as he raced in on horseback.

Xiao Chiye turned and saw his elder brother as well, already dismounting and rushing toward him. Instantly, he was overcome with shame. It was as if he'd been stripped bare of his cultivated bravado and returned to his worthless primal state.

Xiao Jiming dropped to one knee beside them, and Shen Zechuan immediately released Xiao Chiye's hand. The skin between his thumb and forefinger was a mess of flesh and blood, the teeth marks sunk deep.

Zhao Hui, close behind, saw the wound at once. "What happened here?"

"Take him back inside." Xiao Jiming's voice was low. Zhao Hui dragged Shen Zechuan up and into the temple. "The young master

is drunk." Xiao Jiming glanced at the squad leader. "Word of what happened tonight needn't spread; His Majesty will hear the apology from me directly."

The captain kowtowed several times. "Of course, as you say!"

Xiao Jiming rose to leave. Zhao Hui had already shoved Shen Zechuan back into the temple; after appraising the situation, he turned to the squad captain. "Many thanks to our brothers in the Imperial Army tonight for escorting our young master back to the manor safe and sound. It's not easy standing guard on a winter night. I hope our brothers will accept my offer of a round of warm wine."

The squad leader, terrified to offend him, very sensibly agreed.

Only then did Xiao Jiming look silently at Xiao Chiye.

Xiao Chiye hadn't even moved to clean the blood off his hand. By the time he opened his mouth to speak, his brother had already turned away and mounted his horse.

"Dage."[17] Xiao Chiye called to him softly.

Xiao Jiming heard him, but rode away without a word.

---

17 *Dage*, *a term of address for one's eldest brother.*

NEW YEAR

ONCE INSIDE THE TEMPLE, Shen Zechuan's shackles were removed. He stretched his wrists as he listened patiently to the squad leader's grumbling. Ji Gang entered a short time later pushing a wheelbarrow. He nimbly unloaded several jugs of wine for the Imperial Army before sidling up to Shen Zechuan, his linen wrap concealing his face.

After ordering Ji Gang to finish tidying the courtyard before New Year's Day, the squad leader headed outside to warn the guards on duty to keep silent about the night's events.

Only then did Ji Gang take Shen Zechuan's arm. "Are you injured?"

"No." Shen Zechuan rubbed the nape of his neck, where Xiao Chiye's fingers had left livid red marks. "Shifu..." he began.

"Where does it hurt?"

Shen Zechuan shook his head. He thought things over a moment, then said, "He's strong and fierce, and his punches and kicks are powerful; the style felt familiar."

Astonishment spread over Ji Gang's burned face. "Our Ji-Style Boxing has never been shared with outsiders."

"After he struck, I didn't dare counter his moves with my own." The taste of blood seemed to linger in Shen Zechuan's mouth. He ran his tongue over the edges of his teeth and considered. "I was afraid he might notice something, so I didn't fight seriously, but just cowering and playing dumb didn't deceive him either. Shifu, why does he hate me so much? Xiansheng mentioned the current political situation. But should the Hua Clan and the empress dowager not be the ones he hates most?"

"That bastard was drunk!" Ji Gang spat with loathing. "Bullies always pick on the weak, so he turned his hate on you!"

Shen Zechuan extended his left hand. "He was looking for this. Shifu, do you recognize it?"

Lying in his palm was a well-worn thumb ring made of bone.

"Soldiers with exceptional upper body strength often wield great bows; they wear thumb rings like this when they draw." Ji Gang studied it. "This kind of wear and tear almost certainly comes of drawing the Mighty Bows of the Libei Armored Cavalry. But Second Young Master Xiao isn't in the army and doesn't ride into battle—what's he wearing this for?"

Xiao Chiye went home and lost himself in sleep. Lu Guangbai woke him late in the morning.

"You were really something last night." Lu Guangbai made himself at home in a chair. "You've barely landed an official position and you're already out there harassing people. I saw Jiming leave the manor earlier heading for the palace."

There was a lump in Xiao Chiye's throat. He burrowed beneath the quilt. "I had too much to drink."

"We'll be leaving the capital in a few days," Lu Guangbai said, earnest. "You know you can't go on like this. What are you going to do if all this drinking ruins your martial arts and you waste away?"

Xiao Chiye was silent.

"Put yourself in your brother's shoes; they wounded his heart at the banquet last night. He's running himself ragged seeing to Libei's military affairs, all while worrying about your sister-in-law and the baby—and now he has to leave you behind. He feels terrible. Everyone sings his praises in public, but each time he sets out for battle, they secretly hope he never returns. Year after year he leads troops into the field for these people. He doesn't say anything, but he's flesh and blood like anyone else. How could it not hurt?"

Flinging off the covers, Xiao Chiye heaved a sigh. "You think I don't know all that?"

"What do you know?" Lu Guangbai threw a tangerine at Xiao Chiye. "If you know, get up and apologize to your brother."

Xiao Chiye caught the tangerine and sat up.

When Lu Guangbai saw the bandage on his hand, he couldn't help but laugh. Peeling his own tangerine, he said, "What did you go and provoke him for? Are you satisfied now you've been bitten?"

"I told him to sing me a song," Xiao Chiye said. "But he claimed I wanted his life. The guy's a piece of work."

"You're a piece of work yourself, starting a fight with a prisoner in the middle of the street. You're lucky Jiming got there in time, or there would be uproar in the city today. Are you badly hurt?"

"That guy must have been born in the year of the dog," Xiao Chiye grumbled, staring at the teeth marks on his hand.

Xiao Jiming didn't return until afternoon, with Zhao Hui in tow. As they approached, they saw Xiao Chiye waiting under the eaves.

"Dage," Xiao Chiye called out.

Xiao Jiming handed his cloak to Zhao Hui. The maidservant brought out a copper water basin, and Xiao Jiming washed his hands, paying no mind to his little brother.

Zhao Hui peered at Xiao Chiye. "Gongzi, aren't you going to inspect the Imperial Army today? Go get your supreme commander token, then come back for dinner."

"I'll go if Dage tells me to," Xiao Chiye said.

Xiao Jiming dried his hands and finally looked at him. "I didn't tell you to go last night, but didn't you go anyway?"

"I ran in the wrong direction," Xiao Chiye said. "I meant to come home."

Xiao Jiming threw the handkerchief back onto the tray. "Very well. Go get your token, then come back for dinner."

Only then did Xiao Chiye leave.

Ever since the Imperial Army had been relieved from its duty of guarding the capital, the former operations office had fallen into terrible disrepair. When Xiao Chiye arrived on horseback, he caught sight of several men in short pants and waist sashes chatting as they basked in the sun. Their idleness bespoke none of the valor of an "army."

Xiao Chiye dismounted and strode into the courtyard, riding crop in hand. In the center of the courtyard was a balding pine tree ringed by mounds of snow that had been carelessly shoved aside. Icicles no one had knocked down dangled from the walkway eaves, and the rooftop tiles were long overdue for repair.

This army was, in a word, broke.

Xiao Chiye continued inside; the wooden plaque hanging over the entryway had peeling paint. He went down several steps and reached the main hall. Lifting the curtain with his riding crop, he bent to enter.

The men sitting around the stove cracking peanuts whipped around to look at him. Xiao Chiye set his riding crop on the table, pulled up a chair, and sat.

"So, everyone's here," he said.

As one, the men stood with a clatter, noisily trampling the shells on the ground. Most were over forty, hailing from old military households. Even after years in the Imperial Army, they still had no greater talents than shamelessness and petty extortion. Now that Xiao Chiye had appeared, they sized him up and exchanged sly glances, each harboring motives of their own.

"Er-gongzi!" A likely looking fellow wiped his hands on his robe and smiled. "We've been waiting for you to come collect your token today!"

"And here I am," Xiao Chiye said. "Where's the token?"

The man chuckled. "We waited for Your Excellency this morning, but you didn't come. The Ministry of Works was calling for laborers, so Assistant Commander Cao took the token to go deploy the men. Whenever he gets back, I'll send someone to deliver it to Your Excellency's manor."

Xiao Chiye returned his smile. "And you, good sir, are...?"

"Me?" the man answered. "Just call me Lao-Chen! I used to be a company commander overseeing a hundred men in Dicheng. Thanks to Lord Hua Shisan who recommended me for promotion, I'm now the registrar of the Imperial Army."

"How strange." One hand draped over the armrest, Xiao Chiye turned halfway to look at Lao-Chen. "One rank beneath the supreme commander of the Imperial Army should be the vice commander. How did the token end up in the hands of an assistant commander?"

"Your Excellency may not be aware, but..." When Lao-Chen saw the intensity of Xiao Chiye's regard, he straightened imprudently from his deferential bow. "After Zhongbo's defeat last year, the transport of grain levies from Jincheng was blocked. That led to a food shortage in Qudu. The Ministry of Personnel didn't have enough to pay salaries to all the officials, so they cut the staff in the Imperial Army Office by half. Presently we don't have a vice commander, so next in rank is Assistant Commander Cao. There're only a few of us left here."

"So what you're saying is that anyone can get their hands on the supreme commander's token?"

"Usually we just take the token and go. Tasks from the Ministry of Works can't wait; they need men to carry lumber into the palace. Our position is low, and our words carry little weight. We can't afford to offend anyone, so what choice do we have?" Lao-Chen started passing the buck. "If this practice offends Your Excellency, you'd do well to clear it up with the Ministry of Works."

"As the supreme commander, why must I explain myself to the Ministry of Works?" asked Xiao Chiye. "The Imperial Army reports to the emperor. The Six Ministries sought help, and we provided it; it was out of camaraderie that we never settled accounts all this time. But from now on, if anyone wants for manpower, they'll give a proper explanation of the task and a clear account of the schedule before any of my men are expected to lift a finger."

"That's all very well to say," Lao-Chen and the others laughed, "but we aren't in charge of patrols anymore; we're just errand-runners and odd-jobbers! If we lend a hand when the Six Ministries call for it, at least we're still useful. Besides, it's been like this for years, and His Majesty's never said a word against it. Friends in court are better than money in your pocket, Er-gongzi. You come from Libei, but the Imperial Army is nothing like your Armored Cavalry, or even like the Eight Great Battalions! Some things simply won't work here."

Xiao Chiye stood. "Who did you say recommended you to this post?"

Lao-Chen glowed as he straightened proudly; he was only too happy to repeat it. "Lord Hua Shisan! Your Excellency must know him. He's the empress dowager's grandson of common birth, and Third Lady Hua's—"

Xiao Chiye lifted his foot and kicked him square in the chest.

One second Lao-Chen was puffing himself up; the next he was toppling into the table and chairs. A teapot smashed against the ground, splashing tea across the floor and jolting Lao-Chen back to his senses. Trembling, he knelt.

"A loafer raised by some Hua concubine," Xiao Chiye said, sweeping away peanut shells on the table. "Someone fit only to carry my boots, and you think he's a powerful patron? He's small potatoes. I asked for the supreme commander's token. Instead, you lecture me on how things are done. Are you so blinded by your meager gains that you can't see who stands before you? Starting today, my word is law in the Imperial Army!"

Lao-Chen kowtowed at once. It was a rude awakening; he hastily called out, "Er-gongzi, Er-gongzi!"

"Who the fuck is your *Er-gongzi*?" Xiao Chiye's eyes held a piercing chill. "As supreme commander of the Imperial Army, I hold your life in my hands. You dare put on airs and act like some local thug? The Ministry of Works needs manpower for labor, but all the men come from the Imperial Army. If there were no money in it, would you find it worthwhile to throw yourselves at their feet? The men at the bottom are sent to work themselves to the bone, but you've certainly kept yourself fat without lifting a finger. What? Hua Shisan is backing you, so you think you have a token of immunity?"

"I wouldn't dare. I wouldn't dare!" Lao-Chen shuffled forward on his knees. "My lord! This humble subordinate was just talking..."

"Before half an incense stick burns," Xiao Chiye said, "I need to see the token of command, a full staff register, and twenty thousand men. If anything is missing, you gentlemen may bring me your heads in its place."

Lao-Chen leapt to his feet and bolted out the door.

Days later, the frontier generals departed the capital.

The Xiande Emperor led a convoy of court officials to see Xiao Jiming off. He trod through the heavy snow, coughing intermittently, to take Xiao Jiming by the arm. The emperor was frightfully thin under his thick cloak.

"After you leave today, Jiming, we won't meet again until next year. The conflict on Libei's border continues, and though the Biansha Horsemen have retreated after their defeat, they refuse to submit to our Great Zhou. The desperate greed of the Twelve Tribes is clear for all to see. As our trusted official and a fearless general of the empire, we implore you to take care and remain vigilant."

"We were late to the rescue, yet Your Majesty still shows us such great favor. Both my father and this humble subject are struck by the honors Your Majesty has bestowed on us. From this day forward, Libei is at Your Majesty's beck and call, ready to risk life and limb at your word."

"Since your father fell ill, it's been many years since we've seen each other." The emperor slowly turned to take in the massive crowd gathered within the city gates, then raised his eyes to the magnificent palace that had towered over the capital for a hundred years.

"As for the Shen Clan remnant...we failed the loyal soldiers who gave their lives on the battlefield," he said softly. "We have been confined to our sickbed too long; there are too many matters on which our hands are tied."

Xiao Jiming followed his gaze. After a time, he said, "A storm rages in Qudu. Please be mindful of your health, Your Majesty."

The Xiande Emperor slowly loosened his grip on Xiao Jiming. "Good man. Go."

Lu Guangbai rode out of the city. As expected, Xiao Chiye was waiting alone at the pavilion at the foot of the mountain. Sitting astride his horse, he whistled at Xiao Chiye from afar. "Brat, your big brothers are leaving!"

"Turbulence seethes below the surface; only wary travelers stay afloat.[18] Be careful out there."

"If you have something to say, spit it out. Why are you reciting poetry?" Lu Guangbai laughed heartily. "Be patient—you'll go home too one day."

"That's up to fate." Xiao Chiye smiled in return.

The sound of hooves rang out behind them. Lu Guangbai looked back; as soon as he saw the rider kicking up snow, Lu Guangbai turned his horse and shouted, "Grand Marshal! Let's ride together!"

Qi Zhuyin slowed. Her black hair was pulled into a high ponytail, and she wore a sturdy coat over a worn outer robe with a longsword strapped to her back; she traveled light. Going by appearances, she could have been an ordinary woman skilled in martial arts, traversing the world under her own power. Only after the flurries of snow settled could one see that she possessed an extraordinarily charming face.

"That horse of yours is second-rate." She raised her eyebrows and grinned, her commanding air immediately evident. "Will it be able to keep up with mine?"

---

18 *From the poem "Dreaming of Li Bai II" by Du Fu.*

Lu Guangbai was quite fond of his horse. “Perhaps he isn’t as fierce as your steed, but he’s a good lad who’s seen his share of battle. Let’s have a race, and we’ll test his mettle.”

“Now, that mount looks like a rare one.” Qi Zhuyin lifted her chin in Xiao Chiye’s direction. “Swap with me?”

Xiao Chiye stroked his horse’s mane. “No thanks. No matter how I look at it, I’ll be the loser.”

Qi Zhuyin raised her hand and threw something to Xiao Chiye, who caught it with both hands. It was an unusually heavy executioner’s blade, still in its sheath. “Libei raised some fine battle steeds for Qidong last year, thanks to you. That thing was forged by the best craftsman in our camps and cost me a good bit in precious materials too,” Qi Zhuyin said. “How about it? Not losing out now, huh?”

Xiao Chiye weighed it in his hands and laughed. “Marshal, from now on, you’re my dearest older sister! The blade I brought from home is decent but far too light. This one feels much better in the hand.”

“Sister?” Qi Zhuyin echoed. “Show some respect! Wait till you unsheathe the blade; you’ll be calling me grandpa!”

“Does this blade have a name?” Xiao Chiye asked.

“I actually thought of one,” Qi Zhuyin said. “Those who speak of a wolf’s ruthlessness speak of an animal appetite. Isn’t that just perfect for you? Why not ‘Wolfsfang?’”

Lu Guangbai countered, “The word ‘ruthlessness’ is a little too vicious. He’s only—”

“Vicious.” Qi Zhuyin snapped her riding crop, and her horse bolted. Without looking back, she called, “A son of Libei should be precisely that—vicious!”

The mass of troops in the distance had already started moving. A sea of red-tasseled spears from the Qidong Garrison Troops followed at Qi Zhuyin’s heels, surging toward the eastern plains.

Lu Guangbai could tarry no longer. He waved a hasty goodbye to Xiao Chiye, then spurred his horse to catch up.

Xiao Chiye heard the thunder of hooves so loud against the ground it seemed as if the earth itself quaked underfoot. He looked out into the distance and saw his older brother in the lead. Like a black tide, the familiar Armored Cavalry of Libei rose up along the snowy plains and swept north.

The gyrfalcon cut through the air to chase after them. It wheeled over the armored cavalry and screeched. Xiao Chiye stood, clutching his blade, watching until they disappeared into the snowy expanse.

Shen Zechuan's wandering mind was pulled back by a rasp from Grand Mentor Qi.

"The various generals have returned to their bases, and Qudu is once again at an impasse." Grand Mentor Qi, his loose hair spread over his shoulders, craned his neck to look at Shen Zechuan. "Time is short. You mustn't sit back and accept your fate as a turtle trapped in a jar!"

"I'm as much at their mercy as meat on the chopping board." Shen Zechuan looked up. "Xiansheng, is there really a chance I could leave this place?"

"Fortune and misfortune come hand in hand. Confinement may not necessarily be a bad thing." Grand Mentor Qi unstoppered his gourd and took a few gulps of wine. "It's easier to hide your strengths behind closed doors. You will have plenty of opportunities to display them in the future!"

In the distance, the palace bells tolled.

A new year had begun.

DUANWU FESTIVAL

FIVE YEARS PASSED in the blink of an eye. It was midsummer in the eighth year of Xiande.

The round-collared robe of the Secretary of the Ministry of Revenue, Wang Xian, was drenched in sweat. He sat as if his chair was lined with pins and needles. Not for the first time, he lifted his black gauze official's cap to wipe his brow.

"Lord Xiao," Wang Xian hemmed and hawed, "i-it's not that the Ministry of Revenue doesn't wish to disburse the funds. But at the moment, the current expenditure of the treasury has yet to be tallied. Without Pan-gonggong's authorization, there's really no way we can release the sum!"

"It takes time to tally the accounts, certainly." Xiao Chiye sipped his tea. "I'm waiting, aren't I? Take your time."

Wang Xian's throat bobbed. He glanced at Xiao Chiye, as composed as ever, and then at the Imperial Army soldiers standing stock-still on the veranda outside.

"Your Excellency," Wang Xian said, nearly begging. "The day is hot, and I feel terrible keeping the soldiers waiting outside. Let me treat everyone to some cold drinks. We have ice—"

"The Imperial Army has done nothing to deserve your consideration." Xiao Chiye showed him a shallow smile. "We're sturdy men used to manual labor; what's a few hours of standing? Pay us no mind, Your Excellency. Focus on your accounting."

Gripping his account book, Wang Xian held his brush over the page for a long interval. Still, he couldn't bring himself to lower it.

The emperor had fallen seriously ill in early spring of that year. In response, the empress dowager ordered a temple built in the palace where she could recite Buddhist scriptures and gather blessings for His Majesty. The Ministry of Works needed to ship large quantities of lumber from Duanzhou for construction, and to save money, they had called upon the Imperial Army to transport it. Not long after, Secretariat Elder Hai came out in opposition to the project; in the face of his disapproval, the empress dowager withdrew her plan. By then, however, the lumber was already in the capital.

The hole from this abandoned endeavor had never been filled in the Ministry of Works's budget. And thus, for two months, they had dragged the matter out, delaying payment to the Imperial Army.

Money was tight everywhere. Had the state treasury been full, there would have been no issue. Who would be willing to cross Second Young Master Xiao over such a small sum? But the Ministry of Revenue was destitute. Last year, for the empress dowager's birthday, they had lavished close to a million taels of silver on the banquet and pecuniary rewards alone.

Wang Xian set aside his brush and decided to stick his neck out. "Your Excellency, there's no way to settle the payment right now. I'll be honest: looking at the current accounts, the expenses tallied so far this year are well over the budgeted amount. Our own salaries are up in the air. We really have no money to give you. Even if you stab me, Wang Minshen, for saying so, there's nothing I can do!"

"So. The provisions of the Eight Great Battalions are distributed as usual without delay, but when it comes to the Imperial Army, you're flat broke. We all serve the emperor here, but it seems Xiao Ce'an is the only bastard doomed to hold this debt and wait for the treasury to fill itself." Xiao Chiye tossed the teacup onto the table with a clatter. "Every year the Ministry of Revenue cries poverty, but how is that my problem? We do the work, and you pay the money. It's right there in black and white. The work is done, so payment must be made. As for anything else, I don't want to hear it; it's not my responsibility. If everyone has to forgive the problems of the Ministry of Revenue, what's left for you to do? Best vacate the position and let someone else take over."

Wang Xian sprang to his feet, livid. "If we're all serving the emperor, why is Your Excellency intent on pushing me into a corner? Who would be unwilling to settle the account if we had the money? If the Imperial Army is so capable, why bother with manual labor? Go do what the Eight Great Battalions do! Let's see who is so bold as to withhold your money then!"

Just as the atmosphere threatened to tip into violence, another voice rang out. "There's no need for anger, Lord Wang. The second young master is simply a forthright man who speaks his mind." The newcomer took off his wide-brimmed hat and wiped his hands with a handkerchief. "This humble one is the Chief Supervising Secretary from the Office of Scrutiny for Revenue, Xue Xiuzhuo. I'm here regarding this very account."

The Chief Supervising Secretary of the Office of Scrutiny for Revenue was merely a seventh-rank position, technically not even considered a court official in Qudu. However, it was a unique post; not only did the officeholder supervise the works-in-progress of the Ministry of Revenue, he also participated in the reviews and appraisals of officials that took place every six years. On top of that, he could bypass any of the Six Ministries to appeal directly to the emperor himself.

This was a person Wang Xian could not afford to offend; he swallowed his pride. "How could I be angry? The Imperial Army has contributed so much; I don't want Lord Xiao to have worked for nothing. But Yanqing, just look at this account. We simply don't have the funds."

Xue Xiuzhuo, courtesy name Yanqing, had a scholarly and refined bearing. He spoke without even looking at the accounts. "I'm aware of the difficulties faced by the Ministry of Revenue. How about this, Er-gongzi: the city of Quancheng shipped us a batch of silk recently. We'll settle your account with an equivalent value in silk. Would that be acceptable?"

It seemed it was. The instant Xiao Chiye was gone, Wang Xian's expression turned cold. "He's not demanding payment for the Imperial Army," he told Xue Xiuzhuo. "More likely he's squandering it himself. Ever since this second young master took up the reins of the Imperial Army, he's been leading a life of drunken debauchery. Yet he pushes us to our limit every time, unwilling to show a shred of empathy!"

Xue Xiuzhuo smiled and said nothing.

Xiao Chiye left the Ministry of Revenue's office and rode toward Donglong Street. He was much taller now than five years ago, his youthful drive and vigor somewhat faded.

Prince Chu had been waiting for him all morning. As soon as he spied Xiao Chiye, the prince started badgering him. "Where the hell have you been? I nearly died of boredom!"

"Fooling around." Xiao Chiye sat and gulped down a cold drink.

On seeing the basin of ice set nearby to cool the room, he sighed and stretched out on the settee. "This is so comfortable. My head is spinning from the heat outside. I'm going to take a nap."

"You can't!" Li Jianheng waved his bamboo fan vigorously, the front of his robe wide open in the heat. He sighed. "At least let me finish talking before you sleep!"

Who knew what mischief Xiao Chiye had been up to all night, but he was obviously flagging. He hummed absentmindedly.

Li Jianheng sipped some chilled wine out of a cup held in a courtesan's slender hand. "Do you remember that girl I told you about? The one I was keeping in my villa five years ago? I was preparing to take her as my own, until that son of a bitch Xiaofuzi took her and offered her to the castrated bastard Pan Rugui!"

Xiao Chiye murmured acknowledgment.

"Well," Li Jianheng continued, more animated by the second. "I recently left the capital to escape the summer heat and saw her near the villa! The girl's kept herself so smooth and tender, even lovelier than five years ago. My heart was pounding just looking at her. How I hate those eunuchs! That thieving son of a bitch came out of nowhere and broke up a blossoming romance! He thinks that's the end of it? No way!"

Xiao Chiye yawned.

"Are we brothers or not?" Li Jianheng fumed. "Help me think of a way to get back at him! Maybe we can't touch Pan Rugui, but that Xiaofuzi needs a good thrashing!"

Xiao Chiye was truly exhausted. "What do you want to do? Have him dragged out of the palace?"

Li Jianheng pushed aside the courtesan waiting on him and snapped his fan shut. "The Duanwu Festival is around the corner. His Majesty will be at the West Gardens to watch the dragon boat race; Pan Rugui will doubtless be there too. Where he goes, Xiaofuzi follows. We can lure him out during the horse race and beat him to death!"

Xiao Chiye seemed to have dropped off.

"Ce'an, did you hear me?"

"Bad idea to beat him to death," Xiao Chiye said without opening his eyes. "If you make an enemy of Pan Rugui over this, you'll be in for a world of trouble."

"But we can at least give him a beating, right?" Li Jianheng whined. "If I don't vent my anger, I won't even be able to eat. What's up with you lately? You always look half asleep. What are you getting up to at night? And why did you send away the virgin I picked for you last time?"

Xiao Chiye acknowledged Li Jianheng's words with a wave of his hand. There was no ring on his thumb, but the bite between his thumb and forefinger had left its mark.

When Li Jianheng started in on something else, Xiao Chiye turned a deaf ear to it all.

A few days later, on the occasion of Duanwu, the long-absent Xiande Emperor dragged his sickly bones to the West Gardens. The imperial ladies accompanying him donned gauzy robes of sheer silk, while Ji Lei and the commander in chief of the Eight Great Battalions, Xi Gu'an, jointly escorted the emperor. As the Imperial Army had nothing but spare time, they invited Xiao Chiye along as well.

Xiao Chiye was last to arrive. In keeping with custom, the Xiande Emperor had already hung up the willow branch to ward against evil and was waiting for the horse race to begin. The Court of Imperial Entertainments, as part of the entourage, served sticky rice dumplings and pastries at each seat. From his spot in the princes' seats, Li Jianheng waved Xiao Chiye over.

Xiao Chiye tossed his riding crop to his right-hand man Chen Yang, who followed a few steps behind him. He loosened his arm guards as he took his seat.

"What took you so long? The anxiety is killing me!" Li Jianheng complained, clutching the bamboo fan he favored.

"You're anxious every day," Xiao Chiye shot back. "You sure you're all right?"

"I'm just used to saying it!" Li Jianheng responded, fanning himself. "Look, see that? Xiaofuzi is serving over there."

Xiao Chiye followed his gaze and saw Xiaofuzi beaming as he spoke into Pan Rugui's ear. "Hang back later," he said. "We'll get someone to give him that beating."

Xiaofuzi stepped onto the edge of the latrine pit an hour later, ready to relieve himself. Without warning, his vision went black—someone had thrown a sack over his head.

"Hey!" Xiaofuzi shrieked but was quickly knocked down with a blow to the neck. Li Jianheng wasted no time; he lifted his robe and started kicking him. Xiaofuzi, gagged by the sack, groaned in pain as he writhed on the ground.

The race nearby was nearing its midpoint; no one heard a thing.

After beating Xiaofuzi for the better part of an hour, Chen Yang stopped Li Jianheng, who still hadn't had his fill. Chen Yang shot a glance at the prince's manor guards behind them, and they hurriedly darted off with the sack.

"Your Highness," he said, "he would have died if you continued. Perhaps next time."

Li Jianheng straightened his robe and glanced at Chen Yang. "Where are they dumping him?"

"The supreme commander ordered us to dump him in the woods by the lake. Once the banquet begins, the serving eunuchs will pass that way and he will be freed."

Li Jianheng spat on the ground where Xiaofuzi had suffered and finally returned to his seat.

By the start of the banquet, Li Jianheng had forgotten all about the little eunuch. Xiao Chiye kept an eye out, looking over occasionally at Pan Rugui, but saw no sign of Xiaofuzi.

"He was probably humiliated and ran back to change his clothes," Li Jianheng said between bites. "Eunuchs who serve before the emperor have a terrible fear of appearing dirty and being disdained by the masters. Do you want to come to my villa in a few days for some fun? You can see that little lady I was talking about too."

"I'm busy," Xiao Chiye said, sipping his cold tea.

Li Jianheng snickered. "Still putting on an act, even in front of me? You, busy? The Imperial Army is on the verge of dissolution. What could possibly keep you busy in such an idle position?"

Xiao Chiye laughed in return. "Busy drinking." His eyes were fixed on the tea in his hand; his side profile revealed the flippant quirk of his mouth. "The internal reviews are starting in autumn. I have to buy a few rounds if I want to hold onto this idle position."

"Being human—" Li Jianheng tapped the table with his chopsticks "—is about living in luxury and shunning productivity. The constant fighting, the so-called Pan faction, the Hua Clan—aren't they tired? Where's the pleasure in that?"

"Yeah." Xiao Chiye's grin grew wicked. "Isn't that just asking for a hard time? Having fun is life's greatest satisfaction."

Li Jianheng matched his sly expression. "So what's the deal with this review? Who would dare deny my dear brother his post? You were personally appointed by His Majesty; we loaf on imperial orders. How about this? I'll host a flower-viewing feast at my residence before autumn, and we invite them all."

"There's no hurry." Xiao Chiye cast his eyes over the West Gardens and spotted a familiar roof behind the cascade of overlapping eaves. He frowned. "This place is rather close to the Temple of Guilt."

"Still thinking about it, huh? It's been ages since you lost that thumb ring."

Xiao Chiye rubbed his thumb out of habit.

"That Shen Clan remnant has been locked up for five years; there's been no news of him all this time. His Majesty never even inquired whether the boy died or went insane," Li Jianheng said. "If I were locked in there, forget five years; I'd have cracked in a week."

The scar on Xiao Chiye's hand ached. He'd no desire to bring up that person.

The sound of drums rose by the lakeside. Li Jianheng tossed down his chopsticks and jumped to his feet. "Let's go! The dragon boat race is starting. They're definitely taking bets!"

Xiao Chiye made to rise when he saw Ji Lei hurry through the crowd and lean over to whisper in Pan Rugui's ear. Pan Rugui whipped his head around to stare at him. An instant later, he banged heavily on his table.

Xiao Chiye shot a swift glance at Chen Yang.

"My lord—" Chen Yang began, stunned.

"Your Majesty!" Ji Lei was already kneeling before the emperor, his voice carrying. "I'm afraid the dragon boat race cannot go on. Just now, when this humble one was patrolling the grounds with the Embroidered Uniform Guard, we fished Xiaofuzi—a eunuch of the imperial palace—from the water!"

The Xiande Emperor coughed violently; Pan Rugui stepped forward to stroke his back. When the coughing subsided, the emperor managed, "What was he doing in the water?"

Ji Lei raised his head. It wasn't clear if he looked to the emperor or the empress dowager. "He drowned," he answered, voice heavy.

A commotion broke out among the palace ladies, who covered their gasps with silk handkerchiefs.

Li Jianheng had knocked over the teacup on his table. In a panic, he picked it up and looked at Xiao Chiye. "I swear I didn't mean it..."

LITTLE CICADA

XIAO CHIYE RIGHTED the lid of the teacup, carefully not looking at Li Jianheng. "Don't fret," he said.

Li Jianheng slumped back in his chair, scared out of his wits.

"With His Majesty here, and the guards so watchful, how could someone simply drown like that?" the empress dowager asked.

"Your Majesty," Ji Lei addressed her, "this humble subject has already sent the corpse for the coroner's examination. We will have more details soon."

"What do you mean?" The specter of constant illness had cast a pall over the Xiande Emperor. He frowned gloomily. "Was there something strange about his death?"

"He was covered in bruises, Your Majesty," Ji Lei replied. "He had clearly received a beating before he went into the water. Xiaofuzi was a palace eunuch but held no important post in the Twenty-Four Yamen.[19] He was only His Majesty's personal eunuch. If he was tortured, then I'm afraid the murderer might have more sinister motives."

The Xiande Emperor rose, supporting himself on the edge of the table. "We have only just stepped out of the palace," he said coldly, "and somebody's so impatient."

---

19 *An institution of eunuchs serving the emperor and his household in matters of household administration and domestic comforts.*

"Your Majesty." Hai Liangyi stepped forward and knelt. "The Embroidered Uniform Guard and the Eight Great Battalions are on rotation duty today. If the eunuch's murderer really had grander designs, would he have done such a sloppy job of it? Xiaofuzi often left the palace on errands to purchase this or that. It's not impossible for him to have made personal enemies outside."

"I'm afraid I disagree, Renshi," Secretariat Elder Hua Siqian said from his seat. "Any man who dares strike this close to the throne plainly has no regard for His Majesty or the officials here. What commoner outside the palace would have the gall?"

Xiao Chiye sat stock-still as the gears turned in his mind.

Chen Yang had dragged Xiaofuzi into the woods at half past noon. Within the time it took an incense stick to burn, the eunuchs carrying banquet dishes and the Eight Great Battalions' patrol should have passed by. Countless people would've left their seats to change clothes, drink tea, or make a trip to the latrine. The guests present today were of the highest status; moreover, the accompanying guards and eunuchs all had the right to move freely within the garden. As all these people were going to and fro, someone only needed to give Xiaofuzi a light kick, and he would have drowned in the pond.

At this point, the thorniest issue was not the bruises on Xiaofuzi's body, but the fact that Ji Lei had changed the narrative, turning this petty murder case into suspected treason.

Xiao Chiye rested a fingertip on the lid of his teacup.

This fire must never spread to Prince Chu.

The emperor was gravely ill, and even the Court of Imperial Physicians was at its wits' end. No one could predict the moment Heaven's Ordained would depart this world, and the Xiande Emperor had no heirs. Once the inevitable came to pass, Li Jianheng would be next in line for succession. Today, Xiao Chiye had been too careless. Li Jianheng's absence from the banquet earlier was glaring; he couldn't dismiss it with a perfunctory excuse.

The Xiao Clan was already on thin ice. If they were suspected of bringing their swords to bear in the matter of succession, the mere existence of one hundred and twenty thousand Libei cavalry would be enough to drop the executioner's blade on Xiao Jiming's neck. The situation had snowballed; it was already an avalanche bearing down on him. He had to stop it.

Xiao Chiye flung down his teacup, shattering it on the table. The sound rang out crisp and clear, drawing glances from everyone at the banquet.

Looking at him apprehensively, Li Jianheng stuttered, "C-Ce'an..."

Xiao Chiye rose from his seat and strode toward the throne. Sinking to his knees, he declared, "Your Majesty! This humble subject daren't hide this from you. The one who ordered this man's beating was I."

The Xiande Emperor fixed his gaze on him. "He was but a palace eunuch. What grudge did you bear him that you would go so far?"

Ji Lei also looked askance at him. "Lord Xiao, this is a matter of grave importance. You mustn't take the blame for another simply because of personal ties."

"What grave importance," Xiao Chiye said offhandedly. "This humble subject sees no crime here. So what if I beat a lowly eunuch? I am the supreme commander of the Imperial Army and a second-rank official; don't tell me I have to put up with insolence from that bastard?"

"To incite such fury from Er-gongzi, this must be no ordinary grudge," Hua Siqian said. "Except Xiaofuzi doesn't usually cross your path. What happened to anger you so?"

"The secretariat elder is unaware of this," Xiao Chiye began, "but on my way to the drill grounds a few months ago, that bastard's sedan blocked my horse's way. You ought to have seen the pompous display he put on; I'd have thought it was Pan-gonggong himself had he not lifted the curtain. I offered a few words of rebuke, and he boldly mouthed off to me. What real man would allow himself to be humiliated by a filthy, castrated wretch right there in the street? I doubt anyone here could stomach it in silence."

The assembled guests flinched at Xiao Chiye's choice of words. All eyes turned to Pan Rugui, standing conspicuously by the emperor's side.

As the Xiande Emperor deliberated, the empress dowager chimed in: "Be that as it may, killing at the slightest provocation is not the behavior of a gentleman."

These words seemed to move Pan Rugui to tears. The gray-haired man knelt, his eyes red-rimmed. "Your Majesty's mercy is a grace from above. We servants are lowly creatures. How could we compare to the second young master? Xiaofuzi had been spoiled rotten; he was ignorant of etiquette when encountering military officials of the court. Even after receiving the second young master's guidance, he remained unrepentant. This servant has been remiss in his instruction; as his teacher, I am to blame for the faults of the child!"

His tone was conciliatory, but the law was clear: eunuchs were required to dismount and kowtow in greeting upon meeting a minister or official of the court.

The empress dowager was a staunch Buddhist; she was greatly displeased at the wanton taking of lives. She turned to the Xiande Emperor. "It has ever been said that all men are equal in the eyes of the law. Whether it was perpetrated to satisfy sentiment or reason, Xiao Chiye's unruly violence cannot be treated lightly. Besides, the

Xiao Clan are known to be loyal and upright men. The Prince of Libei sent his son to Qudu to be raised under Your Majesty's eye. If we indulge him until he thinks himself above the law, we will have disappointed the Prince of Libei who left him in our care."

Ji Lei, too, was indignant. Unwilling to let the matter go, he spoke up. "The second young master has always been friendly with Prince Chu. As for this act tonight, His Highness is also—"

"This humble subject is not finished." Xiao Chiye cut him off. "I said I was the one who beat him, but I didn't kill him. Your Majesty, I had indeed intended to take his life to vent my fury. But when His Highness Prince Chu found out, he persuaded me against it. The beating today was meant to be carried out by my guards on the sly, yet His Highness noticed something amiss and left his seat to save Xiaofuzi's life. With Prince Chu standing by, this humble subject didn't dare rebuff His Highness's teachings, and thus I let Xiaofuzi off with his life. As for his drowning, I find it strange as well. Who would take up my grudge and do such an unwise thing?

"Lord Ji." Xiao Chiye turned to Ji Lei, his eyes faintly gleaming. "The Embroidered Uniform Guard is usually meticulous and impeccable in their work. This eunuch was left just at the edge of the road today, yet he managed to dodge the patrols and drown in the pond. Perhaps he could not orient himself with his head covered and tumbled in himself."

"A good point," Hai Liangyi agreed. "A person fell into the pond, and the Embroidered Uniform Guard, though they walked back and forth patrolling the grounds, were none the wiser. If assassins were to infiltrate the West Gardens today, they mightn't notice that either!"

Ji Lei didn't dare stir up any more trouble. He dropped to the ground and kowtowed a few times, panicked. "Your Majesty! The Embroidered Uniform Guard have our own constraints! The guards are sharing patrol duty with the Eight Great Battalions today; we organize manpower carefully when relieving each squad. We would never neglect the tiniest detail!"

The Military Commissioner of the Eight Great Battalions, Xi Gu'an, knelt as well. "It's as he says, Your Majesty. The Eight Great Battalions also take this matter very seriously. The patrol rotation follows a fixed schedule. It's not impossible for someone to have memorized it and seized their moment to kill Xiaofuzi. This is a personal grudge. Anyone with grievances against this eunuch, Xiaofuzi, must be thoroughly investigated."

"Do it then." The Xiande Emperor laughed in anger, flinging his teacup at Xi Gu'an. "A man died right under your noses. Instead of reflecting on your actions, you speak only of shirking responsibility! To think we actually put our safety into your—your..." The emperor's voice went hoarse; he covered his mouth as the coughing took him. His rage seemed to scorch his very lungs; he reached down to support himself on the table, then crumpled to the ground.

"Your Majesty!"

Shrill cries of alarm issued from the palace ladies, and chaos spread like fire through the banquet hall.

The empress dowager sank to her knees to support him. "Summon the imperial physician, quickly!"

When Xiao Chiye finally made his way back to Li Jianheng's side, the prince regarded him as his own kin. "Brother of my own blood!" he cried. "You scared the life out of me!"

"I've been kneeling for ages; I'm starving. Is there anything to eat?"

Li Jianheng motioned for someone to run and fetch some food. Standing on a veranda in the West Gardens, the pair looked toward the brightly lit hall.

"When His Majesty wakes, he'll ask for you again," Li Jianheng said. "How did Xiaofuzi end up in the pond? What shit luck I have!"

Xiao Chiye washed his snacks down with cold tea. This was a delicate matter.

Xiaofuzi had always enjoyed Pan Rugui's favor. Even if someone had plotted to take his life, how could the timing dovetail so perfectly with Li Jianheng's beating? If it wasn't a premeditated attempt to kill Xiaofuzi but a spur-of-the-moment decision, it would have been vastly more advantageous to untie him than to kill him.

Pan Rugui and Ji Lei had reacted far too swiftly. The man's body had hardly cooled, yet they had made full use of him. And if they could pin his death on Prince Chu, so much the better.

"Has His Majesty spent his nights with any lady in particular recently?" Xiao Chiye asked offhandedly.

"Sure," Li Jianheng answered. "Lately he favors the lady from the Wei Clan. The empress dowager likes her too."

Xiao Chiye looked thoughtful.

By now night had fallen, but no one dared to leave—the guests from the banquet clustered in small groups along the veranda, waiting for the emperor to wake.

Xi Gu'an had left the courtyard at some point in the evening. When he returned, he went to wait inside the hall on the empress dowager's orders. After an hour, Xiao Chiye saw a footman dressed in clean but simple clothes enter through the side gate, escorted by members of the Eight Great Battalions.

"Who is that?" Xiao Chiye asked.

Li Jianheng craned his neck. "A footman. There are plenty here, aren't there? Why are they bringing in this one?"

Even under the dim light of lanterns, Xiao Chiye's sharp eyes spotted twisting burn scars marring the footman's face. His heart pounded as an ominous premonition took shape in his mind. "The West Gardens are noble grounds meant to host the emperor. Those who wait upon him must please the eye. How could such a footman serve here?"

Some time later, Pan Rugui stepped out of the hall. "Summon the eighth son of the Shen Clan! Bring him at once for an audience with the emperor!"

Uproar immediately broke out among the officials, the sounds of chatter echoing off every wall.

Though no final judgment had been made on the case of Shen Wei's treason, his blackened name had spread far and wide. Zhongbo's wounds had yet to heal; even now, Shen Wei bore the blame for the troops' defeat. That the last member of the Shen Clan had escaped with his life was already cause for resentment on the frontiers; how could he be permitted to walk free?

Li Jianheng panicked. "What's going on? Don't tell me they discovered something more? There's enmity between the two of you; you see red whenever you lay eyes on him. For the sake of the Xiao Clan, they should keep him locked up!"

Xiao Chiye said nothing, but merely shifted his gaze to the door and stared with rapt attention.

In less than half the time it took to burn a stick of incense, a guard strode into the courtyard followed closely by another man. His hair had grown long in the last five years. It cascaded down his back, secured only with a crude wooden hairpin and no crown. His worn, wide-sleeved robe hid his wrists from view, but the hands that peeked from them were fair and lustrous as porcelain. A lantern obstructed Xiao Chiye's sight, but Li Jianheng dropped his teacup when Shen Zechuan walked into view.

"You never told me he looked like *this*..." Li Jianheng muttered.

Xiao Chiye's thumb unconsciously curled.

Shen Zechuan passed before the walkway where they stood. Xiao Chiye watched him with cold detachment. In that split second, he locked gazes with a pair of eyes he remembered well. Those eyes were long and narrow, their ends extending in a delicate upward curve. Even in the dim glow of the lantern, the irises glittered like lost stars. Shen Zechuan's lips seemed to curl in a hint of a smile as he glanced at Xiao Chiye, so faint that once he passed it left no trace—it had come and gone like the chill night wind.

PRAYING MANTIS

SHEN ZECHUAN FOLLOWED THE GUARD inside and knelt before the hanging curtains. The Xiande Emperor leaned against the head of the bed, while the empress dowager sat, straight-backed, beside it. Pan Rugui stepped back with the bowl of medicine he was holding to reveal Shen Zechuan's presence to them.

The emperor made an effort to gather himself. "The patrol from the Eight Great Battalions said they saw your footman beside the pond. We ask you: what was he doing there?"

"To answer Your Majesty," Shen Zechuan said, "Ge-shu was waiting for Fu-gonggong from the palace."

"On whose orders?"

Shen Zechuan paused, then kowtowed. "On this offending subject's orders."

The emperor coughed feebly. "You are confined to the Temple of Guilt, which receives a monthly provision of food and clothing from the palace. What connections do you have with Xiaofuzi?"

"Upon Your Majesty's mercy, this offending subject was permitted to remain in the Temple of Guilt and reflect on past wrongs. Your Majesty even sustained my life with food. Sadly, this offending subject recently fell ill, and coupled with my old ailment, it became increasingly difficult to get up every day."

Shen Zechuan was the very picture of grief. "Although the palace sends my meals, there is no medicine. Ge-shu has been assigned to the temple for a long time. He took pity on this offending subject and, seeing Fu-gonggong out on an errand, asked for medicine from the palace. Later, this offending subject asked Ge-shu again to beseech Fu-gonggong to bring some blessing oil lamps for me."

"You have no family," said the empress dowager. "What use do you have for lamps to pray for blessings?"

"This sinful subject is conscious of my heinous offenses. I've been praying by the lamp in the temple day and night for the health of the emperor and the empress dowager. I also recite sutras for the loyal martyrs who lost their lives in Zhongbo at the Battle of Chashi." Shen Zechuan spoke piously. "This offending subject has planted some vegetables on the temple's grounds and asked Ge-shu to sell them at the morning market. Since this illness of mine is unlikely to improve, it is far better to trade those coins for blessing oil lamps than spend it on medicine."

The empress dowager sighed deeply. "Although you are indeed guilty, your sins are not unforgivable."

The Xiande Emperor closed his eyes, weary. "Xiaofuzi is dead. Do you know of anyone who might have had a dispute with him?"

Shen Zechuan shook his head. He said softly, "Although this offending subject was bold enough to beseech Fu-gonggong to buy lamps, I have never met Fu-gonggong in person nor exchanged letters with him."

"And what about you?" The emperor motioned for Ji Gang to speak. "Tell us. Did he mention anything to you in passing?"

Ji Gang dared not look at the emperor directly. He answered with a mixture of awe and fear, as any ordinary footman would. "Your Majesty, whenever Fu-gonggong left the palace, it was only for procurement. He had such a busy schedule; he usually sent those serving under him to meet this humble one."

On hearing this, the Xiande Emperor cast a self-mocking glance at Pan Rugui, who stood as still as a wooden statue.

"But once," Ji Gang continued, "this humble servant greeted Fu-gonggong in his sedan and heard him talking to his attendants—something about His Highness flying into a humiliated rage and looking to create trouble for him. At the time, this humble servant was anxious to give Fu-gonggong the money for the oil lamps, which was why I stood closer than usual. But Fu-gonggong was pressed for time; he told this humble one to come to the West Gardens today instead to wait for him. That is how the guards on patrol came to see this humble servant lingering by the pond."

"Are you sure you heard it correctly?" Pan Rugui probed. "It was 'His Highness' and not someone else?"

Ji Gang kowtowed repeatedly. "How would I dare deceive His Majesty?! Many people saw this humble servant in the market that day. You have only to ask around to determine whether this humble one is lying."

The emperor said nothing for a long time. The heavy smell of medicine permeated the room. At last, holding a handkerchief over her nose and mouth, the empress dowager leaned over and said, "Your Majesty, we cannot rely on Xiao Chiye's story alone to determine the motives behind Xiaofuzi's death. This incident happened mere steps away from your imperial person. If it is as this man says, and Prince Chu was the one who wanted Xiaofuzi dead, why would Xiao Chiye go so far to muddle the facts?"

"Your Majesty," Pan Rugui added quietly, "Xiaofuzi's life is of little consequence. If Prince Chu killed him out of personal grudge, that is no great matter—but I'm afraid things may not be so simple.

His Majesty hardly steps out of the palace, while Xiaofuzi frequently came and went. Why didn't Prince Chu choose some other day? Why now?"

The Xiande Emperor doubled over with another spate of coughing. He pushed aside Pan Rugui's hand and used his own handkerchief to wipe the blood on his lips.

"Jianheng is our own brother," he said without looking up. "We understand his temperament better than anyone. Since the case has already progressed this far, Ji Lei may see it to its end. All of this happened because Xiaofuzi abused his station, lorded over others, and overstepped his bounds, creating resentment and envy. A-Ye shall be confined to his manor for half a month, while Ji Lei and Xi Gu'an shall have their salaries suspended for three! Pan Rugui, relay the message. When they've heard it, they may be dismissed."

Pan Rugui turned to the empress dowager. "But..."

The empress dowager was silent.

The Xiande Emperor also turned to the empress dowager, his tone earnest. "Imperial Mother, we live in troubled times. Autumn approaches, and the situation on the frontiers is precarious. Trade conflicts there increase day by day. The troops in Libei, Qidong, and its Bianjun Commandery must stand fast; we cannot afford a blow to morale. If we pursue this matter and it ends up implicating certain people, it may produce dissatisfaction at the frontier. In that case, the common folks will be the ones to suffer. Although the pain of Zhongbo has passed, its humiliation has yet to be avenged in the eyes of our soldiers. We mustn't drag this case out, Imperial Mother, lest we lose the faith of the people."

The empress dowager's brow was lined with concern as she tucked the quilt tighter around the emperor. "How blessed the empire is; Your Majesty is still worrying over state affairs while so gravely indisposed. Go on, Pan Rugui."

Pan Rugui acknowledged her orders and slowly backed out the door.

"The way I see it," the empress dowager continued, "the eighth son of the Shen Clan wishes earnestly to repent and mend his ways. He is nothing like Shen Wei. He is a child you can use."

"His health is poor," said the emperor. "We're afraid he's not well enough to take up any duties. Perhaps it's better for him to continue his convalescence in the temple."

The empress dowager slowly drew away from him. "Your Majesty is right, of course. But he is already here. If we send him back now for no reason, it will arouse suspicion about the particulars of this case. Is that not contrary to Your Majesty's desires?"

The Xiande Emperor turned to Shen Zechuan with a smile. "The empress dowager thinks highly of you. You must keep this in mind; don't go down the same path as your treacherous father. Let's send you to the Embroidered Uniform Guard, then. Their Twelve Offices tend to a variety of duties; there will naturally be work for you to do."

Shen Zechuan prostrated himself to thank the emperor for his grace.

When everyone had left, the emperor leaned over the edge of his bed and threw up the medicine he had ingested earlier; his face was ashen under the dim light of the candles. The quilt covering his hands had been wrung into creases. His health was truly dire.

On a veranda that stretched over the pond, the empress dowager walked with Pan Rugui supporting her elbow. Hua Xiangyi, arms full of fresh-picked lotus blossoms, followed at a distance alongside the maidservants.

"Since his last bout of illness, His Majesty has grown more obstinate," the empress dowager said as she walked. "How can a man so gravely ill continue to wear himself down with routine matters of the state?"

"As they say, illness strikes quick as an onrushing avalanche; convalescence comes slow as pulling silk from a cocoon," Pan Rugui said. "His Majesty is merely anxious to get back on his feet."

"When I selected Jianyun back then, it was because I valued his gentle and refined ways, as well as his biddable nature. He has frequently been in poor health over the years, yet he has done his best." The empress dowager glanced at Pan Rugui and continued, "But who could predict his great fear of the Xiao Clan? Every time he must make a choice, he tries to not offend either party. But you can't always please everyone."

"When it comes to Qudu, Your Majesty's words are what matters. Once the imperial concubine, Lady Wei, is pregnant with a son, Your Majesty need worry no longer."

The empress dowager raised her hand and patted Pan Rugui's supporting arm. She said meaningfully, "Before Concubine Wei is with child, we'll need you to keep close watch over His Majesty's health."

"Yes, Your Majesty," Pan Rugui replied. "This servant has been keeping a sharp eye."

The crowd was scattering by the time Shen Zechuan came out with Ji Gang behind him. They emerged just in time to see Xiao Chiye riding out.

"I thought the Imperial Army was a dead end for idlers." Eyeing Xiao Chiye's waist and legs, Shen Zechuan added, "But judging from his physique, he's clearly kept up with his training."

"An expert in horseback archery." Ji Gang narrowed his eyes and studied Xiao Chiye's retreating back. "But without exchanging blows with him, I can't guess the lad's strength. If he could already draw the Mighty Bows of Libei five years ago, I'm afraid he's even stronger now. Don't fight him, Chuan-er, unless absolutely necessary."

Before Shen Zechuan could answer, Xiao Chiye suddenly reined his horse around and charged straight at him.

Shen Zechuan stared Xiao Chiye down without dodging or giving way. He watched the horse draw closer and closer, brushing past him by a hairsbreadth at the last second. Shen Zechuan's wide sleeves fluttered with the gust of wind and settled back down in its wake.

"What does this case have to do with you?" Xiao Chiye's horse circled Shen Zechuan.

"It has nothing to do with me." Shen Zechuan smiled up at him again. "But it has plenty to do with you, Er-gongzi."

"Pan Rugui lost his lapdog, and I took a tumble from grace. No one reaped any benefits today except you." Xiao Chiye leaned over his saddle and peered down at him. "You don't stay down for long, I'll give you that. But how do you get so lucky?"

Shen Zechuan looked back at him and replied with humility, "It's all thanks to association with Er-gongzi's noble aura. If it weren't for the move you made, how would I have seized this opportunity?"

Xiao Chiye's eyes were cold. "You certainly are well-informed."

"A cheap trick is all," Shen Zechuan said.

Xiao Chiye glanced up at the sky. The gyrfalcon had a sparrow in its grasp and was hovering midair, awaiting its reward. "So you've been let out." He whistled, and the gyrfalcon landed on the rooftop and tore apart the little bird in its claws. Turning back to Shen Zechuan, he continued, "Qudu is large. One has to find entertainment somehow."

"A noble truly is a rarefied creature," Shen Zechuan said. "Even the entertainment you seek differs from the common man. Dining, wining, whoring, and gambling are all beneath your station; you prefer to play with lives. But playing alone isn't as fun as playing together. It wouldn't be very interesting to have only me for company."

The corners of Xiao Chiye's mouth quirked up as he said, riding crop in hand, "Looking at you is interesting enough. Why would I want others to come between us?"

"That's an honor too great for me to bear," Shen Zechuan said. "Besides, I've found so many friends for Er-gongzi."

"Better to worry about yourself than me." Xiao Chiye shifted his gaze. "There are such good prospects in the Embroidered Uniform Guard, and Ji Lei thinks so highly of you. I'm sure he'll be looking forward to your eminent presence."

Shen Zechuan chuckled. He looked at Xiao Chiye, eyes curved in a smile, and said gently, "You and I are but birds in a cage. I may have good prospects, but aren't you also confined by your comforts? Yet I am alone with no tethers, and therefore free from worries and concerns. Are *you*, Er-gongzi?"

The backdrop of hanging lanterns haloed Shen Zechuan's jade-like beauty. The gyrfalcon finished with his feast and landed on Xiao Chiye's shoulder.

"If we're all caged birds," Xiao Chiye said, flicking dust from his falcon's feathers, "why pretend to be free?"

Shen Zechuan returned to the temple, took his medicine, and sat in the courtyard across a small table from Grand Mentor Qi. Ji Gang had cleared out the courtyard in the Temple of Guilt and, at Grand Mentor Qi's request, planted bamboo and even a vegetable garden. It had become quite the refreshing place to sit on a summer night.

"His Majesty has no desire to pursue the matter," Shen Zechuan said. "He allowed my release to protect Prince Chu. Xiansheng's foresight truly is incredible."

"Whether it's incredible or not, it's too early to tell." Grand Mentor Qi tapped a weiqi piece on the table and clicked his tongue. "They say His Majesty's been in such poor health since the beginning of the year that he's confined to his bed. The man's in the prime of his life, with the whole Court of Imperial Physicians attending him, yet he's weaker now than he was in his prince's manor. Pan Rugui may very well deserve the credit for this."

Ji Gang squatted at the entrance grinding a stone. "Much of His Majesty's fury was directed at them. Even Ji Lei didn't escape punishment. I'd guess he's been harboring resentment for a long time."

"When one feels their time is running out, they will grow bolder," Grand Mentor Qi said. "As emperor, he's spent his entire life making concessions."

Shen Zechuan finished his medicine and wrinkled his nose at the bitter aftertaste. "The empress dowager has no love for Prince Chu, but he's the only one who can ascend the throne. Ji Lei took several swipes at the prince today. If you told me Pan Rugui put him up to it, I'd believe it. But if Pan Rugui is set on sending Prince Chu to his doom, it'll be because he's no longer concerned about consequences. There must be another heir somewhere in the palace—someone easier to manipulate than Prince Chu."

"The late emperor was a man in control of his appetites." Ji Gang blew the dust from his rock. "So I doubt it. Anyhow, if there was such an heir, how could they have kept him hidden all these years?"

"As long as Li blood runs in him, he's an imperial heir." Grand Mentor Qi held a weiqi piece between his fingers. "The late emperor might not have another son, but can't the current emperor beget one? Once a future emperor is born in the inner palace, after this one breathes his last, the empress dowager will be free to hold court with the babe in her arms—she can set aside the screen altogether. They can appoint Hua Siqian the regent minister. When that time comes, our Great Zhou will truly belong to the Hua."

"But Xiao Chiye is close to Prince Chu. The Xiao Clan has nothing to lose and everything to gain if Prince Chu ascends the throne." Shen Zechuan rolled his own weiqi piece between his fingers. "In no world would Libei simply stand aside and watch. As long as Prince Chu lives, Xiao Jiming and Lu Guangbai of the Bianjun Commandery can command their troops to storm Qudu in his name. The Eight Great Battalions don't stand a chance."

Grand Mentor Qi propped his elbows on the table and scratched at his unkempt hair. "Think, Lanzhou! You think the empress dowager hasn't considered that? Why do you imagine they kept Xiao Chiye here five years ago? With Xiao Chiye in their hands, Xiao Jiming won't make any rash move. Qudu's Eight Battalions don't stand a chance against Libei's Armored Cavalry, but what about the garrison troops of Qidong? The Qi Clan has no dog in this fight. Qi Zhuyin and her troops would be obligated to stop Xiao Jiming, if only for the sake of demonstrating fealty to the throne."

As Shen Zechuan contemplated in silence, Ji Gang asked, "Isn't our emperor still alive? What's the point in worrying about that now? Tomorrow, Chuan-er joins the Embroidered Uniform Guard, directly under Ji Lei's command. Now that's what *I'm* worried about."

"That's why I said I don't have *incredible* foresight!" Grand Mentor Qi snapped irritably. "Sending Lanzhou to the Embroidered Uniform Guard is a means of freeing him, which happens to match the empress dowager's wishes—but does the emperor really not remember who interrogated Lanzhou in the Imperial Prison?

Why do you think he's pushing known adversaries together like this?! Ji Gang, I meant to ask—when you found Xiaofuzi today, was he really still breathing?"

Ji Gang wiped away the dust on the stone with a fingertip. After a moment, he answered, "It's hard to say. There wasn't time to take a closer look."

"And there we are." Grand Mentor Qi turned back to Shen Zechuan. "Think carefully. If Xiaofuzi was already dead before we laid our hands on him—then who did it?"

ORIOLE

EARLY ON THE DAY Shen Zechuan was to visit the Embroidered Uniform Guard offices to accept his post, Xi Gu'an's younger brother, Xi Hongxuan, hosted a feast for the up-and-coming scholars and promising talents in Qudu. All were invited to exchange civil discourse at Chaodong Tavern.

Xi Hongxuan was an obese man; an attendant beside his chair was required to fan him without pause. "It's this humble one's lucky year," he said, another bamboo fan in his own hand. "Although I couldn't get Yanqing to come, I managed to make Yuanzhuo promise to grace us with his rare presence!"

Xue Xiuzhuo had to attend to his official duties, so he was absent. But the "Yuanzhuo" Xi Hongxuan was so proud of was Yao Wenyu, the beloved pupil of the current Secretariat Elder, Hai Liangyi. These three young men addressed each other with great familiarity; they were all of the Eight Great Clans to begin with, and had known each other since childhood.

As if on cue, the bead curtain lifted to reveal an elegant scholar, gentle and pure as jade. He was dressed in a deep-blue wide-sleeved robe with slanting collars, and a small money pouch hung at his waist. Upon hearing Xi Hongxuan's boasting, he merely smiled. The other scholars in attendance rose and offered a chorus of courteous greetings.

Yao Wenyu greeted them all individually. Only after he invited everyone to take their seats did he sit himself. "My dear fellow, we meet every year. How am I worthy of the words *rare presence*?"

As humble as he was, none present were brave enough to tease him. Yao Wenyu had been the child prodigy of Qudu since his early years. He composed poetry at eight years old and verse at twelve. This young man was the "jade" cradled in the palms of the Old Master of the Yao Clan. To prevent his prodigious talents from waning, they had placed him under Hai Liangyi's tutelage. Secretariat Elder Hai was by nature inflexible and stern. To this day, he had only a single student—one he prized greatly.

Greetings and small talk soon yielded to discussions of the latest news.

Xi Hongxuan motioned to his attendants to stop fanning him. "Something truly strange is brewing in Qudu these days. I'm sure everyone here still remembers the Prince of Jianxing, Shen Wei, who self-immolated for fear of judgment five years ago?"

"The vile man who colluded with our enemies and cowered from battle!" One scholar straightened up from his seat. "He should have been beheaded under the law. Even executing his entire clan wouldn't have been unreasonable. How unfortunate that the one wretched remnant of the Shen Clan was spared thanks to His Majesty's benevolence. And just this morning, I heard he's been released! The evidence of Shen Wei's crime is conclusive. How could the son of such a disgraced and defeated subject take up an official post? Are the virtuous talents from across the land expected to lie down and accept this?!"

"Precisely," Xi Hongxuan agreed. "How could it be? There's no precedent for such a thing."

"If you ask me, Her Majesty wants to preserve him," someone else chimed in. "Everyone knows this wretch has ties to the Hua Clan.

But how could personal relationships prevail over concerns of the state? Is this not a violation of our most basic laws?"

Xi Hongxuan sighed, heavyhearted. "I'm afraid this will give all the heirs of future damned officials a loophole to exploit."

The idea incensed the scholars. Shen Wei's crimes were so severe; how could they accept Shen Zechuan's release?

"What does Yuanzhuo think?"

Yao Wenyu drank his tea and answered evenly, "I have been away from the capital for some time, so I'm afraid I'm unfamiliar with the case. I couldn't comment."

"That's right," Xi Hongxuan mused. "You travel so often for your studies; you aren't aware of what's happening in Qudu."

Someone else spoke up: "All of us here tonight are knowledgeable and widely read in the classics. We are men with a sense of honor and shame, and well-acquainted with the law. We cannot stand by and do nothing."

"Then what should we do?" Xi Hongxuan asked.

The same person answered, "We are all students of the Imperial College. If public sentiment opposes it loudly enough, His Majesty will have to reconsider. Why not kneel together before Mingli Hall and beseech His Majesty to retract his pardon and dole out a stronger punishment on that wretch Shen Zechuan?"

The guests roared their assent. Xi Hongxuan clapped his hands and cried, "Excellent! All of you here are indeed the pillars of our empire. You will be remembered throughout the ages for bending your knees today! This humble one is ashamed I can't do more myself. I'm no student of the Imperial College—but I am still willing to join you!"

"That won't do," the scholar replied. "Your elder brother is the Military Commissioner of the Eight Great Battalions. If you're implicated in such an act of dissent, you stand to lose much more than you'd gain. Gentlemen, we'll be the ones to go!"

The feast drew to a close. Yao Wenyu called for the server to steam some tender and palatable meat dishes to take with him. As he stood waiting, he overheard the scholars whispering as they descended the stairs.

"So much for that Unpolished Jade. Unprincipled coward is more like it. Did you see him earlier? He didn't say a single word. Hongxuan-xiong[20] is a model of benevolence compared to him."

Yao Wenyu tossed a pine nut into his mouth and laughed soundlessly. He didn't bother to confront them. By the time he stepped outside with his wrapped-up dishes, the scholars had more or less dispersed.

"Yuanzhuo," Xi Hongxuan called. "Shall I give you a lift?"

"No, thanks." Yao Wenyu lifted the bundle in his hand. "I'm heading for my teacher's manor."

Xi Hongxuan watched Yao Wenyu's departing figure until it was out of sight. Then he sneered, "Let's go."

Elsewhere, Shen Zechuan had arrived at the offices of the Embroidered Uniform Guard. From the moment he stepped over the threshold, all eyes were upon him; every guard rushing through the compound glanced at him as they passed.

Ge Qingqing led Shen Zechuan to the registry. "The Embroidered Uniform Guard is made up of four groups. The first is selected from households designated 'female houses' in the Yellow Register; their sisters work in the palace. These men are exempt from military service, but as their families receive a stipend from the palace, their

20 *Xiong, a word meaning elder brother. It can be attached as a suffix to address an older male peer.*

posts are not permanent, and they don't draw a salary here. An example is Xiao-Wu.

"The second group received a recommendation from a palace eunuch: 'Conferment by Eunuch's Recommendation.' Our chief commander is one of these. The third are those born into military households, who owe their inherited positions to the blessing of legacy. I am one of these myself. The fourth are those with specialized skills. These are directly appointed by His Majesty regardless of background. Those men are formidable indeed; you'll have a chance to meet them later."

Ge Qingqing lifted the curtain and beckoned Shen Zechuan inside. "This is where you come to register your name in the official records and receive your post."

As Shen Zechuan entered, all noise in the registry abruptly ceased. Guards in their various uniforms, authority tokens at their waists, turned their heads as one. A bizarre silence descended on the hall.

"Shen Zechuan?" A man sitting cross-legged at the table pushed aside his records book and looked him over. "So you're the one, huh?"

Noting the flying fish embroidered on the man's robe, Shen Zechuan knew he was an assistant regional commander at least. He bent in a shallow bow and replied, "The very same."

The man's hair flopped over his forehead, and stubble covered his jaw; his manner and bearing were markedly sloppy. With a hand to his chin, he smiled. "As expected of the son of a dancer, you're a looker; whatever fortune in silver Shen Wei spent to win that beauty's smile was clearly worth the expense. Qingqing, give him the token."

He picked up a wooden token from the table—he had obviously anticipated Shen Zechuan's arrival—and tossed it to Ge Qingqing.

Ge Qingqing caught the token and handed it to Shen Zechuan. "This man is Lord Judge of the Imperial Prison here in our

Embroidered Uniform Guard. He made a special trip here today just to deliver your token."

"The name is Qiao Tianya." He motioned for Shen Zechuan to examine his new token.

Shen Zechuan turned it over, read it, then looked at Qiao Tianya again.

"The Elephant-Training Office, isn't it? That's where you'll be going, then. Qingqing will take you over there later. But first, there are some rules. In the Embroidered Uniform Guard, our tokens are as precious as those of the Eight Great Battalions. When you're not on duty, keep it safe. Never lend it to outsiders. Now, everyone is assigned duties within the Twelve Offices, but that isn't your primary duty. Our primary duty is to serve at His Majesty's pleasure and obey his commands.

"On top of your Twelve Offices assignment, we also serve as the emperor's eyes and ears. If something major happens, such as your arrest five years ago, we need His Majesty's imperial edict—with the warrant penned and the arrest token approved by the emperor himself—to carry out the arrest. Allocation of men is never decided by me or the chief commander. Instead, to ensure no one has prior knowledge, we draw lots for every warrant delivered; chance decides."

Ji Gang had briefed Shen Zechuan on most of this beforehand, so he nodded and said nothing.

"One last thing." Qiao Tianya stood; his gaze took in everyone in the hall. "The Embroidered Uniform Guard is of one mind. Once you wear our token, you are our brother. Any past grudges will disperse with the wind. There will be no tricks to frame or make fools of our brothers. If such a thing is discovered, your tokens will be revoked, your names struck off, and your next stop will be the Imperial Prison to be dealt with to the harshest capacity."

Everyone immediately dropped their gazes and busied themselves with their work. Satisfied, Qiao Tianya turned back to Shen Zechuan. "You may go."

Shen Zechuan bowed to take his leave and followed Ge Qingqing out the door.

"I thought it would be a post in the Procession Guard, like the Fan Bearers." Ge Qingqing looked at Shen Zechuan. "The Elephant-Training Office...works too."

Shen Zechuan smiled. "I had my guesses, too, but I never thought I'd be raising elephants."

"The Horse-Training Office is the ideal post. Those golden-saddled horses are raised for the highest nobles. In that post, you get plenty of chances to meet them and get in their good graces, and it's easy to get recommended for promotion. The Elephant-Training Office..." Ge Qingqing had an odd expression on his face. "It's not an idle job, since it involves attending morning court sessions. Furthermore, those lordly elephants are a pain in the ass to serve. On the bright side, the chief commander rarely goes there, so it'll be difficult for him to make trouble for you."

The Elephant-Training Office was close to Mingli public road in the Imperial City, which led right to the Kailing River. When the weather was hot, the guards herded the elephants to the river to drink and bathe. They were also charged with leading six elephants to stand at either side of the stairs daily during morning court. In the event of a major festival or hunt, they increased the number of elephants. These elephants would not only attend morning court sessions like the officials did, they would also be dismissed from court sessions together with their human counterparts. But while the court officials were hard-pressed to take time away to convalesce when they fell ill, the elephants had no such problem;

like the Embroidered Uniform Guard, they worked in rotating shifts.

Shen Zechuan had never raised so much as a dog, and now they were giving him the impossible task of raising elephants. All he could say to that was, *You never know what life has in store.*

He and Ge Qingqing were still on their way to Shen Zechuan's new post when they heard footsteps pelting after them.

"What's the matter?" Ge Qingqing asked, turning back.

The Embroidered Uniform Guard racing up to them looked at Shen Zechuan and said solemnly, "The token has been suspended. He can't take up the post today. Hurry back to the registry!"

"Has the palace issued a new assignment?" Shen Zechuan asked.

"There's no new order from the palace—but three thousand students from the Imperial College are on hunger strike. They're kneeling in protest right now, beseeching His Majesty to retract his order and punish the Shen Clan remnant!"

Ge Qingqing's countenance filled with unease as he looked at Shen Zechuan.

Having been punished with house arrest for his misdeeds, Xiao Chiye spent the morning flipping through a play on his settee. Even when he heard Chen Yang announce Prince Chu's arrival, he could hardly be bothered to rise.

"I'm grounded," Xiao Chiye said without looking up and reached for a piece of fruit. "What are you doing barging in here so brazenly?"

Li Jianheng tossed down Xiao Chiye's supreme commander token, obviously excited. "Ce'an! Something big's happened!"

Xiao Chiye's eyelid twitched.

"Three thousand students have knelt to ask His Majesty to punish Shen Zechuan severely! They've been kneeling there all day, using a hunger strike to force His Majesty's hand. When His Majesty heard about it during dinner, he was so angry he collapsed onto his bed!"

Xiao Chiye looked at the token. "Get that thing out of here."

"The Eight Great Battalions won't do anything to disperse the students, so they asked me to deliver the token to you. If the Imperial Army can disperse the students tonight, the mark against you will be written off!" Li Jianheng stamped his foot anxiously. "If nothing else, can't the Imperial Army deal with a few weak students? This is a good thing!"

Xiao Chiye covered his face with the book. After a moment of silence, he hissed through clenched teeth, "And what a good fucking thing it is."

Not only were students of the Imperial College future candidates for official positions in the imperial court, they had no small influence among local scholars across the country. Xi Gu'an knew it was risky to touch them; if Xiao Chiye laid a finger on these students tonight, he would be the first to perish under the weight of their words in the future.

Sitting up, Xiao Chiye asked with his hands propped on his knees, "Where is Shen Zechuan right now?"

"I heard he went to the Embroidered Uniform Guard's registry early this morning." Li Jianheng watched Xiao Chiye jump up and throw on his clothes. "Where are we going? Are we going to look for Shen Zechuan?"

Xiao Chiye raced down the stairs to where Chen Yang had already prepared his horse. In a flash, he leapt into the saddle and rode hard toward the palace.

16 TEMPEST

As Xiao Chiye set out, the wind rose; rain soon followed. He galloped straight through, arriving at the Imperial College just in time to hear one of the scholars, Gao Zhongxiong, shouting over the crowd: "Until the traitor is executed, the wrath of the public will not be appeased!"

The mass of students kowtowed and echoed in unison. "Until the traitor is executed, the wrath of the public will not be appeased!"

The rain spattered against the ground; the students' robes were drenched.

Xiao Chiye reined in his horse so sharply it danced in place. He looked down at those bent backs for a moment, then raised his voice. "Where were you five years ago? If you gentlemen had knelt to make your case back when that traitor's son first entered the capital, he would never have lived to this day."

Gao Zhongxiong's chest heaved. "Lord Supreme Commander, as they say, better late than never. The Shen remnant has yet to spread his wings. As long as His Majesty is willing to retract his pardon and punish him to the fullest extent, the loyal souls lost in Zhongbo will still be consoled!"

"An imperial edict from the Son of Heaven cannot be issued at dawn and rescinded at dusk," Xiao Chiye said. "You are not beseeching His Majesty by kneeling, you are threatening him. All you gentlemen here are loyal and filial men of the world. There are a hundred ways you can make your appeal—why insist on this unwise course?"

"Your Excellency." Gao Zhongxiong looked up. "Men who wield swords die in battles, while men who wield brushes die in remonstrations! If we watch helplessly while His Majesty is deceived into such decisions, we might as well let our blood spill on the terrace tonight. Let our death prove our faith!"

"You threaten death with every sentence." Xiao Chiye scoffed. "After all this time, is that all civil servants are capable of?"

The rain grew heavier. The students didn't budge.

Xiao Chiye dismounted and squatted before Gao Zhongxiong. Water poured down in sheets. He leaned in and asked, "Who put you up to this?"

A look of great resolve came over Gao Zhongxiong's face. "I am driven to action by my loyalty to my sovereign!"

"I don't think so," Xiao Chiye drawled. "Of course, if you want to protect an outsider, you can. It's just that your actions today have implicated all three thousand of your fellow students behind you. If this angers the Son of Heaven, and it turns into a bloodbath, the lot of you will be no different from that wretched remnant of the Shen Clan—sinners condemned through the ages. And that isn't even the worst part. What's worse is this: even if your head rolls, His Majesty still won't rescind his edict. For a dozen years you devoted yourself to your studies, all to be someone else's tool?"

Gao Zhongxiong lifted a hand to wipe the rain off his face. "I am doing this out of loyalty and righteousness; this is nothing like the Shen Clan's treachery! Even if all three thousand of us were to die here tonight and our blood flooded the terrace, it would all be for the sake of His Majesty!"

"The palace has neither withdrawn Shen Zechuan's post, nor have they issued any edict to appease these students," Xiao Chiye said. "Do you not understand His Majesty's intent?"

"For each day His Majesty does not rescind his order," Gao Zhongxiong persisted, "we will neither rise, eat, nor retreat!"

The thunderstorm raged overhead. Xiao Chiye straightened. Chen Yang stepped forward with an umbrella, but Xiao Chiye raised a hand to stop him. Rain soaked his robe; even the token hanging from his belt dripped with water.

"My lord," Chen Yang murmured, "the Embroidered Uniform Guard is here!"

Xiao Chiye turned and saw Qiao Tianya arriving on horseback through the rain. He dismounted and cupped his hands in salute.

Murmurs rose among the students as they recognized the Scarlet Cavalry.

"What a thorny problem. Nothing to trouble Your Excellency the supreme commander over." Qiao Tianya put a hand to his blade and smiled. "A member of the Embroidered Uniform Guard is the target here, so naturally we should be the ones to resolve this."

"Resolve this." Xiao Chiye raised an arm almost thoughtlessly and rested it on Qiao Tianya's shoulder. "How does Your Excellency propose to resolve this? It's just some unarmed students; nothing to trouble the Embroidered Uniform Guard over."

"The emperor is the highest authority in Qudu." Qiao Tianya glanced sidelong at him. "Any with the gall to defy His Majesty become enemies of the Embroidered Uniform Guard."

Xiao Chiye looked him in the eye. After a moment, both men burst out laughing. "My good man," Xiao Chiye said, "you're certainly of true heart."

"It's cold and wet out here." Qiao Tianya tightened his grip on his blade. "I'll send someone to escort the supreme commander back to your manor."

"I just got here." Xiao Chiye's hand was heavy on Qiao Tianya's shoulder, preventing him from unsheathing the blade. Still smiling, he said, "There's no harm in staying a little longer."

"This is a tricky situation. Why does Your Excellency insist on wading into these muddy waters?"

"It's precisely because it's tricky that I'm wading in; we can't deal with all of them at once," Xiao Chiye said. "Besides, these students are all great minds of the state. None of us can shoulder the blame of losing even one."

At the back of the Embroidered Uniform Guard, a man in a thin, wide-sleeved robe dismounted his horse. He carried no blade; amid the others, he stood out like a sore thumb. Qiao Tianya loosened his grip on his hilt and shouted, "Lanzhou, come here a moment."

Shen Zechuan turned and exchanged glances with Xiao Chiye.

Qiao Tianya shrugged Xiao Chiye's arm off with a languid roll of his shoulders. "The supreme commander's concern is valid. However, the Embroidered Uniform Guard do not simply bludgeon our way through our tasks. I already made arrangements; the imperial order should arrive any minute... Ah, here he is. The two of you are old acquaintances, are you not? Stay with the supreme commander a while, Lanzhou. The students have frightened him."

Shen Zechuan gathered his sleeves and looked out at the students kneeling in the rain. Xiao Chiye shot him a glance. "You sure wasted no time picking up your token."

"Er-gongzi's token was returned quite briskly as well," Shen Zechuan replied.

Xiao Chiye smiled, though his eyes were cold. "This protest appears to take aim at you, but the real target is the palace. You didn't win enough for yourself yesterday and had to whip up this storm the moment you escaped your cage?"

Tipping his head, Shen Zechuan looked at him with eyes full of innocence. "Er-gongzi thinks too highly of me. I certainly haven't the ability to cause such a tempest. If the real target is the palace, one wonders who is praying for His Majesty to fall out with the Hua Clan. Surely Er-gongzi would know better than I."

"I don't," Xiao Chiye said. "All this convoluted stuff is beyond my understanding."

Shen Zechuan smiled. "We are old acquaintances; there's no need to put on an act with me."

Xiao Chiye didn't answer. Instead, he lifted a finger and flicked the token at Shen Zechuan's waist. "The Elephant-Training Office is a good place. You must be pleased."

"That I am," Shen Zechuan said. "It just so happens I have some insight on taming ferocious beasts."

"Wouldn't call that insight," Xiao Chiye said. "More like a conversation between two like creatures."

"I daren't entertain such conversation." Shen Zechuan coughed quietly. "If our talk breaks down and I receive another kick, wouldn't all my efforts be for naught?"

"Use your fangs, then." Xiao Chiye took the umbrella from Chen Yang and held it overhead, covering Shen Zechuan too. "Don't you have sharp teeth and a sharper tongue? What are you afraid of?"

"I value my life." Shen Zechuan heaved an affected sigh. "As they say, the kindness of a drop of water shall be repaid with a gushing spring. There is so much more I wish to repay Er-gongzi for."

Xiao Chiye scoffed. "You must have the wrong person."

"That can't be." Shen Zechuan cast a sidelong glance at Xiao Chiye and said calmly, "I recognize you."

"Fine, then." Xiao Chiye looked askance at him as well. "I also want to see how much I owe you."

The voices beyond the umbrella fell away. The two men stood shoulder to shoulder, accentuating their stark difference in height.

"Regrettably, there's no way you can stay out of this matter." Xiao Chiye gazed at the students in the rain. "If even one of them dies tonight, the blame will fall on you."

"Thirty thousand wrongfully perished souls and counting," Shen Zechuan said nonchalantly. "If they're afraid to die, they shouldn't have become someone else's weapon. Even if someone tries to pin this on me, who says I have to lie down and take it?"

They fell silent again, waiting in the rain.

Qiao Tianya had been sitting under a shed eating melon seeds; when he saw the expected sedan chair approaching, he casually shook the shells off his robe and stood, watching the silhouette sway toward them in the gloom of night.

The curtain lifted, revealing Pan Rugui within. A junior eunuch supported him with a hand, while Ji Lei kept pace at his side, holding an umbrella. Wearing a robe with a mandarin square of tiger, mugwort, and five poisons and a black, wide-brimmed hat, Pan Rugui let Qiao Tianya guide him toward the students.

Qiao Tianya reined in his glib demeanor. "What a downpour. To think they managed to draw the director out in this weather."

Pan Rugui cast a glance at Gao Zhongxiong and asked Qiao Tianya, "He won't back down?"

"Scholars are bullheaded," Qiao Tianya replied. "They're neither enticed by the carrot nor cowed by the stick."

"Then I'm afraid the stick isn't sturdy enough." Pan Rugui had lost his right-hand man only the day before and had nowhere to vent his pent-up anger. With the junior eunuch supporting him, he came to stand before Gao Zhongxiong. "You are well-read in the classics. How is it you can't comprehend the words 'overstepping your bounds'? Affairs of the imperial court are to be discussed *in* the imperial court. Brats as green as grass have no business meddling!"

On seeing this familiar lackey of the Hua Clan's faction, Gao Zhongxiong couldn't help but sit up straight. "Every man has a duty to his country. Since students of the Imperial College benefit from the imperial stipend, we must serve the imperial throne! These days, treacherous toadies abound in every corner of the palace. If we don't—"

"Treacherous toadies!" Pan Rugui sneered. "What a fine way to put it! Who directed you to slander the imperial court and malign His Majesty?"

"It was a loyal—"

"Enough," Pan Rugui snapped. "You act on the instigation of traitors with sinister motives and publicly defy an imperial decree. You incite your clique to slander the imperial court and the people. If this goes unpunished, what use is the law? Men, take him!"

Gao Zhongxiong had never expected Pan Rugui to be so brazen as to arrest him without cause. He braced himself there in the rain and cried, "Who dares lay a hand on me! I was chosen by His Majesty himself to study at the Imperial College! Villains stand before us, and eunuchs endanger the state!" Hoarsely, he continued, "The empress dowager exerts control over state affairs and refuses to return governance to its rightful master. If anyone should be arrested, it's treacherous ministers and traitors like you!"

"Take him away!" Ji Lei snapped, seeing Pan Rugui's temper flare.

The Embroidered Uniform Guard stepped forward; Gao Zhongxiong's attempt to climb to his feet was thwarted. He raised his arms in the direction of the palace and shouted, "Take my death today as a remonstration to the state! If the eunuch wants to kill me, then let him! Your Majesty..."

Qiao Tianya locked his arm around Gao Zhongxiong's neck. The scholar struggled for breath yet still croaked out, "Your Majesty—! With treacherous ministers ruling the court, is there any place for the loyal and righteous?"

Xiao Chiye had a single thought: *Oh shit.*

What happened next was just as he expected. Sorrow and indignation surged through the three thousand students. They gave no thought to life and death amid their fervent aggrievement. As the storm raged above them, the students climbed to their feet and charged the Embroidered Uniform Guard.

"Eunuchs endanger the state!" The young men yanked the pouches off their belts and hurled them at Pan Rugui. Bitter cries rang out: "Treacherous ministers rule the court!"

Ji Lei instantly shielded Pan Rugui, retreating with him toward safety. "What are you doing?" he called back furiously. "Staging a rebellion?!"

"Here is the real traitor to the nation!" The students flung themselves against the Embroidered Uniform Guard holding them back. Their fingers jabbed toward Ji Lei's face, and specks of saliva flew as they shouted, "State traitor! Traitor!"

Xiao Chiye tossed the umbrella to Shen Zechuan and hurried down the steps.

Shen Zechuan stood alone at the top of the stairs and watched the fray with cool detachment. Pan Rugui had been shoved back into his sedan; in the chaos, Ji Lei had even lost one of his shoes. So softly that he could barely be heard, Shen Zechuan said, "Turbulence seethes below the surface. An impressive showing, Lord Ji."

A chuckle rose from beneath the umbrella. He spun the handle leisurely, then turned to watch Xiao Chiye's receding figure.

Grand Mentor Qi and Ji Gang sat beneath the eaves, drinking wine and tea.

"Was killing Xiaofuzi a ploy to get Chuan-er out?" Ji Gang drank his tea.

As though he couldn't bear to drink it all at once, Grand Mentor Qi took tiny sips of his wine. He hugged the gourd and said, "Who knows? Guess if you wish."

"No matter what, his safety comes first." Ji Gang said, turning to him.

Grand Mentor Qi shook his gourd. "On the battlefield, obtaining the element of surprise requires risky maneuvers. You taught him martial arts so he could remain calm and protect himself as he wades into danger. Sometimes, we must cast safety aside; only out of the most desperate situations can one grasp true victory."

Ji Gang watched the rain grow heavier, worry clouding his face. "I've already made arrangements for the task you entrusted me with."

"We're casting a long line." Grand Mentor Qi scratched his foot. "If you don't weather the waves for a few years before you haul it in, all you will catch are foul fish and rotten shrimp. Should there come a day, before this is over, when you and I lose our lives, then today's arrangement will be the killing move that will preserve his life."

TURBULENCE

"WHAT'S ALL THAT RACKET?" The empress dowager, awoken in the middle of the night, sat up and draped a robe over herself.

Hua Xiangyi pulled the bed canopy back and helped her move aside her warm and fragrant bedding. "The students of the Imperial College want His Majesty to rescind his order," she murmured.

Maidservants on either side quietly lit the lamps and raised the curtains as the empress dowager rose. Hua Xiangyi helped her to the arhat bed, then brought soft cushions and a hand warmer while she heated some yogurt.

The empress dowager stirred the bowl, a slight crease between her brows. "How did this happen out of the blue?" She considered a moment. "The order was only given yesterday, and they came to cause this disturbance tonight. It's rather too timely."

"It's students from the Imperial College too." Hua Xiangyi leaned against the empress dowager. "All the learned minds across the land look to the Imperial College. Even the secretariat elder himself would find it ill-advised to interfere."

The empress dowager took a careful spoonful of the yogurt. Her bare face under the lamplight was etched with signs of her years, yet it only added character to her elegant profile. Slowly, she set the bowl aside and leaned back against the cushions, staring at the glazed lampshade.

"That's right," she said after a time. "Shen Wei's crimes are known to all. By all rules of sentiment and logic, the secretariat elder cannot come forward and rebuke the students. If they force His Majesty to rescind his order, I'll have to swallow this bitter pill in silence."

"It was never His Majesty's intent to release Shen Zechuan," Hua Xiangyi said. "Now, because of this order, he has earned a reputation of being misguided. I'm afraid this will open a rift between you."

"No matter," the empress dowager said. "Once Concubine Wei is with child, our Great Zhou will have an heir. An imperial heir is the foundation of an empire; as long as we have one, I'm still empress dowager. The emperor has been at odds with me since he fell ill; even if he's angry now, it's merely a tantrum thrown in a moment of weakness. Let him be."

Since falling ill years ago, the Xiande Emperor had gradually stopped complying with the empress dowager's wishes. His small acts of defiance concerned trivial daily matters, but they were nevertheless an indication of his dissent. The empress dowager had assumed command in the palace with Pan Rugui at her side and Secretariat Elder Hua in the imperial court. If she wanted to cement the Hua Clan's supremacy, she needed a submissive and obedient emperor.

If the Xiande Emperor no longer fit the bill, she would find another.

The empress dowager did not like Prince Chu for one crucial reason: Li Jianheng had already come of age. He was neither a helpless child nor a youth who had grown up at her feet. Should he ascend the throne, he would never be as compliant as an imperial grandson she had personally raised.

"Moreover, the appeal today is a slap across His Majesty's face," the empress dowager said calmly. "In the nine years he has been on the throne, his every concern—his food, clothing, his day-to-day business, whether important or trivial—has gone through me. Now he wants to be an independent and imperious ruler. He emboldened himself to show goodwill to the Xiao Clan—refusing at first to release Shen Zechuan and protecting Prince Chu. But I know him; he is outwardly strong yet inwardly weak. In his heart, he fears me. This is why he aimed from the start to please both parties. Instead, he's ended up thoroughly offending all sides."

"Didn't His Majesty keep Shen Zechuan in detention all these years for the sake of the Xiao Clan?"

The empress dowager took Hua Xiangyi's hand. "What does detention mean?" she said soberly. "Detention is a reprieve from death. His Majesty thought he did the Xiao Clan a favor, but he was sowing the seeds of disaster. Xiao Jiming lost his younger brother to Qudu, so Libei wants Shen Zechuan dead. As long as Shen Zechuan lives, His Majesty is letting down all those hundred and twenty thousand armored cavalry who came to his aid when the Shen Clan failed him. Think about it. Xiao Jiming has worked himself to the bone to prove his loyalty; he even relinquished his younger brother. He has conducted himself with frankness and sincerity toward His Majesty. And yet, to avoid offending me, His Majesty dismissed Shen Zechuan's death sentence and locked him away instead. As long as Shen Zechuan lives, he will water the roots of trouble. This is a struggle between life and death, but His Majesty remains naive.

"And need I mention this disaster? To shield Prince Chu, His Majesty refuses to launch a full investigation into Xiaofuzi's death, thwarting Pan Rugui's attempt to move against the prince. At the same time, he worries I'll hold a grudge, so he reluctantly lets Shen Zechuan out to appease me. He thinks the Xiao Clan will understand his dilemma, but when Xiao Jiming hears of this in faraway Libei, he will certainly not be happy."

"In that case," Hua Xiangyi said, "could someone from the Xiao Clan have put the students up to it? Forcing His Majesty to renege on his word would put him at odds with the Hua Clan *and* prevent both you and the secretariat elder from stepping forward. It would also see Shen Zechuan eliminated without dirtying their own hands."

The empress dowager brushed aside Hua Xiangyi's stray hair. "If it were so clear-cut," she said dotingly, "then Xiao Jiming wouldn't be one of the Four Generals. That young man has always been prudent. If he were the perpetrator, he would not be found out so easily. Besides, Libei has no contact with the Imperial College."

"Well, then I can't guess." Hua Xiangyi leaned on the empress dowager and said like a pampered child, "Tell me, Auntie."

"All right." The empress dowager had no children of her own, nor was she close with any of her maternal relatives; she doted only on Hua Xiangyi. "Look at the eight cities that encircle the capital. These are where the Eight Great Clans originated. Our Hua Clan resides in Dicheng, south of Qudu. When it comes to selecting ladies of the palace, it has always been the city of choice. But only during my time has the Hua Clan reached the height of glory, coming first among the Eight Great Clans. Before that, when the late emperor ascended the throne, the Yao Clan had held the most influence since they had thrice been conferred as the emperor's tutor. If not for Old Master Yao's lack of literary talent, Qi Huilian from Yuzhou might not have become the Grand Mentor of the crown prince during the Yongyi years."

She continued, "From the current Xi Clan, Xi Gu'an is the only one to have been promoted as high as Military Commissioner of the Eight Great Battalions, where he could manage the younger generations of the Eight Great Clans—think of him as a teacher in the military camps. The Xi Clan has always bred men of inferior morals and virtue; they will not achieve great things. As for the Xue Clan, their decline began when the eldest head of their family passed away. Xue Xiuzhuo is the only one now with an official post in the central administration. But the hour is late—I can speak of the Wei, Pan, Fei, and Han Clans some other time."

"I've heard Father speak of them before," Hua Xiangyi said. "So Auntie is saying the hidden instigator of the Imperial College riot might be anyone from the Eight Clans."

"That's what I suspect," the empress dowager said. "Glory is enjoyed in turns. The Hua Clan has enjoyed the sunlight for many years since my ascent. Now that His Majesty is in such poor health, people may begin to entertain certain ambitions. Summon Pan Rugui tomorrow morning; let him instruct the Embroidered Uniform Guard to conduct an investigation—it should be thorough but covert. There's only so much space in Qudu; I don't believe there is not a single loose lip to be found."

Xiao Chiye wrung water from his robes as he entered Mingli Hall beside Ji Lei. It was deep in the night, but the Xiande Emperor was still awake.

"You are under house arrest to reflect on the error of your ways." The emperor was holding a report; after a moment, he glanced at Xiao Chiye and asked hoarsely, "So what are you doing running around with the Embroidered Uniform Guard?"

Xiao Chiye felt truly ill-used. "Military Commissioner Xi personally asked me to go. This humble subject assumed it was by Your Majesty's verbal decree."

"So you went," the emperor said. "And how did it go?"

Ji Lei fell to his knees and kowtowed. "Your Majesty, the students of the Imperial College were instigated to action by an unknown party. They not only spoke presumptuously on state affairs and slandered Your Majesty, they also laid hands on Pan-gonggong. It was utter chaos. This humble subject wished to take them into custody, but the supreme commander refused."

He hadn't been alone, either; the whole Imperial Army seemed cast in the same mold as their commander. They had every one of them shamelessly obstructed the Embroidered Uniform Guard, preventing them from rounding up the students—they may as well have dropped to the ground and thrown a tantrum. This horde of idle ruffians had skins as thick as the city wall.

"You obstructed the Guard from arresting the students?" the emperor asked Xiao Chiye.

"If the students were taken into the Imperial Prison, how many would survive?" Xiao Chiye explained. "Their lives are insignificant, but what if it tainted Your Majesty's good name?"

"They formed a faction and colluded with unknown malefactors," Ji Lei argued indignantly. "They acted with intent to dismantle the rule and order of the court! If we do not send them to trial, then what use is the Embroidered Uniform Guard?"

The emperor coughed for several moments before he said, "Ce'an has done well."

"Your Majesty!" Ji Lei looked back at him in disbelief. "This mob of students gathered to foment a riot. They dared shout the word *rebellion*! If we do not take the harshest hand with them, we endanger the empire and state!"

"They merely spoke their minds," the emperor said mildly. "If they hadn't been pushed this far, why would they set down their brushes to come trade blows with the Embroidered Uniform Guard? That wretched descendant of the Shen Clan should have never been released! If it weren't for... If it weren't for—!"

The emperor cast aside the report as he was wracked by coughs. It was a long time before his breathing settled. "Even so, they must be punished. Reduce the Imperial College's stipend by half and cut their meals from twice a day to once. The punishment shall last for half a year."

When he saw that the emperor had made up his mind, Ji Lei said no more. He remained kneeling in silence, but the emperor sensed his thoughts.

"The Embroidered Uniform Guard are *our* dogs." The Xiande Emperor's gaze bored into Ji Lei. "You are their chief commander. Why are you going around acknowledging others as your godfather or grand-godfather? We've said nothing until now only out of faith in your apparent deference! Tonight, we want you to appease the students of the Imperial College. Do you understand?"

Ji Lei kowtowed. "This humble subject obeys. The Embroidered Uniform Guard serves only Your Majesty!"

By the time Xiao Chiye and Ji Lei emerged, the rain had subsided to a drizzle. Junior eunuchs from the bailiff office ran up to hold umbrellas for the two of them.

Ji Lei's expression was unpleasant as he raised his hands in a departing bow to Xiao Chiye. Xiao Chiye appeared unconcerned. "My hands are tied, Lao-Ji. I was placed under house arrest only yesterday. For the sake of my freedom, I didn't dare lay a hand on the students."

Xiao Chiye's cavalier attitude infuriated Ji Lei, but what could he do? He jerked his chin in a cursory nod, wishing Xiao Chiye would leave.

"But what do you think of my Imperial Army?" Xiao Chiye took the umbrella from the junior eunuch's hand and waved him off, walking out of the palace right beside Ji Lei.

What do I think? Ji Lei fumed. *I think they're a bunch of thugs! They're even more useless now under your command!* But he said politely, "They seem much more spirited than before."

"Right?" Xiao Chiye agreed shamelessly. "Honestly, the Imperial Army's drill grounds are too small for us to properly stretch our legs. Do you think you could ask the commissioner of the Eight Great Battalions if he would allocate some land for the Imperial Army?"

Ji Lei had heard Xiao Chiye was primarily using the drill grounds to play polo with the Imperial Army. He never expected the man would have the guts to ask for more land. But he couldn't very well turn Xiao Chiye down right to his face, so he said, "I'm afraid that would be difficult. When Prince Chu expanded his manor last month, his forced seizure of civilian residences was reported to the prefectural yamen. These days, people are crammed everywhere in Qudu. Where is Gu'an going to find space for you to build a military drill ground? Besides, if there's a spot in the city, it would go first to the Eight Great Battalions."

Xiao Chiye sighed beneath the umbrella. "Well, if we can't get a piece of land in the city, we can make do outside it. As long as the space is large enough for us to play to our hearts' content."

At once Ji Lei grasped the intent behind this conversation. He looked at Xiao Chiye and snorted. "All right, Er-gongzi. You've taken a fancy to a piece of land, have you not? Why play dumb with me?"

"I'm asking you for a favor, Lao-Ji," Xiao Chiye said. "You have more connections than anyone in the capital. If *you* ask, how can the commissioner turn you down? We can negotiate the details once the deal goes through."

"There's no need to talk money with me." Ji Lei's attitude softened. "I've taken a godson, and I was just wondering where to find a good mount for him! When it comes to horses, no one's more knowledgeable than you, Er-gongzi."

"Sure, I'll gift him a few horses to play with," answered Xiao Chiye. "They're bred from the herds in the Hongyan Mountains, no worse than my own. I'll have someone deliver them right to your manor in the next few days."

"I'll speak to Gu'an, then," Ji Lei said. "A drill ground is a piece of cake. Just wait for good news!"

By the time the two parted, the rain had stopped. Xiao Chiye climbed into a carriage where Chen Yang waited. Watching Ji Lei's sedan depart, Chen Yang asked, "Is my lord really going to give him our horses? What a waste!"

"No such thing as a free lunch." Xiao Chiye kicked off his boots, which had long been soaked through. "We need a drill ground. Anything inside the capital will draw too much attention. And if that old crook can't deliver on his promise after accepting the horses," he added coldly, "I'll send his godson to meet his ancestors."

The carriage began to move. Xiao Chiye wiped his face with a handkerchief and asked, "Where is he?"

"He?"

"Shen Zechuan!"

"He went back ages ago." Chen Yang poured a cup of tea for Xiao Chiye. "His steps seemed faltering to me; with a weak constitution like that, how is he going to work in the Embroidered Uniform Guard?"

"He'll be raising elephants." Xiao Chiye took the tea and gulped it down. "That invalid is only too eager to dodge manual labor. He's most definitely the sort who loafs on the job."

The alleged loafer let out a sharp sneeze. He sat in the dimness for a moment, wondering if he'd caught a cold.

The door opened, and a rotund figure strode in. "What a fine spot," Xi Hongxuan marveled. "Not even the Embroidered Uniform Guard will be able to find this place."

"It's a broken-down manor no one wants to rent; that's the only good thing about it," Shen Zechuan replied without turning around.

"But it can't have been easy to get your hands on it." Xi Hongxuan rubbed his palms together as he took a seat at the table and looked at Shen Zechuan. "This is the manor the late emperor bestowed on the crown prince at the time, who then gifted it to Qi Huilian. It was sold off after Qi Huilian died. How did it end up in your possession?"

Shen Zechuan sipped his tea and shot a pointed glance at Xi Hongxuan.

Xi Hongxuan lazily raised his hands. "Look at this foolish mouth of mine, always prying into people's business. I heard on the way here that Pan Rugui got knocked down a peg too. You do move fast, don't you."

"The eldest Lord Xi is Military Commissioner of the Eight Great Battalions," Shen Zechuan said. "The student incident, whether he had a part in it or not, has roused the empress dowager's suspicion. He will have a very hard time in the days ahead."

"The harder it is, the easier I'll sleep." Xi Hongxuan placed his fleshy palms on the table. "Instead of waiting for higher officials of the imperial court to find the nerve to raise it, may as well get the students to speak up first—and we had the advantage of first move. After this incident, you really are free."

Shen Zechuan reached for a dish and grasped some vegetables with his chopsticks. "Just a small trick. It's nothing compared to yours."

Xi Hongxuan watched Shen Zechuan eat before he touched his own chopsticks. "So, what will you do now?"

"Just try to get by in the Embroidered Uniform Guard," Shen Zechuan said. "But Ji Lei is Pan Rugui's godson and the sworn brother of Xi Gu'an. If you want to kill Xi Gu'an, you'll have to get past Ji Lei. Why not split the two of them between us, and they can be brothers for all eternity?"

Xi Hongxuan sniggered. Leaning over the table with a sinister look, he asked Shen Zechuan, "What's your grudge against Ji Lei?"

Shen Zechuan picked out the peppercorns in his dish. Without lifting his eyes, he answered, "I don't like his shoes."

DONKEY ROAST

XIAO CHIYE KEPT HIMSELF out of trouble for the next half month. When he finally received confirmation from Ji Lei that the military drill ground had been secured, he immediately headed out with Chen Yang for a look. The unused plot had originally been a mass burial site, left deserted ever since the platform used for execution was moved elsewhere.

Chen Yang dismounted and looked around. "I knew this place was on the other side of Mount Feng, but this is a little *too* far."

"It's only three hours' ride before dawn." Xiao Chiye pointed his riding crop toward one end of the clearing. "We have to treat those wily old codgers from the Ministry of Works to a good meal if we want them to cobble together some materials to fill up this side. Tidy it a little and we can make do. This place is so remote not even the Eight Great Battalions' patrols come out here."

"I can't explain how unpleasant it feels to spend money on them," Chen Yang said.

"Bear with it," Xiao Chiye answered. "Even if they squat on our heads and piss, we need this place."

"Yes, my lord." Chen Yang didn't complain again.

Xiao Chiye didn't ride back until dusk. The instant he entered the city, he spied Li Jianheng's guard waiting for him at the gate. Xiao Chiye reined his horse to a halt. "What's happened?"

The guard bowed. "His Highness is holding a feast at Huixiang Tavern on Donglong Street. He's waiting for Your Excellency the supreme commander to join him."

After thinking about it for a moment, Xiao Chiye spurred his horse over.

Donglong Street ran adjacent to the Kailing River. Night was falling, and lanterns shone bright along the way. Taverns and pleasure houses lined both sides of the street while all manner of painted boats and light canoes floated on the water.

Xiao Chiye dismounted outside Huixiang Tavern, and the shopkeeper personally led him upstairs. Only when he lifted the curtain and glanced inside did he realize this was no mere feast. Every guest was a well-known personage in their own right or a young master whose father or elder brother held official positions in the court. Next to Prince Chu sat a delicate and fair-faced junior eunuch—no doubt the "grandson" Pan Rugui had found for himself after Xiaofuzi's death.

"Ce'an is here!" Li Jianheng called. "Sit, sit! We were waiting for you!"

Xiao Chiye sat in the first vacant seat. "Quite the turnout," he said with a smile.

"Allow me to introduce you. This is Pan-gonggong's grand-godson, Fengquan, Feng-gonggong!" Li Jianheng turned to Fengquan. "This is my good brother, the second young master of Libei's Xiao Clan and the supreme commander of the Imperial Army, Xiao Ce'an."

Fengquan was a great deal easier on the eyes than the departed Xiaofuzi. He bowed respectfully to Xiao Chiye. "I've heard much about you, Your Excellency."

Xi Hongxuan sat across from them with one leg crossed over the other. His bulk was spread over two seats, his plump face perspiring profusely. "Let's dispense with the formalities. Are we waiting on anyone else, Your Highness? If everyone's here, let's start the feast!"

Li Jianheng quirked an eyebrow at Xiao Chiye. "I did invite one more guest of honor whom everyone has wanted to meet."

Xiao Chiye looked back at him, baffled, until an attendant behind him lifted the curtain and announced, "The distinguished guest has arrived!"

A brief silence fell over the room.

Xiao Chiye turned just in time to see Shen Zechuan stride across the threshold in his Embroidered Uniform Guard attire. Shen Zechuan was visibly stunned to see him—the surprise showed so obviously on his face that Xiao Chiye didn't believe it for a second.

Everyone here knew of the animosity between them, and for a moment, a peculiar tension filled the room. Guests hoping to witness a scene exchanged meaningful glances.

"This is Shen Lanzhou." Li Jianheng introduced him warmly. "You all know of him, right? Take a seat, Lanzhou. Tavern-keeper, let the feast begin!"

Xiao Chiye suspected Li Jianheng must have been bewitched by Shen Zechuan's looks to invite the man to this feast. Of all places to sit, Shen Zechuan picked the seat right beside Xiao Chiye. Their eyes met as he sat down.

"So, this is Shen Lanzhou, whose name has been making waves in Qudu of late." Xi Hongxuan eyed Shen Zechuan. "Seeing truly is believing."

"I heard Lanzhou's mother was an unparalleled beauty in Duanzhou in her youth," Li Jianheng said. "Shen Wei staked half his manor before he won her over! How could Lanzhou be anything but lovely?"

Scattered laughter rose as the guests openly or surreptitiously threw glances at Shen Zechuan. Even Fengquan smacked his lips in appreciation and said, "If this man had been born a girl..."

"Then there'd be no place for the Hua women!"

The group of idle young masters burst into knowing laughter. From the corner of his eye, Xiao Chiye saw Shen Zechuan with his head slightly lowered, his face unreadable.

The nape of this man's neck, bathed in the dim light of the nearby lamp, rose from beneath his collar like creamy white jade. It seemed defenseless, just waiting for the touch of another's hand—as if by caressing it, one could reach ecstasy. The contours of his profile were smooth and beautiful, and the bridge of his nose sloped charmingly. But the corners of his eyes were most devastating: all that could make one's heart itch lay within them, and the shadow of a smile seemed to rest at the tails of those upward crescents.

Xiao Chiye took another look. Shen Zechuan was indeed smiling.

"Have you mistaken me for someone else?" Shen Zechuan shifted his gaze to Xiao Chiye.

"Just seeing you in a different light." Xiao Chiye looked away.

Shen Zechuan looked up and smiled obsequiously at the guests seated all along the table. "Everyone speaks too kindly. This one's appearance is middling at best."

Upon hearing this, those who had been clinging to decorum loosened up, and the conversation grew ever more vulgar.

"Wasn't there a new game getting popular on Donglong Street? It's called 'playing cups,'" Xi Hongxuan said. "You fill a goblet with good wine, place it in the fragrant shoe of a beauty, and pass it around. Your Highness, have you played before?"

Li Jianheng laughed. "I have the wine but lack a beauty."

"Isn't one sitting right here?" Xi Hongxuan flapped his hand.

Shen Zechuan acted as if they were strangers and forced a polite smile. "I'm unworthy of the word *beauty*. If you really want to play with beauties, I'll invite you all to the brothel tonight; play to your hearts' content."

Lovely as his face might be, Shen Zechuan still had the backing of the Hua Clan. The others didn't dare push their luck. Only Xi Hongxuan seemed determined to offend Shen Zechuan, continuing to harass and dismiss him. Rumor had it that Xi Gu'an had fallen out of favor with the empress dowager. It was no surprise, the guests thought, that Xi Hongxuan would vent his anger on Shen Zechuan on behalf of his elder brother.

Shen Zechuan was about to retort when Xiao Chiye spoke up beside him. "How can you ask His Highness Prince Chu to play such a tired old game? Playing cups is a centuries-old party trick. Even prostitutes in the south no longer find it interesting. How about we go about it from a different angle? Take off your shoes, Second Young Master Xi, and we can use them as boats."

Everyone roared with laughter; Xi Hongxuan's feet were indeed much larger than those of the average man. Normally no one would be brazen enough to say so, let alone poke fun at him.

"That works too." Xi Hongxuan gamely raised his foot. "Men! Remove my shoes!"

At this, Li Jianheng laughed and cussed cheerfully at him.

Shen Zechuan hadn't expected Xiao Chiye to come to his aid; he and Xi Hongxuan had merely been putting on a show. Now he looked at Xiao Chiye again. Xiao Chiye ignored him. He picked up his chopsticks and applied himself to his food.

After a while, when Fengquan saw the dishes were more or less served, he said, "Since you gentlemen are here to indulge, let me add another dish to the table tonight." He clapped his hands, and attendants waiting downstairs rushed in on his summons.

The dish in question turned out to be a live young donkey.

"Of all the delicacies in this world, donkey meat is the finest," Fengquan said. "Gentlemen, have you ever tried 'donkey roast'?"

The noise in the room died down. Everyone looked at the donkey in the center.

"What's a donkey roast?" Li Jianheng asked.

The attendants dumped some soil on the floor and deftly heaped it into a tidy mound. They drove the donkey onto it so its hooves were buried and its belly brushed the surface of the soil. Then, they covered the donkey with a thick padded quilt.

"Now, gentlemen," Fengquan said courteously, "watch and see."

An attendant half-crouched as he ladled boiling soup fresh from the pot and poured it over the donkey. His assistants held the quilt over the head of the braying animal. Its fur peeled away. Yet they still weren't done: the attendant who had poured the boiling soup set aside the ladle and started carving meat from the still-living donkey's seared flesh. The meat was placed on a platter for an attendant waiting by the stove. They roasted it on the spot and passed the plates around.

The screams of the donkey grew more distressing every moment; even the guests downstairs were alarmed. Color drained from Li Jianheng's face as he looked at the meat. He covered his nose and mouth with one hand. "Feng-gonggong, isn't this dish a little too..."

"Why don't you try it first, Your Highness? This donkey meat is most delectable when carved immediately after the soup has been poured. Food must be eaten fresh," Fengquan said. "There is deeper meaning behind this donkey roast. If a man falls into the hands of another, he puts himself at their mercy: if his master tells him to kneel, he must kneel; if his master wants him to cry, he must cry; and if his master eyes his flesh, he must allow himself to be carved."

Shen Zechuan knew he was this donkey. As he watched blood run from under the quilt and into the soil until the stench filled the air, it was as if he was looking at Ji Mu five years ago, or at his younger self.

Xi Hongxuan ate a few slices and, as if he didn't grasp the meaning of anything, hollered "Delicious!" Xiao Chiye's chopsticks never touched the meat. Shen Zechuan didn't even touch his chopsticks.

The eunuch's little speech had disturbed Li Jianheng. He said nervously, "It's really too depraved. Take it away!"

"A moment, please." Fengquan finally looked at Shen Zechuan. "My godfather specifically asked me to serve this dish, Shen-gongzi. Why have you not tasted it?"

If Pan Rugui was his grand-godfather, then this godfather he spoke of was Ji Lei. It was certainly a curious thing—what connections did this man possess to obtain Pan Rugui's favor and trust so quickly? Not only had he taken over Xiaofuzi's duties, he was already in Ji Lei's good graces.

Ji Lei had missed his chance to kill Shen Zechuan, and now that Shen Zechuan was under his command, he couldn't touch him. Devising such a disgusting humiliation sent a clear message: their grudge was far from ended.

Shen Zechuan lifted his chopsticks. "I..."

Before he could finish, the chair beside him scraped the floor as Xiao Chiye stood. Picking up the plate of donkey meat, he flung it in Fengquan's direction, where it crashed to the ground.

Li Jianheng scrambled to his feet. "C-Ce'an..."

Xiao Chiye stared at Fengquan. It wasn't his business whom Fengquan wanted humiliated on Ji Lei's behalf. But at that moment, he too was a trapped beast in Qudu, no different from this donkey. This was a slap to his face too. And it stung.

Fengquan looked at him in puzzlement. "Is this dish not to the supreme commander's liking?"

Xiao Chiye grasped the hilt of Wolfsfang at his waist. Screams rang out as he drew his blade; his hand rose and fell, the donkey's head rolled. Its miserable braying ceased as blood seeped out of the soil onto the floor, turning the boards crimson.

The assembly held their breath, waiting for whatever Xiao Chiye would do next.

Silhouetted in the dim light, Xiao Chiye wiped the edge of his blade clean with the tablecloth. Only then did he casually turn and smile at Li Jianheng's guests. "Gentlemen, please continue."

Li Jianheng stared at the blade. "Ce'an, Ce'an," he said, his voice soft, "you can p-put it away."

Xiao Chiye sheathed Wolfsfang and leveled a look at Fengquan. He hooked a chair over with his foot and sat down boldly in the middle of the room. "Go ahead and roast the whole thing. I'll sit right here tonight and watch Feng-gonggong eat."

Shortly after, Fengquan called for his sedan and left in a hurry. Li Jianheng, having had his fair share of the wine, turned to Xiao Chiye with a face full of tears and snot. "I really didn't know that would happen, Ce'an. Who would've thought that castrated bastard was so despicable? We're buddies. You mustn't let this get between us!"

Xiao Chiye's mouth curled. "There's a difference between acquaintances and friends. I understand. You go on ahead."

Li Jianheng tugged at his sleeve, wanting to say more, but Xiao Chiye gestured for Chen Yang to stuff Li Jianheng into his sedan.

"See that Prince Chu gets back in one piece," Xiao Chiye said. "I'll walk."

Observing Xiao Chiye's stormy mood, Chen Yang didn't quibble. He mounted his horse and left with Prince Chu's sedan.

Xiao Chiye stood alone under the lantern. After a moment, he kicked over a potted plant. The helpless plant, which was worth quite a lot, toppled and rolled in a gentle arc before tumbling to the bottom of the stairs.

A pale hand pushed it gently back upright.

Standing on the stairs below him, Shen Zechuan said evenly, "Do you have money? You'll have to pay for this, you know."

"I've got plenty of money," Xiao Chiye replied, his voice cold. He rummaged in his belt's pockets and came up totally empty.

Shen Zechuan waited a moment before turning to the tavern-keeper. "Put it on the good sir's tab. He's got plenty of money."

19
TRUTH AND LIES

A BREEZE BRUSHED THROUGH the hot summer night; the moon hung low over lush treetops. Xiao Chiye was young and vigorous, and the rush of wine had quickly overheated him. He was restless. Staring at Shen Zechuan as he descended the stairs, he said, "So the Temple of Guilt can purify one's heart of desire and change one's temperament."

Shen Zechuan dismissed a runner nearby. "I'm just the kind of person who greets adversity with perfect equanimity."

Xiao Chiye accepted tea from an attendant to rinse his mouth and dried it with a handkerchief. "If you're going to make up stories, at least put more effort in. You probably don't even know how to spell those last two words."

"Aren't we all just playing our parts?" Shen Zechuan wiped his own hands, then smiled. "Yet you took it so seriously."

Xiao Chiye tossed the handkerchief back onto the tray without looking at him. "It was a little over the top; do you think anyone believed it? But someone had to play that role, and I, Xiao Ce'an, happened to be perfect for the part. Did it not please you as well?"

Shen Zechuan's eyes wandered down. "That's a fine blade."

Lifting a hand, Xiao Chiye blocked his view. "And the man isn't?"

One of the lanterns upstairs went out. Shen Zechuan sighed. "How do you expect me to answer that? It's a rather inappropriate question."

"You have a keen eye." Xiao Chiye moved his hand away. The gaze he fixed on Shen Zechuan was ruthless and fierce. "Few people can recognize a good blade."

"When the man himself is finely appointed," Shen Zechuan said amiably, "naturally, everything he wears is quality. It was a lucky guess—even a blind cat will stumble upon a dead mouse once in a while."

"Why is it that when you praise me, I feel as though I've seen a ghost?"

"You don't get praised often, hm?" Shen Zechuan's tone was gentle. "I haven't even voiced my most heartfelt words."

The people around them had dispersed.

"You seem to be good at restraining yourself," Xiao Chiye said blandly.

"Grand schemes are thwarted by a lack of forbearance. You'll experience more of my capabilities soon enough." Shen Zechuan smiled. "Try to be patient."

"Grand schemes. What is there for you to scheme over in this tiny city of Qudu?"

"I say a few words..." Shen Zechuan looked at Xiao Chiye sympathetically. "...and you believe them. I didn't take you for the naive and artless type, Er-gongzi."

"I'm but a frivolous young master, loafing around, drinking and dining and waiting to die," Xiao Chiye said. "How would I know what treachery the world holds? And now there's even someone like you come to deceive me."

"A thousand pardons." Shen Zechuan took a step forward. "I saw how piteous you were with your talons and fangs sealed. That slash of your blade tonight must have been gratifying."

"A little." Xiao Chiye lifted a leg to block Shen Zechuan's way. "Where are you going? We're not done talking."

"Escorting you back to your manor. You helped me out of a bind tonight, and for that I'm so grateful I'm practically on the verge of tears. How can I *ever* repay the kindness?"

Xiao Chiye grinned. "Mouth full of lies. You must have deceived quite a few."

"Not so many." Shen Zechuan looked back at him. "Of course, in this life one must tell a *few* lies. Such as the kind about having plenty of money."

"But I can hardly compare to you." Xiao Chiye dropped his leg.

"You see," Shen Zechuan said pleasantly, "you're being polite again."

There was simply no way to have a conversation with this man. It was impossible to tell which of his words were truth and which were lies, every new sentence drawing a veil over the last. No matter how long they spoke, Xiao Chiye couldn't make heads or tails of it. Xiao Chiye turned and whistled for his horse, then said, "Because of the incident tonight, you speak as if we're close. But your audience is gone now. Why keep up the act?"

"Then what should I do?" Lantern in hand, Shen Zechuan looked at him with soft and obliging eyes. "Bite you again?"

Xiao Chiye took a swift step closer and said lightly, "You use this flesh to bewitch others. What do you expect me to think you're after if you look at me like that?"

Unperturbed, Shen Zechuan answered, soft-voiced, "But I was born with a pair of affectionate eyes."

"And what a waste," Xiao Chiye said derisively, pointing his riding crop at the space between Shen Zechuan's brows. "All they contain are schemes and calculations."

"I was born low." Shen Zechuan lifted a finger and slowly pushed aside the riding crop. "How can I play the game if not by scheming?"

"What I did tonight was for my own sake. Don't go thinking it was for you."

"The moon is so beautiful tonight. Why do you have to spoil the mood?"

Xiao Chiye mounted his horse and looked down at him for a moment with his reins in hand. "I fear, since I've shown you this bit of kindness, you will latch on to me and try my nerves with all that weeping and wailing about your sorry lot," he said archly.

"It's not the alcohol that's addled your mind," Shen Zechuan observed. "Whatever's afflicting you, I'm afraid it's fatal."

"Who can say?" Xiao Chiye said. "It's not like you've never been known to make a scene."

They lapsed into silence, the night around them quiet.

Xiao Chiye turned away, considering this a small victory. He had urged his horse into a trot when he heard the man behind him say with a smile in his voice: "Have you found what you lost five years ago?"

Xiao Chiye whipped his head around and yanked back on the reins. "Give me back the thumb ring," he demanded, his voice like ice.

Shen Zechuan gazed back at him with a wicked look in his eye. "You want the thumb ring? Easy. Bark twice like a dog and I'll give it back to you."

The gyrfalcon swooped down to rest on Xiao Chiye's shoulder. Beast and master stared frostily at Shen Zechuan in the gloom. Nearby, a watchman struck his clapper, startling away the flame in Shen Zechuan's lantern.

The road went dark.

It was several days before Li Jianheng worked up the courage to show his face before Xiao Chiye. He was surprised to find that

Xiao Chiye's anger had yet to subside. Shards of ice were practically flaking off the man as they sat in a pleasure den listening to music, so forbidding the delicate young courtesans were afraid to get close enough to wait on him.

Li Jianheng held his teacup between them as a shield and whispered, "Are you still angry?"

"Nope." Xiao Chiye ground the ice from his drink between his teeth.

Li Jianheng's hair stood on end as he listened to the ice crack. "Autumn is around the corner; don't eat ice like that. It's rather terrifying."

"Such a large cellar of ice is prepared every year. It'd be a waste to leave it." Xiao Chiye propped both his legs on the furniture and leaned back.

"Then I'll tell you something good." Li Jianheng scooted closer. "That Fengquan—do you know who he is?"

"Who?"

"Remember that little lady I told you about?" Li Jianheng beamed, a cunning look in his eyes. "Fengquan is her younger brother. Now that she has Pan Rugui's favor, how could Pan Rugui not promote her kin? That Fengquan's got a silver tongue; Ji Lei was so enamored of his flattery he took that eunuch in as his godson!"

"It seems to me..." Xiao Chiye propped his cheek in one hand and glanced at Li Jianheng. "...you really have your heart set on that girl."

"Of course," Li Jianheng said. "Anyway, that bastard Ji Lei was the one behind the—what happened the other day. As his godson, how could Fengquan defy his godfather's order?"

"Are you saying you want me to let it go?"

Li Jianheng was an adaptable man, lacking the usual aspirations expected of descendants of the imperial family. He slipped from his chair and squatted before Xiao Chiye. "For the sake of my romance, brother, let it go this once. Didn't we make him eat until he puked? That's something. He's Pan Rugui's man; really we can't be too harsh on him. It's only been a few days since the trouble with Xiaofuzi. His Majesty is watching us."

Xiao Chiye sat up straight and nailed him with a stare. "Did you touch her?"

Li Jianheng hemmed and hawed.

"You touched Pan Rugui's woman right under his nose?" Xiao Chiye was incredulous.

"I wouldn't have done it if he were a real man." Li Jianheng reluctantly stood. "But he's just an old eunuch with the same old tricks, and he's beating that delicate beauty all day long until she's in tears! She was supposed to be mine! If you were in my shoes, wouldn't you have done the same?"

Overcome with disappointment, Xiao Chiye snapped, "No!"

"Ce'an, we're brothers! This is such a small thing; turn a blind eye this once. Let Fengquan off and I'll find you something else to amuse you!"

Xiao Chiye slumped back down and said nothing.

If Pan Rugui found out about this, Xiaofuzi's murder would pale in comparison. That old dog would spend the rest of his days trying to see them both dead. His promotion of Fengquan was evidence enough of how he doted on that woman. Pan Rugui was sixty-five. As a eunuch, he had no biological sons, and over the years, none of the pretty women around him had remained by his side for long. If he truly regarded this woman as a beloved wife or favorite concubine, he might very well hack Li Jianheng to death personally.

Xiao Chiye interrupted Li Jianheng's incessant pleading. "Since you already did it, does that mean you have a plan?"

Li Jianheng sat on the carpet and lowered his head to pick at his bamboo fan. "Not really," he answered in a small voice. "It's just that I—I've heard Pan Rugui used to keep a boy toy as well. Maybe all I have to do is send him the right one to play with."

"There aren't many who can surpass that pretty lady of yours, are there?"

Li Jianheng was on tenterhooks, but he couldn't hide this from him. "Lately, quite a few people have been asking around about that...Shen Lanzhou."

"Asking what?"

"Asking his price, and whether they could afford to keep him." Seeing Xiao Chiye's face devoid of expression, Li Jianheng eagerly clung to his chair. "Money is no issue, but I can't approach him myself. If he did something desperate when pushed into a corner... Help me this once, Ce'an! You just need to ensure he gets to Pan Rugui. After the deed is done, I'll give him silver! Or gold!"

Xiao Chiye rested his hands on his knees in silence.

Seeing a glimmer of hope, Li Jianheng pushed ahead. "You hate Shen Wei, right? After this, Shen Zechuan will never throw his weight around in front of you again! Think about it. He didn't die, but life has an interesting sense of humor! If he ended up a eunuch's toy in Qudu, that'd be a fate worse than death! Besides, isn't the empress dowager also..."

"I thought you were using your brain to talk." Xiao Chiye slowly moved his legs away. "Turns out it's all fucking mush in there."

"Ce'an, Ce'an!" Seeing him rise to leave, Li Jianheng lifted the hem of his robe and chased after him.

But Xiao Chiye stepped out of the building. He mounted his horse, and, without a single backward glance, rode out.

Even if they could turn Shen Zechuan into Pan Rugui's forbidden toy, could Pan Rugui accept such a gift? The empress dowager had been adamant about protecting this man. If Pan Rugui took him, he would be burning his bridges. Li Jianheng was out of his mind!

But, if Li Jianheng really dared.

If he really dared…

How could he dare to do it?

At the end of his shift, Shen Zechuan removed his token from his waist. He had scarcely stepped out the door when he spied Xiao Chiye's dashing horse outside and the man himself sitting on a nearby rock.

"Here to ask for your thumb ring back?" Shen Zechuan asked as he descended the steps.

Xiao Chiye had snapped off a twig with a few leaves and now held it between his teeth. After eyeing Shen Zechuan for a moment, he said, "Wake up, it's broad daylight. Cut the bullshit and give it back."

"You weren't this short-tempered the other night." Shen Zechuan glanced up at the sky. "It would be too humiliating for the supreme commander to stand here and bark like a dog, so you aren't here for the thumb ring. What's the matter? Spit it out."

"Don't you know everything that goes on around here?" Xiao Chiye propped his elbows on his long legs. "Prince Chu wanted to give Xiaofuzi a thrashing, and you managed to hear about it from within the temple. I'd forgotten about it—but thinking back, you must have planted a man by the prince's side, right? A spy, or at least someone to egg him on."

"If I were that powerful," Shen Zechuan said, "I wouldn't have been reduced to raising elephants."

"Who knows if that's the truth or a lie?" Xiao Chiye's gaze was aloof and cold. "You had better give me a thorough account so I can decide what to believe."

DECISIONS

"AH, I'M SO MISUNDERSTOOD," Shen Zechuan said. "Nowadays, the minute something happens, somehow it's all Shen Lanzhou's fault."

"There has been wave after wave of trouble since your release," Xiao Chiye replied. "Xiaofuzi, the Imperial College, Pan Rugui. Why is it that every incident leads back to you?"

"That's right," Shen Zechuan said wryly. "Why *is* it that they all have something to do with me? Do you really see no reason for it? If Heir Xiao had ended my life when he fished me out of the Chashi Sinkhole five years ago, none of this would've happened."

Xiao Chiye stripped the twig of its leaves. "Back then, you cheated death and chose to eke out an ignoble existence. Have you only now come to realize how it feels to truly live?"

Shen Zechuan's expression was so tranquil it seemed almost surreal.

What a peculiar man.

It had been the same the day of the feast. His every move carried an undercurrent of having left worldly concerns behind. But Xiao Chiye remembered vividly the look in Shen Zechuan's eyes five years ago, on that snowy night when the boy had bitten him.

This serenity in Shen Zechuan was like peering into a bottomless abyss. Those roiling torrents of hate seemed to have been smoothed to nothing, until no one could tell where his limits lay. Everyone at the feast had humiliated him, yet he merely lowered his head and smiled. When Xiao Chiye said he was seeing him in a different light, he'd truly meant it.

If a man could welcome adversity to this extent, then to Xiao Chiye, the darkness beneath the calm was all the more disturbing.

"How it feels to live." Shen Zechuan laughed again. "I felt it every day and night while I was confined in the Temple of Guilt. Now that I'm out, it's clearer than ever that to live is a difficult thing. I cherish my life and am loath to lose it—but they want me to shoulder someone else's guilt, to pay for countless lives with my own when I have but one life to give. So how does that work? Thus I bow and scrape and try to gain favor, all in the hope that Er-gongzi and your peers will have mercy on me. If you want me to confess today, Er-gongzi, then at least tell me what I'm guilty of."

Xiao Chiye had already given up on getting any truth out of this man. He had a keen nose and always felt vaguely uneasy when Shen Zechuan was docile and compliant. But Shen Zechuan yielded to neither jokes nor coercion. However hard Xiao Chiye tried to pry candor out of him, he couldn't tell the truths from the lies.

He didn't believe a word out of Shen Zechuan's mouth. It was just as Shen Zechuan had said that night: if they were all playing a part, why take it so seriously?

However—people lied, but the traces they left did not. If one were to walk among the gutter-dwellers of Qudu, odds were ten to one they'd come out with useful information. If Shen Zechuan had planted someone at Li Jianheng's side, they wouldn't be any sort of master. Given Shen Zechuan's present circumstances, he could at most bribe a runner or attendant.

This case of Li Jianheng's was fishy inside and out. If he didn't get to the bottom of it now, there would be no end to his troubles in the future. Ever since Xiao Chiye cast his lot with Prince Chu, the stress had kept him up at night.

"I just came to play with you. How did it become an interrogation?" Xiao Chiye blew at the leaves on his twig and lamented, "I hear people are making inquiries about you. This involves Prince Chu's good name, so naturally I have to come and ask."

"Every time you come to play with me," Shen Zechuan said, "I lose a night of sleep."

"Don't say that. You don't have it easy, to be sure, but I'm not doing so great myself. We can turn the page on the old grudges between us, let bygones be bygones."

Shen Zechuan laughed. "Tens of thousands of lives were lost in the six prefectures of Zhongbo. And Er-gongzi wants to let bygones be bygones."

"Things are different now." Xiao Chiye finally tossed away the twig and rose to his feet. "You've got the favor of the Hua Clan and are in the empress dowager's good graces. How would I dare offend you? Don't make me a stranger, calling me Er-gongzi. Are we not close acquaintances now, Lanzhou?"

Shen Zechuan merely smiled. "Goodbye, Er-gongzi."

Xiao Chiye mounted his horse and looked down at him. "When are you going to return that thumb ring to me, Lanzhou? A worn-out thing like that isn't worth much, and keeping it ought to disgust you. Why does it seem like you're treasuring it instead?"

"I keep it with me," Shen Zechuan said, "so I may ward off evil with Er-gongzi's ferocious aura. How could I bear to part with it so easily?"

Xiao Chiye cracked his riding crop. "Don't you know? Your Ergongzi is evil itself."

Shen Zechuan stood unmoving and watched Xiao Chiye ride away. His smile faded, leaving an unfathomable stillness. As that silhouette diminished into the distance, the setting sun dipped below the horizon, its orange light slipping under Shen Zechuan's feet and racing toward the shadow of Xiao Chiye.

Stars glimmered in the sky above the courtyard. Grand Mentor Qi spread a newly drawn map before Shen Zechuan.

"The former Eastern Palace did not have the authority to deploy troops to the border. However, it was thoroughly familiar with the positions of all garrison troops, thanks to information from the Ministry of War. This map shows Libei's."

"Libei is backed by the Hongyan Mountains; to its west is Luoxia Pass, and its eastern side overlooks the grasslands of the Biansha Tribes." Shen Zechuan pointed at the Hongyan Mountains that stood to the east. "Autumn is around the corner. The Biansha lands haven't produced enough grass for their horses this year, so they're bound to raid trade markets along the border. Xiao Jiming must move his troops to meet them; why hasn't he sent an appeal to the capital yet?"

"Because His Majesty is severely ill." Grand Mentor Qi considered for a moment. "Xiao Jiming only submitted one memorial to the throne all of last spring. He surely has informants in Qudu. If he has yet to submit a memorial to request deployment, it can only mean one thing."

"His Majesty hasn't long to live," Shen Zechuan said quietly.

"The question of who could sit securely on the throne keeps Xiao Jiming from making a move." Grand Mentor Qi took out a brush, dipped it in ink, and inscribed a circle around Libei. "Prince Chu's ascension can only benefit the Xiao Clan. They have been at odds with the Hua for too long. Because of Zhongbo, they have fallen into a position of disadvantage where Qudu holds their chain. Now at last they have a chance to cut that collar. Xiao Jiming will not pass up this opportunity."

Shen Zechuan pointed to Qudu on the map. "But didn't Xiansheng say the other day that as long as the gates of Qudu are shut, Xiao Chiye remains the hostage from Libei? The empress dowager still has him in her grasp; how can Xiao Jiming act?"

"Since you bring it up..." Grand Mentor Qi set aside his brush. "I have something else to ask you."

"Yes, Xiansheng."

"In your opinion, what kind of a person is Xiao Chiye?"

Shen Zechuan lowered his lashes to look at the map. "Sharp. Smart. Unconventional."

"I think he's..." Grand Mentor Qi scratched his head as if he couldn't land on a suitable word. After a moment of frustration, he leaned over the table and said cryptically, "I think he's the opportunity heaven sent to Libei to turn the tide—an extraordinary prodigy."

Shen Zechuan swung his brush in his fingers. "Why does Xiansheng say so?"

Grand Mentor Qi ducked under the table and pulled out a number of crudely bound books he had penned himself. As the years passed, he had sensed himself growing old and forgetful, and had committed as much as he could to paper. He riffled noisily through a few, then flopped over the table again and pushed one toward Shen Zechuan.

"These are the details Ge Qingqing managed to obtain from the Ministry of War. In the first year of Xiande—eight years ago—

Xiao Chiye was fourteen. He followed Xiao Jiming into battle against the Biansha. At the height of summer, Xiao Jiming was besieged by three of the tribes on the eastern side of the Hongyan mountain range. His retreat was cut off, and he was trapped on the banks of the Hongjiang River. After three days, their father's reinforcements had yet to arrive, and Xiao Jiming was about to enter his last desperate battle for survival. The horsemen from the third tribe of Biansha are agile; Libei's Armored Cavalry are a wall of iron adept at dealing a powerful head-on blow, but they can't maneuver quickly in a back-and-forth engagement. If a battle drags on too long, Xiao Jiming's army will be the one to tire first."

Grand Mentor Qi paused for a few mouthfuls of wine. "But on the night of the third day, the Biansha troops retreated like an ebbing tide—it turned out that their heavily guarded provisions had been set ablaze. The fire spread from the center of their encampment and threw their rearguard into disarray. Xiao Jiming seized the opportunity; the decisive battle he fought broke through the siege in one night.

"The account Libei delivered to the Ministry of War ended here. What I say next is information your shifu went to quite a lot of effort to find out. Can you guess how those heavily guarded provisions were set alight? Apparently, the third tribe of Biansha had dug a trench near the river as a latrine. Xiao Chiye crept from the Hongjiang to the trench and spent half the night crawling through mud and filth to infiltrate the camp."

Grand Mentor Qi stroked his chin. "Yet Libei suppressed the news of such a remarkable deed. And that's not all. Since Xiao Chiye came to Qudu, he's made a name for himself as an idle loafer—but could a loafer possess that kind of grit? Imagine: his failure on that mission would have spelled death for his brother. He lay dormant for two days, waiting for the Biansha troops to drop their guard, before he set the fire; two days over which his brother's life was in constant danger. What if the fire hadn't caught, or his timing was off? Too early, and Biansha troops would still be solid as a fortress. Too late, and the Libei soldiers might lose morale! Yet he struck at precisely the right time. How could he have done that without extraordinary insight?"

Shen Zechuan looked pensive.

"The boy was positively mad. On this daring adventure, he only brought this many people with him—" Grand Mentor Qi held up two fingers, then paused for a moment. "Lanzhou, I suspect Pan Rugui sent him to the Imperial Army to mitigate risk, and in doing so, has made a fatal error. He thinks the Imperial Army is on its last legs, but consider its background—the men all hail from military households that followed the emperor and settled in and around Qudu. The Eight Great Clans don't think much of them, so this army looked to the emperor alone. Now the emperor doesn't want them anymore, and these twenty thousand men have become weapons without a master. It would've been one thing if they really fell into the hands of a disinterested noble son, but in Xiao Chiye's hands... What could possibly deter Xiao Jiming from protecting Prince Chu now?"

So that was it!

What had previously confounded Shen Zechuan became clear. He had assumed that Xiao Jiming understood, when he left Xiao Chiye in Qudu, that his little brother would become a pawn. Therefore, Xiao Jiming would either abandon the pawn or proceed with caution. But if he was being cautious, he should never have let Xiao Chiye get so close to Prince Chu. It was asking for trouble; Xiao Chiye would always be holding his breath and cleaning up after the imperial prince.

"This autumn chill in Qudu is about to freeze somebody to death. We are few in number and weak in might, so it's best to steer clear." Grand Mentor Qi had spoken so long his throat was parched. "After the riot from the Imperial College, a rift has formed between the empress dowager and Xi Gu'an, and between His Majesty and his imperial mother. If she means to hold onto power, an heir is a matter of critical urgency. By the same token, if anything happens to Prince Chu now, all the Xiao Clan's efforts will have been drawing water through a sieve. Xiao Chiye's urgency to meet you today must have been because he was already on alert.

"But the empress dowager is shrewder still. All those years ago, to orchestrate Prince Ning's ascension to the throne where he now sits, she did not hesitate to wipe out the entire Eastern Palace. Today, to guard against the unexpected, she would happily erase Prince Chu. I'm afraid it will not be easy for Xiao Chiye to ensure the prince's safety."

"If the empress dowager will not use Xi Gu'an, the only one left is Ji Lei." Shen Zechuan's eyes were calm. "Experts abound in the Embroidered Uniform Guard, and they are clean and efficient in their work."

"Set aside this fight between powerful beasts for the moment," Grand Mentor Qi said. "Right now, you must decide whether to cast your lot with Prince Chu or the empress dowager."

Shen Zechuan reached out a hand and laid it over the map.

AUTUMN HUNT

IN THE FIRST DAYS of the rainy tenth month in Qudu, the maple leaves on Mount Feng turned red. When Shen Zechuan herded the elephants to court in the morning, he noticed the thin layer of autumn frost covering the ground. Surprisingly, the Xiande Emperor's illness improved with the change of season—rumor had it that he had resumed regular meals, and his coughing during morning court had eased greatly.

Traditionally, the emperor hosted a hunt at the Nanlin Hunting Grounds in the eleventh month. But despite the Xiande Emperor's improving health, he seemed worried that traveling in colder weather would be too taxing. Thus he had given orders to prepare for the Autumn Hunt at the start of the tenth month.

Chen Yang waited at the edge of the drill grounds, holding Xiao Chiye's blade. "The Eight Great Battalions and the Embroidered Uniform Guard are still responsible for patrol duty. But didn't His Majesty fly into a rage when they patrolled the Duanwu celebration last time?"

"That was last time." Xiao Chiye wiped sweat from his face. "Last time, His Majesty was furious because he felt threatened from all sides. It's different now. Xi Gu'an has been shunned by Her Majesty for two months; by this point, he'll be desperate to put himself back on the board."

"Does the emperor believe such small favors will move Xi Gu'an?" Chen Yang glanced around for eavesdroppers before continuing. "The empress dowager has been accumulating power for a long time, and His Majesty is ill. Even if the emperor's willing to hand Xi Gu'an an olive branch, would Xi Gu'an dare accept it?"

"You said it yourself; these are small favors." Xiao Chiye grabbed an outer robe and slipped it on. "But what if His Majesty handed Xi Gu'an immense power and authority? A few days ago, he asked the age of the Xi Clan's daughter. Prince Chu has yet to take a princess consort. If the emperor really bestowed a marriage on them, even if Xi Gu'an hadn't intended it, Her Majesty would see it very differently."

"A shame we don't have a young miss of our own at home," Chen Yang sighed.

"We're better off without," Xiao Chiye said. "If I had a sister, she would have to be like Marshal Qi; otherwise, she would have no control over her life. She, too, would most likely be forced to marry some husband she'd never met." Xiao Chiye slowed his pace. "Actually, the Hua Clan has always been the first choice for imperial consorts. Hua Xiangyi, who's been raised and nurtured by the empress dowager, has yet to marry. Even His Majesty won't presume to make arrangements for her; he still addresses her as his own younger sister. When it comes to her future, the throne will bow to the empress dowager's wishes."

"Fortunately, our heir is already married," Chen Yang said. "But to whom can Third Lady Hua possibly be betrothed? I really can't guess."

"The Qi Clan is the best choice." Xiao Chiye smiled. "If Qi Zhuyin were born a man, the empress dowager would have sent Third Lady Hua to wed her long ago. What a pity for them that Qi Zhuyin is a woman, and the Hua Clan doesn't have a son of lawful birth in this generation. They can eye that choice cut of meat, but they can't touch it. They're getting anxious."

Xiao Chiye's horse was led over, and he stroked its nose. "Come on. Let's go to Donglong Street—the East Market."

Shen Zechuan had only just stepped onto Donglong Street with Ge Qingqing.

Since he had been officially released from imprisonment, he obviously had to leave the Temple of Guilt. At first, this matter had been set aside. But in the eighth month, Qiao Tianya had taken notice and followed him back to the temple. When he saw Grand Mentor Qi covered in mud and acting like a lunatic, he insisted Shen Zechuan get an advance on his salary from the Embroidered Uniform Guard so he could find proper accommodations. Thus, at the end of the ninth month, Shen Zechuan moved to an old alley house. The rent was cheap, and the place was suitable for his current status.

"Who exactly is this person Shifu wants me to find?" Shen Zechuan picked up the deed of indenture and read the name there: *Songyue*. Where the place of origin should have been recorded above, the deed was blank.

Ge Qingqing looked around at the crowd. "He didn't tell me either. He just said Xiansheng suggested you let this person take care of your day-to-day needs in the future."

Since moving out of the temple, communication with Grand Mentor Qi had become difficult. Shen Zechuan was unwilling to keep messenger pigeons. First of all, they were too easy to intercept, and second, the sight of Xiao Chiye's gyrfalcon disemboweling a sparrow had left a deep impression on him. For now, they were forced to rely on Ji Gang as go-between and meet up whenever he came out to make purchases as a footman. It was less than convenient, but they had few better options at present.

"This Songyue should be in the East Market," Shen Zechuan said. "Let's go have a look."

Donglong Street ran along the Kailing River. The area was a pleasure district, and there was a market on the eastern side that mostly dealt in human chattel. Young people whose parents had died without money knelt here to sell themselves into servitude for burial expenses, and common households all came to this market to pick their attendants and maids.

Xiao Chiye, a register of names in hand, had come to the market to investigate the origins of some of the staff at Prince Chu's manor. He strode out of the broker's and caught sight of a familiar nape.

"Isn't that..." Chen Yang trailed off.

Xiao Chiye raised a hand; Chen Yang fell silent.

Shen Zechuan had just tucked the deed of indenture away when he felt a chill on the back of his neck. Glancing over his shoulder, he saw Xiao Chiye behind him.

"Oh, what an honor," Shen Zechuan said. "What are you doing lurking back there?"

"Looking at you, of course." Xiao Chiye casually stashed the register of names away and strolled to Shen Zechuan's side. "Are you here to buy servants?"

"I'm selling myself," Shen Zechuan answered dryly. "How on earth could I afford to buy someone else?"

"Already reduced to that, huh?" Xiao Chiye sized him up. "I seem to have heard that many people are seeking you at high prices."

"In those cases, sentiment is involved." Shen Zechuan kept

walking. "They have to catch my eye before I decide whether or not to accept an offer."

Xiao Chiye had an inkling of what kind of men were making offers. "It can't be easy choosing between cracked dates and misshapen pears."

"I'm sure Er-gongzi wouldn't know." Shen Zechuan looked at him sidelong. "You must eat well at Prince Chu's side."

"Envious? Come with me."

Shen Zechuan smiled. "I'm not so desperate yet."

When they reached the end of the street, Shen Zechuan turned aside. "I won't trouble Er-gongzi to accompany me further. I'll be going now."

"No hurry." Xiao Chiye remained where he was. "We still have to look out for each other during this year's Autumn Hunt."

"How would I look out for you?" Shen Zechuan met his eyes. "The Embroidered Uniform Guard and the Imperial Army have no common ground."

"You hold me at such a distance," Xiao Chiye said. "If I visit you often to stretch my legs, perhaps we can find some."

Shen Zechuan made no reply.

After they left, Xiao Chiye stood rooted to the spot. "Who is he looking for around here?" Xiao Chiye thumbed the hilt of his blade. "Ge Qingqing again—of course it's Ge Qingqing. Chen Yang."

"Sir!"

"Look into him," Xiao Chiye said. "I want a thorough check on Ge Qingqing's background."

Shen Zechuan's search for Songyue had been derailed by Xiao Chiye, and he'd been placed on consecutive rotational duties ever since. As a result, he hadn't managed to find any more free time to seek out Qi Huilian's mysterious contact. On the eve of the Autumn Hunt, his turn finally came to receive a special assignment. Sure enough, he was to accompany the emperor to the Nanlin Hunting Grounds.

That night, when Shen Zechuan returned home from his shift, he sensed the presence of someone else in the house.

Fengquan's voice floated out from within. "Aren't you coming in?"

Shen Zechuan pushed the door open. There was no light in the house, and with a cloak draped over him so his snow-white face was immersed in darkness, Fengquan looked like a wandering ghost. He took a last sip of tea, his finger sticking up delicately, then set the cup aside. "I've come to convey a message from Her Majesty."

Shen Zechuan tossed his dirty outer robe onto a small clothing rack. "Sorry to have troubled you."

"Yes." Fengquan looked at Shen Zechuan maliciously. "It's quite important, or I wouldn't have needed to come in person. You've been graced with so many favors from the empress dowager; it's time to repay your debts." He tossed him an object. "If this doesn't go smoothly at the Autumn Hunt, it won't go smoothly for you after."

Shen Zechuan caught it; the little object was an eastern pearl wrapped in a strip of cloth. A swipe of his fingertip revealed the traces of half a character on the strip of cloth—*Lin*.

It was the same character that made up the top half of *Chu*.[21] Shen Zechuan's gaze swung back to Fengquan's face.

Fengquan stood and approached him. "If you succeed, the empress dowager will continue treating you as her obedient dog. If you fail, there's no point keeping you."

"Formidable masters abound," Shen Zechuan said. "I'll try my best."

---

21 *林, lin, meaning woods or forest, is the same as the lin in Nanlin Hunting Grounds. The character is also a radical in the character 楚, chu, in Prince Chu.*

Fengquan stared daggers at him for a moment, then smirked. He strode out the door, lifted his hood, and melted into the black of the night.

Shen Zechuan lit a candle and stood beside the table as he burned the strip of cloth. In his hand, the flame licked the fabric, turning that *Lin* to ash.

The Nanlin Hunting Grounds were southeast of Qudu and encompassed a wide area; half the game supplied to the Court of Imperial Entertainments was hunted here. On the day of the hunt, the Eight Great Battalions mobilized a full fifty percent of its forces to accompany the emperor in a grand procession.

Shen Zechuan was traveling with the elephants. When he heard the thunder of hooves rise behind him, he didn't have to turn to know who approached. Sure enough, in the next moment the gyrfalcon swooped over his head and snatched a wild rat from the grass before soaring back into the sky.

Xiao Chiye and Li Jianheng, at the center of a group of rich young masters from Qudu, rode rowdily past and dashed ahead. The jet-black steed with the snowy patch on its chest was impossible to miss.

Xiao-Wu looked toward the sky with some envy. "Supreme Commander Xiao's falcon and horse are both treasures beyond compare!"

"Wild things," Shen Zechuan said.

Xiao-Wu was young and sociable, so he was always eager to make small talk with Shen Zechuan. Sitting astride his horse, he munched on dried sweet potatoes and said in a Huaizhou accent, "Do you know what the horse and falcon are called, Chuan-ge?"

Shen Zechuan smiled. "They're wild creatures, so there's only so much they can be called."

Stretching his hands wide, excitement spread over Xiao-Wu's face. "Well, that falcon is called Meng! It means *fierce*—isn't it a perfect fit? But the horse's name isn't fierce at all. It's called Snowcrest."

He savored each syllable, his wonder so childlike the men around him smiled.

Stopping to catch his breath, Li Jianheng looked back at Xiao Chiye. "I swear, every time I see him, I think, *Why wasn't he born a woman?!*"

Xiao Chiye turned his horse to look at Li Jianheng.

"I know, I know," Li Jianheng said hastily. "I'm not that befuddled!"

"When we arrive later," Xiao Chiye warned him, "tell me before you venture out. Don't go anywhere without your guards, and none of the women you brought are allowed in the tent."

"I didn't bring any women," Li Jianheng said boldly.

Xiao Chiye scoffed, his expression wicked.

Chen Yang overtook them from behind and said, "Supreme Commander, I got someone to send all those women back."

Li Jianheng, thwarted, bit the tip of his tongue. "Ce'an, honestly, if I can't even sleep with a pretty girl, what's there to do at the Autumn Hunt?"

"Plenty," Xiao Chiye said. "Even staring at the sky is more interesting than being cooped up in the tent."

Li Jianheng sighed again and rode on, listless and dejected, all his earlier high spirits drying up in the sun.

By the time they arrived, it was dusk.

Shen Zechuan wasn't on duty the first day, so he stayed with the caravan to help with odd jobs. Qiao Tianya had also come with the group; when they finished, he called their fellow guardsmen over to eat.

"You can hold your drink, huh," he said, spying the bowl in Shen Zechuan's hand.

"No more than a bowl," Shen Zechuan replied.

Qiao Tianya didn't expose him. This man didn't look like an Embroidered Uniform Guard, but more like a free spirit, traveling from place to place at will. Qiao Tianya produced a dagger to slice the freshly roasted game and said, "Eat up; you're at the hunting ground! This happens only once a year. What you are eating now are things usually sent into the palace, so seize the opportunity while you can."

Chewing on the meat, he continued, "You need to be armed while you're on duty. You can use Qingqing's blade during your shift tomorrow night. Why didn't you bring one? Didn't the Elephant-Training Office teach you any moves?"

"Weapons are too heavy," Shen Zechuan replied, looking as though he couldn't lift a thing. "It's too much to carry with me all the time."

"This body of yours..." Qiao Tianya said, "couldn't have been broken by that kick Xiao Er gave you, could it? What a pity. That's a first-grade hoodlum if ever there was one, and we can't extort him either. Otherwise, as your good brother, I'd fleece him out of his whole family fortune in revenge for that kick."

The Embroidered Uniform Guard around them burst into laughter.

Shen Zechuan's lips curled in a smile. Between sips of his wine, he snuck a look over the rim of the bowl. All these men were inseparable from their blades. Other than himself, who else was here to kill Prince Chu?

Apart from those present, there were undoubtedly assassins unseen in the shadows; how many were quietly lying in wait? Even if

Xiao Chiye was a prodigy, could he really preserve Prince Chu's life under such heavy siege?

Across the camp, Xiao Chiye and Li Jianheng were drinking wine and playing dice, heedless of what waited in the dark.

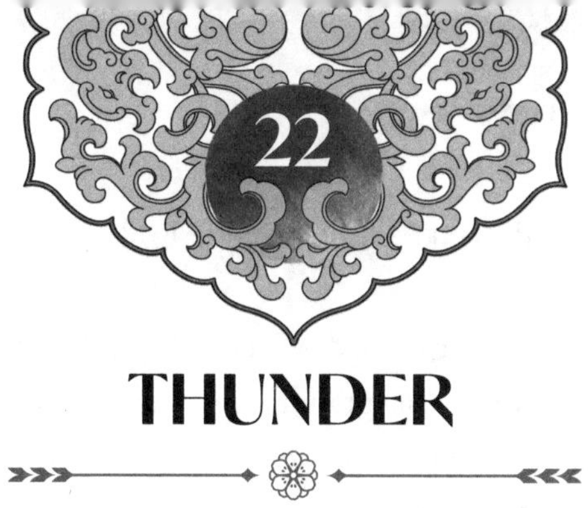

THUNDER

THE NEXT MORNING, the Xiande Emperor assumed personal command of the Autumn Hunt. His health didn't permit him to hunt on horseback, so he prepared some rewards and told the young men around him to vie for their prize on the hunting grounds.

Li Jianheng made several attempts to mount his horse before gracelessly hoisting himself into the saddle. The emperor gave him a sharp look. "Jianheng, you must lead by example. We await a demonstration of your skills!"

The prince gripped his reins. He had already given instructions to his guards; even if he didn't hit the mark himself, he would certainly not return empty-handed. He set out in high spirits, his guardsmen following close and Xiao Chiye at his side.

A stretch of forest lay at the end of a vast expanse of grassland within the Nanlin Hunting Grounds. Morning dew hung on yellowed branches, and freshly released game of all sizes scattered through the undergrowth, startled by shouts and the pounding of hooves.

Brandishing his bow from his seat astride his horse, Li Jianheng drew with considerable effort and fired on a hare. The arrow sank feebly into the ground some distance away from his quarry. Blind applause and cheers immediately rang out around him as the guard who went forward to take a look brought back a dead hare, prepared in advance.

Satisfied, Li Jianheng turned to Xiao Chiye. "My skill with a bow's not bad, right? My imperial grandfather taught me back in the day!"

"Never have I seen such a display of archery prowess even in Libei," Xiao Chiye said sincerely.

Li Jianheng laughed. "You've been in Qudu so long—you haven't forgotten how to draw a bow, have you?"

Xiao Chiye had brought an ordinary bow; the draw weight couldn't match even the ones issued to the Embroidered Uniform Guard. "Let me show you my skill too," he said.

Xiao Chiye drew back the bowstring and loosed an arrow into the clearing before them. His shot was weaker than Prince Chu's; the arrow didn't even stick in the dirt. Another round of sycophantic cheers and exaltation rang out from the watchers, and Xiao Chiye grinned smugly.

Qiao Tianya had grown impatient waiting behind them, but this scene amused him. "See that? If you neglect your training, you'll be treated like a fool!"

Looking at Xiao Chiye's shoulders and arms, Shen Zechuan was once again reminded of that bone thumb ring. He couldn't help but smile.

Prince Chu hadn't been riding long when his legs started to ache, significantly dampening his enthusiasm. He had overdone the drink last night and was feeling poorly all over. He allowed his horse to wander aimlessly through the wood, enduring his discomfort, then urged his men back the moment it was time to return. The guards at the back of his entourage had hardly exhausted the arrows in a single quiver before they were escorting him back. They'd never even made it as far as the eastern woods.

Back at camp, Li Jianheng dismounted and knelt before the emperor. Pan Rugui, standing beside the throne, made an inventory of his kills as the emperor waited. The longer Li Jianheng listened, the more pleased he became. "There's even a red fox, Imperial Brother! It has an excellent pelt that'll make the perfect fur collar for you."

The emperor was equally pleased. "You certainly seem more spirited now than back in the capital! Pan Rugui, reward Prince Chu."

Li Jianheng lifted the silk cover over the tray with delight, only to see, lying beneath, a great iron bow. No ordinary man could draw a thing like that. He instantly lost interest, although he still dutifully said, "Thank you for the reward, Your Majesty!"

The emperor laughed until he coughed. "You don't like it? Don't worry, it's not meant to be used. This bow was left behind by our Great Founding Emperor in the early years of our clan. Legend has it that it's forged of black iron and dragon tendons; it weighs a grand one hundred and twenty catties. Even among the current Four Great Generals, none can draw it. I bestow it upon you now as a reminder: be always diligent. When you see this bow, remember the hardships faced by the Great Founding Emperor and his monumental undertaking to establish our Great Zhou."

Li Jianheng solemnly acknowledged his words and called for his men to carry the bow away.

Over dinner, the emperor called for Li Jianheng to sit at his side. The signal of favor couldn't have been more obvious. Every official in attendance recognized it but played dumb—after all, Secretariat Elder Hua Siqian was still on equal footing with Prince Chu. Later that night, once everyone had their fill of wine and food, the party gathered around a bonfire.

The Xiande Emperor had not yet retired, so no one else could leave. Li Jianheng had long grown weary of sitting, but the emperor showed no sign of retreating to his tent.

What's going on? Li Jianheng cast a questioning glance at Xiao Chiye, who pretended not to notice.

By now, the evening's entertainments had concluded, the singers and dancers were gone, and the bonfire was roaring. Unexpectedly, the emperor gathered his robes around him and called out, "My dear minister Hai."

Hai Liangyi smoothed his robe and respectfully knelt before the emperor. "This aged subject is here!"

"What was it that you wanted to ask today?"

Hai Liangyi kowtowed and replied, "This aged subject would like to recommend the Chief Supervising Secretary of the Office of Scrutiny for Revenue, Xue Xiuzhuo, be permitted to directly petition Your Majesty tonight!"

Sensing something afoot, Hua Siqian stroked his beard and said, "Why put it that way, Renshi? The chief supervising secretary is already permitted to report directly to His Majesty."

"That may be so," Hai Liangyi said, "but Xue Xiuzhuo's memorials have repeatedly failed to reach the throne. What can he do but seek a direct audience?"

"How is it possible that a memorial can't make its way to His Majesty?" Hua Siqian asked.

"We are curious about this, too," the Xiande Emperor said. "My dear minister Hai, call him up to say his piece."

Pan Rugui exchanged looks with Hua Siqian. He strode forward and called out: "Summon the Chief Supervising Secretary of the Office of Scrutiny for Revenue, Xue Xiuzhuo, for an audience with His Majesty!"

When Xue Xiuzhuo appeared, he was not wearing his official's robe. He seemed travel-worn, as though he had just dismounted his horse. As he made his way forward, he looked only at the ground before him, finally kneeling to kowtow to the Xiande Emperor.

"What do you have to report?" the emperor asked over the sound of the wind.

"This subject is the Supervising Secretary of the Office of Scrutiny," Xue Xiuzhuo began. "My key task is to audit the finances of the Ministry of Revenue in minute detail. In the third month of the fifth year of Xiande, this subject audited the expenditure ledger for the fourth year of Xiande and discovered a subsidy of two million taels. The Ministry of Revenue recorded this sum as a subsidy to the thirteen cities of Juexi.

"Out of an abundance of prudence, this subject personally made a trip to Juexi to verify the accounts. Together with the Provincial Administration Commissioner of Juexi, Jiang Qingshan, this subject cross-referenced the accounts and discovered something quite strange. Out of the subsidy allocated in the fourth year of Xiande, only 1,530,000 taels had actually reached Juexi. The remaining 470,000 taels had vanished without a trace.

"The discrepancies did not end there. In the eighth month of the same year, the Ministry of War disbursed salaries and provisions to the troops at our borders. The Ministry of Revenue allocated 2,800,000 taels for this purpose. Of that amount, 1,800,000 were meant for the Five Commanderies Garrison Troops in Qidong, and one million were meant for Libei. But by the time I traced that million back to Luoxia Pass, there were only 830,000 taels left!

"You Majesty, this goes on, incident after incident. There is an enormous avenue of loss in the state treasury. Where did all this money go? Who took it? Even if Secretariat Elder Hua maintains his ignorance, this subject has the records to submit to His Majesty!"

"Nonsense!" Hua Siqian snapped. "The Ministry of Revenue reconciles the accounts every year right in the palace! If there is such dramatic loss, how is it that the Minister of Revenue, the Grand Secretariat, and the Director of Writ at the Directorate of Ceremonial Affairs all have no idea, and you're the only one who does!"

Hai Liangyi raised his head and said steadily, "This aged subject knows how. Since the second year of Xiande, the account books the Ministry of Revenue submits have been split into real and sham copies. When it comes to deciding what is submitted each year, it is not the Minister of Revenue who decides—it is you, Hua Siqian!"

The crackle of the bonfire was like a thunderbolt striking the assembly into silence. No one had expected such a stunt from the Xiande Emperor.

"Fine." Hua Siqian laughed in anger and rose from his seat, slamming his palms on the table. "So are we fabricating wild charges now? You people speak of a 'Hua faction'—there is no such thing! All under heaven belongs to the emperor. I, Hua Siqian, have been open and aboveboard in everything I have done. All along, I've placed His Majesty first! If there are any dubious accounts, bring them out now. Zheng Guoshi, tally it with him!"

The Minister of Revenue, Zheng Guoshi, knelt in a panic. "Your Majesty, this subject begs to ask Chief Supervising Secretary Xue a question. If the accounts from the fourth year of Xiande are those at issue, why did he wait until today to bring it up? If there is a true problem, he has delayed the matter for years!"

Xue Xiuzhuo quickly returned fire. "Nowadays, local officials who enter the capital do not meet their superiors nor pay respects to Your Majesty. Instead, they send visitation cards and go first to the Hua manor and Pan-gonggong's secondary manor to fawn and flatter. With so much power and influence in the hands of the Hua faction, who dares defy Secretariat Elder Hua!"

Hua Siqian was incensed. "Every year, I tell the investigating censors to speak openly if there is a problem! What have I to fear? The Hua Clan's ledgers have been presented to His Majesty; we've nothing to hide!" He stared at Xue Xiuzhuo. "Xue Yanqing, have you forgotten? Back in the years of Yongyi, who recommended you for the opportunity to enter Qudu as an official? You ought to respect me as half your teacher, but instead you frame me before the entire court!"

Xue Xiuzhuo raised his head and met Hua Siqian's eyes. "There is no place in the court for teacher and pupil, only the sovereign and his ministers."

Hua Siqian turned to the emperor. "Does Your Majesty believe this slander?"

The emperor lowered his gaze and said, "We believe the accounts."

Hua Siqian threw his head back and laughed. He clapped his hands together. "Excellent! Back then, when all of Qudu was in tumult, the late emperor chose you on his deathbed. Who here supported you, protected you, and guided you through that period of upheaval? Yet tonight, you would rather believe the words of this disloyal and unfilial scum?!"

Lashes lowered, the emperor raised his teacup to his lips. When he finally looked at Hua Siqian, his eyes brimmed with loathing. "Was it protection, or was it coercion? Who would know better than you?"

"Ji Lei!" Hua Siqian called out, shoving his table aside.

Steel sang as the Embroidered Uniform Guard drew their blades in unison.

"You would dare?!" Hai Liangyi cried.

"I wouldn't," Hua Siqian said, "but you've pressed the blade to my throat. Surely you don't expect me to take it lying down?"

"What do you want?" the emperor said coldly. "Xi Gu'an!" Soldiers from the Eight Great Battalions stepped swiftly forward to stand before the emperor. "Take down Hua Siqian!" the emperor commanded.

"Don't move!" Hua Siqian bellowed. "Xi Gu'an, your wife and child are having tea with the empress dowager as we speak. One more step, and it'll spell the end of the Xi Clan lineage! The empress dowager has always treated you well. You have repeatedly let others lead you astray, but it's not too late to turn back."

Xi Gu'an had been forced reluctantly into this position to begin with. Now, he took a small step back, afraid.

"Not too late?" The emperor's tone was venomous. "Xi Gu'an, was it *not too late* for the former crown prince? Was it *not too late* for Shen Wei? Which of them was less loyal than you? They gave way, but did the empress dowager let them be? We have already drafted an imperial edict. As long as Prince Chu ascends the throne, the Xi Clan's daughter will be empress!"

"His Majesty has a nasty habit of reneging on his word. Do you dare harbor such outrageous ambitions?" Hua Siqian snapped his sleeves. "His Majesty's mind is addled with illness! Imperial Concubine Wei is already half a month pregnant; how can Prince Chu possibly take the throne!"

Xi Gu'an gripped his blade. His forehead was sheened in sweat.

Dark clouds shrouded the stars. The wind that had blown through the hunting grounds earlier with the promise of rain also ceased. Flags and banners drooped lifelessly in the stillness.

No one moved.

Xi Gu'an gritted his teeth; he drew his blade and turned to the emperor. With some difficulty, he said, "His Majesty's illness is—is beyond cure."

The emperor looked at Xi Gu'an and began to laugh. "We gave you a chance," he said. The longer he laughed, the louder it grew. And the louder it grew, the more he coughed. At last he braced himself against the table and said frostily, "If we did not have total confidence in our preparations, how could we flush out treacherous ministers and traitors like you! Qi Zhuyin is on her way now with her troops. She'll be here within four hours! So whom will you kill? Hm? Who dares!"

Ji Lei piped up. "Marshal Qi is far away in the Cangjun Commandery in Qidong. The Embroidered Uniform Guard handles all incoming and outgoing correspondence with the garrisons. Your Majesty, it's time for you to wake up!"

The emperor glared furiously at him. "Qi—"

Pan Rugui hastily clamped a hand over the emperor's mouth and forced him to sit. He smiled at the crowd. "His Majesty is experiencing a relapse of his illness."

The civil officials were trembling in their seats. Hua Siqian looked at Li Jianheng with a nasty smile. "Prince Chu intends to stage a revolt at these hunting grounds. The evidence against him is conclusive—he even wields a bow! What are you waiting for? Kill him!"

Except for the guards who stood beside the prince, steel suddenly glittered all around the clearing as men drew their blades.

Li Jianheng dropped his chopsticks in shock. He backed away, tumbling to the ground in his haste, his stool falling behind him. "S-Secretariat Elder! I have no designs on the throne!"

"Your Highness," Hua Siqian said, "do you understand the words, 'out of one's hands'?"

Thunder shook the sky.

Li Jianheng could hear the swarm of approaching footsteps as he cowered among his personal guards. He said tearfully, barely able to stand without support, "I'm only an idle prince! Why go this far?"

A blade flashed before him. Li Jianheng cried out and clutched his head in terror. Just before it struck, he heard the table overturn with a tremendous crash. Someone gripped the back of his collar and lifted him bodily off the ground.

"His Majesty bestowed the Conqueror Bow upon you, so you are the crown prince of Great Zhou." Xiao Chiye smiled grimly. "You stand before the supreme commander of the Imperial Army. Who's so eager to meet their maker under my blade?! Chen Yang, help the crown prince onto his horse!"

"Xiao Er." Ji Lei slowly drew his own weapon. "We've always been on friendly terms. Why are you wading into this tonight?"

"Been fooling around too long." Xiao Chiye flung Li Jianheng at Chen Yang. "I'm itching for a fight."

"Seize Er-gongzi," Ji Lei ordered. "Preserve his life, but break his arms and legs if you have to."

Xiao Chiye shook off his cumbersome outer robe; underneath, his clothes were fitted, designed for ease of movement. He swept a look around. "If anyone is able to break my arm or leg, I'll not only award him a hundred taels of gold, I'll kneel and call him Master."

Wolfsfang, that killing blade that had almost never left its sheath in Qudu, slid steadily out, its frosty glint blinding and deadly.

"But if he fails," he said, "I will take his life."

DOWNPOUR

A GALE BATTERED THE GRASS of the hunting grounds. The clang of weapons rang out as the flames of the bonfire leapt and crackled.

The feast rapidly devolved into chaos. Hai Liangyi climbed up from the ground, and with a burst of unexpected energy, slammed headlong into Pan Rugui. "Castrated traitor! Unhand my master!"

Li Jianheng had been pushed onto his horse and sat trembling as he watched cold steel flashing all around him. Clinging to the horse's neck, he closed his eyes and cried out, "Ce'an! Ce'an, save me!"

Xiao Chiye sent Ji Lei staggering with a kick; he didn't even turn as he put his blade through an Embroidered Uniform Guard trying to sneak up behind him. Warm blood spattered his back. He freed his blade and took two steps forward to meet an Eight Great Battalions soldier charging at him headlong; Xiao Chiye struck him to the ground with one blow.

Chen Yang had already leapt onto his own horse; he hauled Li Jianheng upright, let out a piercing whistle, and shouted to Prince Chu's guards, "Follow me! Protect His Highness! Break through the siege from the east!"

As the horses shifted, Ji Lei commanded coldly, "Stop them—"

Before he could finish, a blade came swinging down over his head. He brought up his own to block it; at once, his arms sank down nearly to his chest from the numbing force of Xiao Chiye's blow. Ji Lei groaned and staggered under the impact; astonished, he stared at the man before him.

Xiao Er!

"You played us for fools." Ji Lei took a wide stance and lifted his blade against the weight with shaking arms. He bellowed furiously, "I misjudged you!"

A gust of wind at his side warned Xiao Chiye of an oncoming assault; he turned his head to dodge. He swept his blade in a diagonal arc, leaving a stream of blood glistening in its wake. Then Wolfsfang collided with Ji Lei's sword once again. Snowcrest charged in, knocking over tables and dragging the tablecloth along as it galloped through the bonfire. The flames surged in its wake, setting the tents and withered grass alight. In the split second Snowcrest rushed past him, Xiao Chiye flipped atop its back. He swatted the flank of Prince Chu's horse with the flat of his blade and growled, "Go!"

"Protect His Majesty!" Xue Xiuzhuo rushed forward to pull Hai Liangyi away from where he was tussling with Pan Rugui. "Elder Hai! We must escort His Majesty away!"

The Xiande Emperor gasped for breath, lips and face pale. Xue Xiuzhuo hoisted the emperor over his shoulder and fled the fire alongside the panicked civil officials.

Xi Gu'an turned to give chase, but Hua Siqian pointed in the direction Prince Chu had ridden. "His Majesty's fate is sealed; it matters not whether we kill him now. But Prince Chu must die tonight! If he slips through our fingers, you and I will be branded traitors! Ji Lei—recall the Embroidered Uniform Guard and rally the two thousand garrison troops in the city of Chuancheng; surround the hunting grounds. Prince Chu *must* die! Xi Gu'an, hurry back to the capital! The Eight Great Battalions will guard Qudu!"

With the most urgent instructions issued, his usual calm returned. "We have an imperial heir in our hands and the empress dowager in command. As long as Qudu remains stable and Prince Chu is eliminated, not even Qi Zhuyin can do anything about it. As for the Xiao Clan, let them run; there will be plenty of opportunities to deal with them in the future."

The stench of blood on Xiao Chiye was thick; he pursed his lips against the smell. Any who blocked his path lost their heads to Wolfsfang, regardless of their allegiance. Li Jianheng's stomach lurched, but he didn't dare puke now; he closed his mouth tight.

The remaining forty men with them were all Xiao Chiye's personal guards. His steed galloped swiftly beside Prince Chu's. Behind them, the Embroidered Uniform Guard followed hot on their heels.

Just as their group reached the edge of the forest, Xiao Chiye barked, "Scatter!"

The guards tore off their uniforms to reveal forty riding outfits identical to Li Jianheng's. In unison, they turned their horses and charged into the forest in all directions. Dark clouds veiled the moon; no one could distinguish Prince Chu among them, especially at a distance.

Ji Lei reined his horse to a halt at the edge of the trees and spat. "Surround the grounds! Search every inch of the forest! If you encounter Xiao Er, do *not* engage him one-on-one. Form a team of at least four men and attack from all sides!"

Branches whipped across Li Jianheng's face; the pain spurred him to raise an arm to shield himself. The guards had already dispersed, leaving only Xiao Chiye and Chen Yang riding beside him.

"Get off." Xiao Chiye lifted Li Jianheng from the saddle and threw him to the ground; it was time for Chen Yang to take over.

Li Jianheng was sent tumbling face-first in the dirt. "Ce'an, Ce'an," he whined, "what are you doing?"

"Please follow me, Your Highness the Crown Prince." Chen Yang pulled Li Jianheng to his feet. "It's too conspicuous to travel through the forest on horseback. The Embroidered Uniform Guard are experts at ambush and assassination. You're a live target atop a horse—we can't take the risk!"

"I won't go!" Li Jianheng fearfully yanked his arm back and pleaded, "Ce'an, you're the only one who can protect me!"

"Knock him out; get him out of here!" Xiao Chiye commanded. Without waiting for Li Jianheng to reply, he turned and galloped deeper into the woods.

Lightning flashed, its sharp light deepening the endless layers of ghostly shadows among the trees. The sounds of hooves, of drawn blades and racing footsteps, rang out in succession. Only the sound of human voices was absent.

The wet smell of the impending rainstorm hung on the breeze. Xiao Chiye didn't know how long he'd been riding when Snowcrest gradually came to a stop. Everything around him, suddenly, was still.

The clouds at last broke open, raindrops pattering down before Xiao Chiye's eyes. Amid the downpour, a monstrous creature seemed to creep slowly out of the darkness. Countless Embroidered Uniform guards advanced through the trees toward Xiao Chiye like a net of densely woven shadow.

No one gave orders. The rain drummed on the ground.

The sharp, curved edge of a Xiuchun saber sliced through the water, reaching Xiao Chiye's neck in the blink of an eye. In a single motion, Xiao Chiye bent his head and Wolfsfang left its sheath. The spine of his blade clanged against the Xiuchun saber. With an ear-piercing shriek, the saber cracked; Xiao Chiye slid Wolfsfang back into its sheath and kicked out, sending the broken blade and its master tumbling into the rain.

More swordsmen surged up, surrounding his horse.

Xiao Chiye clapped his palm to Snowcrest's flank, leaping out of the saddle. Wolfsfang again sprang from its sheath. This time, the glint of the blade swept in a flat arc, splitting skin and flesh in a ring around him. Blood splashed onto his face and trickled down his chin as he listened to the sound of human bodies collapsing.

Xiao Chiye landed back in a crouch on the saddle, blade still half-drawn.

The sound of breathing. The patter of rain.

In this pitch-dark night, one was as good as blindfolded; Xiao Chiye stretched his hearing to the maximum. Not one of the Embroidered Uniform Guard who had been wounded earlier made a sound. Closely matched footsteps circled around him, too close, forming an unbreakable ring with him at the center.

Whoever broke first would fatally expose his weakness.

Xiao Chiye waited in silence. In this moment, Qiao Tianya, who was among those hiding in the darkness, truly realized what it meant to be called a lone wolf. Xiao Chiye was preternaturally calm, as if the more danger he faced, the more coolheaded and unpredictable he became. The blade he wielded was a set of fangs freshly bared.

Qiao Tianya felt a rare sense of restlessness. They had been ordered to take Xiao Chiye alive—but when it came to a dangerous predator like this, it was far more difficult to trap and thwart him than it was to kill him. They would likely have only one chance to get close. If they could not take him down swiftly, this man would slaughter them. He closed his eyes. When he opened them again, they were sharp and merciless.

He pulled out his own Xiuchun saber and stepped forward. The next moment, his figure was a blur as he burst into action, slashing down toward Xiao Chiye's back like lightning.

Xiao Chiye swung his blade back to parry the blow, then spun to kick Qiao Tianya in the gut. The men on the other three sides fell upon him as one. He stopped their blade hands with one arm, exposing his left side; someone seized the opening and sliced up toward his face. Xiao Chiye's elbow struck the flat of the saber, knocking it off course. He drove that elbow into the face of the man behind him, dropping him with a sharp blow.

Qiao Tianya followed closely on his heels.

The rain slashed down. There was no shouting, only the sound of blades. Rainwater had scrubbed away at Xiao Chiye's features until they looked still more ferocious. Trapped within this never-ending perimeter of steel, he maintained an acuity that was unique to him alone. Time and again, in the darkness, he warded off the onslaught led by Qiao Tianya as if treading on thin spring ice.

Qiao Tianya pressed his offensive. These men were indeed experts at drawn-out siege. Was a lone wolf so terrifying? They had only to surround him and wear him down. Once he was tired, his patience and calm exhausted, he was bound to reveal weakness. Sure enough, Xiao Chiye's breathing gradually became labored under the intense flurry of blades. The downpour masked his view of the finer details around him. He never saw the crossbow being pulled out under the cover of darkness.

The longer Xiao Chiye fought, the fiercer he grew. Blood flowed endlessly beneath his horse's hooves. But suddenly, Qiao Tianya waved his hand. The shadows surrounding him melted back into the night, plunging Xiao Chiye once again into silence and bringing the momentum he had gained to a screeching halt.

Rainwater washed over the backs of his hands. Xiao Chiye could no longer hear any footsteps. The heavy rain that drenched him was the only sound. Under him, Snowcrest anxiously stamped its hooves.

Click.

The sound of the crossbow trigger was soft, yet deafening in Xiao Chiye's ears. He slapped his horse, and Snowcrest lunged forward—but instead of riding to safety, he rolled off its back. There was a succession of thuds as a row of short arrows sank into the mud behind him. Xiao Chiye wiped the rain from his face, only to hear the twang of bowstrings from all directions. He jumped to his feet at once and started running. Footsteps followed him relentlessly.

An arrow grazed Xiao Chiye's arm. He felt a numbing itch as blood oozed from the cut.

Tranquilizer. They were herding him into capture like a wild beast.

There was a narrow dip in the terrain ahead. Xiao Chiye sprang up with all his might and leapt the gap. He had just landed on his toes when he felt a sudden chill.

With the momentum of his leap behind him, Xiao Chiye rolled forward to avoid the blade that hacked down into his footprints. That strike had been meant to kill. Before this new foe could extract his blade from the dirt, Xiao Chiye slipped behind him, shoved him down into the mud, and crushed his neck with a hand.

A cluster of arrows nailed themselves into the tree trunk beside him. Before Xiao Chiye could rise, he was kicked in the back. Caught by surprise, he tumbled into the undergrowth. But after a split second to get his bearings, he braced a hand against the ground and readied himself to face his new assailant.

When Xiao Chiye got a clear look at the man before him, he licked away the blood between his teeth and called out to him as though to a lover. "Oh, Lanzhou."

Shen Zechuan also had one hand on the ground; thin blades were held between each of his fingers. He stared at Xiao Chiye through the rain, then pounced.

Xiao Chiye's palm was already on the hilt of his blade, but Shen Zechuan got there first, knocking Wolfsfang away with one hand and grabbing Xiao Chiye's collar with the other, flinging him to the ground. Mud splashed. Xiao Chiye hooked his arm around the back of Shen Zechuan's neck, fumbling a moment for Wolfsfang and slashing toward Shen Zechuan.

Shen Zechuan immediately dropped down and came face-to-face with Xiao Chiye. The instant their eyes met, he swatted Wolfsfang aside with the heel of his hand. Beads of blood from the edge of the blade splashed onto Shen Zechuan's face, where they slid along his jaw and mingled with the rain before dripping into the space between Xiao Chiye's brows.

The Embroidered Uniform Guard closed in on them from behind. Shen Zechuan moved to rise, but Xiao Chiye slid his palm up Shen Zechuan's neck to press him down until they were close enough to hear each other's breath.

Xiao Chiye was panting slightly. He whispered, "Are you so desperate to court death with me?"

But Shen Zechuan bowed his head and murmured, "Not even a wolf can run once it's struck by the arrow. You've already slowed so much. How much longer can you go on?"

Xiao Chiye's fingers teasingly caressed the nape of Shen Zechuan's neck. His thumb slipped to the hollow of Shen Zechuan's throat and pressed firmly. "I can still break a neck like this with no problem."

A figure came rustling out of the underbrush. Without turning, Shen Zechuan raised his hand to fling a thin blade. The man crumpled. The murderous intent in Shen Zechuan's eyes had yet to fade, but he pushed away Xiao Chiye's wandering hand and dragged him along as they slid down another slope.

Qiao Tianya came too late. By the time he arrived, all he found were the corpses of two strangers. He flipped them over for a look and plucked a thin blade from the throat of one of the dead men. "This doesn't seem to belong to Xiao Er." He narrowed his eyes. "The second young master is the leash holding Libei in check. He must not die. Wasn't that the fucking consensus? So who has sent assassins?"

RAINY NIGHT

LIGHTNING FLASHED and thunder boomed. The rain came down like a curtain.

Qiao Tianya straightened and handed the thin blade to the man behind him. "Xiao Er was hit by an arrow. He won't get far."

At the bottom of the slope, Xiao Chiye and Shen Zechuan lay flat in the mud catching their breath.

Right this moment, not only were the Embroidered Uniform Guard everywhere around them, there were also unknown assassins in the forest. Hiding from them would be harder than ascending to heaven. But breaking through the perimeter was even tougher. Their biggest problem was Xiao Chiye himself. His left arm, grazed by the arrow, had already gone numb. In another hour, the tranquilizing drug would spread through his body and paralyze him.

Qiao Tianya nudged the trampled grass aside with a toe and spotted the mess of footprints. Without a word, he raised a hand and pointed down the slope.

The Embroidered Uniform Guard filed around him, crouching as they approached and surrounded the ditch.

Xiao Chiye's body tensed as he listened to the sound of squelching footsteps getting closer and closer. He clutched the hilt of his blade. If someone jumped down, he would end them in a single blow.

The Xiuchun sabers had made their way over the edge of the slope. Xiao Chiye was about to jump up and fight when Shen Zechuan grabbed hold of his soaked robe. Xiao Chiye looked down and was met with Shen Zechuan's calm eyes. At that moment, several figures dropped down from the trees and engaged the Embroidered Uniform Guard. By the time Qiao Tianya saw the flash of flying blades and drew his saber, several guards had already collapsed to the ground. Seizing their advantage, the shadowy figures pounced.

As chaos broke out above them, Shen Zechuan stowed his few remaining blades. He didn't need to say more; Xiao Chiye had already leapt to his feet. He climbed up the other side of the muddy slope and rolled into the thick grass.

"Catch them!" Qiao Tianya bellowed.

The Embroidered Uniform Guard streamed after them. Xiao Chiye reached up and grasped a tree branch, swinging himself up. Below him, Shen Zechuan had only just reached the trunk when the guards behind him caught up. Like a tiger springing down the mountain, Xiao Chiye hacked viciously down at them with Wolfsfang, forcing the guards back, then landed in a crouch on the ground.

Qiao Tianya sprang up from behind and swung his blade toward Xiao Chiye before he had a chance to retract Wolfsfang. Xiao Chiye ducked his head just in time, as, with a *clang*, the edge of Qiao Tianya's saber collided with a sheath.

Shen Zechuan pressed Wolfsfang's sheath against Qiao Tianya's blade. He stepped with one foot onto Xiao Chiye's back; his bulk lifted Shen Zechuan's whole body up to close in on Qiao Tianya. The thin blade between the fingers of his other hand shot toward Qiao Tianya's eyes.

Qiao Tianya made no attempt to dodge; the guards on either side of him swiftly brought down their blades to block the attack.

Xiao Chiye sent Qiao Tianya stumbling back with a kick square in the chest, and both parties retreated simultaneously. Qiao Tianya flung droplets of blood off his blade. Shen Zechuan had sliced off a lock of hair on the judge's forehead.

Xiao Chiye and Shen Zechuan took two steps back, then turned without a word and made a run for it.

Qiao Tianya stared at their backs. "After them!"

"East!" Xiao Chiye reached out and dragged Shen Zechuan over.

Shen Zechuan brushed aside stray branches as he ran. "There's a man every five steps and a squad every ten. Not to mention there are still the Chuancheng Garrison Troops in the east!"

Xiao Chiye slowly retracted his hand but stubbornly insisted, "The east is our way out."

"We're done for." Shen Zechuan backhandedly tossed one of his blades, and the Embroidered Uniform Guard lying in wait up a nearby tree crashed headfirst to the ground. Shen Zechuan drew the man's Xiuchun saber from its scabbard as he passed.

Xiao Chiye grasped the hilt of his own blade in a reverse grip. The next moment, he sliced through the pitch-black night, blocking the attack of a man wielding two steel swords in the rain. He had already lost all sensation in his left arm. Even the fingers on his right hand were becoming stiff.

This wasn't going to be easy.

Shen Zechuan lopped the attacker's head off with the borrowed saber, then kicked the body aside.

With his next stride, Xiao Chiye staggered, knocking his chest against Shen Zechuan's back and sending them both tumbling forward into the billowing waves of grass before rolling into a creek. The rain was still falling, and the freezing water rushed over them. Xiao Chiye's heavy breaths pressed down on the back of

Shen Zechuan's neck as he lay face-down in the water, producing a bizarre duality of scalding heat and piercing cold.

"Killing me won't do you any good." Levering himself up slightly with Wolfsfang, Xiao Chiye said, "So I'm counting on you to take us the rest of the way."

Shen Zechuan wiped the dirt and blood from his face with water from the creek. "There's no point in saving you either."

Xiao Chiye pinned him down again. "You're looking for Prince Chu. What are you going to do now? The Embroidered Uniform Guard will never flush him out; I'm the only one who knows where he is. You've already missed your opportunity. The empress dowager will fail tonight! Treat me well and I could be your ticket out of here."

Shen Zechuan glanced over his shoulder; the two faced each other with the tips of their noses barely touching. "I'll hack you to death," he said coolly. "Then we'll die together."

"You expended so much effort to free yourself from that temple just to die with me in the name of love?"

"Why don't you use that smart mouth to chat with Qiao Tianya." Shen Zechuan grasped Xiao Chiye's blade hand with icy fingers. The next instant, Wolfsfang swept back and momentarily beat back their pursuers. Shen Zechuan seized the opening to knee Xiao Chiye aside; he held the Xiuchun saber in one hand and grabbed Wolfsfang with the other, taking deep, steadying breaths.

"Put that life of yours on your tab," he said. Watching Qiao Tianya run toward them, Shen Zechuan tightened his grip on both hilts. "After tonight, I own you."

A snow-white flash cut through the inky night. Shen Zechuan gave Qiao Tianya no chance to speak but slashed at him head-on. He sent up a spray of water with every step. Each of Shen Zechuan's blows was deadly. As blade met blade, chips formed on the edge of his borrowed Xiuchun saber. At last, Qiao Tianya parried it with a sharp sweep of his own and sent it flying.

The two men sprang apart. Shen Zechuan sank his empty left hand into the creek, washing away the blood that had trickled down.

"A porcelain beauty like yourself should sit safely behind a curtain on the high dais of a pavilion." Qiao Tianya looked as though he had caught a whiff of copper on the wind. "Carrying a blade will hurt your hands. What if you snap them right off?"

Shen Zechuan weighed Wolfsfang with his right hand. "Without my arms and legs, perhaps I'll be more compliant."

"There's a type of person in this world one should never provoke," Qiao Tianya said. "It's those who are ruthless even to themselves—people like you."

Shen Zechuan lunged forward to attack.

Wolfsfang was so heavy in his hands as to be unwieldy, but its weight also had an advantage: with its added heft, the power of his Ji-Style Blade kept Qiao Tianya too occupied to counteract his blows.

The force of his attack had Qiao Tianya nearly bent over backward as he retreated. As he drew nearer the creek, he had a terrible sense of foreboding. Sure enough, Shen Zechuan's injured left hand suddenly splashed up from the water. Mud spattered into Qiao Tianya's eyes; in this crucial moment of weakness, Shen Zechuan delivered yet another heavy blow as he kicked Qiao Tianya and sent him crashing down into the water.

More guards would arrive any second. Shen Zechuan took several steps back, eager to end the engagement. Unfortunately, Xiao Chiye was so tall, and with such long legs, Shen Zechuan could hardly lift him; he started half-dragging Xiao Chiye away.

The search intensified, yet time seemed to slow to a crawl.

All the Guard managed to find in the forest were Xiao Chiye's decoys. They were every one of them well-trained suicide agents—once they fell into the Embroidered Uniform Guard's hands, they took their own lives by biting off their tongues, denying Ji Lei any chance at interrogation.

Where exactly was Prince Chu? Only Xiao Chiye knew.

"That little bastard!" Driven mad with frustration, Ji Lei rose to his feet to survey his surroundings. "Get the Chuancheng Garrison Troops to search along the edge of the hunting grounds!"

Shen Zechuan climbed out of the water, dragging Xiao Chiye out after him. But the creek bed was too steep; in the end, he bit down on Xiao Chiye's back collar and hauled with all his might to drag the man the last few feet.

The cut on Shen Zechuan's left hand bled incessantly. He tore a strip off his robe, rinsed it in the creek, and clumsily bound the wound.

"There's a handkerchief in my lapels," Xiao Chiye said, leaning against a moss-covered rock.

Shen Zechuan reached in, fished a sodden handkerchief from inside Xiao Chiye's robe, and squeezed the muddy water onto Xiao Chiye's chest.

"When will the effects of this drug pass?" Xiao Chiye asked.

"Two hours or so. Soon."

"Crouching in a tree is better than lying in a creek."

Shen Zechuan was soaked through. Xiao Chiye could see where the back of his collar gaped open, revealing specks of dark mud on his pale neck. The contrast was very...

"The Embroidered Uniform Guard has offices for training beasts. Animals can smell the scent of blood." As Shen Zechuan spoke, he lowered his head and sniffed lightly at fingertips that had been tainted with red.

Very seductive.

Xiao Chiye watched him.

What sorcery was this? Only a moment ago this man was killing people with a blade, and even now, nothing about his actions was like a woman—so why had Xiao Chiye thought such a thing?

It must've been Li Jianheng's influence. Day in and day out, the prince had gone on about Shen Zechuan's beauty, until even Xiao Chiye himself had come to think and see the man this way, like those old men in Qudu with their unusual predilections.

"Your swordsmanship's not bad." Xiao Chiye's gaze was so intense it could've peeled back Shen Zechuan's collar. "You must have trained hard in the temple. And yet it's impossible to tell from your physique. Did you use some kind of medicine?"

Shen Zechuan looked sidelong at him. Noting the direction of Xiao Chiye's gaze, he raised a hand to the back of his neck. "How many times a day do you have to look at it? Are you that obsessed?"

Xiao Chiye savored the residual taste of blood on the tip of his tongue. "When you put it like that, it's so suggestive. You make it sound like I'm some pervert."

Shen Zechuan reached over and covered Xiao Chiye's face with the dirty handkerchief. "I thought you indulged in powders and perfume. I didn't expect you to have a taste for men and women both."

"What's with the flirting?" Xiao Chiye said. "Er-gongzi only wants you to wipe the mud off your neck."

"You want me to wipe it?" With the handkerchief between them, Shen Zechuan's fingertip stopped between Xiao Chiye's brows. "Or you want to wipe it for me?"

Icy rain trickled down his finger and dripped between Xiao Chiye's brows. As if they had fully absorbed Shen Zechuan's allure, the droplets that seeped into Xiao Chiye's collar blossomed into ripples of temptation; he was overcome with a restless itch.

Xiao Chiye wanted very much to drink some water. At the same time, he wanted Shen Zechuan to stay a little farther away from him. After a moment of silence, he laughed. "You really are something."

"You think too much." Shen Zechuan gathered his collar tighter, hugged Xiao Chiye's blade to his chest, and spoke no further.

The rain gradually slowed.

The barking of hounds rang out from somewhere deeper in the woods. Neither man moved. The rock they huddled against jutted out over the side of the creek's steep bank, with shrubs overhanging it from above. It was a small and narrow hiding place, just large enough for one man, and Xiao Chiye was already in it.

Waiting, Xiao Chiye listened as a guard leading a hound closed in on them. Shen Zechuan wedged Wolfsfang into a crevice above them and crept up the bank to climb his way into the small space beneath the rock.

Xiao Chiye felt a weight on his body as the man inched up his legs to his chest. Pressed tightly, the two men managed to squeeze together into the narrow space. Xiao Chiye could feel the heat of their thighs rubbing against each other as Shen Zechuan straddled him. He could feel Shen Zechuan's breath by his temple as he leaned in close.

With his eyes still covered by the handkerchief, Xiao Chiye was free to visualize Shen Zechuan's current pose. He couldn't shake off the image of that lotus-white neck.

"I beg of you." Xiao Chiye sighed. "Sit on my stomach. Don't sit down there."

Shen Zechuan didn't move; the rustling from above was getting closer.

Xiao Chiye tried to calm his breathing, but if he raised his head an inch, he would touch Shen Zechuan's chin, and if he bowed his head an inch, the tip of his nose would graze the curve of that neck.

Shen Zechuan had been listening for movements above. Now, he suddenly lifted the handkerchief off Xiao Chiye's face and eyed him wordlessly.

Xiao Chiye looked back at Shen Zechuan. He didn't know if the scent of blood had gone to his head tonight, or what kind of madness this was. In any case, something hot and hard was pressing up against Shen Zechuan, making both of them uncomfortable. Their clothes, soaked by rain, clung so close to their skin it was almost as if there was nothing between them at all, as if the slightest movement would constitute the spark that lit a fire. Above them, the hounds were hunting.

DAYBREAK

FEET TRAMPLED THE UNDERGROWTH, and the hound, as though it had caught a scent, nosed aside branches and leaves as it pawed at the earth just over their heads.

Dirt rained down on Shen Zechuan's neck. Movement in any direction was out of the question, so he could only remain frozen in place.

Xiao Chiye felt increasingly uncomfortable. This position made it impossible for him to settle. He remained in constant contact with that delicate firmness, as if the man astride him was not human at all but a cloudbank, enveloping him like mist—ubiquitous and pervasive.

This atmosphere lit a fire in him. He hadn't satisfied himself in far too long and was still so hard that all he could think about was being in a tub of ice, alone, immediately. Raindrops pattered against the ground, soaking through the brush and drenching his hair. As they lay locked in this endless stalemate, Xiao Chiye finally regained some feeling in his arms. His fingers twitched as the nerves awoke.

The hunter above them finally moved away, but Shen Zechuan didn't relax. Pressing up against each other in this precarious crevice now became a different kind of danger. Xiao Chiye did not avert his gaze.

He must not look away. If he appeared the least bit evasive, it would seem as though he really had a thing for Shen Zechuan.

"You're way too close to me," Xiao Chiye said nonchalantly.

Shen Zechuan did not reply.

For the first time, Xiao Chiye understood the meaning of the saying, "he who rides a tiger finds it difficult to dismount." He wanted to raise his head and gasp for air, but he didn't dare—doing so would make him look even more like an impatient pervert. He swore he had no such intentions. It was just that they were too close. Bewitched by the exquisite friction of their bodies and Shen Zechuan's distinctive scent, his body merely submitted to his base desires.

Xiao Chiye felt Shen Zechuan slide down his chest. The instant he peeled himself away, Xiao Chiye breathed a small sigh, as if he had been relieved of an unsupportable burden.

But before the breath had fully escaped him, his collar tightened around his neck, and he was hurled head-first toward the creek, chest scraping the moss.

He reached back and grabbed hold of Shen Zechuan's wrist, hooking a foot around Shen Zechuan's ankle to trip him. They splashed into the creek together. Xiao Chiye rolled them over, took Shen Zechuan's wrists in either hand and pinned the man heavily under his body.

"Romantic problems should be solved in a romantic way." Xiao Chiye refused to let Shen Zechuan move. "Why raise your hand to me?"

All ten of Shen Zechuan's fingers were splayed, his hair scattered in the water. He gasped for breath, his chin slightly raised. A grim smile tugged at the corners of his lips as he said, "Forcing yourself on others is not a smart thing to do."

"I have no such intentions," Xiao Chiye hissed, grinding every word to pieces between his teeth.

Shen Zechuan pressed his knee to Xiao Chiye's groin and looked at him meaningfully.

Xiao Chiye answered him with a long-suffering look. Then he hung his head and shook his dripping hair like a dog, sending droplets splattering across Shen Zechuan's face. Without waiting for Shen Zechuan to react, he rubbed the back of Shen Zechuan's neck ruthlessly in the water until that maddening bit of mud was washed clean. When he was satisfied, he drew Shen Zechuan's collar closed and fastened it securely.

"The night is wet and cold." Xiao Chiye released Shen Zechuan and climbed off him. "Cover up."

He dunked his head into the water without giving Shen Zechuan a chance to reply. When he surfaced again, he'd mostly calmed down. Wiping water off his face, Xiao Chiye's eyes became clearer, sharper. "It's almost dawn. Let's go," he said, and took up his sword.

Ji Lei was increasingly agitated. Dawn glimmered on the horizon, yet the hunt had turned up nothing.

Qiao Tianya peeled away the collar of one of the suicide soldiers but found nothing that identified them. "These men belong to Xiao Er." He squatted down and pondered. "In Qudu, his every move is under watch. When did he find the time to train a suicide guard?"

"We *must* find him now!" Ji Lei looked to the northwest, where Qudu lay. "The Eight Great Battalions should already control the city gates. We can't lose our heads now." Ji Lei's hand had not once left his blade. Watching him, Qiao Tianya felt he was restless not merely because Xiao Chiye and Prince Chu eluded them, but for some other reason.

"Xiao Er is our lifeline if we want to keep Libei at bay." Qiao Tianya maintained his composure and watched Ji Lei. "Yet there are assassins in the woods tonight. Does Your Excellency know anything about this?"

"The Xiao Clan has offended quite a few people. It seems one of them wants to fish in troubled waters." Ji Lei turned to stare at Qiao Tianya. "How would I know who it is?"

Qiao Tianya spread his hands helplessly. "The fact is, we can't find Xiao Er. He must have come prepared—that's why he's slipped through our fingers all night. He's had us running circles for hours, and it's almost dawn. I'd say *we* have fallen into *his* trap."

"Fallen into his trap?" Ji Lei furrowed his brow.

"I'm afraid he's used himself as bait to buy time." Qiao Tianya stood and looked out over the distant grassland. "If I had to wager, I'd say he has reinforcements."

"The troops on all four borders are accounted for. Where are these reinforcements coming from?"

Qiao Tianya didn't answer; he couldn't begin to guess.

Xi Gu'an rode hard back to the capital. As he entered the city gates, he was greeted by a pervasive silence. Instantly suspicious, he drew his blade and turned to his deputy. "Has there been anything odd in Qudu tonight?"

Even the deputy general who had come to lead Xi Gu'an's horse could see he was nervous. "No, nothing out of the ordinary."

"Gather the men," Xi Gu'an ordered. "Other than those guarding the city gates, everyone else follows me to surround and defend the palace!"

With that, he spurred his horse toward the palace. His wife and son were still within, and while the danger lasted, there was no way the empress dowager would let him anywhere close. On pain of death, he had to ensure the empress dowager's safety.

The deputy general went to mobilize his men as ordered. But as he led the patrol squad out, his path was blocked by a group of drunk men from the Imperial Army. The Eight Great Battalions had always looked down on Qudu's errand boys. From atop his horse, he snapped his riding crop and barked, "Scram!"

The vice commander of the Imperial Army was a man with a vicious blade scar marring his face. After taking the lash from the crop, he unexpectedly grinned and dropped to the ground nearly under the horse's hooves, rolling in the dirt and shouting, "We are both military men. I'm higher ranked than you. Why did you strike me? How dare you!"

The deputy general scoffed. "Lowlife pests sponging off the imperial coffers. Scram! Don't hold up the Eight Great Battalions on important business!"

The man rose to his feet in a single fluid move and sneered up at the deputy general. "Important business? Showing the Imperial Army a good time *is* your business tonight!"

His words were still ringing when the Imperial Army, who had by all accounts been three sheets to the wind, drew their swords in unison. By the time the deputy general reined his horse in shock, the line of men behind him were crumpling to the ground, their throats slit.

"Is this a revolt?!" the deputy general cried. "The Eight Great Battalions—" A blade flashed before him, and he toppled from his horse, his blood painting the ground.

The vice commander kicked the deputy general's head aside and wiped his blade clean on the dead man's chest. "In your fucking dreams." His voice was steady. "The tides have turned. It's time for the Imperial Army to piss on your heads!"

Faint white light bled over the horizon. Dawn was fast approaching.

Qiao Tianya gulped some water and tossed the waterskin to the man behind him. He wiped his mouth and commanded, "Keep searching." But as he strode forward, something fell into place. He turned his head and carefully sized up his subordinates.

Where could Prince Chu be hiding?

There was no way he could have escaped the hunting grounds, so why couldn't they find him? The Embroidered Uniform Guard had been pursuing "Prince Chu" all night—was it possible that the one they sought had been among them the whole time?

Qiao Tianya instantly gave the order: "Verify everyone's authority tokens! All guards on the duty roster tonight must be accounted for. Start checking now!"

As the vice commander walked the lines, the guards removed their tokens of authority and presented them. The vice commander checked the token and swept a glance over the man it belonged to, matching each name to a face. Relying on his keen memory, he checked one by one, until he came to the very end of the line.

"Token." He looked up and studied the guard before him with eyes like an eagle. "Hand it over."

The man slid his token onto the tray. The guard beside him began to tremble; he ducked his head, not daring to raise it.

The vice commander seemed not to notice. He lifted his brush to make a tick in his book and said, "Which office?"

"The Swords Office," Chen Yang replied.

"I've never seen you on a mission before," the vice commander said. "First time?"

Li Jianheng was trembling badly; Chen Yang knew it was only a matter of time until they were caught. Still, he remained unruffled. "Strangers at first meeting, friends at second. You'll find me a familiar enough face after a few more missions."

The vice commander pointed his brush toward Li Jianheng. "Token."

Even after a few attempts, Li Jianheng's fumbling fingers hadn't managed to remove the token from his belt. The vice commander smiled and reached out to remove it for him; Chen Yang tensed. Unfortunately, Li Jianheng seemed to have lost his nerve. The instant the vice commander moved toward him, the prince flinched back and cried, "Don't hurt me!"

Shit!

At that moment, they heard a shrill whistle, and a black horse with a snowy white chest thundered out of the forest, a troop of cavalry close behind. As dawn broke over the trees, the gyrfalcon led the way, wheeling toward them.

Hearing the commotion, Hua Siqian turned to see men and horses charging across the grass. "The Eight Great Battalions?!"

But these men bore no insignia on their armor; they didn't even carry banners.

Chen Yang immediately took hold of Prince Chu and called out, "His Highness the Crown Prince is under protection of the Imperial Army. All who bear swords before him shall be slain without exception. Stand aside!"

Hua Siqian took a few stumbling steps forward in disbelief. He looked back at the ranks of the Embroidered Uniform Guard and shouted, "Prince Chu is held hostage by traitors. What are you waiting for?!"

Qiao Tianya lunged toward the prince. Cornered with nowhere to retreat, Li Jianheng couldn't help but scream.

A long blade suddenly shot out of the woods and buried itself in the ground before Li Jianheng's feet. Xiao Chiye leapt down from his horse, tore off his token, and threw it onto the tray.

"Our main forces are on their way; who has the guts to make a move?" he growled.

Ji Lei, too, had just reached the clearing on horseback. Encountering this scene, he bellowed, "What a load of horseshit! The Imperial Army is—"

The gyrfalcon landed on Xiao Chiye's shoulder. He stroked the raptor approvingly. "Give it a try, Lao-Ji, if you have the balls."

Ji Lei looked toward the grassland. The vanguard of the Imperial Army was already here, yet the mass of mounted soldiers behind them seemed to stretch without end. Then the Cangjun Commandery banners of Qidong unfurled; he saw that the one at the head of these galloping horses was none other than Qi Zhuyin herself.

Hua Siqian retreated several steps. He gripped Pan Rugui as he said in a hoarse voice, "The message to Qidong was intercepted. How could they secretly—"

Xiao Chiye sheathed his sword. "If all written communication in Qudu had to pass through the hands of the Embroidered Uniform Guard, how troublesome would that be?"

The situation was beyond salvation. Hua Siqian sank to the ground and murmured, "The empress dowager is still in the palace..."

"The empress dowager is advanced in years. In order to attend to her health, she has handed all matters pertaining to the patrol and defense of the capital to the Imperial Army." Xiao Chiye, disheveled from hours of fighting, now pulled the tidy Li Jianheng to his feet.

"Your Highness has been on the move all night. It can't have been easy on you."

Qi Zhuyin's horse had cut through the crowd. Now she dismounted and knelt to Li Jianheng to make her obeisance, her voice ringing clear through the hunting grounds: "Rest assured, Your Highness! The two hundred thousand men and horses of Qidong stand at the ready. This subject, Qi Zhuyin, swears to ensure the safety of Your Highness the Crown Prince!"

As if in a dream, Li Jianheng looked blankly at Qi Zhuyin, then to his left and right. Qiao Tianya was the most astute of his companions. Seeing the writing on the wall, he knelt at once. The moment he did, the Embroidered Uniform Guard around him threw down their blades and knelt one after another.

"I..." Li Jianheng clenched his empty palms as though clutching at a lifeline. He was weeping with joy, the tears in his eyes spilling down his cheeks as he struggled to speak. "Now that I'm the crown prince...I'll surely reward the great kindness everyone has done me today!"

26 BITTER FROST

IMPERIAL CONCUBINE WEI looked around nervously as she followed the eunuch to her audience. Seeing only unfamiliar palace walls around her, she asked, "Gonggong, where are we? Where is Her Majesty the Empress Dowager?"

The eunuch leading the way ignored her.

The eerie silence made her hair stand on end. She stopped in her tracks and complained of a stomachache, making a great scene about wanting to head back. This eunuch before her was one she'd never seen. His face was young and unfamiliar when he turned back to look at her. "We will be there soon," he said gently. To the eunuchs accompanying them, he said, "Support Lady Wei as she walks. We mustn't let her fall."

The eunuchs on either side immediately grasped Imperial Concubine Wei's arms. She struggled, raising her voice to yell, but more hands gagged her mouth. The eunuchs nimbly hoisted her off the ground and sped down the corridor.

In a small, deserted courtyard lay a well; some water remained at the bottom. The eunuch craned his head and looked in. "Right here. Send the lady in."

Imperial Concubine Wei fought with all her might. Her manicured fingernails scratched the arm of the leading eunuch, her hair disheveled as she shook her head and sobbed, clinging to the edge of the well.

The eunuch stroked her pretty hand. When he told the men to lift the stone over her fingers, his voice held pity.

Far below, there was a *plunk*. The sound startled the birds on the branch overhanging over the vermilion wall, and they scattered in flight.

The Xiande Emperor lay inside the carriage. Li Jianheng knelt by his side, cradling a bowl of medicine. The emperor's breaths came so weak he hadn't even energy to cough. He beckoned to Li Jianheng, who quickly put the bowl aside and shifted over.

"Imperial Brother, are you feeling better?"

"Jianheng," the emperor croaked, placing a hand on the back of Li Jianheng's.

"Your subject and brother is here." Li Jianheng started crying again. "I'm right here."

"The late emperor, in his final years, ruled under the control of others. At that time, our eldest brother was the crown prince of the Eastern Palace, while we..." The emperor met his eyes. "We were like you, an idle prince. The whims of fate are unpredictable. In the end, this empire fell into our hands. But since our ascension, we have been constrained at every turn. Each move was like a puppet dancing before a screen. If Imperial Mother wanted us to laugh, we laughed. Now she wants us to die, so we must die."

Li Jianheng was choked with emotion.

"In the future," the emperor continued, "just as our father was, and just as we have, you will become that same lonely man on the throne."

Li Jianheng burst into tears. He held the emperor's hand and pleaded, "Imperial Brother! How could I rule? I'm but a worm in this Li Clan's empire. How can I possibly sit at its peak? Imperial Brother, I'm scared, I'm so scared."

"Don't be." With a sudden surge of energy, the emperor gripped Li Jianheng's hand and opened his eyes wide. "You are different from us—the empress dowager's kin have lost! Death is all that's left for Hua Siqian and Pan Rugui. Kill them, and the empress dowager will have no one left to aid her! Power will fall back to you, and you will be...the ruler of all lands under heaven! What we couldn't do...you can... We..."

The emperor coughed so violently, his whole body shook, but he was unwilling to release Li Jianheng. He continued with blood in his mouth, "Eliminate the empress dowager's kin and keep close watch on the court officials. The Hua Clan has lost today, but there are... others...you must bear in mind. Allow no one to sleep too soundly in the bed of imperial power! Those...who save you today...can kill you...tomorrow! Military power is like a tiger... Xiao..."

The emperor vomited fresh blood, sending Li Jianheng into a panic.

"You must not..." The emperor gasped for breath and gripped Li Jianheng's hand so hard it bruised. "Must not...release...A-Ye..."

You must not release A-Ye back to Libei!

It didn't matter if he was an idle young master or an extraordinary prodigy. The Xiao Clan would only remain a loyal dog if he remained in Qudu. Even if the empress dowager's kin had been defeated, it didn't mean the frontier garrisons would never consolidate their power and assemble an army to challenge the throne. Without the Hua Clan, who could hold the Xiao Clan in check? If Xiao Chiye had the capacity to endure in silence for five whole years in Qudu, making a miracle out of the degenerates in the Imperial Army, imagine if they gave him another five years in Libei. He would surely become their most lethal threat!

"Imperial Brother." Li Jianheng was dazed. "How can we do that? Imperial Brother!"

"Strip the territories of their power and reduce their troops," the emperor said weakly. "If necessary...kill...kill..."

Kill him.

When Li Jianheng saw the emperor close his eyes, he let out a wail. Until the very moment of his death, the Xiande Emperor never released his hand; the resentment and gloom between his brows never dissipated so long as he lived.

He had sat upon the throne for nine years, yet never had he made a single decision without a nod from the empress dowager. It was the empress dowager who had final say over his meals, clothing, expenses—even over which woman would spend the night in his bedchamber. The boldest move he made in this life was to establish covert communication with Qidong and draw Xi Gu'an over to his side to pave, at the Nanlin Hunting Grounds, what seemed like a smooth path to the throne for his brother Li Jianheng.

As soon as the emperor's death was known, the long procession making its way to the capital stopped, and cries of grief and sorrow rent the air. The crowd of ministers went to their knees. At their fore was Hai Liangyi, wracked with sobs. His devastated cries of "Your Majesty!" were the final honors accorded to the Xiande Emperor.

The funeral bell in Qudu tolled without end, and the nation mourned.

Empress Dowager Hua sat on her settee, feeding the Xiande Emperor's parrot with a wooden spoon. At the sound of the bell, the parrot screamed, "Jianyun! Jianyun! Jianyun is back!"

The eastern pearls dangling from the empress dowager's ears swayed as she nodded. "Jianyun is back."

The parrot screamed, "Imperial Mother! Imperial Mother!"

Empress Dowager Hua remained motionless save for the rhythmic tapping of her spoon. As she sat within the slanting shadow, the streaks of white in her hair could no longer be covered, and the fine lines at the corners of her eyes resembled the cracks on a prized porcelain antique.

The parrot screeched a few more times before falling headlong from its perch, permanently silenced. The empress dowager set the spoon aside and sat quietly until the bell rang no more. "Where is Imperial Concubine Wei? What's taking her so long?"

With the death of the Xiande Emperor, Xiao Chiye's return to the capital was so busy he could hardly breathe. For several days, he knelt together with hundreds of other officials; by the time he could finally lie down, he was exhausted.

But exhausted as he was, he still had to bathe. As Xiao Chiye wiped his body, he saw that the wounds on his shoulders and arms had already scabbed over. He pulled on a clean robe and came out to ask Chen Yang, "Where is he?"

This time, Chen Yang knew who he meant. "The Embroidered Uniform Guard is being reorganized, so he's been in the process of re-enlistment the past few days. He's barely been home."

"I was asking," Xiao Chiye said, "about Ji Lei. Whom are *you* talking about?"

Chen Yang scratched his head abashedly. "Oh, Ji Lei. He's been detained. He'll probably face beheading after the new emperor ascends the throne. But Your Excellency, weren't you the one who locked him up a few days ago?"

Xiao Chiye shrugged on another layer and said in all seriousness, "I forgot."

Shen Zechuan, Ge Qingqing, and Xiao-Wu were eating noodles at a street stall. They were halfway through their meal when Xiao-Wu suddenly looked up and stared fixedly ahead.

Shen Zechuan turned to see Xiao Chiye tossing some silver to the stallkeeper. He lifted his robe to sit beside Shen Zechuan as he called, "Two bowls of noodles."

Xiao-Wu slurped his meal down. Taking hold of the bowl, he shuffled his butt away to another table like a hunted quail. Under Xiao Chiye's gaze, Ge Qingqing took his own bowl and joined him.

Shen Zechuan picked at his noodles. "I'm full."

"Finish it." Xiao Chiye pulled out a pair of chopsticks and clacked them at Shen Zechuan. "Afraid to see me? Look how anxious you are to flee."

"Of course." Shen Zechuan slowly took the last bite. "Anyone who's been pinned down once would be afraid."

"You ran off pretty fast the other day, too, when we were protecting the new emperor." Xiao Chiye's noodles came, and he poured vinegar into the bowl. "It was a great opportunity for a promotion. Why did you run?"

"I didn't do anything." Shen Zechuan blew at the soup and drank it. "So there was no reason for me to stay."

Xiao Chiye ate his noodles in silence. When he had almost finished the bowl, he said, "Come to think of it, you must've crouched behind me for a long time that night, mustn't you? Deciding whom to choose? Why not play it by ear? If Xi Gu'an captured Qudu, you'd give me a stab. If he failed, you'd give me a hand. Keeping an eye out for the perfect opportunity, just waiting for me to take a fall before you made your move."

"Then you're lucky." Shen Zechuan turned to him with a smile. "You're still alive."

"You wouldn't be the one who shot that arrow at me, would you?" Xiao Chiye wondered aloud. "If I weren't in such a perilous position, how could you have emphasized the significance of your favor?"

"I haven't even asked for anything in return. Why do you assume I'm plotting against you?"

"Not asking for anything in return is the problem." Xiao Chiye still seemed hungry. He set down his chopsticks and said, "You couldn't risk appearing before Prince Chu that day. Was it because you were afraid of Ji Lei, or because you were afraid Hua Siqian would let something slip?"

Shen Zechuan stacked his copper coins neatly on the table, then leaned close to Xiao Chiye and whispered, "Wrong. I was afraid of you."

"Afraid of me?" Xiao Chiye echoed.

"Of that hard thing."

The sounds and voices around Xiao Chiye seemed far away. All that remained in his ears was this warm puff of *hard*. He realized that Shen Zechuan was wearing a collar that fastened high on his neck today, denying him the chance to lay wanton eyes on it again. His face moved through several expressions; finally, he looked at Shen Zechuan and squeezed out through clenched teeth. "You don't need to worry."

"Er-gongzi has come of age now." Shen Zechuan straightened. "It's about time you find yourself a wife."

"What do you know of it? Your Er-gongzi is more seasoned than you realize." Seeing Shen Zechuan rising to leave, Xiao Chiye grabbed his wrist and pulled him back into his seat. "You're always trying to go before I'm done talking. That's against the rules."

"And you're always laying your hand on me at every turn," Shen Zechuan said. "Tell me again about the rules."

Xiao Chiye released his wrist. "I'll repay you for the favor."

"Call me Master and I'll consider it even."

"But first, there's something you owe me. Surely you don't want me to keep chasing you for that thumb ring, right?"

Without another word, Shen Zechuan tossed the bone thumb ring to him.

Xiao Chiye caught it and looked at him skeptically. "What kind of gimmick is this? Returning it the moment I ask for it?"

"This is the way honest people handle matters," Shen Zechuan said. "Quick and straightforward."

At this point, there was nothing more to say.

Xiao Chiye watched Shen Zechuan rise to his feet. He turned the thumb ring in his fingers, thinking it had been far too easy.

"Going home?" Xiao Chiye asked behind him.

"I'm on duty tomorrow."

"The Embroidered Uniform Guard is being reshuffled; what duty?" Xiao Chiye asked. "Winter is bitter in Qudu. Take care."

"Small fry like me drift with the current and go with the flow." Shen Zechuan turned around. "I'm not the one who needs to take care."

Xiao Chiye rubbed his knuckles. "While you're at it, send my regards to Ji Gang-shifu."

Shen Zechuan paused mid-step and swiveled to face Xiao Chiye.

Slipping on his thumb ring, Xiao Chiye smiled carelessly. "So, Lanzhou, want to come play with me?"

AUTUMN CHILL

SHEN ZECHUAN immediately smiled. "This is no big secret. Goodbye."

"Why not hear me out first?" Xiao Chiye was in a good mood after recovering his lost thumb ring. "Ji Gang is your shifu, so we're fellow disciples of the same martial lineage. I'm older than you, so it would only be proper for you to call me *shixiong*."

"The Ji family has no connections in Libei." But even as he said this, Shen Zechuan recalled his fight with Xiao Chiye in the snow five years ago. Back then, he'd felt a sense of familiarity that had nagged at him.

"Perhaps they do, perhaps they don't," Xiao Chiye said. "It's hard to say for sure when it comes to things like fated meetings."

Shen Zechuan gestured for Ge Qingqing and Xiao-Wu to wait and sat back down beside Xiao Chiye. "You looked into Ge Qingqing."

"I couldn't forget it," Xiao Chiye looked at him. "He fled from me so quickly five years ago, and now, five years later, he's so close to you. How could I not be suspicious of such a glaring coincidence? So, following that thread, I managed to find out all about him."

"What do you want?" Shen Zechuan asked with a smile.

"Nothing." Xiao Chiye raised a finger and gestured at Shen Zechuan's eyes. "No need for your fake smiles. We're practically sworn friends in life and death by now; why put on a brave face? You're panicking. Scared now, huh?"

"Not quite yet," Shen Zechuan said.

Xiao Chiye spun his chopsticks around and tapped the table absently. "If Ji Gang is your shifu, it makes sense that the Embroidered Uniform Guard led by Ge Qingqing spared your life back then."

"You're overly suspicious." Shen Zechuan looked down at the brown oil stains on the tabletop. "Just because that kick didn't kill me, you kept nosing around. You sure are dogged."

"It's one of the few virtues I have," Xiao Chiye said, "and I spent it all on you."

"Since you say we are of the same martial lineage," Shen Zechuan said, "it wouldn't be proper of you to keep your shifu's name from me, would it?"

Xiao Chiye tossed the chopsticks back into the bamboo holder, which promptly toppled over. "Let's hear you call me shixiong first."

Shen Zechuan said nothing.

"Ji Gang is an impressive man," Xiao Chiye said. "I sent someone to Duanzhou to make inquiries; everyone there thought he died in a fire. Say, was he the one who killed Xiaofuzi?"

"Nope." Shen Zechuan righted the chopstick holder. "My shifu is of an advanced age. How could he take a life?"

The wind picked up. Neither man moved.

"You seem like you've done nothing," Xiao Chiye said. "Yet I feel like you've done everything."

"Whether I did it or not, you all refuse to let me go." Bracing his hands on the bench, Shen Zechuan turned to Xiao Chiye and laughed quietly. "Well then—so you can be justified in hating me, why don't I do all those bad things?"

It was only when Xiao Chiye entered the palace the next day that he learned of Imperial Concubine Wei's death.

Li Jianheng had already adopted the emperor's robes. He looked drained and sallow from the days he'd spent crying. Seated on the dais, he said, "They say she slipped and fell into the well. They didn't find her body until last night."

How convenient this slip was.

Seeing no one around, Li Jianheng whispered, "Ce'an, don't tell me it was you."

Xiao Chiye shook his head.

Li Jianheng looked immediately relieved. He shifted uncomfortably in the emperor's seat. "Now that I live in the palace, whenever I open my eyes at night, I can see eunuchs waiting. It's quite terrifying. They used to call Pan Rugui *lao-zuzong*, and now their lao-zuzong is locked up in prison! Ce'an, do you think they hate me?"

He loosed a stream of grumbles, all revolving around the topic of how fearful he was. In the end, he convinced Xiao Chiye to send the Imperial Army into the palace to take over the important tasks of guard and patrol duty, at least for now. Xiao Chiye naturally would not refuse. After another moment, Li Jianheng said, "Libei has sent a letter: the Prince of Libei and your brother are on their way. You'll see them in a just few more days, Ce'an."

Li Jianheng was nakedly playing up to Xiao Chiye with this. Now that he stood on the cusp of becoming master of all the lands, he was more timid than he'd ever been; his insufferable arrogance seemed to have been stripped away entirely during the Autumn Hunt. Finally, he understood who held the real power.

Not that Xiao Chiye intended to seek rewards or accolades. Li Jianheng knew more than anyone the thing he most wished for. Yet to date, Li Jianheng had said nothing about letting him go home to Libei.

Xiao Chiye's face remained impassive, hiding his sinking heart.

Five days later, the Prince of Libei arrived in Qudu. Autumn rain had fallen uninterrupted all day. Still, Xiao Chiye rode his horse out of the city early in the morning and stood in the pavilion where he had seen them off years ago. After four hours' wait, he finally saw several falcons materialize on the distant horizon. On his shoulder, Meng grew excited and charged into the rain, drawing great arcs in the sky as he caught up with his brothers and sisters.

The armored cavalry burst from the curtain of rain like a stroke of dark ink drawn through water, sweeping toward Xiao Chiye. Unable to wait, he leapt out of the pavilion and dashed into the rain to greet them.

"Father!"

Atop his horse, Xiao Jiming laughed loudly and said to his father, "He looks so big and strong now, but the instant he sees you, he shows true colors."

Xiao Fangxu took off his bamboo hat and leaned over to drop it onto Xiao Chiye's head. "You've grown taller," he said after studying his son a moment.

Xiao Chiye grinned wide. "That's right; even Dage is half a head shorter than me now!"

"What a smug little brat," said Xiao Jiming. "Ever since he outgrew me, he's been mentioning it every year when we meet."

Xiao Fangxu handed his reins to Zhao Hui and dismounted. Then he reached out and pulled his youngest son into a hug, clapping him heartily on the back. "Silly boy!"

Xiao Chiye laughed. "I've been waiting a while. Did something keep you on the way?"

"The little master caught a chill before we left home," Zhao Hui explained, "so the prince made a detour through Dengzhou to invite the Venerable Master Yideng for a look."

"A-Xun is sick? Since when? Why didn't Dage mention it in his letter?"

"It's only a minor illness," Xiao Jiming replied. "Yizhi is looking after him at home. You don't need to worry."

Xiao Chiye couldn't help his disappointment. When he'd left Libei five years ago, his sister-in-law was pregnant. Now, little A-Xun was already four, but Xiao Chiye hadn't seen him yet. All he learned about his little nephew came in scraps gleaned from his father and elder brother's letters.

He wanted to go home.

But Xiao Chiye's low spirits were fleeting. He smiled. "I've got a birthday present ready. When Dage returns home, please give it to him for me."

Xiao Fangxu dusted off the brim of his bamboo hat. "Before we set off, Xun-er specially painted a picture for you. I'll have Zhao Hui bring it over later. Let's not chat here. We'll make our greetings in the palace first and talk when we return to the manor tonight."

They mounted their horses and rode together into Qudu.

As summer turned to autumn, Grand Mentor Qi ate so well he put on weight for the first time in years. He was presently washing his feet in the rain, wiggling his toes.

It had been many years since the Prince of Libei had shown himself in the capital. Now that the names of the Four Generals had spread far and wide, few still remembered the Prince of Libei, Xiao Fangxu.

"If we're speaking of the Four Great Generals of the land," he began, "we had the same twenty years ago. Back then, Xiao Fangxu of Libei, Qi Shiyu of Qidong, Lu Pingyan of Bianjun, and Feng Yisheng of the Suotian Pass were the leading commanders of the military forces at the four corners of the empire. Feng Yisheng died in battle, and the Feng Clan had no surviving heirs. I doubt anyone remembers this name today. But back then, they were valiant warriors all who took their horses to the frontier pass and wiped out the Biansha troops."

"Feng Yisheng?" Ji Gang called out from where he was cooking inside. "What do you mean no one remembers? Chuan-er! Both of General Feng's sons died on the battlefield. But he later adopted a son—my dage."

"Shifu's eldest brother?" Shen Zechuan asked as he scooped rice into bowls.

"I forgot to tell you!" Ji Gang smacked his forehead.

"Is the food ready?" Grand Mentor Qi yelled. "Aye, isn't his eldest brother Zuo Qianqiu? What's there to tell? Anyone could guess!"

Shen Zechuan brought the dishes and laid out chopsticks for Grand Mentor Qi. "Dinner is ready, Xiansheng," he said respectfully.

Grand Mentor Qi gulped down a mouthful of wine. "Being waited on like this really is the most satisfying feeling."

Ji Gang wiped sweat from his brow and sat across the small table from them. "You were saying Xiao Er told you he hails from the same martial lineage as us. I'm afraid his shifu must be Zuo Qianqiu!"

Shen Zechuan listened as he ate.

"I haven't seen him in years," Ji Gang lamented. "Did you exchange blows with Xiao Er this time? How did it go? Were the strokes of his blade strong and forceful?"

"Let Lanzhou eat first," Grand Mentor Qi said. "We'll talk once we're full. This was a dangerous situation, but we don't need to rush into our next steps. We can rest for a few days."

"I should have known," Ji Gang said. "Xiao Er wore a bone thumb ring. If anyone in the world knows how to wield a heavy bow, it's Zuo Qianqiu."

"Perhaps you'll be able to meet your dage now that Xiao Fangxu is in the capital," Grand Mentor Qi commented, picking at the dishes on the table. "Zuo Qianqiu gave everything he had at Tianfei Watchtower. He warded off the Biansha Horsemen, but it cost him his wife. That battle earned him the moniker 'Thunder on Jade Terraces,' but he never recovered from it. Rumor was that he left home to become a monk. It's not impossible that he instead buried his name and took refuge with Xiao Fangxu, and has been teaching his son all these years."

"A general's success is built upon the sacrifice of tens of thousands," Ji Gang said sorrowfully. "So what if he's renowned for his exploits on the field? In the end, he'll still become no more than a handful of yellow sand. Those who die in battle are loyal to the end; those who survive suffer onward. Zuo Qianqiu buried his name, Xiao Fangxu has stepped down because of illness, and Lu Pingyan has grown old. Twenty years from now, where will the current Four Generals be? They're all but waves crashing on the shore, each generation overtaking the last."

Grand Mentor Qi had become slightly tipsy as he watched Shen Zechuan eat. After a time, he said, "What a waste, to come into this world and suffer a lifetime for naught. We will all of us die, so why not reach for the heavens and realize our ambitions before the time comes! Here, Lanzhou! Have another bowl!"

By the time they had eaten and drunk their fill, night had descended.

Grand Mentor Qi lay on a mat under the eaves while Shen Zechuan sat and wiped his teacher's feet. Ji Gang draped outer robes over each of them, then squatted in the corner to smoke his pipe.

Resting his head on a papaya, Grand Mentor Qi said, "Lanzhou, tell me again what happened at the hunting grounds."

Shen Zechuan repeated his detailed account.

Grand Mentor Qi listened with his eyes closed. He was still silent when Shen Zechuan finished. The vines in the courtyard basked in the downpour, each drop pattering onto the leaves. After the rain had drummed uninterrupted for some time, Grand Mentor Qi finally spoke. "On the surface, Xiao Er seems to have come out of this battle covered in glory, but he is caught in the same snare that trapped his father and elder brother. The new emperor has called him friend for five years. Yet Xiao Chiye concealed his true character so deeply for so long; how could anyone not be wary of him now? Today, the new emperor warmly remembers the kindness Xiao Chiye did him in saving his life—but how much can this friendship endure until it's worn away to nothing? I had imagined the second young master would be able to hide it a little longer, given his demonstrable endurance. There were countless ways he could have let Qi Zhuyin take the lead here, yet he had to do it himself."

Ji Gang knocked off some ash under the dim light. "The wolf pup wants to go home. All he dreams of are the grasslands of Libei. How old is he? This kind of spirit is the essence of youth."

"A little impatience upsets great plans," Grand Mentor Qi said. "Had he endured it this time, wouldn't he even now be returning home as a scoundrel young master?"

At that very moment, Xiao Chiye was standing outside the palace gates, gazing up at rooftops cast in shadow. The overhanging eaves of these vermilion walls seemed a trial given to him by the heavens. Beneath his frivolous mask, a ferocious beast writhed and howled in silence. In the Temple of Guilt, Shen Zechuan suddenly, strangely, understood the meaning behind Xiao Chiye's actions.

He wanted to go home.

He wanted to go home, proudly and honestly, as himself.

DRUNK IN THE ALLEY

THE AUTUMN RAIN in Qudu had fallen without cease since the new emperor's coronation. White mourning lanterns hung high beneath the old black tiles. Were someone to stand atop the wall overlooking the city, they would have seen a bleak chill shrouding every corner.

After the events of the Autumn Hunt, every member of the Embroidered Uniform Guard had their authority tokens revoked. All those of fifth rank and above, such as Ji Lei and Qiao Tianya, were imprisoned. Together with Hua Siqian and Pan Rugui, they were due to face a joint trial by the Three Judicial Offices.

Xue Xiuzhuo was transferred out of the Office of Scrutiny for Revenue and promoted to Assistant Minister in the Court of Judicial Review. This new position appeared to have less authority than the Chief Supervising Secretary of the Office of Scrutiny for Revenue, but in truth, it gave him an inroad to the central administration of the Three Judicial Offices. Now, he not only had the authority to examine any case reviews, but also the power to participate in the deliberations and rebuttals of proposals from the Ministry of Justice and the Chief Surveillance Bureau.

"Xue Xiuzhuo." Empress Dowager Hua reclined on her settee, idly tapping a black jade weiqi piece against the board. "I had never heard of this child before the Nanlin Hunting Grounds incident. Who is he to the Xue Clan?"

Fanning the incense burner, Aunt Liuxiang answered, "Your Majesty, he is the third son of common birth in the Xue Clan. This lowly one had also never heard this man's name and went specifically to inquire about him."

"It appears the Xue Clan has found a worthy successor," the empress dowager said. "All these years, Yao Wenyu has been the one garnering renown. I thought that old fox, Hai Liangyi, would eventually recommend the boy into the Grand Secretariat. Who would have expected him to put the unremarkable Xue Xiuzhuo forward instead?"

"This Xue Xiuzhuo first joined forces with the Provincial Administration Commissioner of Juexi, Jiang Qingshan, to secretly gather evidence, then secured the support of Secretariat Elder Hai," Aunt Liuxiang said. "As the Chief Supervising Secretary of the Office of Scrutiny for Revenue, he had full access to the Six Ministries. Now that he's been promoted to Assistant Minister of the Court of Judicial Review, he'll be hearing the case of our Secretariat Elder Hua. I fear he's made up his mind to see it through; he will not let the matter go easily."

"I can't go out at the moment." The empress dowager looked contemplative. "If Xue Xiuzhuo wishes to investigate, then let him. The Hua Clan is at a critical juncture. Go tell my brother he needs to be ready to cut his losses if we have any hope of staging a comeback."

Aunt Liuxiang murmured in acknowledgment and quietly withdrew.

Shen Zechuan shook rainwater off his umbrella and took a seat on the run-down veranda of the deserted courtyard. Less than an hour later, Xi Hongxuan's monumental figure appeared beneath an umbrella as he strode through the round arch of the moon gate and approached.

"Spies abound these days. I barely managed to slip away." Xi Hongxuan gathered up his wet clothes and frowned. "Did you call me here for something urgent?"

"Xi Gu'an is in prison," Shen Zechuan said. "Your long-cherished wish is about to be realized, yet you've made no move to secure your victory. Are you waiting for him to take desperate action and foil your plans?"

"His death warrant is all but signed," Xi Hongxuan said. "Any further move now would be as redundant as drawing legs on a snake."

"Nothing in this world is certain." There was no trace of a smile on Shen Zechuan's fair face. "The more critical the situation, the less you can afford to be negligent. As long as he lives, there's a chance he'll survive this."

Xi Hongxuan studied his side profile. "The case of the Hua faction has already been handed over to the Three Judicial Offices. Under so many watchful eyes, how do you plan to make *your* move?"

"I'm not making any moves." Shen Zechuan glanced over. "Xi Gu'an has been the Hua Clan's lackey for years; his crimes while in office are too numerous to count. But only if the right ones are handed over to the Court of Judicial Review will his death be etched in stone."

"Bearing arms before the emperor, surrounding and hunting down the successor to the crown—are these two alone not enough to put him to death?"

"As the Military Commissioner of the Eight Great Battalions, it's his prerogative to bear arms before the throne. The hunt for the crown prince has nothing to do with him. He could simply claim he headed back to the capital for reinforcements upon seeing things go awry. The new emperor is wary of the Imperial Army. He has taken down the Hua Clan, yes, but this is precisely the time he needs the help and cooperation of the other Eight Great Clans. When it comes to this, he is timid—but the longer it drags on, the harder it will be to guarantee the death of Xi Gu'an." Shen Zechuan smirked. "And as long as Xi Gu'an lives, you will remain 'Xi Er,' second in line, never stepping into the light."

At length, Xi Hongxuan asked, "What do you plan to do?"

"Xi Gu'an was assigned to the Eight Great Battalions in the fourth year of Xiande. In the four years since, the Eight Great Battalions have received a total of nine million taels in military funds and provisions. Yet only seven million of the disbursement is accounted for. What of the remaining two million taels?" Shen Zechuan asked. "They disappeared after passing through Xi Gu'an's hands.

"Audits of the account books were always Xue Xiuzhuo's job," he continued. "Once he checks, he will very likely uncover even more missing funds. Pan Rugui and Hua Siqian might take such a large sum for themselves—they are greedy and corrupt. But Xi Gu'an cannot afford to be merely greedy or corrupt. He holds the reins of the Eight Great Battalions, whose key task is to patrol and defend Qudu. If he can't explain where the money went, one must suspect him of embezzling funds to raise and pay his own private army under the aegis of the Eight Great Battalions."

"His own private army." A chill ran down Xi Hongxuan's spine.

"He stands at the bedside of the Son of Heaven. What other reason is there for him to raise such an army?" Shen Zechuan said.

"No way!" Xi Hongxuan vetoed it. He wiped sweat off his face. "Do you think me mad? If it's only a question of associating with the Hua faction, he's the one who dies. But if it's treason, my whole family dies! This is a crime punishable by extermination of the entire clan!"

Shen Zechuan laughed aloud, then lowered his voice. "A change of sovereign brings a change of ministers. This is a precious opportunity for you to distinguish yourself before the new emperor. Xi Gu'an is giving you his life as a congratulatory gift for your promotion."

"You want me to..." Xi Hongxuan stared at Shen Zechuan and burst out laughing. "You certainly are ruthless. The empress dowager has saved your life twice. You really have no regard for the kindness shown to you."

"Kindness, huh?" Shen Zechuan picked up his umbrella. "It's not too late to repay it after the kill. Besides, this is a power game between Xiao and Hua. What does it have to do with me?"

With that, he opened his umbrella, nodded to Xi Hongxuan, and stepped into the rainy night. Xi Hongxuan was left alone on the veranda, watching Shen Zechuan disappear. When he touched his back, he found it drenched in cold sweat.

A few days later, the Court of Judicial Review began the serious trials of the Autumn Hunt.

Jiang Xie, the Chief Minister of the Court of Judicial Review, served as the presiding judge, while Hai Liangyi served as the overseeing supervisor and Xue Xiuzhuo as associate judge. This was a major case examined and prosecuted by the Chief Surveillance Bureau, submitted to the Court of Judicial Review with the criminal charges of formation of political factions, embezzlement and corruption, and endangerment of the state.

Of these, the charge of formation of political factions caused some small panic among civil servants in the Six Ministries. All those who had paid visits to the Hua manor, or had received recommendations from Hua Siqian and Pan Rugui, found themselves in a precarious position. Countless officials scrambled to submit memorials criticizing Hua Siqian and Pan Rugui, each hoping to avoid implication with an impassioned statement of loyalty.

Unfortunately, memorials of any kind gave Li Jianheng a headache. He had never been one to sit still for long periods. Even so, he didn't dare mess about during a time of national mourning. He had seen the way Hai Liangyi confronted Hua Siqian that night, and was, as a consequence, very much afraid of the man.

Secretariat Elder Hai was rigid and inflexible. His neatly trimmed beard always hung properly before the second clasp on the front of his robe, his crown was always perfectly placed, and his hair meticulously combed. During the dog days of summer, he would never let his robe hang open even in his own home, and in the coldest winter months, he would never warm his hands in opposite sleeves when going to court. When he stood, he was a tall pine tree high on the mountain ridge, and when he walked, he was the swift wind blowing through a tranquil valley. He was never sloppy in his work and could listen attentively to details of a case for three days and three nights without showing any sign of weariness.

Li Jianheng spent all his days fooling around; he went weak at the knees at the sight of upright and scholarly ministers like this.

But because of the Hua faction case, Hai Liangyi was constantly seeking him out to report various details. Li Jianheng had found the dragon throne in Mingli Hall so hard that his behind hurt from prolonged sitting, so he ordered several layers of soft padding. When Hai Liangyi saw it, he roundly chastised him, advising him to be steadfast in character.

The heady thrill of having power within his grasp was fleeting as a flake of snow; what had followed was an avalanche of responsibilities. Li Jianheng found it difficult to keep up with the never-ending morning court sessions. He looked down every day from the dragon throne, yet often didn't understand what the people below him were arguing about.

No money? Collect taxes, then! Kill some corrupt officials—that way the money could be recovered, no? What's there to argue about?

Li Jianheng didn't dare reveal these innermost thoughts. He feared Hai Liangyi, and feared even more these civil servants and military commanders. He didn't understand what they fought over, or why the Hua faction could not be executed immediately, and least of all why the empress dowager was sending him snacks every day. He curled up on the dragon throne as if this was all merely a dream.

"Is His Majesty ill?" Xiao Chiye, on his way to answer a summons, entered the palace and ran straight into an imperial physician outside Mingli Hall.

"His mind is plagued with worry, and the autumn chill has gotten to him," the physician said. "When you see His Majesty, you must counsel him, my lord."

Xiao Chiye set Wolfsfang aside before striding into Mingli Hall.

Li Jianheng had just taken some medicine and was staring into space on his settee. On hearing that Xiao Chiye had come, he hurriedly slipped on his shoes and called him in.

"Ce'an," Li Jianheng said, "you're just in time. The bakery will be sending some silk-nested tiger's eye candy later. You should try it too; we had it at that official's banquet a few years ago."

Xiao Chiye kowtowed. "Thank you, Your Majesty, for the gift."

His emperor's robes draped around him, Li Jianheng went silent for a moment. "Take a seat, Ce'an."

Xiao Chiye sat, and those serving at the sides of the hall withdrew. Li Jianheng stood and restlessly turned in several tight circles on the spot. "Ce'an, why aren't they beheading Hua Siqian yet? The Court of Judicial Review is talking about a retrial—what more is there to try? Ugh!"

"The Court of Judicial Review has to triple-check every case," Xiao Chiye explained patiently. "This is the rule to prevent miscarriage of justice. The evidence against Hua Siqian is conclusive. No doubt he will be executed before the new year."

"A long night is fraught with dreams—drag something on long enough, and complications arise," Li Jianheng said nervously. "The empress dowager doesn't look like she's panicking to me. Did you know, she sends people to deliver snacks to me every day. What does she want? Does she plan to poison me to death?"

"The Hua Clan is the target of public condemnation, so the empress dowager is putting on a show of maternal affection." Seeing Li Jianheng's flustered expression and the dark circles under his eyes, Xiao Chiye asked, "Is Your Majesty not sleeping well?"

"How can I sleep?" said Li Jianheng. "As long as they live, how would I be able to sleep? Ce'an, how about this—why don't you go tell Hai Liangyi on my behalf to skip the retrial and carry out the execution on the spot!"

But how could he do such a thing? Xiao Chiye was the supreme commander of the Imperial Army. He had no involvement with the Three Judicial Offices, so how could he interfere in the judicial process? Moreover, after what happened at the Autumn Hunt, the person who posed the next greatest danger was Xiao Chiye himself. The civil officials, with Hai Liangyi at the helm, were unwilling to let Xiao Chiye go. Even Xiao Fangxu had gotten wind of this attitude in the past days.

No one was willing to gamble when it came to this matter. Only with Xiao Chiye safe in Qudu could Libei be counted on. The plight of the six prefectures of Zhongbo remained a sore spot. Xiao Jiming could save Qudu once or twice, but could he save Qudu countless times without reservation? Even if he swore he would, who would believe it?

Xiao Chiye ought definitely to avoid any disputes with ministers at this point.

Even as Li Jianheng said it, he knew it wouldn't work. He became more dispirited by the minute. When the silk-nested tiger's eye candy finally arrived, he took a few cursory bites but tasted nothing.

After Xiao Chiye left, Li Jianheng lay sprawled across the settee, thinking what a rotten deal it was to be an emperor.

Shuanglu, a eunuch who had served him since he ascended the throne, knelt at his feet and whispered, "Your Majesty, how about this lowly one accompanies you for a stroll outside?"

"Not going," Li Jianheng replied. "We're tired."

The eunuch suddenly seized upon an idea. "Then why not invite Miss Mu Ru to play the pipa?"

Li Jianheng turned over and glanced toward the open doors of the hall. Seeing no one, he asked, hesitant, "Seems inappropriate, no? The nation is officially in mourning. Besides, she's still in Pan Rugui's manor. Wouldn't we be reproached for bringing her into the palace right now?"

Shuanglu giggled. "Your Majesty, you are the *emperor*. You have the final say within the palace. How would those outside officials know what we in the inner palace are up to? We'll do it on the sly."

Li Jianheng instantly felt his spirits soar. He set aside the candy and asked, "Secretariat Elder Hai won't know?"

"No one will know." Shuanglu shuffled forward on his knees. "You are our master, not him. When we lowly servants run errands, if Your Majesty doesn't want someone to know about them, they will certainly never know."

"Great!" Li Jianheng clapped his hands. "Great! Finally, an opportunity. Go quickly, the sooner the better. Bring Mu Ru in. Since Pan Rugui is about to die, remaining in that compound will only bring her bad luck!"

It was raining again when Xiao Chiye left the palace. He was vexed, though he couldn't say why. The zeal and drive he had before the Autumn Hunt seemed to have dissipated overnight; he didn't even feel like drawing his blade.

Chen Yang and Zhao Hui had come to pick him up, and Xiao Chiye stepped through the rain and into the carriage. Halfway through the journey, Xiao Chiye abruptly lifted the curtain and said, "Tell my father and brother I won't be back tonight."

Without waiting for a response, he jumped out of the carriage and headed for Donglong Street, taking nothing with him.

Zhao Hui got off the carriage behind him. "He's gone drinking again," he told Chen Yang. "You head back and inform the prince and heir. I'll follow him. It won't look good if he gets drunk and makes a scene during a time of national mourning."

"In the time it took you to say that, you lost him," Chen Yang said. "His Excellency doesn't want anyone to follow; you had best let him be."

Xiao Jiming had mentored Zhao Hui as his deputy general, while Xiao Chiye had trained Chen Yang to be his. Perhaps it was no surprise that Zhao Hui was more like an older brother. Though both were members of the Xiao Clan, the subjects of their consideration were ultimately different. Zhao Hui turned, and sure enough, the rain had already washed away any sign of Xiao Chiye.

The Embroidered Uniform Guard, having had their authority tokens revoked, were all temporarily assigned to the Imperial Army to serve on patrols. Shen Zechuan had just finished his rounds for the night and was walking home through the alley behind Xiangyun Villa on Donglong Street. The rain was coming down in a light drizzle, and he hadn't bothered to open his umbrella.

From up ahead, he suddenly heard the sound of retching. A courtesan wearing wooden clogs and no socks trotted out in pursuit and was gently fended off by the man bent over in the alley.

Xiao Chiye propped himself against the wall and pointed at the back door, motioning for the woman to stay back. The courtesans of Xiangyun Villa were well-acquainted with his habits. She knew he wouldn't let others touch him while drunk, so she merely folded a handkerchief and laid it at the side. "Come back in once you feel better, Er-gongzi. I'll prepare some hot soup for you," she said quietly.

Xiao Chiye did not respond. When the sound of wooden clogs had receded into the distance, he squatted down. His stomach was churning unbearably. This was how a man should live—eat, drink, and make merry until you fell into a stupor. It was his only way out.

He felt a sudden weight on his back.

Xiao Chiye looked over his shoulder with a stare so cold it froze the blood. On seeing who had touched him, he thought for a moment before saying, "Why did you kick me?"

"I didn't," Shen Zechuan replied without blinking.

Xiao Chiye reached behind and touched his own back, then tugged on his clothes. He insisted stubbornly, "This is evidence of your guilt!"

Shen Zechuan studied him. "Have you drunk yourself foolish, Xiao Er?"

"Do I look like a fool?" Xiao Chiye demanded. He answered himself without waiting for a reply. "I'm not a fool."

Smelling the wine on him, Shen Zechuan said, "Don't block my way. I want to go home."

Xiao Chiye looked away and stared blankly for a moment before saying to the wall, "Don't block *my* way. I want to go home too."

Shen Zechuan was about to laugh when he heard him continue.

"If I can't go home, then you can forget about going home as well."

FATE

"AH," SHEN ZECHUAN SAID.

That wasn't the response Xiao Chiye wanted; he looked back at him and asked, "Why aren't you arguing?"

Shen Zechuan opened his umbrella. "I have neither family nor friends back there. Why would I want to return?"

Xiao Chiye picked up the handkerchief and wiped rain off the back of his neck before rising. "Right. They already got rid of the Prince of Jianxing's manor in Dunzhou. Being who you are, you'll be cursed by the whole prefecture if you go back."

"In this life,"—here, Shen Zechuan looked at Xiao Chiye quietly for a moment—"you will suffer for being born into the wrong family."

Xiao Chiye didn't look at him as he brushed away raindrops on his forehead. "Then why are you still alive?"

Shen Zechuan smiled. "Millions of people want me dead, but how could I rest easy if I bowed to the wishes of others?"

"If you want to survive, you should've remained in the Temple of Guilt."

Taking two steps to avoid the puddle on the ground, Shen Zechuan answered, "If I remained there, you would still try to see me executed. Xiao Chiye, even if you try to hide it, you are used to looking down from above. You are no different from the people who look down on you today, though all those eyes must agonize you."

He laughed and patted Xiao Chiye on the back. "I seek to live. You seek to die. The Xiao Clan once trapped me, and now the Li family does the same to you. Are not the ways of this world strange? The bird in the cage longs for its former woods, while the fish in the pond misses its familiar deep.[22] Your lot in life has been laid out from the beginning. If you can't go home, you are nothing but a husk, with nothing but hollow aspirations. The most devastating thing in the world is to train a wolf into a dog. How long can your fangs remain sharp in Qudu?"

Xiao Chiye turned to look at him. "You followed me during the Autumn Hunt and saved my life, what, all for this moment of gratification?"

"I am an insignificant nobody," Shen Zechuan said softly. "Even if I didn't show up, you would have survived."

"What are you up to?" Xiao Chiye's inebriation had worn off.

"Repaying a debt of gratitude." They stood so close that the brim of Shen Zechuan's umbrella sheltered Xiao Chiye. "Repaying all of you for your mercy in not killing me."

Xiao Chiye suddenly grabbed Shen Zechuan by the collar. "I thought you had repented and turned over a new leaf."

"What have I done wrong?" The glint in Shen Zechuan's eyes was chillier than the autumn rain. He closed in, almost pressing up against Xiao Chiye, and asked, "What is my crime?"

"Did you not spare a look at the cities of Duanzhou when you climbed your way out of the Chashi Sinkhole?" Xiao Chiye tightened his grip. "The eight cities were massacred. When our horses galloped through the city gates, the blood that splashed under their hooves was the blood of the people."

---

22 *From the poem "Return to Nature (or the Fields) Part 1" by Tao Yuanming, also known as the Poet of the Fields.*

"Shen Wei's troops were defeated." Shen Zechuan at last tore off his mask, exposing his burning hatred. "Thirty thousand men of Zhongbo were buried in the Chashi Sinkhole! I lost my elder brother and shiniang that same day! Why am I to blame?"

"Shen Wei deserved to be killed!" Xiao Chiye, too, had lost control; he shoved Shen Zechuan backward. "Shen Wei deserved death! You are a Shen! How can you be without blame?!"

The oil-paper umbrella tumbled to the ground as Shen Zechuan was slammed against the wall in Xiao Chiye's grip, his toes barely touching the ground. He drew his knee in and stomped on Xiao Chiye's chest. Xiao Chiye retreated a few steps in pain but didn't loosen his hold. Pulling Shen Zechuan by the collar, he flung him to the ground.

The drizzle quickly intensified into a downpour. A series of crashes rang out from the dark lane as odds and ends were overturned and trampled underfoot. Inside Xiangyun Villa, the commotion startled the courtesans who had been waiting for Xiao Chiye. They clung to the doorframe and peered out with their wooden clogs in their hands.

"What's all this?!" Xiangyun, the madam of the house, hastily draped a robe over her shoulders and slipped on her wooden clogs before rushing over. "My dear lords! Let's have a civilized discussion! This isn't worth coming to blows over!"

Shen Zechuan straddled Xiao Chiye and landed a punch that knocked his head to the side. Xiao Chiye grabbed Shen Zechuan's wrist and tugged him hard toward himself. Running his tongue over bloody teeth, he said, "Neither you nor I can dream of having an easy time!"

Xiangyun had already called for her attendants, who joined forces to drag the two apart. Xiao Chiye jerked his arms free, and those strapping footmen felt their hands go numb. Yet he did not pounce again. He wiped his fingers over the broken skin on his face and snapped, "Piss off."

Xiangyun saw things had gotten out of hand; with quick motions, she instructed the footmen to hurry to the prince's manor for help. But before they could move, Xiao Chiye said, "I'll break the legs of whoever dares to alert my father!"

Xiangyun followed his lead and softened her voice. "What's this about, then? Er-gongzi has always shown tenderness toward the fairer sex. Why have you frightened the ladies tonight? It is common for gentlemen to disagree after a few drinks. Let's bury the hatchet with a smile, all right?"

Xiao Chiye rose to his feet, stripped off his dirty outer robe, and threw it to Xiangyun. "You go in."

Clutching the robe, Xiangyun attempted again to persuade him, "Er-gongzi, it's so cold outside..." But her voice trailed off as her courage waned. She waved her hand discreetly at the courtesans and led them back inside. The door was left slightly ajar, and girls clung to its side and crowded at the windows to steal a peek.

Shen Zechuan picked up the umbrella. His clothes were filthy. Strands of dark hair, wet from the rain, stuck to his cheeks and made his fair skin look all the paler.

"Next time," Shen Zechuan said, "come to my door if you're looking for me. I won't pass through this alley again, even in eight hundred years."

"If I knew you'd be passing by," Xiao Chiye retorted, "I'd rather have puked inside than come out here."

Shen Zechuan smirked. "It must really be a small world for enemies to meet on such a narrow path."

"When two meet on a narrow path, the best man triumphs."

Xiao Chiye took a step up to him. "I'll be watching you closely from now on."

"You can hardly look after yourself, yet you still find time to worry about me?" Shen Zechuan raised his umbrella to put some distance between them. "An insect with a hundred legs won't fall even in death. One Autumn Hunt and you think you've brought the Hua Clan to their knees? You really are delusional."

"You had best think about preserving your own life." Xiao Chiye pressed his chest against the edge of the umbrella and looked skeptically at him. "How long can you live without the backing of the empress dowager?"

"A new master sits in the imperial court," Shen Zechuan said. "Isn't it time to change these old assumptions of who holds the power?"

"But you can't kill anyone," Xiao Chiye said. "The ones who've wronged you are the Biansha Horsemen and Shen Wei."

"Whatever you say." Shen Zechuan once again let the veneer of docility settle over him like a coat. He drew his umbrella back and said gently to Xiao Chiye, "I'll listen to you, okay?"

That inscrutable rage within Xiao Chiye surged. "Sure you will. Then you're staying with me tonight."

"You sleep under the bed canopy of a sweet, tender lady," Shen Zechuan said, "yet you want to share it with another man? I'm sorry, but I don't have that kind of predilection."

No matter how Xiao Chiye looked at Shen Zechuan, this man was up to no good. "So you're running now? What happened to *whatever I say*?!"

"Are you," Shen Zechuan pointed at his head, "out of your mind?"

"All the idlers in the Embroidered Uniform Guard are under command of the Imperial Army," Xiao Chiye reminded him. "Who's the one out of his mind?"

Shen Zechuan paused for a moment before responding. "What would *Your Excellency* like me to do?"

The red imprint of Shen Zechuan's fist was still stark on Xiao Chiye's cheek. The hostility between his brows eased, and he took on the countenance of a lazy slacker. He turned to sit on the platform beneath the eaves and pointed to his boots.

The corners of Shen Zechuan's lips curled. "Sure."

Early the next morning, when Chen Yang came to retrieve Xiao Chiye, he was stunned to see Shen Zechuan hugging Wolfsfang at the entrance of Xiangyun Villa on Donglong Street.

Shen Zechuan, who had been leaning against the door, straightened and bowed a greeting toward Chen Yang.

Chen Yang instantly had a bad feeling. "Shen—what is the Scarlet Cavalry doing here?"

"Ji Lei remains in prison and has not yet been sentenced," Shen Zechuan said. "The Embroidered Uniform Guard is temporarily serving as part of the Imperial Army under the supreme commander's orders."

Taking in his calm mien, Chen Yang felt a chill down his spine. He dipped his chin in a slight nod and bounded up the stairs. Shen Zechuan watched him go up. At the same time, Xiangyun was coming down with the hem of her skirt in her hand.

"You haven't eaten yet, right?" she asked sympathetically. "You haven't changed out of those dirty clothes of yours either. Ling Ting—"

A woman upstairs leaned against the railing and said wearily, "Why are you still calling for Ling Ting? That girl's already paid her debt and been redeemed."

It dawned on Xiangyun as she spoke. "Well, I've gotten used to calling for her! Bring some food for this gentleman from the Scarlet Cavalry."

Upstairs, Xiao Chiye was sprawled on the settee, sleeping, with no one to attend him. Chen Yang entered and called softly, "My lord?"

Xiao Chiye groggily buried his face in the blanket and dozed a moment longer. Then he suddenly sat up. "Why are you here? Where is Shen Lanzhou?"

"He's keeping watch downstairs—Your Excellency, what happened to your face?" Chen Yang asked in astonishment.

"Got punched while I was hunting." Xiao Chiye stood and stretched his shoulders and arms. "Did Dage ask you to come for me?"

"It was His Lordship the Prince," Chen Yang clarified. "We received information early this morning. Biansha Horsemen raided the Shaqiu Trade Market last night. We need to enter the palace to discuss this matter in detail. Secretariat Elder Hai has convened the Ministry of War and the Ministry of Revenue. Libei will have to deploy troops again."

Xiao Chiye gave his face a cursory wipe with some water and stepped out the door. As he descended the stairs, he saw Shen Zechuan standing with a courtesan. He strode down the last few steps and reached over them to grab a small plate, then tossed a pastry into his mouth.

Shen Zechuan looked up. "Slow down. No one can save you if you choke."

Xiao Chiye swallowed the mouthful and grinned at him. Slinging an arm around his shoulder, he led him outside. "Oh, Lanzhou..."

Shen Zechuan stared at him.

"Why do you hold a grudge overnight?" Xiao Chiye asked wistfully. "After a good night's sleep, I've forgotten all about it. Come on. Er-gongzi will take you to have some fun."

Shen Zechuan swatted Xiao Chiye's hand away with his own scabbard. "Er-gongzi, don't take advantage to touch the back of my neck."

Mingli Hall was full.

Li Jianheng remained seated on the dragon throne, not daring to move a muscle. His eyes landed first on Hai Liangyi in an attempt to scrutinize his expression before shifting to the others, all the while doing his best to look dignified and imposing.

"Seeing as the Director of Writ at the Directorate of Ceremonial Affairs's position is vacant, before signing off on them, this aged subject will present the various ministries' accounts directly to His Majesty once they are sent to the Grand Secretariat," Hai Liangyi began. "What does Your Majesty think of the accounts from last night?"

Li Jianheng had spent the night listening to pipa music with a beautiful woman in his arms. When Hai Liangyi kowtowed to him, he shifted his buttocks guiltily and said, "They look good, it's all good!"

Xue Xiuzhuo, who had been kneeling expressionlessly behind Hai Liangyi, furrowed his brow.

Hai Liangyi waited, but when it was clear Li Jianheng had no intention of saying anything further, he turned to Xiao Fangxu. "This autumn is cold, and the frost comes apace. If Libei is to deploy troops, they must report to Qudu the military salaries and provisions required in advance. Your Lordship, how much do you need this time?"

Xiao Fangxu smiled. "I have been ill and out of commission for quite a while. All military affairs have long since been entrusted to Jiming. Jiming, tell Secretariat Elder Hai what money we lack."

Xiao Jiming kowtowed. "The Biansha tribes raided the market now because winter snow is about to fall. The various tribes have exhausted their stores of grain, so they plunder the trade market. In prior years, the military fields were sufficient to furnish our provisions, and Libei would not need assistance with army supplies. But with the late emperor so recently passed, the Biansha tribes are likely planning to take advantage of our vulnerability. If we mobilize troops, we must not only expel them from our territory but be prepared to guard the border for as long as it takes. I have already submitted the required sum to the Ministry of Revenue."

The newly appointed Minister of Revenue produced the memorial, and Shuanglu presented it to Li Jianheng.

Li Jianheng looked at it for a moment. "One million two hundred thousand taels. What's so hard about that? What's important is that our soldiers don't go cold and hungry."

The Minister of Revenue, Qian Jin, looked embarrassed. "Your Majesty may not be aware, but...we have yet to make up for last year's deficit. The state treasury cannot make that sum available on such short notice."

"Then," Li Jianheng said, "just one million taels should be fine, right?"

Qian Jin kowtowed. "During the Autumn Hunt, the mobilization of the Eight Great Battalions cost us two hundred and thirty thousand taels, and the late emperor's funeral rites...required five hundred and forty thousand taels. The remaining funds in the state treasury must be used to pay out salary arrears to the officials in Qudu. The end of the year will soon be upon us, and the civil officials all need to celebrate New Year's. We definitely do not have one million taels, Your Majesty. We have but six hundred thousand taels to give the Libei Armored Cavalry."

Li Jianheng truly never expected to be poor as an emperor. He had wanted to do Libei a favor, and in doing so placate Xiao Chiye. Who would have thought he would be so broke? This sudden revelation put him in such an awkward spot he wanted to dig his way under the table. Instead, he mustered a few vague sounds of acknowledgment.

A hush fell over Mingli Hall.

It was Xue Xiuzhuo who spoke up. "Your Majesty, this humble subject has a suggestion."

Li Jianheng looked at this man as though he was seeing his savior. "Speak. Please speak."

"When the Hua faction was in power, they put a price on sinecures and welcomed anyone who could pay up," Xue Xiuzhuo began. "The 'ice respects' bribes they collected every year were large sums. And Pan Rugui took advantage of loopholes in procurement to blatantly amass wealth for himself. Both men are now in prison. Why not search both the Hua and Pan residences and confiscate their possessions to subsidize this military effort? As for the Xi Clan, their second young master, Xi Hongxuan, has already made what amends he could and submitted a report to the Court of Judicial Review just yesterday to accuse Xi Gu'an of keeping his own private army. He even leased out the Xi Clan's residence in Qudu to repay the money that went missing within the Eight Great Battalions while Xi Gu'an was in office."

When Li Jianheng heard this idea of raiding the residences, he instantly showed interest. He said, eager, "Sure! I—we've long been wanting to do this!"

Hai Liangyi hesitated. "This would be inappropriate. The Court of Judicial Review's retrial has not yet concluded. How can we bypass the law to mete out the sentence?"

"It's an emergency," Xue Xiuzhuo countered. "We don't have a choice. Qudu may wait for the retrial, but the Biansha Horsemen will not. We cannot let the Libei Armored Cavalry fight a war on empty stomachs."

Hai Liangyi still wavered, but Li Jianheng had already given his approval. When they finally left the hall, Xiao Jiming asked Qi Zhuyin, who had been silent the whole time, "How is the Bianjun Commandery holding up?"

Qi Zhuyin looked up at the rain beyond the eaves. "As long as Lu Guangbai is in Bianjun, the Biansha tribes will not make a move there. But Libei is lacking a chief commander, which makes things tricky for you."

Xiao Jiming stood for a moment and sighed. "Talent on the field is hard to come by."

"Regardless of what passes in Qudu, it's the duty of commanders and generals to protect their home and defend their country," Qi Zhuyin said. "Jiming, talent is hard to come by, but it is even more difficult to cultivate. Libei is an important fortress guarding our Great Zhou's frontier—it needs a successor. It will only damage you to hold off on your choice any longer."

Each and every one of them had aspired to be a valiant general of the land, an impregnable fortress of the Zhou empire. But even generals would eventually age. Tethering the lives of an army to one man could be overlooked for a few years, but let it continue for a decade, or worse, several, and the Libei Armored Cavalry would turn into a force that could not go on without Xiao Jiming.

If the Libei Armored Cavalry were to lose Xiao Jiming one day with no clear successor to the command, what would become of this army and its sterling reputation that had reigned supreme on the battlefield for decades?

"I know you have high hopes for A-Ye." Qi Zhuyin descended the steps and turned back to look at him. "But he is destined never to fly out of Qudu. Do you think he hasn't noticed the regard you hold for him all these years just because you never spoke of it? The more expectations you have for him at home, the more agony he'll be in. Libei is not his wings, but his cage. Jiming, you and I have been friends for many years. Let me give you a word of advice: choose someone else."

KING OF WOLVES

IN THE LIGHT OF MORNING, Xiao Chiye seemed to have put his loss of composure the night before completely out of his mind. He raced his horse through the streets to cries of discontent from vendors on either side and reached the palace gate just in time to see his family's carriage still outside.

"Er-gongzi is here." Zhao Hui lifted the curtain for Xiao Fangxu.

Resting a hand on his knee, Xiao Fangxu looked out of the carriage. His gaze swept past his younger son and landed on the man riding poorly behind him—Shen Zechuan. He paused for a moment but said nothing.

When Xiao Chiye arrived before him, he noticed the injury on his son's face at once. "What were you up to last night?"

"I went drinking." Riding crop in hand, Xiao Chiye reined in his horse and laughed. "I lost track of time. When I woke up, it was already late. Father, are you done with the meeting?"

Xiao Fangxu nodded. "Is that Shen Wei's son?"

The autumn wind blew sharply in Shen Zechuan's face. He met Xiao Fangxu's eyes and was gripped by an inexplicable shudder. Shen Zechuan tightened his grip on the reins uneasily.

But Xiao Fangxu did nothing.

Powdery white mixed with dark at the temples of the old King of Wolves. Though he sat hunched in the carriage, one could make out his exceptional height and build. His commanding presence was no false front; this was a majestic dignity tempered amid a mountain of corpses and a sea of blood. It was a formidable strength, embedded so deeply in blood and bone that even his recent illness could not overshadow it.

Xiao Chiye's extraordinary physique was familiar now; his shocking upper body strength, remarkable height, wide shoulders and back, and long legs with their explosive speed—all were bequeathed entirely by his father. In contrast to the gentler and more elegant Xiao Jiming, Xiao Chiye was the true wolf pup. One had only to look at the two brothers standing together to banish all doubt that Xiao Chiye was the more threatening presence.

And now, this King of Wolves had his gaze fixed upon Shen Zechuan. Despite having learned long ago to suppress his emotions, Shen Zechuan felt a powerful urge to flee. The feeling was utterly different from being pinned down by Xiao Chiye. This man's gaze made one shiver by sheer instinct. At once, Shen Zechuan recalled Grand Mentor Qi's words:

"Now that Xiao Fangxu has stepped back to convalesce, his heir's star shines bright—everyone fears Xiao Jiming. But Lanzhou, twenty years ago, the one who secured that frontier with his steed was Xiao Fangxu. Today, Qi Shiyu's authority as the grand marshal of the five commanderies is clearly greater than Xiao Fangxu's—but he has not been conferred the title of prince. I will tell you why: Qidong is merely a bestowed fief belonging to the emperor. The five commanderies are all founding lands of our Great Zhou that belong to the Son of Heaven. But Libei is different. The vast territory of Libei stretches from Luoxia Pass to the edge of Hongyan Mountains in the northeast. All this hard-won land was conquered inch by inch by the Libei Armored Cavalry under Xiao Fangxu's personal command during the years of Yongyi.

"Xiao Jiming is now the commander in chief of Libei's Armored Cavalry. *Iron Horse on River Ice*—an awe-inspiring title! But it was Xiao Fangxu who established this unstoppable cavalry. The Libei troops do not have the long history of the Bianjun Commandery Garrison Troops. They are a heavy cavalry conceived by Xiao Fangxu to counter our foes during the years of Yongyi, when the Biansha Horsemen repeatedly assaulted Luoxia Pass. Libei's battle steeds, Libei's soldiers, and Libei's steel broadswords with their trailing chains—every emblem of the current Libei Armored Cavalry originated with Xiao Fangxu.

"The Eight Great Clans have entrenched themselves in Qudu for decades. They are sores and ulcers on the body of our Great Zhou. The Xiao Clan can stand as equals with the Hua Clan only because of Xiao Fangxu's firm seat in Libei. As long as Xiao Fangxu lives, the Xiao Clan is a towering tree, its roots digging deep into the soil of Libei. The title of the King of Wolves is by no means undeserved."

Xiao Chiye looked back at Shen Zechuan and said after a pause, "He is Shen Wei's son."

Shen Zechuan dismounted and knelt to Xiao Fangxu.

Xiao Fangxu appraised him for a moment. "Shen Wei is dead. Since the late emperor released you, he absolved you of your father's guilt. You are innocent and free. So why are you following *this* brat around?"

With one knee bent and his head bowed, Shen Zechuan said, "This humble one was taken into the Embroidered Uniform Guard. It is temporarily under the command of the Imperial Army, and I am thus at the supreme commander's disposal."

"So I see." Xiao Fangxu looked toward Xiao Chiye. "Why are you making life difficult for him?"

Xiao Chiye licked at the wound in his mouth. "Why would I do such a thing? We're friends who've faced death together. Isn't that right, Lanzhou?"

Apparently satisfied, Xiao Fangxu continued chatting with Xiao Chiye without sparing Shen Zechuan another glance.

Shen Zechuan remained on one knee. He saw, reflected in a puddle on the ground, Xiao Chiye's unrestrained smile, and the way Xiao Fangxu looked at his son. Raindrops distorted the scene in the puddle. Shen Zechuan averted his eyes.

Xiao Fangxu had left by the time Xiao Jiming emerged from within the palace, Qi Zhuyin beside him. "Who's that?" she asked abruptly.

Xiao Jiming looked at the man standing beside Zhao Hui and replied, expression unchanging, "That's Shen Zechuan."

Stopping in her tracks, Qi Zhuyin blurted, "Shen Wei's son? Why is he following *A-Ye* around?"

"A-Ye has a mischievous streak," Xiao Jiming said. "He's probably just harassing him."

Qi Zhuyin eyed Shen Zechuan for a long moment. "A remarkable beauty. I heard his mother was a dancer in Duanzhou. Lucky for us it was Duanzhou and not the Cangjun Commandery."

Grand Marshal Qi Shiyu was famously fond of beauties; he wouldn't budge an inch when a pretty woman was in sight. Her father kept countless concubines at home, though Qi Zhuyin had very few brothers to show for it.

"Speaking of which." Qi Zhuyin turned aside. "A-Ye is twenty-three this year. When is he going to get married?"

"Yizhi is also getting anxious about that," Xiao Jiming said. "Libei doesn't need him to marry a noble lady from a powerful clan; a girl from an ordinary, decent family will do. Yizhi's sent portraits to

Qudu every year, but not one of the Libei daughters she picked ever caught his fancy."

Qi Zhuyin laughed. "Noble girls are too haughty to tolerate him, and common girls are too timid—they'd be frightened at the sight of him. Besides, how many maidens can handle his temper? Finding someone he likes who would like him back is harder than ascending to heaven. Not to mention he spends half his nights in pleasure houses. You'd better watch it, or he'll bring a courtesan home one day."

Xiao Jiming knew every one of her stepmothers had been prominent courtesans in Qidong before marrying her father; they quarreled in the inner courtyards all day long and drove the grand marshal mad every time she went home. She'd detested courtesans since youth.

"If he really meets someone he fancies, who can stop him?" Xiao Jiming sighed; just the thought of it made his head ache. "Not even ten bulls would be able to haul him away."

"You'd better prepare for rainy days." Qi Zhuyin thought about it for a moment. "Disregard the rest if you want, but really, the girl can't have a fiery temper. Your Yizhi is so gentle. If he brings home someone fierce, wouldn't Yizhi suffer every day?"

Xiao Jiming laughed out loud. "This is all just talk. It's much too early to worry about that."

"The heart is an unpredictable thing." Qi Zhuyin laughed too. "Perhaps someday he'll see the light?"

Xiao Chiye felt a shiver down his spine. He threw a wary glance over his shoulder and saw Shen Zechuan looking contemplative beside Zhao Hui.

"Go to the Imperial Army office later and collect your token of authority." Xiao Chiye stepped in front of Shen Zechuan, blocking the light. "Until the reassignment of the Embroidered Uniform Guard is finalized, you'll attend me day and night."

"Day and night," Shen Zechuan repeated and looked up at him. "Will I have to carry the chamber pot for Er-gongzi too?"

"If you want to, sure." Xiao Chiye stepped closer. "I'll be busy for the next few days, so I'll stay in the courtyard behind the Imperial Army office." Without waiting for an answer, Xiao Chiye turned to greet Xiao Jiming.

The retrial in the Court of Judicial Review still hadn't concluded by the time the Hua and Pan residences were searched and their assets seized. Li Jianheng took the opportunity to bar access to the Enci Palace, where the empress dowager resided, on grounds that she was "troubled by worries to the point of anxiety."

After much difficulty, sufficient funds were gathered to make up Libei's military salaries and provisions, though Xiao Jiming's original number had been humbly rounded down. Xiao Fangxu and Xiao Jiming could not tarry, and set out for the frontier a few days later.

Unexpectedly, Xiao Chiye did not look reluctant to part with them. It was as if after that drunken night, he'd abandoned all the focus and ambition he'd possessed during the Autumn Hunt. From time to time, Li Jianheng would bestow rewards upon him, and he would accept them graciously.

On top of that, he started to loaf on the job. The Imperial Army had originally been assigned the important task of conducting city patrols, but Xiao Chiye worked in fits and starts like the fisherman who fished for three days and rested for two. There was often no sign of him when he was sought out. Murmurs of doubt gradually swelled in the Ministry of War, and many expressed an inclination to have him replaced.

But Li Jianheng vociferously refused, going so far as to throw a tantrum and threaten to fall out with the Vice Minister of the Ministry of War who had presented the petition. Flinging away the memorial, he fumed, "Xiao Ce'an has shown true valor in coming to our rescue. How does he not deserve to be supreme commander of the Imperial Army? He's not made any mistakes. We won't hear of replacing him!"

And so it was that the two of them reverted to the easy camaraderie they'd shared before the Autumn Hunt, and Li Jianheng felt a little more at ease. The Xiao Chiye of that night was like a figment of his imagination, while this young man without an ounce of decorum was his familiar friend.

Li Jianheng was additionally relieved Xiao Chiye made no mention of returning to Libei. He believed this was his friend's way of showing consideration for his constraints—after all, there was really nothing he could do. And couldn't Xiao Chiye have plenty of fun right here in Qudu? Now that Li Jianheng had become the emperor, his good friend Xiao Chiye could throw his weight around as he pleased. Why return to Libei? How could that bitter land be as comfortable and carefree as the capital?

When Xiao Chiye wanted to head out of the city to run his horse, Li Jianheng approved it. When Xiao Chiye wanted to expand the Imperial Army office, Li Jianheng approved it. And when Xiao Chiye wanted to be on duty for half a day and laze at home the other half, Li Jianheng not only approved it, he approved it with great delight.

The two of them often rode horses and played polo together. Perhaps Li Jianheng couldn't fool around on Donglong Street anymore, but he could invite Xiao Chiye to listen to the pipa in the palace with him. The young lady Mu Ru had taken up permanent residence in Mingli Hall. Li Jianheng had feared at first that Xiao Chiye would disapprove, but his friend said nothing and merely enjoyed the merriment.

It felt so fucking good to be emperor!

As the last autumn rain washed the roofs of Qudu, the Court of Judicial Review sentenced Xi Gu'an to execution by beheading. Xi Hongxuan, his younger brother, had done what he could to make amends by distributing his clan's wealth; for this, he earned a place in Li Jianheng's good graces and was transferred to the Ministry of Revenue, where he took up a modest position. Xi Hongxuan had always been an expert organizer of frivolities, which was exactly to Li Jianheng's taste. He would go looking for the emperor every day with new ideas for a good time.

Not long after Xi Gu'an was sentenced, Hua Siqian committed suicide in prison by biting off his tongue. He left behind a written confession in which he shouldered all responsibility for his crimes and did not implicate the empress dowager in the slightest. This left only Ji Lei and Pan Rugui yet to be sentenced. Hai Liangyi had dearly wished to pry a confession from their mouths, but he never succeeded.

It was damp in the little house when Shen Zechuan returned home. The moment he opened the door, he saw the eastern pearl waiting on the table. He closed the door quickly behind him and had only just picked it up when he heard Chen Yang knocking.

He opened the door, and Chen Yang said, "The supreme commander is calling for you."

Shen Zechuan curled his fingers around the eastern pearl. The strip of cloth it came wrapped in was rain-soaked. "I'll go after I change my clothes," he said evenly.

"Don't bother," Chen Yang said. "Just go as you are; His Excellency doesn't like to wait." He stepped aside, ready to leave together. Shen

Zechuan could do nothing but let his hand drop to his side and stride out the door with Chen Yang.

They found Xiao Chiye with a heavy overcoat on. When he saw Shen Zechuan, he said, "Take my sword and come with me."

Shen Zechuan followed him out. It was only when Xiao Chiye led his horse over himself that Shen Zechuan realized Chen Yang was gone.

As Xiao Chiye mounted his horse, the gyrfalcon shook droplets off his neck and landed on his master's shoulder. Shen Zechuan followed him out of the city; they braved the rain and headed for the drill grounds at Mount Feng.

There was hardly anyone there when they arrived. Xiao Chiye removed Snowcrest's bridle and gave it a pat as permission to run freely around the grounds. Meng glided under the eaves of the walkway, unwilling to stay in the rain.

Halfway through taking off his overcoat, Xiao Chiye turned to Shen Zechuan. "Take your clothes off."

Holding Xiao Chiye's sword in his arms, Shen Zechuan raised his chin high. Water trickled down his collar, exposing his fair, delicate neck. Every time Xiao Chiye looked at that neck, he felt like someone seeing a cat—he couldn't help but want to give it a few strokes.

What the hell was wrong with him?

Thus distracted, he shrugged off his damp outer layer. When he saw Shen Zechuan still standing there, he said again, "What are you waiting for? Hurry up and take your clothes off!"

Shen Zechuan's fingers hovered at his belt. He glanced at Xiao Chiye and said slowly, "If I take these off, there will be nothing left."

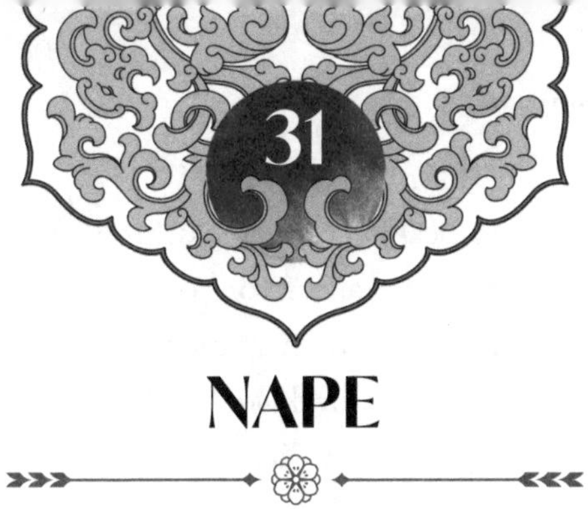

NAPE

"ALL THE MORE REASON for you to take them off."

Xiao Chiye removed his arm guards and set them on a wooden stand placed under the eaves along with his overcoat and outer robe. The soldiers in the inner hall of the compound approached in greeting, but he raised a hand to forestall them. He turned and gave Shen Zechuan a slow once-over. "I'd like to see with my own eyes how a body trained in the Ji mental cultivation techniques differs from mine."

"Seeing as we hail from the same martial lineage," Shen Zechuan said as he set Wolfsfang down, "our stances and moves will naturally be the same."

"Not necessarily," Xiao Chiye replied. "My shifu incorporated boxing techniques from other schools, so his style had already deviated greatly from Ji-Style Boxing by the time it was imparted to me. If our training were identical, you wouldn't have been totally oblivious when we fought before."

"If you want some pointers, say so." Shen Zechuan drew an arc on the ground with his foot. "All this about taking your clothes off just makes you sound like a beast."

For an instant, Xiao Chiye felt as though Shen Zechuan had turned into an entirely different person. The falling rain overlapped with the mist from the mountain, washing out Shen Zechuan's features and emphasizing his tall and slender figure.

"My wish is to be a beast in human clothing." Xiao Chiye strode down the steps and into the curtain of rain. "I almost killed you five years ago with that kick. Do you hate me for it?"

"If I say yes, would it not sound like I've been tossing and turning at night thinking of you?" Shen Zechuan said. "Nope. I don't hate you at all."

Xiao Chiye struck a starting stance. "Pity. If you did, today would be the chance for you to take your revenge." Facing into the biting cold wind, Xiao Chiye slowly added: "That is, if you can."

The raindrops drummed down; Meng hopped a few steps before spreading his wings on the veranda. Xiao Chiye sprang up in the rain to make his move.

His punch struck empty air as Shen Zechuan avoided his fist, but the unyielding strength of his blow sent water droplets spattering across Shen Zechuan's cheek. Xiao Chiye swept his fist to the left. Shen Zechuan reached up to block his blow, then frowned in pain and took a few steps back.

Ji-Style Boxing!

Shen Zechuan pressed his lips into a tight line, but in the next moment he laughed out loud. His shifu's boxing style was steady and robust. It was clear Xiao Er lacked somewhat in steadiness, but his ferociousness more than made up for it. His strength was astonishing—one impact had numbed Shen Zechuan's arm from the shoulder down.

Ji-Style Boxing was meant to be imparted to a man like Xiao Chiye; both his internal and external constitution were uniquely suited for it. He was privileged with a powerful physique that allowed him to hold all others in contempt—but was a mere advantage of birth, bestowed by the heavens, the true key to victory?

The last thing Shen Zechuan believed in was heaven's plans.

With one kick, he sent raindrops splashing toward Xiao Chiye. The sweep of his leg was quick and brutal. Any ordinary person would have weighed their chances and done whatever they could to avoid it, but Xiao Chiye met the challenge head-on. He raised his arm to block Shen Zechuan's leg with a heavy *thud*, then took one steady step forward.

It was too late for Shen Zechuan to retract his leg. Facing Xiao Chiye was like facing a tiger; this man was waiting for an opportunity. If his opponent showed any sign of weakness—a wavering heart, an evasive gaze, an avoidant stance—he would pounce. Forcing Xiao Chiye on the defensive was vastly preferable to letting him go on the offensive.

Leg still raised, Shen Zechuan bore down on Xiao Chiye's arm; the force slowed Xiao Chiye's forward motion slightly. In a fraction of a second, Xiao Chiye threw his arm up, flinging Shen Zechuan into the air. Shen Zechuan arced his body back, pushed off with both hands on the ground, then sprang up like a willow after a gust of wind. The moment he regained his balance, he swept his leg toward Xiao Chiye's head again.

Xiao Chiye once again brought his arm up to block the blow. His eyes were calm. "An ant trying to shake a tree. Should I scold you for not knowing what you're up against, or commend you for your courage?"

He reached around and grabbed Shen Zechuan's calf, dropping his shoulder as he attempted to slam Shen Zechuan to the ground. But having already been swung up, Shen Zechuan took advantage of his momentum to plant his foot on Xiao Chiye's shoulder. His astonishing waist strength came into play again as he got both legs around Xiao Chiye's neck and twisted with all his might, taking them to the ground together.

Xiao Chiye's hand slid up Shen Zechuan's leg and wrapped around his waist. The flesh under his palm was unbelievably supple and smooth.

It was true that he'd been trying to touch Shen Zechuan's body. He couldn't figure it out, as much as he tried. Whether it was Ji-Style Boxing or the Ji-Style Blade, any individual who trained in them year-round should have the muscle to show for it. But Shen Zechuan had not only concealed his strength so well he looked as if he'd never trained a day in martial arts, he'd also deceived both Chen Yang and Qiao Tianya into believing he was morbidly weak from a deficiency in qi and blood.

Shen Zechuan surged up and threw an elbow at Xiao Chiye's head. Bending his neck to dodge, Xiao Chiye held tight to Shen Zechuan's waist and pulled his back flush with his own body, feeling his way up from Shen Zechuan's waist to his chest.

The eastern pearl was still hidden in his lapels. Shen Zechuan slammed his back into Xiao Chiye, grabbed hold of his arm, and flung him over his shoulder into the rain.

The spray of water instantly drenched Shen Zechuan's hair.

Shen Zechuan made to retreat, but Xiao Chiye hooked one long leg out and sent Shen Zechuan tripping toward himself. Shen Zechuan was already starting to pitch over; at the last second, he trod upon the water and steadied himself, body swaying like the reverberations of the strings on a guqin.

Xiao Chiye leapt to his feet and threw himself forward. His next punch struck at empty air, but as Shen Zechuan spun to evade the blow, Xiao Chiye's hand brushed against a lock of inky hair that had fluttered up in the rain.

The rain-soaked lock slipped reluctantly past Xiao Chiye's fingertips, leaving them damp and tingling, as if wanting more.

"We're done here." Xiao Chiye suddenly clenched his fist and looked at Shen Zechuan. "The rain is getting heavier."

Shen Zechuan glanced back. "Are you done feeling me up?"

"Not soft, but not hard either," Xiao Chiye answered without batting an eyelash.

"I thought you were going to start tearing my clothes off." Shen Zechuan's tone was mocking.

"If that's what I was after," Xiao Chiye said, "we would certainly be baring more than our hearts to each other right now." He raised his other hand and waved a thin blade between his fingers—the same ones Shen Zechuan always carried. "The Ji mental cultivation techniques need to be paired with a proper saber. If you use these things every day, you'll never beat me in this lifetime. And if you can't beat me, how will you get your revenge?"

Shen Zechuan carried his thin blades strapped to the outside of his thighs. He glanced down, then looked back up at Xiao Chiye. "Fighting and killing will only cause strife. Wouldn't it be more fun to play the fool together?"

"I fear you're hiding a blade behind that smile, waiting to stab me when I'm least aware," Xiao Chiye said.

"The only blade is the one painted as a warning above the word *lust*."[23] Shen Zechuan spread his hands and shrugged. "Er-gongzi is a righteous man. What's there to fear?"

Xiao Chiye placed the thin blade in Shen Zechuan's palm and said lightly, "I've just said your Er-gongzi is a beast in human clothes. What makes you think I'm a righteous man?" Shen Zechuan was about to pull his hand away when Xiao Chiye caught him by the wrist. "Since you've been so good today, Er-gongzi will take you somewhere to relax."

---

23 *Refers to the radicals that make up the word 色, se (lust). ⺈ (a component form of 刀, which means blade) is written above 巴 to form the character 色.*

"Your Excellency," said Shen Zechuan, suddenly stern, "please, I'm not into men. Let's part on good terms with no hard feelings. Why are you pestering me?"

Xiao Chiye was momentarily dumbfounded. He glanced to the side and saw a crowd of soldiers from the Imperial Army clustered around the doors and windows of the inner hall, watching the show.

The vice commander of the Imperial Army, Tantai Hu, was the scar-faced man who had led his men to slaughter the Eight Great Battalions the other night. Leaning out the window, he took the lead to jeer, "You're fighting like a lecher taking liberties. What the hell, Your Excellency?! You never smile when you lecture us!"

"Pestering!" More soldiers winked meaningfully at each other and heckled, "How can we compete with someone he wants to *pester*?! The supreme commander is twenty-three now. He has no wife to dote on at home, so his energy must be spent on someone else. We can't compare!"

Sensing Shen Zechuan about to run, Xiao Chiye yanked him closer and flashed a shallow smile. "That's right. I love to pester. What are you running for, Lanzhou? I'm not done with you! You aren't into men because you've yet to taste the sweetness of a good one. Er-gongzi will teach you."

When it came to shamelessness, Xiao Chiye would only concede defeat to Li Jianheng. Did Shen Zechuan think to scare him with this act of being forced against his will? The man was belittling him with a cheap trick like this.

Xiao Chiye dragged Shen Zechuan off before he could make any more trouble.

Behind them, Tantai Hu stroked his scar and asked the soldier at his side, "Who is that man? I've never seen him in the Imperial Army before."

"His surname is Shen." The man beside him winked. "The one from Zhongbo."

Tantai Hu's smile instantly cooled. He braced himself on the windowsill to stick his head out again, then looked back. "The same fucking Shen Clan who brought Zhongbo to ruin? What's His Excellency doing with *him*?! Shen Wei caused the deaths of thousands. Eight of his heads aren't enough for us to cut off! The Prince of Jianxing's manor has been ransacked, yet this remnant eats and sleeps in comfort in Qudu. Orphans along the Chashi River are still gnawing on mud! Fuck this! Why didn't you say so earlier?!"

Xiao Chiye led Shen Zechuan up Mount Feng.

A narrow flight of stone steps had been carved into the mountainside. Water seeped through the soles of their shoes, chilling them to the bone, but Xiao Chiye did not look back. He parted branches of maple leaves dripping with rain and left the staircase for an out-of-the-way path. Their shoes sank into mud as they trekked through the trees on uneven steps.

Almost an hour later, Xiao Chiye finally stopped. The thatched cottage sitting in the mist was small and finely constructed, but it did not look like a place where people lived. He turned to Shen Zechuan. "You saved me once in the Nanlin Hunting Grounds. As a reward, I'll share half this place with you."

"The reward I seek is gold and silver," Shen Zechuan said. "Not a bath together."

"Money and fame are but worldly things." Xiao Chiye lifted the curtain to step inside. He stood near the entrance and began to strip, shouting back, "Not even the emperor has enjoyed this place."

Shen Zechuan lifted the curtain and saw Xiao Chiye's bare upper torso. The lines of his back and shoulders were sharp and sleek, as if carved out with a chisel. Other than a small clothing rack, the only thing in the cottage was a stretch of bare floor ending in a hot spring that was open to the mountain air. Xiao Chiye's clothes hung on one side of the rack. The other had clearly been reserved for him.

Xiao Chiye kicked off his boots and looked back at Shen Zechuan. "Do you want to turn your back to me and strip, or do you intend to strip while watching me?"

Pulling at his belt, Shen Zechuan turned around. The eastern pearl rolled into his palm, and he slipped it into the pocket of his sleeve. The eyes on his back never wavered. Shen Zechuan paused, then pulled off his outer robe.

As Xiao Chiye watched that garment slip to the floor, he finally saw how the fairness of Shen Zechuan's neck extended downward, like pear-blossom rice paper under moonlight. His back looked surpassingly fine and smooth.

Xiao Chiye thought: *Of course.*

It was as if he had been staring at Shen Zechuan's nape all this time, waiting for this moment. How could the back of a man's neck possess such breathtaking beauty? It was beyond anything Xiao Chiye had experienced in the past; it amazed and baffled him.

The fangs of the Libei wolf pup were sharp, but they had never bitten such a neck before; never such a man. His gaze slid down from the nape of Shen Zechuan's neck with an intensity that felt like a caress, moving farther and farther down the smooth curve of it, down his back.

Smooth.

Xiao Chiye's mouth was dry. With a jolt, he snapped back to his senses and averted his gaze.

I must be mad! he thought. All those ladies on Donglong Street, every one of them more beautiful than the last—so why was he looking at a man's back as though burning with thirst?

Xiao Chiye had always turned up his nose at men who were seduced by beautiful women; those he admired were men of resolute will. Every one of them was a righteous gentleman, untempted by lust even if it were to sit in his lap. Like his father, his brother, and his shifu.

Famous generals of the land came and went, but among them, he had never admired Qi Shiyu, precisely because of this man's lascivious habits. And after the battle in Zhongbo, the one he loathed most was Shen Wei. Not only was the man guilty of monstrous crimes, he was also lustful enough to sire a horde of sons.

But at this moment, he felt dizzy. That instinct, captivated by beauty and stirred by desire, once again reared its head.

Xiao Chiye struggled to rein in his fevered gaze. He felt vividly the contradiction between his reason and his desire: He had no love for this man. But because of his beauty, the desire to embrace him, to ravage him, to tear at him with tooth and claw sprang up within him for the second time.

"Aren't you getting in?" Shen Zechuan was oblivious as he turned back around and approached, unperturbed.

Xiao Chiye responded fiercely, "Yes."

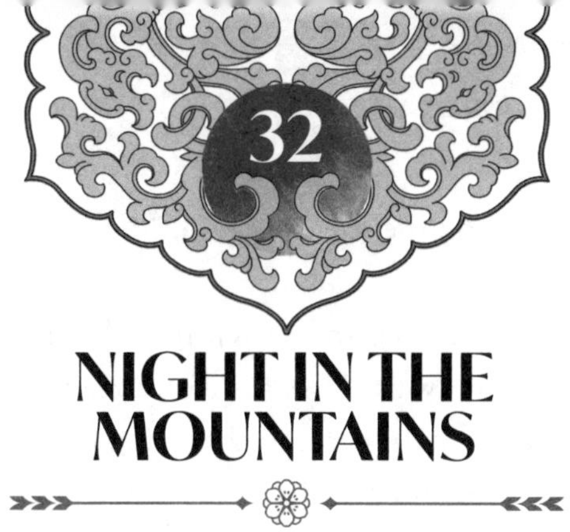

NIGHT IN THE MOUNTAINS

MIST HUNG LOW over the water and the drumming of rain filled the air.

As Shen Zechuan bent to enter the spring, Xiao Chiye had a clear view of the contours of his waist and buttocks from behind, the curves of which became more conspicuous with every move he made. Muscular, but not obviously so. He didn't look trained in martial arts; to Xiao Chiye's eye, he didn't appear threatening.

Shen Zechuan submerged himself. His feet, frozen from the rain, gradually warmed. Xiao Chiye slid into the water and leaned against the side, as far from him as the pool allowed.

"Why are you all the way over there?" Shen Zechuan asked incredulously.

"I want to be." Xiao Chiye roughly folded a wet handkerchief and covered his eyes, then draped his arms along the spring's edge, blocking Shen Zechuan from sight. But after a moment, he thought better of it and pulled off the handkerchief to stare fixedly at Shen Zechuan. It seemed to Shen Zechuan that, just now, Xiao Er was very much like his gyrfalcon—one little jab and the talons would come out.

"What do you want to see?" Shen Zechuan's expression was as mild as a spring breeze. In the tone of one cajoling a child eating candied hawthorns on the street, he said, "Tell me, and I'll show it to you."

Xiao Chiye curled a leg and surreptitiously tugged at the only remaining cover at his waist. "I've felt it all already."

Shen Zechuan sank deeper into the water, leaving only his eyes above the surface, watching him.

The scrutiny made Xiao Chiye even more irritable. "What?!"

Lifting his chin above the surface, Shen Zechuan said, "You were in a pretty good mood earlier. Why the sudden change?"

"I'm still in a pretty good mood. You can shut up in the bath; there's no need for chat." A moment later, he said, "Can you stop looking up at me like that?"

Shen Zechuan slowly stood. Droplets traced the contours of his chest, and his hair scattered like ink in the water, as if he were a pale magnolia emerging from this heavy mist.

Xiao Chiye couldn't stand it anymore. Why had he thought of a *flower*? He watched, wide-eyed, as Shen Zechuan drew closer. When he sat beside him, Xiao Chiye caught his scent.

Mild—not fragrant. He wanted to smell it again.

Xiao Chiye reached an arm back to pull a garment from the clothing rack, then shoved it into the water to cover his lap. He looked calmly at Shen Zechuan. "What? Surprised? I was afraid you'd get funny ideas at the sensual sight of Er-gongzi, so I covered up for you."

Shen Zechuan scowled. "Thanks a lot..."

Xiao Chiye looked down and realized that, in his distraction, he had grabbed Shen Zechuan's robe.

"...For washing my clothes," Shen Zechuan finished. "I suppose I'll have to soak in here until tomorrow." Awkward silence filled the air as the two men looked at each other. Outside, the wind sighed through the dismal autumn rain.

After a long interval, Xiao Chiye finally said, "It was already wet anyway. Meng can go summon Chen Yang." He raised his head and whistled. There was a moment's stillness in the hot spring. Neither Snowcrest nor Meng appeared. Xiao Chiye whistled again.

Outside, Meng buried his head deeper under his wing and ignored the call. He had absolutely no wish to fly out in such a downpour.

The silence stretched.

"I'll wring it dry," Shen Zechuan said eventually, reaching for the garment.

Xiao Chiye pressed the robe down more firmly and gnashed his teeth. "Hold on!"

In the end, they were stranded in the hot spring all night. By the time their clothes had dried, it was nearly dawn. Shen Zechuan finally shrugged back into his robes. He could sense, as he fastened the belt around his waist, the ravenous gaze of a tiger eyeing its prey. He feigned ignorance and said nothing.

Xiao Chiye lifted the hanging curtain. It was still dark, and the air was thick with mist and the smell of petrichor. A thin film of ice covered the stone stairs; it was not an ideal time to head down the mountain.

They walked in single file, one behind the other.

"The drill grounds occupy the land to the southwest of Mount Feng." Shen Zechuan peered down the mountain. "It's close to Qudu, but completely obstructed by the mountain. The Eight Great Battalions won't patrol this far. You chose an excellent location."

"I wouldn't have chosen it if not for Mount Feng." Xiao Chiye pushed aside the maple branches and gestured for Shen Zechuan to pass under his arm.

Shen Zechuan ducked through; the view before him suddenly opened up as the trees and mist fell away. He could see the Imperial Army's drill grounds clearly. At this early hour, there were already squads training below.

He studied them for a moment. "The Imperial Army didn't turn out in full force during the Autumn Hunt, but I can see they're well-equipped. Hua Siqian is dead. The instant they finish seizing his assets, the Chief Surveillance Bureau will come for you."

Xiao Chiye obviously couldn't afford to keep twenty thousand Imperial Army soldiers fed and equipped on his own salary, nor could he appropriate military provisions meant for the Libei Armored Cavalry. Even a cursory glance at the annual budget allocated to him by the Ministry of Revenue before the Autumn Hunt would reveal that the Imperial Army hadn't the money to establish themselves on such a scale. Xi Gu'an had died because of his failure to account for his funds, and now the accountants would be coming for Xiao Chiye.

"Let them come," Xiao Chiye said. He did not offer more, and Shen Zechuan did not inquire.

After a pause, Xiao Chiye seemed to relent. "The Ministry of Works relegated many tasks requiring manual labor to the Imperial Army. For the last five years, every sum paid to the Imperial Army for these assignments was marked down in black and white in the account books. Even if the Chief Surveillance Bureau investigates, they won't find anything to complain about."

So this was why Xiao Chiye had become the infamous debt collector of the Ministry of Revenue. Everyone thought he spent the money on wine and women; in truth, he had been living frugally and saving year over year. His only extravagant expenditure was wine. Li Jianheng might be without good sense, but he was generous with his friends. Whenever he'd invited Xiao Chiye to Donglong Street, he paid for the girls and the feasts for his whole disreputable circle.

In those days, Li Jianheng had lived off the imperial coffers, and with no wife keeping him in line, he'd asked the palace for money whenever he wanted. The late emperor had never been stingy with his brother's spending; he'd always indulged Li Jianheng even if he had to take funds from his personal coffers. Thus Li Jianheng had never lacked for money.

Xiao Chiye hadn't gotten to return to Libei, but he never resented Li Jianheng for it. He knew better than anyone that Li Jianheng truly regarded these layabouts as bosom friends.

"The empress dowager saved your life, so of course she planned to use you," Xiao Chiye said. "If all was well, you might have enjoyed a steady rise to the top in the Embroidered Uniform Guard. But the late emperor began to resist her control. The empress dowager—she reached out to you, didn't she?"

Shen Zechuan met Xiao Chiye's eyes.

He couldn't evade that gaze, not even for a moment. Xiao Chiye had a keen nose; he had only to reveal the barest trace of guilt for Xiao Chiye to sniff it out.

"No." Shen Zechuan's voice was firm with certainty.

The chill wind brushed past them and tugged at the hems of their robes. Xiao Chiye slowly exhaled a cloud of white and smiled. "Then you must be lucky."

It was already daybreak by the time they reached Qudu.

"I have to rush over for morning court," Xiao Chiye said as they rode through the city streets. "You can head back."

Shen Zechuan nodded and watched Xiao Chiye gallop off. When he returned to the courtyard of the Imperial Army office, Chen Yang was gone; he must have left to wait for Xiao Chiye at the palace gate.

Removing the eastern pearl from his sleeve, Shen Zechuan held it between his fingertips and scrutinized it in the dim light. But before he could unwrap the strip of cloth around it, he paused.

When he undressed, he had placed the eastern pearl into the right sleeve pocket of his robe. But just now, he had found it in the left.

Shen Zechuan clicked his tongue and frowned.

When Xiao Chiye arrived at the gates of the palace, he dismounted and made his way to his family's carriage, where he quickly changed into court attire. Chen Yang had also prepared breakfast, and the porridge was still hot.

Chen Yang knelt beside the curtain and whispered, "I went to look for you at the drill grounds last night, but you weren't there. Qudu isn't safe these days. Someone ought to accompany you when you're out."

Xiao Chiye set the bowl aside. "Get someone to keep a close watch on Shen Lanzhou at all times."

Chen Yang nodded his acknowledgment. "Our men are stationed all around the outside of the office. If he leaves, it won't escape our eyes. But Your Excellency, the Hua Clan has fallen; what need is there to keep such close watch on him now?"

Xiao Chiye didn't answer. His face clouded, and he lowered his lashes in thought for a long time. It was not until Chen Yang reminded him of the morning court that he wiped his hands with a clean handkerchief and answered, "I find that man unpredictable. If you look at him, can you tell he's trained in martial arts at all?"

"He looks even frailer now than when he joined the Embroidered Uniform Guard," Chen Yang replied. "If Your Excellency hadn't mentioned his assistance during the Autumn Hunt, I would've never suspected. But get Zhao Hui to take a look; he might catch something."

"Zhao Hui met him face-to-face the last time he was in the capital, but he didn't notice anything out of the ordinary," Xiao Chiye said. "That physique of his—" He stopped abruptly. "Send a letter to Libei at once and request my shifu's presence here."

Stunned, Chen Yang said, "You want to ask..."

"No matter what method he used to cover it up, it will not escape Shifu's eyes," Xiao Chiye said coldly, spinning his ring around his thumb. "Besides, there's...something else I need to speak with Shifu about."

Li Jianheng had shelved the morning court session in favor of a warm bed. He had yet to sleep his fill when Shuanglu reported that Hai Liangyi was kneeling outside. Li Jianheng was instantly wide awake, but Mu Ru still slumbered in his arms. Unable to free himself, he craned his neck and commanded Shuanglu in an urgent whisper, "Go! Send him away."

Shuanglu was only gone a moment before he returned to kneel once again. "The secretariat elder says he must see Your Majesty. This lowly one informed him that Your Majesty still sleeps, so the secretariat elder said he will kneel and wait."

Li Jianheng panicked. Mu Ru blinked open sleepy eyes in his embrace, and he hurriedly coaxed her, "Dearest, get dressed quickly and go out the back to Chenming Palace for your meal! We have to receive the secretariat elder!"

Mu Ru was a dainty woman with a delicate disposition and hair like a dark waterfall. She did not pester him or raise a fuss, but simply dressed herself as instructed. When she had finished, she rose and glanced coyly at Li Jianheng with eyes full of adoration, as if overwhelmed by his favor.

Li Jianheng loved this look of hers to bits. He tugged at her hand, reluctant to part, wanting desperately to cradle her on his lap while holding court.

"Next time." Li Jianheng rained kisses on her upturned face. "Next time, we won't ask you to retreat like this." He took her into his arms and spoke a while longer, until Shuanglu again entered to hurry him. Finally, Li Jianheng reluctantly released Mu Ru.

Minutes later, Hai Liangyi entered with a solemn expression and kowtowed.

Seated on his dragon throne, Li Jianheng said, "Please rise, Secretariat Elder."

Hai Liangyi remained in place and kowtowed again.

Looking to the left and right, Li Jianheng felt his face burn. He coughed. "We've recently caught a cold, so we wanted to sleep in a little longer in the morning..."

"This aged subject heard Your Majesty has been working diligently every night," Hai Liangyi said. "But there have been no responses to all the memorials submitted. After giving the matter careful thought, this aged subject has come to advise Your Majesty in person. Your Majesty is now in the prime of life. If Your Majesty exercises diligence in governing the state and does away with prior slothful habits, then I foresee a bright, thriving future for our empire."

Li Jianheng managed a few awkward chuckles. "Right..."

"However—Your Majesty resides deep in the inner palace served by castrated dogs. If impulses are indulged without restraint, over time, Your Majesty will become deaf to advice and distant from the concerns of the court," Hai Liangyi said resolutely. "This subject has heard that Shuanglu, the eunuch personally serving Your Majesty, has been bribed into filling Your Majesty's chambers with lowly and unscrupulous individuals. According to the rules, anyone so audacious as to bring outsiders into the palace without imperial orders shall be flogged to death!"

Shuanglu dropped to his knees with a thud and looked to Li Jianheng in horror. "Your Majesty, Your Majesty!"

"Mingli Hall is a sacred place. How can we tolerate eunuchs making a racket here?" Hai Liangyi looked at Li Jianheng. "Your Majesty!"

Li Jianheng's heart was pounding. He looked at the stern Hai Liangyi and recalled the unfathomable terror he had felt that night at the hunting grounds. His palms were clammy with sweat, which he meekly wiped on his dragon robe. He didn't dare say a word in reply.

The guards outside had already entered to take Shuanglu away. Shuanglu cried out as he was dragged across the floor, "Your Majesty, Your Majesty!"

"His crime," Li Jianheng began uncertainly, looking at Shuanglu. "His crime is not deserving of death..."

"Your Majesty," Hai Liangyi said firmly, "Pan Rugui formed a clique of eunuchs and colluded with Hua Siqian to wreak havoc within and without Qudu. Now is the time to nip such behavior in the bud as a warning to others! Not only that—promiscuous members of the imperial harem who seduce and bewitch the sovereign in an attempt to sway him should also be flogged to death!"

"We wouldn't dare, we wouldn't dare!" Li Jianheng said, heart hammering with alarm. "With such a virtuous subject as the secretariat elder to supervise and guide us every day, how would we dare fool around? Secretariat Elder, you mustn't be taken in by these baseless rumors."

But Hai Liangyi replied mercilessly, "There's no smoke without fire. Beautiful women are the source of all trouble; Your Majesty must not allow any such temptresses to remain!"

Li Jianheng was terrified now. How could he bear to let Mu Ru die? He rose to his feet in a panic, cutting a sorry figure as he said, "Secretariat Elder, we've realized our mistakes. Shuanglu has served me for many years, and now he—well, never mind that; we will surely pay diligent attention to affairs of state in the future!"

Hai Liangyi kowtowed but said no more, leaving him with some semblance of dignity.

Gripping the table, Li Jianheng listened to the sound of flogging outside. Blow after blow, one after another; it was as if the strikes were landing on his own body. He looked at Hai Liangyi with a mixture of feelings—aggrievement as well as fear.

Xiao Chiye came just in time to see servants mopping the courtyard. There were bloodstains under his feet, the red chilling and vivid. All the eunuchs in Mingli Hall were quietly kneeling outside, not one of them daring to raise his head.

Xiao Chiye stepped inside and saw Li Jianheng sitting frozen on the dragon throne. He stared blankly at Xiao Chiye for a time, then burst into sobs. He stood and began to smash anything in reach as he cried and shouted, "What good is an emperor? To be confronted and humiliated like this! What land under the heavens is not the emperor's land?![24] What's so wrong with doting on a woman? Where's the wrong in that?!"

24 From "Northern Mountain," one of the Minor Odes in The Book of Songs, the oldest existing collection of Chinese poetry, and one of the Four Books and Five Classics in Confucianism.

UNCLE AND NEPHEW

When Li Jianheng's tantrum was over, he covered his face and wept.

Avoiding the shattered fragments on the floor, Xiao Chiye knelt. After a while, when Li Jianheng had calmed somewhat, he looked back at Xiao Chiye. "Get up! There's no need for you to kneel like this. You and I are friends. This will only make us distant."

Xiao Chiye rose. "The secretariat elder is merely upright and frank by nature."

Li Jianheng was in very low spirits. He buried his face in his hands and said, "They come here every two or three days to ask for money, all of which I've approved. Even when money flows out like water, I've not said a word. I'm on pins and needles all day long; I've lost my appetite. I'm so unhappy. Can't I ask for even a few days off now that Hua Siqian is dead and Ji Lei is about to be executed? Ce'an, you have no idea how dissatisfied they are with me in this position. If they had any other choice, they would never accept me."

At this point, he grew upset all over again. "I never wanted to be the emperor. They were the ones who pushed me onto the throne, and now they're the ones who condemn me! The Censor of the Chief Surveillance Bureau watches me day and night. If I so much as go for a walk in the garden, they submit memorials about it to reproach me in that erudite way of theirs! So be it if he kills a eunuch—what's done is done—but can't Hai Renshi allow me some dignity? At the very least, I'm still the emperor of our Great Zhou!"

The longer Li Jianheng ranted, the angrier he became; with nothing left on the table to smash, he pounded his own thigh in indignation. "He made Mu Ru out to be a lowly and unscrupulous person, but these officials—who are they to speak of nobility and virtue?! When we used to go drinking on Donglong Street, who among them didn't drop that dignified air right along with their pants?! I picked Mu Ru from an ordinary family. If it weren't for that dog Xiaofuzi who got in the way, would she have fallen into that traitor Pan's hands? My heart aches for her so much it's fit to break!"

Xiao Chiye merely listened in silence as Li Jianheng vented his grievances. By the time Li Jianheng finished, his anger had mostly subsided. "If they truly see me as the emperor and respect me, I'm willing to be diligent and learn. My imperial brother entrusted this vast empire to me. I want to be a sovereign of a flourishing era as much as anyone," Li Jianheng said resentfully. "But Hai Renshi just doesn't think much of me."

Only then did Xiao Chiye speak. "On the contrary, it's precisely because the secretariat elder has high hopes for Your Majesty that he boldly spoke such blunt admonitions. Your Majesty must not hold a grudge against him. Remember, Secretariat Elder Hai is equally stern and exacting with that Unpolished Jade Yuanzhuo, Yao Wenyu."

"Really?" Li Jianheng asked, skeptical.

"If not, why would the secretariat elder kill Shuanglu today?" Xiao Chiye replied with a question of his own.

"That...is true," Li Jianheng said after mulling it over. If Hai Liangyi thought so poorly of him, why would he insist on asking his opinions on every matter? Li Jianheng recalled the first days after he had ascended the throne. When Hai Liangyi learned that the empress dowager had sent him snacks, he instructed him in private to switch all his utensils to silver to better test for poison.

Hai Liangyi was an inflexible man; he conducted himself seriously in both speech and manner. Unlike Hua Siqian, he kept no apprentices, and had only one student—Yao Wenyu. Yet because Hai Liangyi wished to avoid a conflict of interest, Yao Wenyu had stayed away from court politics despite his extraordinary talent. During his time in the Grand Secretariat, Hai Liangyi never formed factions or alliances. It was also he who put everything on the line at the Nanlin Hunting Grounds and charged out by himself to save the Xiande Emperor.

He was the lone minister memorialized in history books—as proud and isolated as a steep precipice, as righteous as a lofty pine without branches.

While Li Jianheng reminisced, Xiao Chiye lost himself in his own thoughts.

One thing was true in what Li Jianheng had said: had there been any other choice, the one to sit on the dragon throne would not be Li Jianheng. But even the Xiande Emperor never managed to do anything about that; Li Jianheng was the one and only candidate for this honor in all the wide world. Those who had thrust him into power must now teach and guide him. Their Great Zhou was an empire beset by difficulties. It seemed as if a wave of troubles had just calmed in Qudu, but in truth, the next storm had already begun to stir.

The loyal ministers of the court, led by Hai Liangyi, all watched Li Jianheng. In their eyes, he was perhaps a hopeless case. But Hai Liangyi had raised both hands to prop Li Jianheng up with that aging frame, urging him to hang on, to turn over a new leaf, to be an emperor who would leave a glorious legacy.

Xiao Chiye and the civil officials had never gotten on; the central administration in Qudu feared the military power at the frontiers too much. These very men were the reason for the invisible cage in which he was trapped. However, they were also men of indomitable will, the rigid backbones allowing the Zhou empire to hobble forward.

Military generals did not fear death, for they could not avoid it. Civil ministers did not fear death, for they would not compromise. Li Jianheng was used to being fawned over. He needed a teacher like Hai Liangyi who could briskly point out his failings.

"When all is said and done," Xiao Chiye finally said, "Lady Mu has no place in the palace. If Your Majesty is truly set on her, why not have a heart-to-heart with the secretariat elder? Now more than ever our Great Zhou would benefit from an abundance of imperial heirs. As long as Your Majesty speaks to him honestly and sincerely, the secretariat elder will surely return your sentiments. As for Ji Lei and Pan Rugui, I heard the Court of Judicial Review has yet to reach a verdict?"

Preoccupied with thoughts of Hai Liangyi's virtues, Li Jianheng nodded absently and replied, "The accounts don't tally. They will have to be questioned again."

The eastern pearl was hollow. When Shen Zechuan fished the thin fabric strip out, it was sodden, the writing on it already too smudged to read. He burned it.

Xiao Chiye's every action last night played before his eyes. He couldn't have seen what was written inside the pearl, but he knew it was there, and now he would be suspicious. Shen Zechuan had answered wrongly on Mount Feng. Xiao Chiye had gone so far as to tell him the source of the Imperial Army funds and waited for him to offer truth in return. Yet he had denied it with absolute certainty.

Shen Zechuan brewed his medicine and drank it in a single gulp. The bitterness pervaded his mouth. He endured it, just as he did the anguish that dogged him day and night. At last, he smiled in self-mockery, wiped his mouth, and lay down to sleep.

He dreamed again.

In the dream, the cold wind was howling across the Chashi Sinkhole. This time, he was no longer lying at the bottom, but standing alone at the edge of the pit, overlooking those thirty thousand soldiers struggling like ants to survive. The Biansha Horsemen surrounded the sinkhole, a black tide in the pitch-dark night. They blotted out the earth and sky, swallowing up the Zhongbo Garrison Troops' chances of survival and turning the place into a charnel house.

A hand reached out from the roiling waves of withered bones. Jerking like a puppet on a string, Ji Mu lifted his arrow-pierced body and sobbed as he called out to Shen Zechuan, "It hurts so much..."

Shen Zechuan seemed to be a statue carved of wood or clay; he could neither move nor shout. He panted for breath and gritted his teeth as cold sweat poured from him in streams.

The Biansha leader's face was concealed by a helmet. His long, wind-tossed hair had turned a blood-crimson in Shen Zechuan's recurring nightmare. He lifted his arm and swung it toward the sinkhole, and a swarm of arrows flew out from behind him like locusts. They punctured the dying men's bodies in dense clusters, piercing flesh, splattering warm blood across the ground. The heavy snow bloomed red. Shen Zechuan watched Ji Mu sink into the mud as churning waves of blood swallowed him whole. His hands were cold. The blood on them was colder.

Shen Zechuan woke up.

He sat up with his back to the window's light as though nothing had happened. In the silence, he bowed his head for a moment, then rose from his bed and got dressed.

The two guards lurking in the courtyard watched Shen Zechuan step out of his room. They saw him eat his meal before heading to the bath hall. An hour later, one of the guards, whose eyes had never strayed from the entrance, frowned and asked the man beside him, "Why hasn't he come out yet?"

The pair exchanged glances as they both came to the same terrible realization. By the time they rushed into the bath hall, there was only a neat stack of clothes. Shen Zechuan was gone.

Xi Hongxuan had booked the whole of Bu'er Tavern to host an honored guest. Feeling the call of nature as he waited, he got up to head to the latrine. He had only just stepped out and walked a few steps back toward the room when someone tapped him on the shoulder.

Startling backward, Xi Hongxuan turned. "How did you—why do you come and go as quiet as a shadow?!"

"There's a lot going on lately," Shen Zechuan said. He invited himself in and settled at the table, pouring cold tea into his cup. "Ji Lei and Pan Rugui have yet to be sentenced in the third trial by the Court of Judicial Review because Hai Liangyi and Xue Xiuzhuo haven't pried out what they need from them. Am I right?"

Xi Hongxuan glanced around, sat, then whispered, "You want to kill Ji Lei, but what can you do with so many eyes watching? The Hua faction case involves too many, and countless more fear those two will implicate them in a confession. It's precisely to prevent them dying a sudden and inexplicable death that Hai Liangyi set such a strict guard. There's no opening for you to strike."

"I don't plan to." Shen Zechuan smiled derisively at Xi Hongxuan. "But I have a way of getting Ji Lei to talk."

Xi Hongxuan looked at him a long time. Then, he personally lifted the teapot and poured for him. "What way?"

Shen Zechuan sipped his tea. "Just let me see him."

Ji Lei had been tortured for days. He lay shackled in his cell, hair disheveled and feet bare. The only warning he had was the sound of footsteps down the hall before someone burst into his cell, covered his head, and dragged him out. From there, he was shoved into a carriage, and after an indeterminate amount of time, hauled back out and flung to the ground. Wherever he was, it was quiet, with only the sound of water dripping in some far corner.

The black sack still over his head, Ji Lei raised himself onto all fours and asked, "Who's there?"

A water droplet landed with a *plink*. No one answered.

Ji Lei felt a chill down his spine. Raising himself onto his knees, he guessed tentatively, "Secretariat Elder Hai?" Still, no one answered.

His throat bobbed. He shuffled forward and bumped into metal bars. Fumbling around, he steadied himself and shouted, "If you aren't Secretariat Elder Hai, you must be Xue Xiuzhuo! How do you plan to torture me today? Bring it on!"

"Say something. Why won't you say something?!"

Silence.

"Who are you? Who exactly are you? What do you want?! Do you think by staying silent, you'll make me afraid? I'm not afraid—I'm not afraid!"

Ji Lei ducked his head down between his arms and managed to nudge the sack off. Looking sidelong, he saw Shen Zechuan sitting in a chair right in front of him.

Shen Zechuan was dressed in robes as coldly white as the moon, legs crossed, with one elbow on the chair's armrest as he propped his chin in a hand and stared expressionlessly at Ji Lei.

Laughter escaped Ji Lei's throat. He grabbed the bars and squeezed his face between them, then said sinisterly, "Oh, it's you. The stray dog of Zhongbo. What does the vile animal want from his shishu?[25] Revenge for Ji Gang, or for yourself?"

Shen Zechuan said nothing. Whenever the smile slipped from those tender, affectionate eyes, it left only a dark, heavy gaze.

Looking into them, Ji Lei couldn't even find hatred. He felt as if the man before him was not a person of flesh and blood, but a stray cur whose desperate hunger had led him to feed on human flesh. Ji Lei lowered his eyes. "The Ji Clan has no descendants, and the one who severed Ji Gang's bloodline is you," he spat. "So what are you looking at me for? Shen Zechuan, it was your Shen Clan who killed Ji Mu, your Shen Clan who violated Hua Pingting. How do you face yourself, having lived so long with your sins? You are the devil beneath tens of thousands of wronged souls. You are the ignoble continuance of Shen Wei's existence. You deserve to be hacked to pieces, to die by a thousand cuts..."

Low laughter bubbled out of Ji Lei. He looked deranged. "Do you think I'm scared of you? The little bastard nobody wants. You think taking off your pants to follow Xiao Er will grant you better days ahead? Ha ha!"

Shen Zechuan laughed then too.

Ji Lei's cackling gradually came to a stop. "You think that's funny? My plight today will be your predicament tomorrow." His voice was cold.

---

25 *Shishu, a term of address for one's martial uncle, someone who studied under the same master (or shifu) as one's own master.*

Shen Zechuan uncrossed his legs and leaned against the chair as if pondering those words. "Oh, yes, I'm terribly frightened."

His words were breezy with sarcasm.

"Devil. Bastard. Stray dog. Vile animal." Shen Zechuan rose to his feet and crouched outside the bars. He began to laugh at Ji Lei, speaking in a tone so level it sounded crazed. "You're right. I'm the devil who climbed out of the Chashi Sinkhole, the bastard Shen Wei left behind after he burned himself to death, the stray dog without a home to return to, the vile animal despised by thousands. Shishu, I'm delighted you know me so well."

Ji Lei began to tremble uncontrollably.

Shen Zechuan glanced at him, his gaze far more sinister than it had been five years ago. As if a man had already died under that layer of breathtaking skin, and all that survived was an unnamed beast.

"Five years ago," Shen Zechuan said softly as he drew closer to the bars and scrutinized Ji Lei's terrified expression, "the one kneeling here was me. What was it you said, the day you sent me into the Temple of Guilt?"

Ji Lei's throat tightened. He wanted to answer, but he couldn't find his voice.

"I have been remembering all your kindness with deep gratitude," Shen Zechuan said with utmost sincerity. "Every day. Every night."

34 INTERROGATION

"YOU—WHAT EXACTLY are you..." Ji Lei took one look at Shen Zechuan's smile and backed swiftly away from the bars. "What is it you want?!"

"You're asking me?" Shen Zechuan said cheerfully. "Are you asking me?" Shen Zechuan's gaze turned ominous as he beckoned haughtily to Ji Lei. Ji Lei was frozen in place. He pressed his back to the wall and refused to move a fraction closer to Shen Zechuan.

"Prisoners are livestock waiting to be slaughtered," Shen Zechuan said. "Shishu, how dare you ask me?"

"What can you possibly do?" Ji Lei countered. "Kill me?"

"It's not often this martial uncle and nephew have a chance to come together. There's scarcely time for us to play as it is; how could I kill you so quickly?" Shen Zechuan slid his thumb across the bars and softened his tone. "You're keeping your lips sealed because you think your secrets are your salvation—as long as you keep them, no one will risk laying a hand on you. Your days in prison will be more comfortable, and you won't worry over daily necessities or fear for your life. You'll have Pan Rugui for company and plenty of leisure time. A carefree and happy life."

Ji Lei broke out in cold sweat. He plastered himself to the wall, no longer meeting Shen Zechuan's eyes.

"But happy days are so often fleeting. As long as the tongue still works, it shouldn't much matter if a leg is missing, an arm is broken, or both eyes gouged out. A few months ago, Shishu treated me to a donkey roast. I didn't get to taste it then. But we have a long night ahead of us, and it's the perfect time for wining and dining." Shen Zechuan slipped a thin blade from between his fingers and tapped it on the bars. "Ji Lei. Let's feast."

"You—are—insane!" Ji Lei stretched his neck out and enunciated each word. "Shen Zechuan, you're *insane*!"

"I'm insane," Shen Zechuan agreed, looking at him steadily.

"You wouldn't dare lay a finger on me!" Ji Lei snarled. "The empress dowager holds your life in her hands. You wouldn't dare touch so much as a strand of my hair!"

This seemed to cheer Shen Zechuan up again. He smiled. "Shishu, you're so funny tonight. Who do you think sent me here?"

Enraged, Ji Lei thundered, "Don't even think of bluffing—"

"Shen Wei is dead. The day Shen Wei set himself alight, I heard the Prince of Jianxing's manor in Dunzhou went up with him. His body was burned beyond recognition when the Embroidered Uniform Guard dragged him from the ruins and hung him atop the city walls to be reviled by all. I didn't see it with my own eyes, but I've attempted to imagine it over the years. After turning it over and over in my mind, I finally realized something."

Ji Lei gulped.

"His grand plan to collude with the enemy had succeeded. Would it not be preferable to defect before the battle? Duanzhou had already fallen. If he led his troops out of the city to receive their conquerors with a welcome, he could have joined forces with the Biansha Horsemen and toppled Qudu before the Libei Armored Cavalry crossed the Glacial River. Yet he didn't do this; he recoiled in fear and retreated." Shen Zechuan stood. "If his goal was to hand Zhongbo to the enemy, he had already done so. Forward was the only way out, but he withdrew again and again. Even if he was an idiot, he should have known that retreating would lead to his doom."

"Because he didn't have the balls," Ji Lei's voice dripped with loathing; he was panting heavily. "Who in the Twelve Tribes of Biansha would give a damn about him? The moment he sold his nation to the enemy, he was a dead man!"

Shen Zechuan tossed the eastern pearl into the cell, where it rolled and knocked its way to Ji Lei's feet. He observed Ji Lei's face as it gradually drained of color.

He laughed.

Ji Lei's hands shook. He stared at that eastern pearl and said with difficulty, "No... Impossible..."

"The Xiande Emperor is dead." Shen Zechuan leaned forward. "So is Shen Wei."

Ji Lei kicked away the pearl. "You conniving snake, don't even think of deceiving me!"

"Hua Siqian committed suicide by biting off his tongue," Shen Zechuan said blithely. "Who will be next? You, or Pan Rugui? Shall we draw lots? Shishu, you first." He flipped two more thin blades up between his fingers and presented them to Ji Lei through the gap. "If it's chipped, we'll kill Pan Rugui. If it isn't, we'll feed your flesh to the dogs. Don't be afraid. Draw one."

Ji Lei looked at the cold glint on the blades. His lips opened and closed. "Ridiculous..."

"The empress dowager instructed me to be quick." Shen Zechuan stared at him. "Yet I'm letting you choose. Shishu, as long as you're alive, there's a chance for things to take a turn for the better."

After being tortured for days, Ji Lei was already half-delirious. Now, in this bizarre circumstance, Shen Zechuan's words confused him until he couldn't tell truth from lies. He fixed his eyes on the two blades. Finally, as if compelled, he raised a hand. As his trembling fingers touched the thin blade, he saw the corners of Shen Zechuan's lips slowly curl.

"Ah." Shen Zechuan smiled, all regret. "I forgot I only brought along new blades today. The chipped ones have already been disposed of."

The shame of being played overwhelmed Ji Lei. He finally lost control, throwing himself forward and shouting hysterically as he yanked at the bars, "Go ahead and do what you want—kill me, cut me to pieces! I won't say a word of what you want to know! Do it, kill me!"

"Wrong." Shen Zechuan remained in firm control. "I'm not the one who wants to kill you."

"You are!" Ji Lei's fingers dug into the bars. "It's you!"

"Me?" The eastern pearl had rolled back between the bars; Shen Zechuan nudged it over and stepped on it. Looking coldly at Ji Lei, he asked again, "Is it really me?"

Ji Lei held his head and tore at his unkempt hair. He slid down the bars and repeated over and over again, "It's you...you..."

"Shen Wei killed the crown prince," Shen Zechuan said abruptly.

Ji Lei looked up at him in terror, shivering as if he had plunged into a cave of ice. "You—"

"You and Shen Wei killed the crown prince together," Shen Zechuan continued.

"It wasn't me!" Ji Lei clutched at his hair. "It wasn't me! It was Shen Wei who killed the crown prince!"

"You conspired with him to frame the crown prince for treason," Shen Zechuan said, the words rushing out now. "*You* were the one who forged the documents. Your people forced the crown prince into the Temple of Guilt. He wanted to see the Guangcheng Emperor, but you drew your blade and killed him."

"It wasn't me!" Ji Lei was mad. He raged in the face of Shen Zechuan's relentless interrogation. "I wasn't the one who drew my blade! It was Shen Wei—Shen Wei who insisted on killing him!"

"That's why Shen Wei is dead," Shen Zechuan repeated. "Shen Wei set himself on fire and was burned beyond recognition. And now you are the only one left."

Ji Lei cowered under the weight of these insinuations until *kill* was the only word remaining in his mind. He could still see clearly the former crown prince's face as he was cut down. Then, he had stood just where Shen Zechuan was standing now, looking down at the crown prince from above as if looking at swine. Tonight, by a stroke of fate, his position had been reversed. The cell gave him the feeling of a caged beast. He had become the ant under Shen Zechuan's boot. All he could do was stretch out his neck and wait for the slaughter.

He didn't want to die.

His desire to survive had never been so strong. He beat his forehead against the bars. "We were all just following orders. We had no choice! You want to avenge Shen Wei? I can help you! Shen Wei killed the crown prince and was conferred the title of Prince of Jianxing. He fled to Zhongbo!"

Ji Lei became a sniveling mess as he started to heave with sobs. He had no idea where this fear came from; it was as if he had really become livestock at the mercy of his master's blade. He craned his head back to look up at Shen Zechuan. "I didn't kill the crown prince; I wanted to save him! But my father died unexpectedly," Ji Lei said, helpless. "My father died, and they wanted to pin it on me! If I took the blame, my eldest brother would kill me, and so would Ji Gang. What could I do? I begged Pan Rugui for help! In exchange for his protection, I had to forge the documents. I was trapped. I only wanted to live!"

"How did Ji Wufan die?" Shen Zechuan asked abruptly.

"I don't know. I don't know how he died. He fell ill because Ji Gang left—the sons he favored were both gone." At this point, Ji Lei turned vicious again, his hatred boiling over. "I was the one who was with him until the end! Yet he said I was rotten to the core. He regarded Ji Gang and Zuo Qianqiu as real sons and passed the mental cultivation techniques to them, but not to me. But my surname is Ji too; I did nothing wrong. How could he treat me like that?!

"Shen Wei couldn't sleep at night after killing the crown prince. He was afraid. When we went drinking, he told me he sensed someone watching him. He said he could hear someone moving on the roof of his manor in the middle of the night. I told him it wasn't us Embroidered Uniform Guard, but in the capital, what could hide from their eyes? I presumed there were traitors in the Guard; men from the Eight Great Clans were everywhere.

"The Hua Clan was already in power, so we were careful. But Shen Wei's paranoia worsened. He wanted to flee, so he bribed Pan Rugui, hoping to leave Qudu. In those years, Libei was a rising force to be reckoned with. The empress dowager had no army aside from the Eight Great Battalions. To guard against the Xiao Clan, Shen Wei was conferred the title of the Prince of Jianxing. He went to Zhongbo, the prefecture one must pass through to travel between Qidong and Libei, and Libei and Qudu. The empress dowager made him her watchdog with his eyes on Libei and Qidong."

Ji Lei spoke with increasing urgency. "Who would have expected Shen Wei to turn? He was asking for death! He saved all his correspondence with Qudu. If the documents fell into Libei's hands, Xiao Jiming wouldn't waste the opportunity to deal Qudu a heavy blow! Shen Wei *had* to self-immolate! Do you understand now? Shen Wei turned to the enemy because he was no longer willing to be controlled. Back then, the Hua Clan had a son of common birth. According to the empress dowager, once that child came of age, there would be no need for outsiders to govern Zhongbo. Shen Wei had committed so many heinous deeds in Qudu on behalf of the Hua Clan. If Zhongbo no longer needed him, he would be nothing but a discarded pawn. He was driven into a corner, but no one expected him to lash out so disastrously. To let the Biansha Horsemen in to massacre the cities...that was his vengeance! It was his revenge on Qudu, on the empress dowager, and on our Great Zhou!"

Ji Lei grasped the bars and pleaded, "I've said all I have to say. The empress dowager was the one who drove Shen Wei to his death. She was also the one who drove the crown prince to his death. And the Guangcheng Emperor, the Xiande Emperor, Hua Siqian—all of them were weiqi pieces discarded by the empress dowager! And now you're doing her bidding too. Look at me. I didn't tell her you've already thrown in your lot with the Xiao Clan. You saved Xiao Chiye that night, didn't you? But the Xiao Clan won't help you. So long as Xiao Chiye is in Qudu, the Xiao Clan can't lift a finger. They can hardly look after themselves; why would they care about you?!"

He had wanted to prove his usefulness, but after this confession, his fear only intensified. His defenses had crumbled; he was utterly defeated. And the more inferior he felt, the more terrified he became.

Shen Zechuan asked him one last question through the bars. "Five years ago, my shiniang died when Duanzhou fell. No one knew about this, so how did you come to know it so well?"

In the awful silence, cold sweat trickled down Ji Lei's back as he saw the look in Shen Zechuan's eyes.

Xi Hongxuan waited so long he fell asleep. It wasn't until a stack of paper smacked him in the chest that he jolted awake. He took the papers that had been tossed at him and shook them open for a look; even in the dark, the fingerprints at the bottom were a vivid red. He let out a perfunctory laugh. "You really are good."

A faint metallic smell lingered around Shen Zechuan. He smiled and said, "Whether or not this confession can be submitted to the top will depend on what Secretariat Elder Hai thinks of it."

"This is quite the favor you've done me," Xi Hongxuan said. "Surely it wasn't for nothing?"

"There's a man named Qiao Tianya in the Embroidered Uniform Guard," Shen Zechuan said calmly. "He's good with the broadsword. I want him."

"Not a problem." Xi Hongxuan hesitated for a moment. "I'll talk to Yanqing."

"Thank you for taking the trouble," Shen Zechuan said. "It's late. I should go."

With that, he opened the door and took his leave.

It was a rainy night. Xi Hongxuan thought to call Shen Zechuan to join him in his carriage home, but suddenly changed his mind. It occurred to him that everything had gone too smoothly. He flipped through the confession statement and read it over. Thinking he should show it to Xue Xiuzhuo before anything else, he said to his attendant, "Go. Drag Ji Lei out and send him back."

The attendant acknowledged his order and went to open the door to the cell. He had taken but one step inside when he collapsed backward onto the ground, screaming as though he'd seen a ghost.

Looking through the open door, Xi Hongxuan saw Ji Lei. His stomach churned and he covered his face as he retreated, desperately knocking aside tables and chairs as he dashed out into the rain and violently retched.

Shen Zechuan scrubbed his hands until they were raw before wiping them with a handkerchief. His white robe was unstained, but the stench of blood lingered. Taking the front hem of his robe, he frowned as he sniffed it.

Disgusting.

Heedless of the rain, Shen Zechuan squatted by the edge of the water; he was almost immediately drenched. He slowly turned his face up to the starless sky and gazed until his neck was sore. Then, he rose to his feet and walked back.

When Shen Zechuan reached the alley where the Imperial Army's office stood, he saw a figure waiting at the entrance. Shrouded in darkness, Xiao Chiye leaned against the door with arms folded, watching him like a cheetah.

At some point, snow had begun to fall with the rain, its damp chill seeping down to the bone.

FIRST SNOW

THE SHARP WIND slipped under collars and into sleeves. Shen Zechuan suddenly turned his head and sneezed, breaking the spell. Soaking wet, he waved a hand at Xiao Chiye and asked in a muffled voice, "Got a handkerchief?"

Xiao Chiye stepped forward and handed him one.

The tip of Shen Zechuan's nose was frozen red, and so were his fingertips. He took the blue handkerchief and covered his mouth and nose.

Xiao Chiye leisurely opened his umbrella but made no move to get out of the way. "Where have you been?"

"Out having fun," Shen Zechuan replied.

"Well, you're my personal guard. You need to inform the duty office when you head out," Xiao Chiye said. "It worries me so, when you run off without a word."

"I left my authority token in the bath hall. Did Er-gongzi not see it?" Shen Zechuan sniffed the handkerchief. The scent was rather pleasant—not the usual incense used by nobles of Qudu, but one that reminded him of the strong, valiant wind, sweeping the land under a blazing sun. It was the scent of Xiao Chiye.

What a nice smell.

Shen Zechuan lowered his eyes, fascinated by this scent. It was the sunlight beyond his reach, the bright spirit he no longer possessed.

There was a part of him that didn't want to return it. He peeked at Xiao Chiye out of the corner of his eye, as if there was something he wished to say.

"Nope, didn't see it." Xiao Chiye felt around his own lapels but didn't find what he was looking for. He glanced over just in time to see Shen Zechuan's gaze on him. Taken aback, he said, "What conscienceless deed have you done tonight to look at me in such a way?"

"Who knows?" Shen Zechuan said with a hint of smugness. "I've done plenty."

"Let's hear a couple," Xiao Chiye said.

"If you want to have a heart-to-heart, let's do it inside. It's too cold to be standing out here." Shen Zechuan coughed. "Is the bath hall still open?"

"Closed," Xiao Chiye replied. "You'll have to go to my room if you want a bath. You seem unwell again; should I call for a physician to take a look at you?"

"That'd be great." Shen Zechuan replied. "If Er-gongzi steps in, I'll save on consultation fees."

"You still haven't recovered from your illness, and this running about in all weather has me worried sick. I'll get someone to follow you from now on." Xiao Chiye chivalrously stepped aside and made way. "Let's go. Er-gongzi will hold the umbrella for you."

Shen Zechuan looked at Xiao Chiye's shoulder, which rose taller than the top of his own head. He smiled up at him. "I can stand on tiptoe and hold the umbrella."

"I don't want it knocking into my head." Xiao Chiye had a charming profile, with a straight nose and crisp contours. "You're too short."

Shen Zechuan strode through the main entrance with him. "You're the one who's too tall."

"When I was young, I was a few heads shorter than my elder brother, and with such a name to boot—*Chiye* means galloping through the wild, and here I was lagging behind. It made me anxious, so I trained hard every day and drank milk every night before bed." Xiao Chiye stretched his long legs to stride over a puddle and continued, "But when I reached thirteen, my height began to shoot through the roof."

"Good for you," Shen Zechuan said. "My elder brother was very tall too."

The rain had almost stopped, yielding to drifting snow.

Xiao Chiye tilted the umbrella to gaze up at the flurries. "It's the end of another year."

"Another year," Shen Zechuan echoed, eyes on the sky.

"The new emperor has ascended and granted amnesty to all." Xiao Chiye paused. "The empress dowager's power and influence have waned. You can leave Qudu and go anywhere you want."

"So I can conceal my name, forget my past, and scrape by in mediocrity for the rest of my life." Shen Zechuan continued evenly, "This isn't something a man who hates me should say."

"I hate the Biansha Horsemen," Xiao Chiye said coldly, "and Shen Wei."

"You should hate me too."

Something in Xiao Chiye's eyes stirred.

"I'm a person who survives on hatred," Shen Zechuan said.

Snowflakes landed on the stone slabs and melted in the blink of an eye.

"Those words from five years ago—you understand them now more than ever," Xiao Chiye said.

"Living is much more painful than dying." Shen Zechuan suddenly laughed. He exhaled and said to Xiao Chiye, "No, I'm not in pain. Hatred itself is death by a thousand cuts; it's a knife gouging into your flesh. Hating day after day—anyone would grow numb eventually. There's nothing in the world that can make me feel pain again. I'm comfortable living like this. You've advised me repeatedly to let the past go. But you understand as well as I: stopping was never an option for us. If a little show of warmth and tenderness makes you feel better about it, then I don't mind; I'll play along as long as you like."

As he spoke, Shen Zechuan raised his hand and drew an icy finger down Xiao Chiye's sturdy back. He said in a voice so low it was almost a whisper, "Some things are achingly beautiful when seen through the mist, but when you take a closer look, it's just a pile of dead men's bones."

Xiao Chiye waited for him to retract his hand before shaking his umbrella impatiently. "Dead men's bones don't touch people like that."

Shen Zechuan grinned and was about to walk off when Xiao Chiye slung a heavy arm around his shoulders.

"You sure have guts," Xiao Chiye said, tightening his grip, "putting your hands all over your Er-gongzi while reeking of blood. A dozen men in the courtyard can't keep an eye on you, so where do you think you're going? You're sleeping with me."

Shen Zechuan was caught off guard. Xiao Chiye continued, "The favor you did me by saving my life has never left my mind. I've given you plenty of chances, yet you continue to treat me like a fool. Does mocking me make you happy? If so, then why don't you smile? Come, Shen Lanzhou, didn't you say you don't mind playing along?"

He tossed away the umbrella, and in one swift step, hoisted Shen Zechuan over his shoulder. Head dangling, a wave of dizziness washed over Shen Zechuan. He covered his nose and mouth with the handkerchief and fumed, "Xiao Er—!"

"If you dare to move a muscle," Xiao Chiye said, "I'll turn Qudu upside down to find out who helped you kill someone in the middle of the night."

"Go investigate, then!" The moment Shen Zechuan opened his mouth, Xiao Chiye jostled him so hard he almost threw up.

"You slipped out so fast there must be a hole in the wall of the bath hall." With Shen Zechuan still over his shoulder, Xiao Chiye leapt over the railing and passed through the withered greenery of the courtyard. He made his way swiftly through the moon gate and headed for his own room.

The young man sprawled on the rooftop poked his head out for a look and clicked his tongue in wonder. "Just a second ago they were smiling and chatting in the snow, looking all courteous and refined. Why the sudden urgency?"

"That guy doesn't want to be with our Er-gongzi, okay?" The guard who had been shadowing Shen Zechuan took a gulp of his shaojiu. "Considering how quick he was to flee yesterday, he was probably afraid Er-gongzi would force himself on him tonight. I asked around the Imperial Army this afternoon—everyone knows about it."

"Do we report this to Shizi?" The youngster, Ding Tao, fished out a little notebook, licked his brush, and pondered. "Ugh, this isn't going to be easy to write."

"He carried him into the room so brazenly." His companion Gu Jin took another swig and snuck a glance. Xiao Chiye had already kicked the door closed with a *bang*. He thought for a moment, then said, "Or let's just not. Being a cut-sleeve isn't necessarily a major problem, but it's not a minor one either. It'll put us in a tight spot with both sides if we choose the wrong words. I'm afraid our Er-gongzi will be in for a beating."

Ding Tao frowned and set down a few strokes of ink. "Well… then I'll just record it but not report it yet. If the heir comes to settle scores later, we'll just say we buckled under pressure from Er-gongzi and didn't dare run our mouths."

"But how on earth did he escape from the bath hall in the first place?" Gu Jin drank, then pillowed his head on his arms in thought, but he still couldn't figure it out.

The room was hot from the brazier. Xiao Chiye kept Shen Zechuan slung over his shoulder with an arm looped around his waist as he crossed the room and rummaged through his clothes chest. "There's more than enough hot water. Pick whatever soap and fragrances you like." As Xiao Chiye spoke, he turned his head to sniff openly at Shen Zechuan's waist. "You're not the kind of person who needs to bathe in milk and flower petals and pearl powder, are you?"

"Put—" Shen Zechuan said. "I'm going to puke!"

"Then puke from there." Xiao Chiye pulled out some old clothes stowed at the very bottom of the chest and closed it. Ignoring the mess now dangling through the gap, he carried Shen Zechuan farther into his quarters.

Xiao Chiye lifted the hanging curtain. The room beyond was divided into two smaller spaces by a screen in the middle. One side was supplied with a large pool full of hot water, while the other held a clothing rack. Xiao Chiye hung the clean clothes on the rack and shifted the screen effortlessly aside with one arm. Finally, he set Shen Zechuan down by the edge of the pool and hooked his foot around a chair to drag it over.

"Go ahead and bathe." Xiao Chiye sprawled in the chair and jerked his chin at Shen Zechuan. "Everything you need is here. Let's see you run now."

Shen Zechuan's face paled as he asked in astonishment, "You're going to sit there and watch?"

Xiao Chiye stretched out his long legs and folded his arms. "What, are you shy? Shouldn't have run, then."

"I'm afraid I'm not the one who'll have cause to be shy," Shen Zechuan retorted.

"Go on, strip." Xiao Chiye was unruffled. "Let's see which of us throws in the towel first."

Without another word, Shen Zechuan untied his belt. Xiao Chiye stared at him determinedly, gaze unwavering. By the time Shen Zechuan had stripped to his inner robe, his knuckles were white with anger.

"Whether you are in pain or not, I wouldn't know," Xiao Chiye teased, "but from the looks of it, I'd say you're pretty angry."

He was still speaking when Shen Zechuan's clothes hit him in the face. Xiao Chiye caught them and laughed. When he untangled himself, Shen Zechuan was already in the water.

Shen Zechuan settled on the other side of the bath without turning or looking back. Water droplets clung to his back, silky and fair as dew on jade petals.

"My, what a temper you have," Xiao Chiye said after sitting for a while. "You weren't so stiff with me before; you had quite the silver tongue."

"I'm not as *stiff* as the second young master," Shen Zechuan said.

Having heard such an insinuation more than once, Xiao Chiye had already snuffed out whatever shred of shame he had over it. Thus he remained firmly seated and answered with perfect composure, "As you say." After a moment, he probed, "Aren't you going to tell me where you went on your little adventure tonight?"

"Aren't you omniscient?" Shen Zechuan said. "Figure it out."

"There are only a few places where you can kill people at this time of night." Xiao Chiye fished in Shen Zechuan's robe and produced the eastern pearl, studying it between his fingertips. "If nothing else, the empress dowager is still rich. Even in dire straits, she has to send secret messages in such an ostentatious way. Don't tell me you were dazzled by this little bead and set your heart on being her lackey?"

"Who doesn't love money?" Shen Zechuan said. "His Majesty favors and trusts you, yet you still had to make up for the Imperial Army's equipment shortfall on your own. You know better than I the benefits of wealth."

"So she told you to kill someone," Xiao Chiye said, "and you went ahead and did it?"

Shen Zechuan was done soaking. He reached for the clean clothes Xiao Chiye had hung on the rack, but Xiao Chiye nudged it away with his foot. He rose from his chair. "Answer me."

"Yes," a bare-chested Shen Zechuan replied.

"Liar." Xiao Chiye took the clean clothes from the rack. "That pearl was soaked through. There was no way you could decipher the empress dowager's instructions. The person tonight was someone *you* wanted to kill, am I right?"

"Uh-huh," Shen Zechuan said.

"Don't *uh-huh* me." Xiao Chiye rubbed the fabric between his fingers. "An ambiguous answer is equivalent to none at all."

"It was someone I wanted to kill." Shen Zechuan held out a hand. "You were right."

"Ji Lei?" Xiao Chiye guessed. "Or Pan Rugui?"

Shen Zechuan's fingertips had already touched the fabric. "Why can't it be you?"

There was a *swish* as the clothes were lifted high out of reach. Xiao Chiye said, "Only a few words and you've changed your tune.

Er-gongzi doesn't accept sarcasm. Whether you killed Ji Lei or Pan Rugui, by morning, the Court of Judicial Review will certainly have begun a serious investigation. You saved my life during the Autumn Hunt. The empress dowager doesn't know yet, but I can let her know. Once she finds out, you'll be my man whether you want to or not. So speak properly and don't tease your Er-gongzi."

Each time Shen Zechuan attempted to reach for the clothes, Xiao Chiye raised them higher. Shen Zechuan endured it several times before he finally rose from the water to grab them. "Speak properly—while I'm naked?!" he cried angrily.

Xiao Chiye leaned in for a closer look. "See, this is what I mean by speaking properly. What's all that enigmatic stuff about dead men's bones? Ghost stories don't scare me." He paused for a moment. "Since you touched me earlier, it's only fair that I touch you back. We aren't on such good terms that I can just let it go. So, where do I touch?"

SCENT

SHEN ZECHUAN MIMICKED Xiao Chiye's move from before and splashed water all over his face, then seized the chance to grab the clothes.

Eyes closed from the spray, Xiao Chiye reached toward the clothing rack and pulled off a dry cloth. He draped it over Shen Zechuan's head and rubbed aggressively. Shen Zechuan was still putting on his clothes, but Xiao Chiye's motions sent half his body swaying. Seething with contempt, Shen Zechuan used his bare foot to kick out at the chair. Just as the seat under Xiao Chiye slid back across the floor, Xiao Chiye clamped his legs tightly around Shen Zechuan and dragged the other man toward him. Then he continued to dry Shen Zechuan's hair as though he were toweling down a puppy.

"If that's the way it is, I'll do as I please!" Xiao Chiye snapped.

"As you—you...son of a—er!" Shen Zechuan's words fragmented under the rough treatment.

Xiao Chiye pulled the cloth off, and without another word, pinched Shen Zechuan's chin with one hand while sliding the other from the nape of Shen Zechuan's neck down to his lower back.

"Son of a bitch," Xiao Chiye said. "You called me a son of a bitch?"

Shen Zechuan hadn't had a chance to tie his belt properly, and Xiao Chiye's old clothes hung loosely on his body, exposing his collarbones. The lingering water on his skin soaked through the cloth and dampened Xiao Chiye's fingertips, the sensation melding with that satiny touch.

"I didn't." Shen Zechuan reached back and grabbed Xiao Chiye's hand to hold it in place. "They say one should reflect daily on one's faults. That's some good reflecting, Er-gongzi."

"You don't understand." Xiao Chiye's nimble fingers twisted to grasp Shen Zechuan's hand instead. "The first phrase I ever learned was 'son of a bitch.' Everyone knows your Er-gongzi is a scoundrel—that's not something I need to reflect on. This waist of yours is far too slender, isn't it?"

"To your inexperienced hands, maybe," Shen Zechuan said callously.

"You're right." Xiao Chiye pretended not to understand. "I haven't touched your waist many times."

Shen Zechuan had no desire to continue this charade. He tightened his belt with one hand and said, "Since you've touched me, we're even, and that's that."

Xiao Chiye withdrew the legs he'd wrapped around Shen Zechuan, and Shen Zechuan fastened his belt properly. His face had gone red from the haphazard toweling Xiao Chiye had foisted on him.

Feeling the heat, Xiao Chiye rose and picked up the eastern pearl from the ground, whereupon he caught sight of Shen Zechuan's bare legs again. After a brief daze, he swiftly straightened and took two steps back, then reconsidered and took another two steps forward. "Sleep."

Shen Zechuan sat and drank a bowl of hot ginger soup to counteract the cold. After rinsing his mouth, he sneezed again. The way he sneezed amused Xiao Chiye; he thought it resembled a cat. Soaking his handkerchief in cold water, Xiao Chiye wiped his own face clean.

"Don't go anywhere." Xiao Chiye undressed and pointed. "You're sleeping in my bed."

Shen Zechuan wiped his mouth. "Your wish is my command." Dispensing with formalities, he sat down on Xiao Chiye's bed.

Xiao Chiye moved tables and chairs before dragging the settee to the vacated spot next to the bed, only a stool's width from Shen Zechuan. He rolled onto it, folded his arms beneath his head and said, "Lights out, Lanzhou."

Shen Zechuan blew out the candle and lay down under the covers with his back to Xiao Chiye.

It was still snowing outside, but the room was quiet and warm.

Xiao Chiye shut his eyes, preparing to sleep. The feeling of Shen Zechuan's body lingered on his fingertips, more vivid in the darkness. Xiao Chiye opened his eyes, stared at the ceiling, and thought resolutely of the blue skies of Libei.

Only without desire could one become a sage.

His shifu had taught him to hold a bow at a time of year when the pastures of Libei were luxuriant. Xiao Chiye had sat on the fence at the edge of the paddock, resting his chin in his hand and gazing up at the cerulean sky.

"What are you thinking about?" Zuo Qianqiu had asked him.

Hanging around Xiao Chiye's neck was a bone thumb ring. He swung his stubby legs and said, "I want a falcon, Shifu. I want to fly."

Zuo Qianqiu joined him on the fence and looked at him. He patted the back of the boy's head and said, "You are a child filled with desires, but in this world, it is only one without desire who can become a sage. There are many things that will become your cage if you desire them."

Restless, the young Xiao Chiye grabbed the fence with both hands and hung upside down from it, his little robe covering his face in a cloud of grass and dust. "It's human nature to want," he said.

"Wanting is prelude to both joy and misery." Zuo Qianqiu polished the great bow in his arms with care. "If you acknowledge your desires, you will be obsessed with gains and losses. If you want something, you must have it; that is your nature, little wolf pup. But A-Ye, there will be many things in the future that you want but can never have. What will you do then?"

Xiao Chiye landed on the grass. He grabbed the hem of his robe and caught a large grasshopper. Picking up the struggling insect between his fingers, he said distractedly, "My father said, where there is a will, there is a way. There's nothing that can't be obtained."

Zuo Qianqiu sighed. The child was still too young after all. Resigned, he pointed up at the sky and said, "All right—you say you want to fly, but can you really?"

Releasing the grasshopper, Xiao Chiye craned his neck to look up at Zuo Qianqiu, saying in all seriousness, "I can learn to tame falcons. Once I tame one, his wings will belong to me. Wherever he flies, I will have flown there too. A man has to adapt, Shifu."

Zuo Qianqiu looked at him for a long time. "Then you are stronger than me. I'm a fool who cannot adapt."

Imitating a falcon, Xiao Chiye spread his arms wide against the wind and went running into the field. "I want to tame horses too."

"Falcons and horses are both strong-willed." Zuo Qianqiu walked after him and said, "Looks like our A-Ye likes whatever is hard to tame."

"Taming," Xiao Chiye had said then. "I like the process."

Xiao Chiye realized now he didn't just like the process, he reveled in it; he was fascinated by it. Just like conditioning a falcon—he kept the falcon awake for seven days and hungry for four, depriving it until the feathers on its head puffed, until its gaze was as concentrated as a sesame seed, until it obeyed his commands. Only then would he bring it hunting.

And now, this lust was his newly acquired falcon.

He tilted his head slightly to study Shen Zechuan's back, where his collar had once again slid down to expose the nape of his neck. In the gloom, it looked like a piece of natural jade, soft and smooth to the touch.

Xiao Chiye was hard again.

He neither moved nor averted his gaze. He didn't believe something so shallow as lust could dominate him. He didn't believe he would succumb to such base instinct.

The next day, before dawn had fully broken, both men sat up in unison as if they had finally had enough.

Outside, Ding Tao, who had been lying awake on the roof the whole night, huffed a cloud of white into the chill air and watched maidservants file into the room. "Huh. I didn't hear anything last night."

"Duh," said Gu Jin, "he didn't succeed."

Ding Tao, brush and ink already in hand, paused skeptically. "How would you know?" Gu Jin shifted his position and watched Shen Zechuan step outside. "Look at him. He's moving normally. Other than some dark circles under his eyes, he looks rested enough."

The two turned their heads as one to follow Shen Zechuan. Then they looked back at Xiao Chiye as he stepped out.

"Er-gongzi doesn't look too happy," observed Ding Tao.

"He's deprived," said Gu Jin.

Chen Yang draped an overcoat around Xiao Chiye. Noting his grave expression, he asked, "Did he spoil your plans, Your Excellency?"

"You could say so," Xiao Chiye replied.

Alarmed, Chen Yang said, "Last night, he—"

"He's pretty good at feigning sleep." Xiao Chiye secured Wolfsfang around his waist and descended the steps into the snow. "Come on. We're going to the drill grounds."

Chen Yang caught up to him. "There's no training today, Your Excellency, and with the snow—"

Xiao Chiye mounted his horse and said gruffly, "I'm going to see the new gear. Tell Gu Jin and Ding Tao to keep an eye on him."

Chen Yang nodded. Xiao Chiye looked up and shouted at the two on the roof, "If you lose him again, both of you can get lost too."

The two heads that popped out from the rooftop nodded once and shrank back again.

"Great. We've turned from Er-gongzi's personal guards into *his* personal guards." Ding Tao stowed the brush and book carefully back in his lapels.

"That guy could fight eight men on his own. We'll just have to keep an eye on him." Gu Jin shook what was left of his wine.

"Just keep an eye on him." Ding Tao readied himself and placed both hands neatly on his knees. After sitting a while, he asked, "But where is he?"

They looked at each other, then rose at the same time and swore: "Shit!"

Steamed bun in one hand, Shen Zechuan opened the back door to the Temple of Guilt.

Ji Gang was shadowboxing in the courtyard. When he saw Shen Zechuan coming, he wiped his face with a cloth and asked, "What are you doing here?"

"I had time today; in a few days I'll be busy."

Grand Mentor Qi was sleeping on a stack of papers inside. His snores rumbled like thunder, so Shen Zechuan and Ji Gang sat under the eaves to chat instead. Still mopping his brow, Ji Gang asked, "You've been keeping up with your training, right?"

Shen Zechuan lifted his sleeve to reveal the bruises left behind by his sparring match with Xiao Chiye the day before. "I fought with Xiao Er."

Stunned, Ji Gang instantly flew into a rage. "He dared to hit you?!"

"I think he wanted to test my fighting skills." Shen Zechuan shook his sleeve back down. "Shifu, he's truly blessed by heaven. His physique is a league above the Prince of Libei's. I countered his blows with Ji-Style Boxing, but it was as futile as an ant shaking a tree—I couldn't move him at all."

"Back then, Zuo Qianqiu left the capital and headed to Suotian Pass, where he met Feng Yisheng," Ji Gang said. "Feng Yisheng took Zuo Qianqiu in as his adopted son and imparted to him the Feng Broadsword. By the time his practice was passed down to Xiao Er, it was probably an amalgamation of various schools of techniques. But the Ji style naturally has its own advantages. If you spar with him using broadswords alone, you'll be able to see the difference."

"His Wolfsfang was forged by a master swordsmith under Grand Marshal Qi. It slices through metal like mud. Common blades are useless against it."

"The broadswords forged by the Qi Clan's smiths are all 'general's blades,' designed for combat on the battlefield. Take Xiao Er's Wolfsfang: if he takes it into battle, it'll split human bone with one straight slash. It was designed to make the most of his arm strength." Ji Gang stamped the snow off his shoes as he spoke. "As for us, even if we had the opportunity to wield one, such a sword might not be a good fit. But you don't have to worry about your blade. Shifu has already found one for you."

"A blade for me?" Shen Zechuan was taken by surprise.

"The Embroidered Uniform Guard is a good place." Ji Gang smiled at him. "You haven't been there long, but you'll soon see it harbors all the hidden talents of Great Zhou. Qi Zhuyin might have her acclaimed swordsmith, but we have no lack of them in the Embroidered Uniform Guard either. I've been thinking of that blade Ji Lei has. Once I get it for you and hand it to an old friend to reforge, it will be comparable to Xiao Er's Wolfsfang!"

"Isn't Ji Lei's blade a Xiuchun saber?"

"He usually carries a Xiuchun saber, but he also has my father's old blade in his collection," said Ji Gang with a snort. "Why isn't he dead yet? Once the Court of Judicial Review sentences him, that blade will be sealed in the palace armory. As long as it's in there, your shifu will find a way."

"He has been tortured for such a long time," Shen Zechuan said softly. "He won't hold out much longer."

Ji Gang then remembered something else and asked, "Did you find the person I asked you to look for before the Autumn Hunt?"

"I found him." Shen Zechuan smiled. "I'm just waiting for him to come out."

Xiao Chiye didn't return for dinner, so Shen Zechuan retired to his own room. In the middle of the night, he heard rapid footsteps outside, followed by a knock on his door. Shen Zechuan was about to feign sleep when he heard a sound from the window; Xiao Chiye lifted the wooden pane with his scabbard and whistled at him through the opening. Meng landed on the sill and tilted his head to look inside too.

"We agreed to sleep together." Xiao Chiye was displeased. "What are you doing back here?"

Shen Zechuan threw a pillow through the window; Xiao Chiye caught it. He had no choice but to get up. Blanket bundled into his arms, he opened the door.

Xiao Chiye carried Shen Zechuan's pillow and sniffed the air. "Are you wearing some fragrance?"

"I apply ten catties of rouge a day," Shen Zechuan replied.

"Is that so?" Xiao Chiye laughed.

Shen Zechuan walked ahead while Xiao Chiye followed, blocking the night breeze from brushing against Shen Zechuan. Sensing a sudden coolness on the back of his neck, Shen Zechuan's head whipped around.

Xiao Chiye scraped a fingertip lightly over Shen Zechuan's skin, then held it up to his nose, puzzled.

"What is this smell?" Xiao Chiye wondered aloud. "It's like—"

Shen Zechuan threw the blanket over Xiao Chiye's head and replied coolly, "That's the smell of gunpowder on your own body."

After standing still a moment, Xiao Chiye lifted the edge of the blanket with lightning speed and draped it over Shen Zechuan's head as well.

Sticking his head out from the eaves of the roof, Ding Tao fished out his little book and exclaimed, "Way to go, Er-gongzi! You got him!"

FIREARMS

THE WORLD DARKENED before Shen Zechuan; crowded under the blanket with Xiao Chiye, he heard him say, "So the smell is coming from me. It sure is pungent."

"You got firearms for the Imperial Army?"

"Brass muskets." Xiao Chiye held his finger to Shen Zechuan's nose to let him take a sniff. "Mixed with your scent, I couldn't tell it apart for a moment."

"I don't have a scent." The tip of Shen Zechuan's nose twitched. "Did you raid the Eight Great Battalions' armory?"

Firearms were strictly regulated by the imperial court. In recent years, the earlier bamboo barrel design had been exchanged for brass barrels and improved on considerably; this new design became the weapon of the Eight Great Battalions' Chunquan Battalion. These weapons were lethal but difficult to control. The projectiles had a limited range and loading and re-loading took time. Since the Eight Great Battalions were tasked with guarding the capital, and their battlegrounds were most often the alleyways of Qudu itself, not only were these firearms wasted in their hands—they became a burden. The Eight Great Battalions had eventually set them aside; they were brought out only during annual training exercises at the drill grounds.

But what might not have suited the Eight Great Battalions was perfect for the Libei Armored Cavalry. The famed fighting force was a heavy cavalry, with a very small number of infantry and light cavalry. They favored direct attacks that struck like monstrous waves. In the early years, before Xiao Fangxu, the Zhou empire had set up a garrison cavalry at Luoxia Pass. To counter the speed of the Biansha Horsemen, the empire spared no expense purchasing horses in an attempt to build their very own herd. But the horses they purchased from the Biansha Tribes were often their inferior steeds; true Biansha horses were fierce breeds that had been crossed with the wild wolves at the foot of the Hongyan Mountains. Paired with scimitars and sturdy warriors, they reigned invincible wheresoever they rode.

It was with this in mind that Xiao Fangxu established the Libei Armored Cavalry as a force of heavily armored men and horses. They formed a living barrier of steel in the northwest, preventing the Biansha Horsemen's furious assaults from breaching this armored wall.

The northwest was a boundless sea of grass. If the Libei Armored Cavalry could be equipped with muskets, the long distance the Biansha Horsemen had to ride to engage them would become an advantage for the Libei Armored Cavalry, leaving enough time for the firearms to be loaded. By the time the Horsemen arrived before them, they would be within shooting range. For Libei, a bird-gun like this would be akin to bestowing wings on a tiger.

"Even with Xi Gu'an removed, the Eight Great Battalions remain the Eight Great Battalions." Xiao Chiye took a step closer and nudged Shen Zechuan toward the room with his chest. "There's been no raid on the imperial armory; they've only changed hands. Don't worry, I'm just playing with them."

Shen Zechuan looked as if he couldn't care less. He took a few steps forward and said, "Can't you at least take the blanket off to walk?"

"The days are short and the nights are long. Why not carry a candle for a moonlit stroll?" Xiao Chiye grinned. "Do you want to come play with me too?"

"If they weren't obtained through official channels, you're better off keeping them hidden." Shen Zechuan lifted the blanket and ducked out. "Stalking through Qudu reeking of gunpowder—you're lucky it's the middle of the night."

"It wouldn't matter if it were noon." Xiao Chiye tucked the pillow under one arm and raised the other high to hold the blanket up as he walked. Sweeping his eyes across the eaves, he said, "Everyone knows Xiao Ce'an loves to play. They'll think the guns are for shooting little *birds* off roofs." Ding Tao and Gu Jin, sprawled on the roof above, shuddered in unison.

Once inside, Xiao Chiye threw the blanket and pillow onto his bed, kicked off his boots, and crossed the woolen rug to the bath. He was halfway undressed when he leaned out from behind the curtains. "Have you bathed?"

Shen Zechuan rinsed his mouth and said, "Yes."

So Xiao Chiye took a bath by himself. He moved fast, but still, when he stepped out to dry himself, Shen Zechuan had already lain down and turned away from him. Xiao Chiye glanced at the back of Shen Zechuan's neck, which he had covered up tightly, then hastily toweled his hair and blew out the candle.

Shen Zechuan listened as Xiao Chiye sat on the edge of the settee and opened a box to look for something.

"Lanzhou." Xiao Chiye closed the box. "Are you asleep?"

Shen Zechuan answered flatly, "Yep."

"The Court of Judicial Review summoned a great number of physicians today, yet they didn't alert the Court of Imperial Physicians," Xiao Chiye said. "What did you do to Ji Lei?"

"You want to hear horror stories this late at night?" Shen Zechuan asked.

"They're going to interrogate the guards at the Imperial Prison tomorrow morning."

Just going through the motions, Shen Zechuan thought. He didn't know whether Hai Liangyi could tolerate such a heinous act, but Xue Xiuzhuo certainly could; he had gotten the confession he wanted, so Ji Lei was a loss that could be written off. This was a mess of Shen Zechuan's making, but he had never had concerns about it; he knew Xue Xiuzhuo and Xi Hongxuan would be forced to clean up after him. He said, "I've been toeing the line. Even if they investigate—"

"Dry my hair for me." Xiao Chiye had lain down, but now quickly sat back up.

Shen Zechuan closed his eyes and pretended to sleep.

"Stop faking it. Hurry up," Xiao Chiye said.

"Lanzhou."

Then again: "Shen Lanzhou."

Shen Zechuan suddenly felt the bed dip under new weight. He opened his eyes in shock. The covers had been lifted. Xiao Chiye had squeezed in and was nuzzling his sopping hair against Shen Zechuan's back, instantly making a wet patch on his clothes. Tugging on his blanket, Shen Zechuan blurted, "Xiao Er, are you three?!"

"More or less," Xiao Chiye replied lazily. "Weren't you asleep? Don't let me wake you."

The more Shen Zechuan feigned sleep, the wetter he became. That cold mop of hair stuck to him, and behind it was Xiao Chiye, who smelled just like the scent on the handkerchief last night.

"My clothes are wet," Shen Zechuan said, opening his eyes. There was no reply.

"Stop pretending to sleep."

Then: "Xiao Er."

Shen Zechuan propped himself up and said into the darkness, "Xiao Ce'an, you're an asshole."

The asshole considerately handed him a dry cloth, then turned his back to him expectantly.

On the rooftop, Ding Tao tucked his hands into his sleeves. "It's so cold even on days it's snowing. I'm afraid it's going to be a hard winter."

Gu Jin handed him the wineskin and rubbed his hands. "We've kept watch for two nights. There should be a shift change tomorrow morning."

Ding Tao took a sip of the wine, which warmed him a little. Burrowing his hands even deeper into opposite sleeves, he lay down beside Gu Jin and looked at the night sky. "Nothing's happening tonight, either."

"The task is arduous; the road is long." Gu Jin corked the wineskin. His ears suddenly twitched, and he rolled onto his stomach, eyes darting back and forth like a falcon's in the dark.

The soft creak of trodden snow carried over the wind. Gu Jin didn't think twice—with a flick of his hand, he threw out a blade. "The northwest corner!" he hissed.

Ding Tao leapt up, soared across the rooftop, and struck out into the darkness with one hand.

A figure in a jet-black robe dodged his blow smoothly. He moved like a specter, concealing himself in shadows as he attempted to flee. Ding Tao, flexible thing that he was, dropped at once and hung upside down from the eaves, only to see three steel needles flying right for his face. Using the handle of the brush in his hand, he swept aside the needles with a wooden *thwack*. By the time he looked again, the stranger was gone.

Ding Tao landed soundlessly on the ground. His qinggong[26] was outstanding; even when landing on such a fragile crust of snow, he left no footprints.

Gu Jin surveyed the courtyard from the rooftop. "That man's no amateur if he can escape my eyes. Tao-zi, could you tell who it was?"

Ding Tao picked up the steel needles and held them between his fingers to examine them. In an instant, he learned a great deal. "Fine as a hair and dipped in snake venom. This is no product of Qudu, but a foreign gimmick imported through the Port of Yongquan in the thirteen cities of Juexi. His qinggong was good, and his ability to mask his breathing was exceptional. Although he carried no saber, I'd bet he's an Embroidered Uniform Guard."

He carefully stashed the steel needles in his own bamboo tube and somersaulted back onto the rooftop.

"The Embroidered Uniform Guard have had a number of officials removed from office. Skilled masters of the fourth rank and above are few and far between," Gu Jin said. "Who would come sniffing around our manor at this hour?"

"Hard to say." Ding Tao touched a hand to his lapels with trepidation. "He almost poked a hole in my book."

Gu Jin drank his wine, lost in thought.

Ding Tao sat cross-legged and whispered, "You know, I've carried this book for years. It was a reward from the heir consort herself! Even when I went to fight those Biansha baldies, it never got stabbed before. What a close call—really too close of a call. I've written practically everything in it. Did I ever tell you? My father's book

---

26 *Literally "lightness technique," the martial arts skill of moving swiftly and lightly through the air.*

was stolen when someone slit his throat. Good heavens, the things that were written in there! I almost lost my life chasing after that book. Jin-ge, I'm telling you—everyone should keep a journal; you get forgetful when you grow old. Look at you! You drink wine all day long; you'll probably have forgotten how much money you have hidden away before you turn forty. Why don't you tell me, and I'll write it down in here for you..."

Gu Jin stuffed cotton into his ears and began to meditate.

The next morning, Shen Zechuan was first to wake.

In fact, he'd hardly slept. With Xiao Chiye crowding behind him, the two of them had fought over the blanket all night. Besides, Shen Zechuan couldn't relax with such a hulk of a person curled up at his back.

Xiao Chiye was still sound asleep, clutching the pillow in his arms.

As Shen Zechuan waited for him to wake, he felt something else awaken instead. Xiao Chiye's erection pressed against him from behind, hot and hard and impossible to ignore.

The temperature on the bed quickly rose by several degrees. Xiao Chiye soon woke, though from the heat or hardness was anyone's guess. He swore hoarsely and sat up. Xiao Chiye tossed the pillow aside and cast a glance at Shen Zechuan, only to find Shen Zechuan looking steadily back. He grabbed at his own hair and flung out a hand to cover Shen Zechuan's head with the blanket, blocking that gaze. Then he climbed out of bed and plunged straight into the pool without even stopping for his shoes.

Chen Yang was waiting outside, listening for signs of activity, when he saw Shen Zechuan step out. He didn't know what to say as they came face to face. Shen Zechuan pointed calmly in the direction of the bath hall and sauntered off.

By the time Xiao Chiye emerged from the bath, his head was clear. He ate a little breakfast and listened to Chen Yang's report of the intruder the night before.

"Embroidered Uniform Guard?" Xiao Chiye thought for a second. "He didn't come for me; he must've been here to keep an eye on Shen Lanzhou."

"Then he's the empress dowager's man," Chen Yang said. "But the Guard is severely lacking in manpower at the moment; how could there still be such skilled men to send?"

"The Embroidered Uniform Guard's still got plenty of secrets." Xiao Chiye rose to his feet. "I'm going to morning court. We'll talk when I return."

After formally dismissing the morning's court session, Li Jianheng, holding his hand warmer, sat on the dragon throne and watched as the various officials split up to stand on either side of the hall.

"So the verdict has been rendered?" he asked apprehensively.

Xue Xiuzhuo knelt to answer. "Yes, Your Majesty. Ji Lei made a full confession regarding his intent to commit treason at the Nanlin Hunting Grounds. The evidence against him is conclusive. The Court of Judicial Review has worked through the night to sort through the confession, and Secretariat Elder Hai has submitted it to Your Majesty. In the fortnight since the Hua faction case, the Three Judicial Offices have conducted a number of joint trials. In addition to their leader, Ji Lei, the two vice commanders and four assistant commanders of the Embroidered Uniform Guard have all been sentenced to immediate execution by decapitation, while the judge and accompanying battalion commanders present at the Nanlin Hunting Grounds have been sentenced to prison to await execution pending review."

"As long as a verdict has been reached, then good," Li Jianheng said. "Secretariat Elder, you've worked hard. Come, it's not good to kneel for too long. Bring him a seat."

When Hai Liangyi was seated, Li Jianheng continued. "The Hua Clan colluded with eunuchs and the Embroidered Uniform Guard to stage a coup—it's really too abominable! Pan Rugui abused his office as the Director of Writ at the Directorate of Ceremonial Affairs; he was greedy for power and wealth and wicked beyond remedy. This man mustn't be held in custody to await execution; he should be beheaded immediately! After the secretariat elder's previous admonishments, we have tossed and turned through many sleepless nights. After much thought, we are determined to work diligently toward the prosperity of the state from now on."

Hai Liangyi rose at once to bow again.

Li Jianheng raised his hands. "Sit, Secretariat Elder, please sit. There are so many matters that require the secretariat elder's counsel. It wouldn't be a stretch for us to refer to the secretariat elder as *xiansheng*. In the future, we hope everyone will work as one to assist us. If you have something to say, you may boldly speak your mind."

Xue Xiuzhuo looked up in surprise, though his expression remained neutral. He knelt in unison with the officials on his left and right and sang the emperor's praises.

Li Jianheng excitedly motioned for everyone to rise. After a few more words, he dismissed the audience and invited Secretariat Elder Hai alone to stay and share a meal with him.

Xiao Chiye found himself walking out beside Xue Xiuzhuo.

"I wonder what Your Excellency said to His Majesty," Xue Xiuzhuo said, "that His Majesty is now willing to show such respect to his wisest subjects."

"His Majesty is young and strong; this is precisely the time for him to show his mettle and realize his potential. Even if I said nothing, he'd have come to the same conclusion," Xiao Chiye replied. "The Court of Judicial Review has been busy these days. Thank you for your hard work, Lord Yanqing."

"It's only natural to concern oneself with all matters pertaining to one's post; I have merely done my duty." As Xue Xiuzhuo spoke, he looked at Xiao Chiye with a smile. "I hear Your Excellency has traveled to Mount Feng often these last few days. Is there any fun to be had there?"

Xiao Chiye smiled in return. "The first snow on Mount Feng is a sight to behold. Several deer have been spotted recently as well. I've been thinking of capturing a few for fun; if you're free, would you like to go and have a look together?"

Xue Xiuzhuo gave an airy wave of his hand. "I am but a frail scholar. What do I know about hunting? I wouldn't want to dampen your spirits."

The two parted ways at the palace gates. As Xiao Chiye watched him recede into the distance, his smile started to fade.

Chen Yang was standing beside the carriage. He waited until Xiao Chiye arrived before lifting the curtain for him. "Your Excellency, Shifu has departed for Qudu," he said.

Xiao Chiye nodded.

After hesitating for a moment, Chen Yang continued, "Our man in the Court of Judicial Review brought word that Ji Lei is dead."

"How did he die?" Xiao Chiye asked.

Chen Yang gestured sharply but kept his voice down. "He was skinned. When they found him, he looked like neither human nor ghost. He should've died last night, but Xue Xiuzhuo kept him hanging on until the confession was presented to His Majesty. Only then did he let him breathe his last."

Xiao Chiye sat down in silence.

"Five years ago, Ji Lei interrogated Shen Zechuan in the Imperial Prison. Later, Ji Lei sent Fengquan to publicly humiliate him with the donkey roast," Chen Yang said. "Now Shen Zechuan has repaid the favor in kind, and turned Ji Lei into… Your Excellency, this man is vindictive. There's already bad blood between him and us; it's far too dangerous to keep him at your side."

Xiao Chiye twisted the bone ring on his thumb and said nothing.

MILITARY DISCIPLINE

WINTER DEEPENED, and snow fell for days at a time. Xiao Chiye grew lazier, making fewer and fewer trips to the drill grounds. He made the acquaintance of several of the famous Longyou merchants and procured a number of valuable items, including pearls imported from the Port of Yongquan and jade from Hezhou—exquisite little trinkets all.

Li Jianheng had become diligent indeed. He attended court sessions without fail, no matter how cold the weather, and sought daily tutelage from Hai Liangyi. When he saw Xiao Chiye slacking on the job, he gently advised him against it. It seemed he really had changed.

Xiao Chiye was happy to see it. He felled two deer on Mount Feng and offered them to the palace. Still traumatized from the donkey roast, Li Jianheng kept his distance from game; he bestowed the venison on Hai Liangyi instead.

As the end of the year approached, so did two major proceedings: the sacrificial ceremony to the gods and ancestors, and the officials' banquet. The Six Ministries and Twenty-Four Yamen of the imperial palace were up to their necks in work. Since the Directorate of Ceremonial Affairs was still without a leader, someone had to sign off on the decisions—for this, they turned to Li Jianheng. But Li Jianheng was baffled by such things; he had to trouble Hai Liangyi and the Ministry of Rites each time.

Qudu was bustling. When Li Jianheng saw that Xiao Chiye alone was idle, he assigned him the important task of reviewing the Eight Great Battalions' roster, effectively putting all patrol and defense of the capital entirely in Xiao Chiye's hands.

This was one responsibility Xiao Chiye couldn't shirk; he had no choice but to throw himself into his task. And since Shen Zechuan was consigned to following Xiao Chiye wherever he went, it was inevitable that he came into frequent contact with the Imperial Army.

On one such day, when Tantai Hu had just returned to the duty office at the end of patrol—so recently he had yet to remove his weapon—he saw Shen Zechuan standing outside. He rubbed his frozen, scar-ridden face and marched over.

Shen Zechuan turned and watched as Tantai Hu stormed toward him.

"The eighth son of Shen Wei?" Tantai Hu stopped in his tracks. Coldly, he said, "Shen Wei *is* your old man, is he not?"

"Are you looking for my old man, or for me?" Shen Zechuan asked.

"Of course I'm looking for you. Shen Wei was reduced to fucking ashes five years ago." Tantai Hu paced around Shen Zechuan. "Your days in Qudu must've been comfortable. Check out this figure—you look like one of those pampered courtesans on Donglong Street with a taste for food and wine."

It was obvious Tantai Hu had come to make trouble. Chen Yang stood silent off to one side, while the rest of the Imperial Army men in the courtyard craned their necks to watch the show.

Tantai Hu continued, "A perky ass and a slender willow waist, cheeks like peach blossoms and eyes like a fox—you'd be a first-class courtesan in Xiangyun Villa. Why are you running about in the wind and snow with our supreme commander instead of living the good life?" Coming to a stop, Tantai Hu fixed his sharp gaze on Shen Zechuan. "It was only because Shen Wei licked the hooves of the Libei Armored Cavalry's horses five years ago that the six prefectures of Zhongbo didn't become manure pits for Biansha horses. I see you've learned from your old man. So, which part of His Excellency will you be licking? Behind their curtains, the brothel girls are all top of their field in certain *techniques*, so what's your talent? What makes you worthy of standing alongside men who have been to war?"

"If I'm not worthy, will the vice commander revoke my authority token and kick me out?" Shen Zechuan said with a smile.

"Why would I go to the trouble? You're a dog sitting at the doorstep of the Imperial Army. Even a kick is an honor you don't deserve. It's only because of our supreme commander that your granddaddy here is talking to you today. Since you've become a man's plaything, it's time you were enlightened to your new reality: you're no man."

"Under orders of the Son of Heaven, I carry the authority token of the Embroidered Uniform Guard. I'm here as a servant to the throne, not anyone's plaything," Shen Zechuan said. "If I'm the Imperial Army's dog, then you gentlemen are no different. We all walk around Qudu on the same imperial salary. If there is any enlightenment to be had, then we must be enlightened together."

Hands on his twin blades, Tantai Hu widened his tiger-like eyes in anger. "You, the same as men like us? Fucking Shen dog! I was the senior battalion commander of the Dengzhou Garrison Troops in Zhongbo." He lurched forward, seething. "My brothers were in the sinkhole at Chashi River! Do you have any idea what that was like? Those men were still alive when they were shot with arrow after arrow until they looked like pincushions! Thirty thousand men were buried in the sinkhole! *Thirty thousand men!*"

Shen Zechuan's expression remained unchanged.

"My old man and mother were in Dengzhou too," Tantai Hu continued. "When the Biansha Horsemen came, the treacherous Shen bastard fled. He abandoned those who couldn't run, all the old and vulnerable in Dengzhou—my parents! Those Biansha bastards massacred city after city; they dragged my little sister for two li before raping and killing her at the city gates. And here you are, living a comfortable life without a care in the world! Stick your ass out for someone to fuck and you can be pardoned of all sins."

A freezing wind swept the courtyard. By the time Chen Yang realized the situation was getting out of hand, it was too late. Tantai Hu gripped Shen Zechuan by the collar, eyes red. "How *dare* you talk back to me? All you young masters born with silver spoons in your mouths; how would you know how many died in that battle? How would you know there are people starving to death in Zhongbo to this day?! How's life in Qudu, huh? You sleep well, eat well, and people absolve you of blame over and over. But what about the dead of Zhongbo? Who's going to pay for their lives?!"

Without warning, Shen Zechuan grabbed Tantai Hu's arm and flung him to the ground.

It was such an earth-shattering move that everyone around them took a halting step backward. Shen Zechuan wiped his hands clean in the snow and looked at Tantai Hu. "Who? Why don't you settle the score with your own people. It took a month for the Biansha Horsemen to enter our territory, cross the banks of the Chashi River, and reach Dengzhou. When Shen Wei shrank back from battle, you valiant, iron-willed men should have snapped his neck and risen up to fortify the city's defenses."

Shen Zechuan straightened. "Humiliate me, hate me; it's no skin off my back. This world demands a debt of blood be repaid in kind, so killing me would be meting out heaven's justice and appeasing the wrath of the people." He spat at Tantai Hu and laughed cruelly. "What a fucking load of shit. The Biansha Horsemen massacred the cities. The Biansha Horsemen killed those thirty thousand soldiers. If you want to fuck with me, wash the Biansha Horsemen's piss off your head first. My life is cheap and I won't be missed in death, but will it write off the Biansha Horsemen's debts?"

"Don't you fucking try to absolve yourself of guilt!" Tantai Hu snapped. "Wasn't your old man the one who let the Biansha Horsemen in?!"

"Then kill me." Shen Zechuan raised a finger and made a slashing motion across his neck. "Please, hurry up and kill me. Kill me, and the bloodline of the traitor Shen will be severed."

Tantai Hu roared to his feet, pulled out his twin blades, and charged at Shen Zechuan.

Ding Tao had only just woken and come into the courtyard when he was met with this scene. In a panic, he shouted, "Lao-Hu, don't hurt him! I'm supposed to be watching him!"

But Tantai Hu was beyond reason. His twin blades whistled through the air. Ding Tao leaped three feet in alarm and tried to charge in, but Gu Jin grabbed the back of his collar and held him in place.

"Lao-Hu lost his entire family in Zhongbo," Gu Jin said. "You can't expect him to let Shen Zechuan go."

"But wasn't the culprit Shen Wei?" Ding Tao exclaimed. "What does it have to do with Shen Zechuan?!"

Gu Jin hesitated a moment but didn't go on.

Tantai Hu's blade sliced down inches before Shen Zechuan's face; Shen Zechuan spun, kicking his assailant's wrist askew. Tantai Hu's arm numbed as his blade flew from his hand. At that moment, the curtain in front of the office lifted. Yang Zongzhi, the Vice Minister

of the Ministry of War, stared with wide eyes at the blade hurtling toward him.

Chen Yang raised a hand to grab the hilt, but Xiao Chiye was faster. With a swing of his sheathed blade, he struck the blade down into the snow. The steel pierced the ground with such violent force that it shook the entire courtyard. The men of the Imperial Army fell to their knees.

"Please pardon our offense, Supreme Commander!" they chorused.

Xiao Chiye ignored them. He returned his blade to his waist and raised a hand to lift the curtain for Yang Zongzhi. He smiled apologetically. "My failure to discipline my subordinates caused alarm for Vice Minister Yang today."

Yang Zongzhi didn't dare tarry. After stumbling through a few awkward pleasantries, he hurried out of the courtyard, leapt into his carriage, and, after declining a farewell, was soon on his way.

Once the guest had left, Xiao Chiye turned back and swept his eyes over the courtyard of kneeling men.

Chen Yang was aware he had blundered. He hastened to say, "Your Excellency, this subordinate was negligent in my supervision of the men; I didn't—"

"You've watched the show long enough." As Xiao Chiye spoke, Meng came to land on his shoulder. He took some white meat from a waist pouch and fed it to the gyrfalcon. "Zhao Hui wouldn't have done such a thing."

Chen Yang paled.

Xiao Chiye didn't reprimand Chen Yang in front of the men. Chen Yang was the chief of his guards and his most trusted aide. Under the watchful eyes of others, he could not shame Chen Yang by berating him publicly; Chen Yang would lose his authority among his Imperial Army brothers and be unable to hold up his head before them. But Xiao Chiye knew these words cut Chen Yang deepest.

Chen Yang and Zhao Hui were both promising young men handpicked by Xiao Fangxu. Zhao Hui was calm and steady, and under Xiao Jiming's command, his meritorious military deeds were innumerable. He was a deputy general whom few were bold enough to disrespect even in Qudu. Meanwhile, Chen Yang had remained in the Libei Prince's Manor until he finally followed Xiao Chiye to Qudu five years ago. He was prudent, and what he feared most of all was being told he was inferior to Zhao Hui. This was a contest between brothers of the same clan.

These words were more than a wake-up call; they shamed him to the core.

Xiao Chiye turned to Tantai Hu. "When I assumed command five years ago, the Imperial Army was a bunch of rotten thugs with no regard for military discipline, who held their supreme commander in contempt," he said as he stroked Meng. "I can't lead soldiers like that. If you want to stay in the Imperial Army, either sort yourself out and abide by the rules, or pack up and fuck off."

Tantai Hu's chest heaved. He said indignantly, "Your Excellency is right, of course. We have all listened to you in the past. But what's *he* supposed to be? Can someone like this be considered a soldier? As vice commander, I outrank him; is it wrong of me to dress him down? There's no way I'm going to kiss the ass of someone who sells it!"

"The authority token hanging from his belt belongs to the Embroidered Uniform Guard, and his current duty is as my personal guard. Once you get to where I am, you can shame him however you like; that will be your prerogative." Xiao Chiye looked down at him. "You think you did nothing wrong?"

Straightening his spine, Tantai Hu said, "That's right!"

"Then why stay here and suffer this indignity?" Xiao Chiye said. "Go."

Tantai Hu raised his head in disbelief. "For this man, you would dismiss me from my post?"

"There are no personal grudges within the Imperial Army, so don't fucking try to play matchmaker for me. I'm not doing this for anyone." Xiao Chiye's voice was dangerously low. "I have final say in the Imperial Army. If you can make your own decisions, why bother calling me your commander? Strip off this armor and remove your blades; then you're free to demand repayment of any blood debt you're owed. If you can take him down in three moves, I'll get on my knees and acknowledge my mistake. But when you don this armor and wear the token of the Imperial Army, you listen to me. All of you enjoyed quite the spectacle today, trampling all over my reputation to amuse yourselves. You've got guts and backbone to spare; why bother with military discipline? Wouldn't it be more gratifying to fuck off and be bandits in the mountains?"

The soldiers hung their heads, too cowed to utter another word. Meng finished his meat and raised his head to stare at them.

"Don't you all love calling me a fool blinded by lust?" Xiao Chiye continued. "I'll be exactly that today. Remove Tantai Hu's authority token and send him out the door!"

"Please have mercy, Your Excellency!" Cries rose from the Imperial Army.

Tantai Hu refused to back down. He tore his authority token off with trembling fingers and said, "I've regarded Your Excellency as a brother and have been grateful to you for the past five years. I would've laid down my life for you! What wrong have I committed today? If Your Excellency wants to break my heart and dismiss me from my post because of a pretty man—fine! I, Tantai Hu, concede defeat!"

With that, he placed his authority token and helmet together on the ground and kowtowed thrice to Xiao Chiye, then rose to his feet and stripped off his armor. Wearing nothing but his inner garment, he turned to Shen Zechuan.

"See how long you can survive seducing those you serve! I'll seek my vengeance on the Biansha baldies in days to come, but you won't escape either!" Tantai Hu wiped his eyes and cupped his hands to everyone around him. "My brothers, until we meet again!"

Turning his back, he walked out of the courtyard and disappeared from view.

VICIOUS BEAST

A CHARCOAL FIRE BURNED in the hall, warming the room. Chen Yang had been kneeling for almost an hour. Xiao Chiye sat in the principal seat reading a book on military strategy, while the Imperial Army generals knelt just beyond the screen. It was silent inside and out.

As the saying went, "If a general has yet to be revered, he must establish reverence through a show of force."[27] When Xiao Chiye took command of the Imperial Army five years ago, he had put on just such a show of strength and power. He required absolute authority over these men, and that required their respect. Over the last five years, he had fairly meted out reward and punishment, never skimping on salaries nor supplies. He went so far as to spend from his own pocket to make up any deficiencies. He was a generous superior to his subordinates, though the overcoat on his back was the same sent to him by his sister-in-law three years ago.

The Autumn Hunt incident allowed the Imperial Army to hold their heads high. Their name was lauded now; their prestige overshadowed that of the Eight Great Battalions, and for the moment, they had the world at their feet. The same browbeaten soldiers who used to cower before the Eight Great Battalions were now bold

27 *From New Treatise on Effective Military Discipline, a military manual written in 1560 by Qi Jiguang, a Ming dynasty general who defended China from invasion by Japanese pirates.*

enough to boss them around. This was not a blessing, but a curse. A head swollen with success would lead one astray. Xiao Chiye needed an opportunity to knock some sense back into the Imperial Army, and Tantai Hu had given him one.

Chen Yang didn't dare raise his head. When Xiao Chiye rapped on the table, he got up immediately to refill the tea. Once the cup was filled, he returned to kneeling.

Xiao Chiye hadn't said a single word the entire night, so Chen Yang knelt on the ground until dawn.

Many times, leaving words unsaid made one more ashamed than if they'd been spoken aloud.

The next day, Xiao Chiye was due to attend morning court. After dressing, he said to Chen Yang, "You don't have to follow me today. Take a break."

Chen Yang's legs were numb from kneeling. Palms splayed on the ground, he kowtowed and called in a hoarse voice, "Master..."

He had always addressed Xiao Chiye as *Your Excellency*. This plea came from his heart. Xiao Chiye paused in his steps but did not look back.

Chen Yang kowtowed again. "I implore Master to dole out whatever punishment he deems fit."

Xiao Chiye raised a hand and dismissed his attendants. Only when the hall had emptied did he turn to look at Chen Yang. "If a man has done nothing wrong, what need is there for punishment?"

The sweat on Chen Yang's forehead dripped into his eyes. "I was wrong."

There was a long silence. Finally, Xiao Chiye said, "Zhao Hui has followed my elder brother to war on the frontier for years; he has climbed the ranks. Within five years, he may receive his own manor and a conferred title. You are both good men handpicked by my father. Why is it that he, Zhao Hui, enjoys such an honor while you, Chen Yang, have to follow a hoodlum rotting away in captivity?"

Chen Yang's lips were bloodless. "How could I think that way? The heir has his strengths to be sure, but Master holds up the sky above my head! Zhao Hui and I are brothers of the same clan. Our glories and failures are one and the same."

"I hope you truly understand this principle," Xiao Chiye said. "Brothers who fight among themselves and families who draw swords on each other are a rotten lot—they'll destroy themselves before outsiders ever lift a finger. By remaining in Qudu with me, you left all our family matters back at home in Zhao Hui's care. When his younger sister married the Deputy Director of the Ministry of Rites here in Qudu, you stood in as her family here so she wouldn't be stranded in a strange house and would have a brother beside her during the Spring Festival and other holidays. You must contend with will and spirit if you want to accomplish great things, but not at the expense of moral principles. Righteous ardor and heroic spirit make a good man.

"Why are you anxious about being compared to him? Zhao Hui wouldn't have done what you did yesterday, because he would've considered Dage's reputation. You are now the chief of the Imperial Army's bodyguards, yet you rely on cheap tactics like a scapegoat to unite your men. For an ounce of gratification, you'll stand by and watch your master's dignity trampled. Tantai Hu is from Zhongbo. You knew that; you assigned him to yesterday's shift so he could vent his anger. What happened, Chen Yang? In following me, have you fallen so low you've resorted to tricks like these to win people over? You've traded your master's name for a moment's satisfaction."

Overcome with remorse and self-reproach, Chen Yang hung his head. "I've let Master down—"

"You've let yourself down," Xiao Chiye said coolly. "Get your head on straight before you resume your duties. Gu Jin will follow me for the next few days."

Dazed, Chen Yang remained kneeling. He raised his head just in time to watch as Xiao Chiye lifted the curtain and stepped out.

Shen Zechuan had finally gotten a good night's sleep. At present, he was waiting beside the carriage, puffing warm air into his hands as he watched the gyrfalcon wheel in the snowy sky.

When Xiao Chiye emerged, he stepped straight up into the carriage. Gu Jin picked up the riding crop and looked at Shen Zechuan. Shen Zechuan did not return his gaze. The curtain was partially open, and he could see Xiao Chiye looking at him meaningfully.

Shen Zechuan felt eyes on his back as the Imperial Army, who had been freezing in the courtyard the entire night in penance, all raised their heads to stare. He smiled at Xiao Chiye, then made his way up.

The carriage started to sway as Gu Jin drove the horses forward.

Xiao Chiye passed a hand warmer to Shen Zechuan. When Shen Zechuan accepted it, Xiao Chiye pressed the back of his hand to Shen Zechuan's.

"So cold," Xiao Chiye said.

Shen Zechuan raised a finger to push Xiao Chiye's hand away, then leaned against the side of the carriage and held the hand warmer close.

"You don't look happy," Xiao Chiye said.

"I'm happy." He looked at Xiao Chiye and continued with a smile, "I'm overjoyed that Er-gongzi spoke up for me and helped me out of my predicament."

"Er-gongzi wasn't speaking up for anybody," Xiao Chiye said.

"Perhaps not," Shen Zechuan said. "Now that reverence has been established, it's time for you to make friends of them again. When will the favors be doled out? There aren't many days left for me to be your bodyguard. You should hurry if you want to use me."

Xiao Chiye looked at him in silence.

Shen Zechuan lifted his chin slightly in a careful pose of relaxation and exhaled. After a pause, he said, "I'm no match for you when it comes to governing others. Shen Lanzhou is a good target. Place him at your side, and you can defend your authority, intimidate the tiger, and maybe even warm your bed. It's hard to find a situation where you can kill three birds with one stone. *Quite* impressive, Xiao Er."

Voices from the street clamored outside the carriage; inside, the tension grew thick as the silence stretched. They were just a few inches apart, yet they seemed to be separated by a natural chasm. When the carriage at last arrived at its destination, Gu Jin tactfully said not a word to interrupt them. Shen Zechuan returned the hand warmer to the small table. "Such a pity though."

"What's a pity?" Xiao Chiye asked.

"Everyone thinks you spend your nights indulging in pleasures of the flesh," Shen Zechuan ran his tongue over the sharp edges of his teeth and said placidly, "Who would have suspected Xiao Er to be a diligent and conscientious man of honor? You haven't so much as touched my lips, let alone fucked me."

He made to lift the curtain and exit the carriage, but Xiao Chiye swiftly grabbed onto his belt. "I see." Xiao Chiye grinned wickedly. "If you're so eager to cross swords on the bed, I shall comply with your wish."

"I don't want anyone with eyes so fierce," Shen Zechuan said.

The curtain swayed as he stepped down from the carriage, leaving Xiao Chiye's fingers empty. They twitched once, left wanting.

After Tantai Hu's dismissal, the Imperial Army buckled down. The soldiers tucked their tails between their legs and behaved, falling back into their discipline from before the Autumn Hunt. Chen Yang became even more prudent and no longer turned a blind eye when others stirred up trouble.

Chen Yang had hurt his foot years ago in Libei, and the injury still plagued him. During a harsh cold spell in Qudu a few days later, his foot ached whenever he was on duty. One evening, Xiao Chiye tossed Chen Yang several bottles of medicinal ointment after dinner. When Chen Yang opened them that night, he found an incredibly rare ointment that Xiao Jiming had received from Master Yideng a few years ago. He couldn't help but reproach himself again and threw himself into his work with renewed diligence.

Tantai Hu, on the other hand, went home and found himself immediately in dire straits. Though everyone in his family was dead, he had adopted three children from Zhongbo, all of whom lived off his salary. He was unmarried and had no wife to manage household affairs; every month he drained his salary down to the very last copper. Now their stores of grain were empty, and the new year was fast approaching. Tantai Hu was a veteran of Dengzhou and had many friends in Qudu. All these years, he had been the one taking care of others. Now that it was his turn, he couldn't bring himself to ask for help—yet tightening his belt to feed the children was hardly a long-term solution either.

Tantai Hu had reached the point of considering taking work as a debt collector for loan sharks when Chen Yang arrived on his doorstep.

"New Year's is right around the corner," Chen Yang said as he set down a money purse. "The supreme commander remembers that you have three children at home."

Sitting in his chair, Tantai Hu turned his face away. "Since I'm no longer on the Imperial Army's payroll, there's no reason for me to accept money from the Imperial Army."

"You have *tiger* in your name, but it doesn't mean you have to be a brute," Chen Yang said severely. "Why do you still hold a grudge against His Excellency? You struck out at Shen Zechuan in front of everyone that day; where is your respect for the supreme commander? Lack of discipline is a major taboo in the army. You've been a vice commander all these years; don't tell me you don't understand that."

"What was I supposed to do?" Tantai Hu asked. "Whenever I see that Shen guy, I think of my parents!"

Chen Yang sighed. "Even so, you shouldn't have humiliated him—by extension, that insults the supreme commander. You've followed him for years; shouldn't you know his temperament? Yet you still shot your mouth off."

Tantai Hu ran a hand through his hair.

"I was at fault, too," said Chen Yang. "I knew you were rash, but I didn't stop you. Admit your mistake if you make one, and accept your punishment if you receive one. A real man knows when to resist and when to submit. Must you burn your bridges just to prove yourself a hero?"

"What can I do? I've already handed in my authority token!" Tantai Hu felt aggrieved all over again. "I followed His Excellency for five years. I risked my life during the Autumn Hunt. It wasn't easy for the Imperial Army to make a name for itself after all this time—so it unnerves the hell out of me to see that cunning fox going freely in and out of our office! The way he looks... I worry he'll lead His Excellency astray! I was anxious, and I hate him to death! I heard Ding Tao say something about how it's not his fault. Sure, who doesn't know that? But could you stand it if you were in my shoes? It wasn't some dog by the roadside that died—my parents and siblings are gone!"

Chen Yang was silent.

Tantai Hu stomped his foot in grief and wiped haphazardly at his eyes. The thought of it still brought the scarred man to tears. Chest heaving with sobs, he said, "Anyone would be appalled to see a man they despise waved in front of their face, let alone one with whom they have a blood debt. The year the Zhongbo troops were defeated... those of us who survived were left with broken families and ruined homes, while we ourselves barely escaped with our lives! Chen Yang, who's going to take pity on us? Look at the three children in my house. They became orphans before they could talk, digging mud under the hooves of the Biansha horses to survive. Our lives are worth nothing."

Chen Yang patted his shoulder and waited for him to take a few steadying breaths. "But now that you have joined the Imperial Army, our supreme commander's word is law. Hu-zi, five years ago, when His Excellency cleaned up the Imperial Army, he wanted to take in soldiers like you who were not native to Qudu, but the Ministry of War disapproved. Do you remember what His Excellency said then?"

Tantai Hu's shoulders trembled.

Chen Yang went on, "His Excellency said the same thing that drives you to be a soldier now: 'The wrongs suffered by our families have yet to be avenged, and the humiliation of our nation has yet to be redressed.' The Imperial Army will one day ride our horses out of the mountain pass. When the time comes, won't slaying the enemy with your own hands be more gratifying than giving a tongue-lashing to some stranger today? How is it that you've forgotten this?"

"How could I forget?" Tantai Hu said. "It's never left my mind. I gave this life to His Excellency to use as he wished, all in hopes that such a day would come."

"Then we're done here." Chen Yang got up and pushed the money across the table to Tantai Hu. "Brothers don't hold grudges. The supreme commander treats us as brothers and took this money from his own account. After the new year, return to your original squad, hang up a squad commander token, and resume your duties."

Filled with mixed feelings, Tantai Hu saw Chen Yang out of the door.

When Chen Yang returned, he ran into Shen Zechuan; the two men greeted each other on the veranda. Chen Yang lifted the curtain and went in, and Shen Zechuan knew the matter was resolved.

He watched the falling snow, his thoughts drifting.

A vicious beast like him could pass as fake even if he were real, and be made real even if he were fake. No one could tell whether happiness or anger hid behind his smile, nor could they distinguish his sincerity from his deception.

It wasn't long before Chen Yang stepped out again. He lifted the curtain and nodded toward Shen Zechuan. "His Excellency is ready for you to eat together."

Shen Zechuan turned around and saw Xiao Chiye waiting inside, already watching him.

40 TEARING AND BITING

FRESH VEGETABLES were a rare sight in winter, and they fetched a high price in Qudu at this time of year. But thanks to the generosity of Li Jianheng, Xiao Chiye's dinner table tonight included a plate of crisp, shredded cucumber.

"Side dishes that accompany the main course invigorate the spleen and eliminate toxins."[28] Xiao Chiye ladled hot soup into a bowl and pushed it toward Shen Zechuan. "You've been standing outside for so long. Warm yourself up and fill your stomach before you rest."

"As the saying goes," Shen Zechuan said, wiping his hands as he took a seat, "one who is solicitous without reason hides nefarious intent. So, what commands does Er-gongzi have for me?"

"Plenty," Xiao Chiye said. "We'll talk as we eat."

So they ate.

There was no one else in the room. The two bowls of rice quickly disappeared, as did the plate of shredded cucumber, split between them. Neither touched the meat dishes.

"New Year's is right around the corner, and my shifu is coming to the capital," Xiao Chiye said between mouthfuls of soup. "If Ji Gang-shifu is free, we can arrange a dinner for the two elders."

---

28 *From Recipes from the Garden of Contentment, a culinary treatise written by Qing dynasty scholar Yuan Mei.*

Shen Zechuan set down the chopsticks. "A New Year celebration, or a Hongmen banquet? You'll have to make that clear. My shifu doesn't stake his life on games."

"New Year celebration," Xiao Chiye said. "They're the only members of the Ji family left in this generation, and it's been many years since they've seen each other."

"Sure. I'll prepare a big gift later and ask Shifu to come out of seclusion." Shen Zechuan was full; he pushed himself away from the table.

Watching him get up, Xiao Chiye said, "You'll sleep in my room as usual tonight."

Shen Zechuan looked back and smiled placidly. "I'm not going anywhere. Let's take turns in the bath. Take your time eating. I'll go first."

He lifted the curtain and headed to wash up.

Xiao Chiye called for the servants to clear the table. As he stood by the window, he noticed it was snowing. He turned his head and saw Shen Zechuan's silhouette, hazy through the screen.

Shen Zechuan removed his outer robe as if prying away a layer of coarse shell to reveal the soft, tender flesh within. When he lowered his head to untie his belt, butter-yellow light danced along the curve of his nape, a velvet touch upon that pristine surface. Looking at him through the screen was like scratching an itch through a boot. It magnified Xiao Chiye's desire and scattered it aimlessly through his body; it equally tickled and irritated him, eliciting a violent yearning. It was said a gentleman possessed all the virtues of jade, yet the jadelike qualities Shen Zechuan possessed gave him a wholly different kind of allure.

With those eyes and that smile, he exuded a sensual appeal even without meaning to.

Come hold me.

Come touch me.

Come tangle your limbs with mine to your heart's content.

This kind of appeal was harmless yet persistent as a drizzle, and at some point unbeknownst to Xiao Chiye, it had invaded his mind. Meanwhile, Shen Zechuan seemed entirely oblivious to it. He retained a kind of aloofness that was diametrically opposed to lust, making himself a study in contradictions for others to puzzle out.

Xiao Chiye didn't want to keep thinking about it. He was keenly aware that this "falcon" was not so easily tamed. Above all things he must remain the master of himself; he couldn't tolerate this—becoming a stranger to himself whose basest impulses were so easily roused.

Turning away, Xiao Chiye closed the window and went to the bath hall.

As before, the men slept each to their own bed, with the stool's distance between. Their backs were to each other, their breathing steady, as if they had fallen asleep.

Xiao Chiye touched his thumb ring as his mind drifted in memory.

This thumb ring didn't originally belong to him. Its first owner was Feng Yisheng of the Suotian Pass. When Feng Yisheng died in battle, he left it to Zuo Qianqiu. Wearing this thumb ring, Zuo Qianqiu made a name for himself at the battle of Tianfei Watchtower, where he shot the fatal arrow that killed his wife. It was for this reason that Zuo Qianqiu's hair had turned white, and also why he fell from the peak of prestige and never recovered. The general had achieved fame and glory; the man himself was dead. Zuo Qianqiu could never again step onto the battlefield. His hands, which had achieved incredible feats at Tianfei Watchtower, could never again wield a bow.

Xiao Chiye had learned from Zuo Qianqiu as a child. One day he asked him, "How did you end up shooting your wife?"

Sanding his bowstring, Zuo Qianqiu asked in return, "Do you really want to be a general?"

Xiao Chiye nodded.

"Then don't start a family," Zuo Qianqiu said. "Dying after a hundred battles is nothing for a general to fear. Far more terrifying are the choices a general will come to face in life. What you want for yourself, and the burdens you must shoulder as a commander, are not the same." Zuo Qianqiu looked at the bow, his face a mask of desolation. The wind rushing over the grassland caressed his white hair. "I hope you never find yourself in such a desperate situation," he said, eyes unfocused. "When a man faces such a decision, he will die no matter what he chooses."

"You saved tens of thousands of lives at Tianfei Watchtower." Xiao Chiye leaned against the fence. "Why didn't you want to be conferred a title?"

"Because I died in that battle." Zuo Qianqiu laughed with no joy.

It was not until Xiao Chiye was several years older that he understood Zuo Qianqiu's words. In the battle at Tianfei Watchtower, Zuo Qianqiu's wife was taken hostage. Between opening the gates to surrender or barring them and fighting to the death, he could only choose one.

Zuo Qianqiu chose neither. He rode out of the city alone, drew his bow, and killed his beloved wife.

Those who were there said it was the steadiest shot he had fired in his life. He sighted his target among a crowd of thousands. The rain was pouring that night; no one knew later if he had cried himself hoarse, or when his hair had turned white. When the invaders retreated at dawn, Zuo Qianqiu stood upon the white expanse of bones and collected his wife's cold corpse.

From then on, his reputation as the general of "Thunder on Jade Terraces" spread far and wide. Yet those who respected him also cursed him behind his back—a man as heartless as he became a specter in the minds of ordinary people, as if all generals were naturally so cold-blooded.

Xiao Chiye treasured this thumb ring greatly. But he also feared it. He was afraid that he, too, would one day find himself caught in such a dilemma. So he never spoke freely of what he liked. Even Chen Yang, who had served at his side so many years, still had no idea of Xiao Chiye's real preferences: the wine he loved, the food he liked, or the clothing he preferred. The truth was so mixed up with falsehood that no one could really tell.

But Libei. *Libei!*

This word was the one vulnerability he could not obfuscate or conceal. He'd already had a taste of falling under someone else's control because he failed to keep his desire in check. So how could he court trouble again?

Xiao Chiye sat up soundlessly and looked at Shen Zechuan. He raised his hand. He had only to bring it down, and he could smother this desire in its crib. But when he bent over to look at him, he saw a Shen Zechuan he had never seen before.

He looked like he was having a nightmare. He was frowning, and his temples were drenched in a cold sweat that had already dampened his back.

Trapped in a tide of blood, the dreaming Shen Zechuan was soaked to the bone. He reached out a hand; it dripped crimson. The dream repeated itself every night without fail. He was on the verge of going mad.

Shen Zechuan twitched a few times, ever so slightly. Clammy with sweat, his tightly pursed lips slowly parted as he muttered something in his sleep.

How helpless he was.

Xiao Chiye suddenly plucked another thought out of that deep-seated wariness he carried. He studied Shen Zechuan, like a great beast observing its prey. Shen Zechuan was not invincible. Beyond their cryptic challenges and dread of each other, they shared the inexplicable empathy of fellow sufferers.

In the dream, Shen Zechuan was weary. He no longer cried in these visions, nor struggled to dig through the corpses. He had seen through the nightmare. He already knew Ji Mu was dead.

Hurry up.

He watched the scene dispassionately.

Get it over with.

He urged both the Biansha Horsemen and the dead on ruthlessly, wanting the blood to spill faster and the snow to fall harder. How else would this nightmare end? He no longer had any fear. The blood had eaten through his flesh, down to his marrow. He was a stray dog feeding on rotting meat and filthy water, the hatred he received the only evidence of his existence.

Shen Zechuan's eyes flew open, and he reached out a hand that braced against Xiao Chiye's chest. A brief moment later, even as cold sweat covered him, he asked calmly, "Can't sleep?"

Xiao Chiye's chest was searing. He could feel the chill of Shen Zechuan's palm through the thin fabric. "I ate too much."

"Someone more faint of heart would be scared to death to open his eyes in the middle of the night and find someone right above him," Shen Zechuan said.

"I heard you calling my name," Xiao Chiye lied without batting an eyelid. "I had to see if you were cursing me."

"If I wanted to curse you, I wouldn't do it in my dreams." Scorched by the heat of Xiao Chiye's body, Shen Zechuan retracted his fingers.

But Xiao Chiye pressed Shen Zechuan's hand back to his chest. "Are you cold?"

Shen Zechuan's temples were soaked with sweat. He smiled. "Yeah. I'm freezing."

He had reverted back to that alluring Shen Lanzhou, though it was clear he didn't care in the least whether Xiao Chiye was tempted. This kind of ability was innate; it came to him naturally. He was a terrible person.

Xiao Chiye gripped Shen Zechuan's hands and pinned them above his head. Surrounded by Shen Zechuan's scent in the darkness, he said, "You sleep in my bed. You know very well what I think about every night. You call me impressive, but Shen Lanzhou, the impressive one is you."

"Ah. What's to be done, then?" Shen Zechuan's voice was a little hoarse. He said nonchalantly, "I didn't do anything."

"But *I* want to." Xiao Chiye leaned in and stared down at him. "I want to do it."

"Choose some other death for me." Shen Zechuan allowed Xiao Chiye to gather his wrists into one hand. "Dying in bed is too embarrassing."

"I changed my mind." Xiao Chiye brushed aside Shen Zechuan's damp hair with the hand he'd freed as if examining a newly purchased jewel. "I don't want you to die."

"I advise you not to bite this neck," Shen Zechuan said.

"Lanzhou." Xiao Chiye sighed his name and jested, "If I don't, will you let me off for the rest?"

Shen Zechuan looked at him.

"Is it fun teasing me?" Xiao Chiye asked.

"Yeah." Shen Zechuan sensed Xiao Chiye gradually closing in. "It's fun to see the pitiful look of a little lost wolf."

"Then, let's have even more fun," Xiao Chiye said. "The empress dowager has been biding her time without making a move. What did she promise you? Throw it away, Lanzhou, and I'll give you much, much more."

"Uh-huh." Shen Zechuan laughed. "I'm guessing freedom is not among the things you're offering. Maybe you don't know, Xiao Er, but everything you want is written in your eyes. And at this moment, you want to chain me up, am I right?"

"I want to forge a golden chain," Xiao Chiye said. "It's a pity this neck is so bare."

"Dog collars were first used to leash wolves," said Shen Zechuan. They were so close now they could hear each other's breathing. "I'd like to put a golden chain around your neck too. For every sentence you speak, I'll yank it once."

"Let's not." Xiao Chiye arched a brow. "With your salary, you wouldn't be able to afford it even if you emptied your pockets."

The tips of their noses were about to touch. Xiao Chiye's thumb ring was digging into Shen Zechuan's wrist, already red in his grip.

Xiao Chiye continued, "Since it's—"

Shen Zechuan lifted his head and kissed Xiao Chiye's lips. The soft touch was accompanied by icy derision. "Want to go wild with abandon?" There was a madness in Shen Zechuan's eyes as he murmured, "Do you dare? Try tearing me apart, Xiao Er. See if I care."

The tightly wound string of Xiao Chiye's control finally snapped, and those tempestuous waves of emotion rushed out with the force of the tide. In answer to this mockery and provocation, he ruthlessly pinned Shen Zechuan down and ravaged him with kisses as sharp as bites.

Lust entangled with murderous intent; hatred entangled with pity. Which of them was more contemptible, which more pathetic? Their mouths opened to each other, wet and hot; where Xiao Chiye kissed Shen Zechuan, Shen Zechuan gave his all in response. The sound of ragged breath carried between tongue and teeth as two wayward souls met the flames of lust and were consumed.

Suddenly releasing his grip on Shen Zechuan's wrists, Xiao Chiye lifted Shen Zechuan's back as he tried to press them closer together, to eliminate the last whisper of distance between their bodies.

So let's hate each other.

Each would stain the other, letting mutual hatred spin a thread that couldn't be severed. It was too agonizing to live like this, alone, with only the snow to listen to their howls in the night. They had no one to lean on but each other—so why not tear into each other until they were bloody?

This life was already rotten enough.

LANZHOU (PART 1)

WITH SHEN ZECHUAN'S CLOTHES shoved out of the way, his skin spilled out like moonlight under Xiao Chiye's hands, ice-cold to the touch. There were no soft caresses, only desperate need. Shen Zechuan was a pool of spring water, slipping through Xiao Chiye's fingers and melting into the thick darkness of night. Xiao Chiye struggled to brace himself before the tidal wave of desire and saw Shen Zechuan watching him as he gasped for breath.

In those eyes was none of the heat of lust. They only reflected Xiao Chiye's own absurd behavior.

Xiao Chiye felt a thrill cut through him like a blade. He rubbed at Shen Zechuan's skin until it rippled hot and pink under his fingers. He dragged Shen Zechuan down from high in the clouds and bound him in the crooks of his arms, pressing hard against him as he put his mouth everywhere he could reach. Biting down on the back of Shen Zechuan's neck was like taking a mouthful of the most intoxicating elixir.

The night had been soaked through, and now so too had the sheets; their tangled limbs dragged at the ruined bedclothes. Xiao Chiye's thrusts were urgent; within them, he gradually grasped at joy. He was a quick study, surrendering himself in that soft bank of clouds, rising only to fall again. In silence, he pushed hard into Shen Zechuan, so hard Shen Zechuan strained for breath, even as his neck arched fearlessly under Xiao Chiye's eyes.

Xiao Chiye kissed that neck and scooped up both of Shen Zechuan's knees. He was no longer a hypocrite pretending to be immune to lust. He was an ordinary man who stormed the enemy's den and went for the kill in the dark. He would make it impossible for Shen Zechuan to remember the Chashi Sinkhole; impossible for Shen Zechuan to forget this intense merging of bodies.

They had no lifesaving hopes to clutch at. This was a night of indulgence to break free of their misery. Pleasure blazed through their bodies like an inferno. Shen Zechuan reached out for the headboard, but Xiao Chiye dragged him back and locked him in his embrace.

"Go on, show me how feral you can be," Xiao Chiye breathed into his ear. "You wanted me to go wild with abandon, yet you dare to run? Don't you want to see which of us is more ruthless? I'm not afraid."

Shen Zechuan's cheek chafed against the sheets as he closed his eyes and gasped for breath. His expressions of pain, of being on the verge of collapse—on his face, all utterly captivated Xiao Chiye.

How did he blossom into such a tender sight?

Xiao Chiye took Shen Zechuan's chin and lifted it to capture his lips, giving him no chance to rest or catch his breath. Shen Zechuan shuddered at his touch; in that moment, Xiao Chiye released everything into him.

While Shen Zechuan was still trembling from the aftershock of his own climax, Xiao Chiye turned him over and thrust desperately in once more.

The cold wind howled outside the window. Only the sounds of ragged breathing cut through the darkness as Xiao Chiye kissed Shen Zechuan again and again.

He didn't want to surrender.

But he had already lost.

THE STORY CONTINUES IN

Ballad of Sword and Wine

VOLUME 2

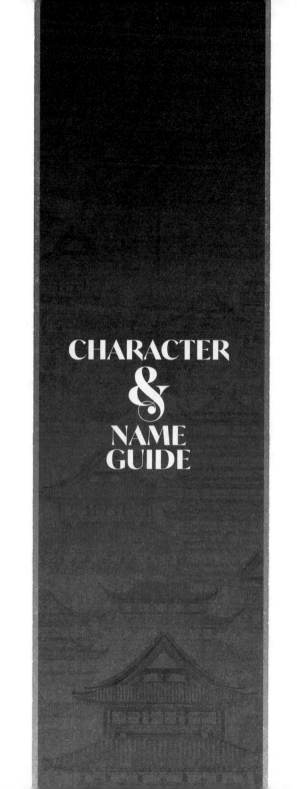

CHARACTER & NAME GUIDE

CHARACTERS

MAIN CHARACTERS

Shen Zechuan

沈泽川 SURNAME SHEN; GIVEN NAME ZECHUAN, "TO NOURISH THE RIVERS"

COURTESY NAME: Lanzhou (兰舟 / orchid; boat)

TITLE: Member of the Embroidered Uniform Guard

The eighth son of common birth to Shen Wei, the Prince of Jianxing. Due to his father's alleged collusion with the enemy during the invasion of Zhongbo that led to the slaughter of thirty thousand soldiers in the Chashi Sinkhole, he was sentenced to imprisonment and was obligated to pay his father's debt as the last surviving member of the Shen Clan.

Xiao Chiye

萧驰野 SURNAME XIAO; GIVEN NAME CHIYE, "TO RIDE ACROSS THE WILD"

COURTESY NAME: Ce'an (策安 / spur; peace)

TITLE: Supreme Commander of the Imperial Army

WEAPON: Wolfsfang (狼戾 / Langli): A single-edged executioner's blade forged by the best craftsman in Qidong.

The second and youngest son of lawful birth to Xiao Fangxu, the Prince of Libei. Sometimes called Xiao Er, or Second Young Master Xiao.

QUDU

CHEN YANG 晨阳 ("MORNING SUN"): Leader of Xiao Chiye's guards.

DING TAO 丁桃: Young guard to Xiao Chiye. He carries a little notebook everywhere he goes.

FENGQUAN 风泉: A junior eunuch, Pan Rugui's "grand-godson" and Mu Ru's younger brother.

GE QINGQING 葛青青: A member of the Embroidered Uniform Guard who served under Ji Gang when the latter was still the vice commander.

GU JIN 骨津: Guard to Xiao Chiye. He has excellent hearing.

HAI LIANGYI 海良宜 ("VIRTUOUS AND PROPER"): Courtesy name Renshi. Deputy Grand Secretary of the Grand Secretariat and teacher to Yao Wenyu.

HUA HEWEI 花鹤娓: The empress dowager, widow of the Guangcheng Emperor.

HUA SIQIAN 花思谦: Grand Secretary of the Grand Secretariat. Brother to the empress dowager and current head of the Hua Clan.

HUA XIANGYI 花香漪 ("RIPPLES OF FRAGRANCE"): The third lady of the Hua Clan, adored niece of the empress dowager.

JI GANG 纪纲: Shen Zechuan's shifu. Once the vice commander of the Embroidered Uniform Guard, he is one of the three adopted sons of Ji Wufan, the former chief commander of the Embroidered Uniform Guard.

JI LEI 纪雷: Chief Commander of the Embroidered Uniform Guard. One of the three adopted sons of Ji Wufan and "godson" to Pan Rugui.

LI JIANHENG 李建恒: Prince Chu, the idle younger brother of the Xiande Emperor.

LI JIANYUN 李建云: The Xiande Emperor. Son of the Guangcheng Emperor and elder brother to Li Jianheng.

MU RU: The daughter of a common family and sister to Fengquan. Adored by Li Jianheng.

PAN RUGUI 潘如贵: Director of Writ at the Directorate of Ceremonial Affairs, a high-ranking eunuch who closely serves the emperor.

QI HUILIAN 齐惠连: Grand mentor to the deceased Crown Prince of Yongyi, and later, Shen Zechuan's teacher.

QIAO TIANYA 乔天涯: The scruffy judge of the Embroidered Uniform Guard.

TANTAI HU 澹台虎 ("TIGER"): Vice Commander of the Imperial Army

XI GU'AN 奚固安: Military Commissioner of the Eight Great Battalions. Elder brother of Xi Hongxuan and first son of lawful birth in the Xi Clan.

XI HONGXUAN 奚鸿轩: Xi Gu'an's brother and the second son of lawful birth in the Xi Clan.

XUE XIUZHUO 薛修卓: Courtesy name Yanqing. Chief Supervising Secretary of the Office of Scrutiny for Revenue A capable young official and son of common birth in the Xue Clan.

YAO WENYU 姚温玉 ("GENTLE JADE"): Courtesy name Yuanzhuo. Hai Liangyi's only acknowledged pupil, said to be an extraordinary talent.

LIBEI

XIAO FANGXU 萧方旭 ("RISING SUN"): Prince of Libei. Father to Xiao Chiye and Xiao Jiming, and one of the past Four Great Generals of the empire of Zhou.

XIAO JIMING 萧既明 ("APPROACHING BRIGHTNESS"): Heir of Libei and commander of the Libei Armored Cavalry. Xiao Chiye's elder brother; he is married to Lu Yizhi, Lu Guangbai's sister. One of the current Four Great Generals, he's known as "Iron Horse on River Ice."

LU YIZHI 陆亦栀: Heir Consort of Libei. Xiao Jiming's wife and Lu Guangbai's sister.

ZHAO HUI 朝晖 ("MORNING SUN"): Xiao Jiming's dependable deputy general.

ZUO QIANQIU 左千秋: Xiao Chiye's shifu and one of the current Four Great Generals, he's known as "Thunder on Jade Terraces."

QIDONG

QI ZHUYIN 戚竹音 ("SOUND OF BAMBOO"): Grand Marshal of the Qidong Garrison Troops. One of the current Four Great Generals, Qi Zhuyin is known as "Windstorm through the Scorching Plains" and commands all five garrisons in the commanderies of Qidong.

QI SHIYU 戚时雨 ("TIMELY RAIN"): Qi Zhuyin's father and one of the past Four Great Generals of the empire of Zhou.

LU GUANGBAI 陆广白 ("EMPTY EXPANSE"): Commanding general of the Bianjun Commandery in Qidong. Brother to Lu Yizhi and one of the current Four Great Generals, known as "Beacon-Smoke and Rising Sand."

LU PINGYAN 陆平烟 ("PACIFY BEACON SMOKE"): Lu Guangbai's father and one of the past Four Great Generals of the Zhou empire.

PAST

SHEN WEI 沈卫 ("DEFENSE"): Prince of Jianxing and Shen Zechuan's father. Found guilty of colluding with the Biansha Horsemen to invade Zhongbo, he self-immolated to evade justice.

JI MU 纪暮: The only son of Ji Gang and Hua Pingting, and Shen Zechuan's adoptive elder brother.

HUA PINGTING 花娉婷: Wife of Ji Gang and mother of Ji Mu; Shen Zechuan's shiniang. She was born in the Hua Clan.

INSTITUTIONS

The Embroidered Uniform Guard 锦衣卫

The Embroidered Uniform Guard, sometimes referred to as the Scarlet Cavalry, are the elite bodyguards who report directly to the emperor. They are a non-military secret police and investigative force. The Embroidered Uniform Guard is organized into the Twelve Offices, which include the Carriage Office, Umbrella Office, Elephant-Training Office, and Horse-Training Office, among others. The Xiuchun saber, a single-edged blade, is their signature weapon.

The Imperial Army 禁军

The Imperial Army of Qudu was once the Imperial Guard of the eight cities and the impregnable fortress of the imperial palace in Qudu. However, with the rise to power of the Eight Great Battalions, their duties were reduced significantly, and the Imperial Army became a dumping ground for sons from old military households. They are one of the two major military powers in Qudu.

The Eight Great Battalions 八大营

Led by a member of the Eight Great Clans, the Eight Great Battalions are one of the two major military powers in Qudu, tasked with patrolling and defending Qudu against external forces. Responsible for defending Qudu, the capital city and heart of the Zhou empire, the Eight Great Battalions hold the empire's life in their hands.

The Eight Great Clans 八大家

The Eight Great Clans originated from the Eight Cities of Qudu. One clan holds sway in each city—the Xue Clan of Quancheng, Pan Clan of Dancheng, Xi Clan of Chuncheng, Fei Clan of Chuancheng, Hua Clan of Dicheng, Yao Clan of Jincheng, Han Clan of Wucheng, and Wei Clan of Cuocheng.

The Six Ministries 六部

The Six Ministries comprise the primary administrative structure of Great Zhou's government and include the Ministry of Works, Ministry of Justice, Ministry of Personnel, Ministry of Rites, Ministry of Revenue, and Ministry of War. Coordinated by the Grand Secretary of the Grand Secretariat, the heads of these ministries report directly to the emperor.

The Six Offices of Scrutiny is an independent agency set up to inspect and supervise the Six Ministries. It includes the Office of Scrutiny for Revenue.

The Libei Armored Cavalry 离北铁骑

The Libei Armored Cavalry is a heavy cavalry established by Xiao Fangxu to counter external foes at the northern front during the Yongyi era, when the Biansha Horsemen repeatedly assaulted Luoxia Pass. Currently commanded by Xiao Jiming, the Heir of Libei.

The Qidong Garrison Troops 启东守备军

Under the command of Qi Zhuyin, the Qidong Commandery Garrison Troops are stationed across five commanderies. They watch over the Qidong territories in the southern regions of the Zhou empire, which are led by the Qi Clan.

The Biansha Horsemen 边沙骑兵

The Biansha Horsemen are the aggressor forces against the empire of Zhou. The story begins with the aftermath of the war, where the Biansha Horsemen ravaged the six prefectures of Zhongbo and left them piled high with bodies. Also referred to in derogatory form as the "Biansha baldies."

NAMES GUIDE

NAMES, HONORIFICS, AND TITLES

Courtesy Names vs Given Names

Usually made up of two characters, a courtesy name is given to an individual when they come of age. Traditionally, this was at the age of twenty during one's crowning ceremony, but it can also be presented when an elder or teacher deems the recipient worthy. Though generally a male-only tradition, there is historical precedent for women adopting a courtesy name after marriage. Courtesy names were a tradition reserved for the upper class.

It was considered disrespectful for one's peers of the same generation to address someone by their given name, especially in formal or written communication. Use of one's given name was reserved only for elders, close friends, and spouses.

This practice is no longer used in modern China but is commonly seen in historically inspired media. As such, many characters have more than one name. Its implementation in novels is irregular and is often treated malleably for the sake of storytelling.

Diminutives, nicknames, and name tags

A-: Friendly diminutive. Always a prefix. Usually for monosyllabic names, or one syllable out of a two-syllable name.

XIAO-: A diminutive prefix meaning "little."

-ER: An affectionate diminutive suffix added to names, literally "son" or "child." Not to be confused with Xiao Chiye's nickname, Xiao Er, in which "er" (二) means "second."

LAO-: A diminutive prefix meaning "old."

-ZI: Affectionate suffix meaning "son" or "child."

-XIONG: A word meaning elder brother. It can be attached as a suffix to address an older male peer.

Family

DI/DIDI: Younger brother or a younger male friend.

GE/GEGE/DAGE: Older brother or an older male friend.

JIE/JIEJIE: Older sister or an older female friend.

-SHU: A suffix meaning "uncle." Can be used to address unrelated older men.

Martial Arts and Tutelage

SHIFU: Teacher or master, usually used when referring to the martial arts.

SHIXIONG: Older martial brother, used for older disciples or classmates.

SHIDI: Younger martial brother, used for younger disciples or classmates.

SHISHU: Martial uncle, used to address someone who studied under the same master (or shifu) as one's own master.

SHINIANG: The wife of one's shifu.

XIANSHENG: Teacher of academics.

Other

GONGZI: Young man from an affluent household.

-NIANGNIANG: Term of address for the empress or an imperial concubine, can be standalone or attached to a name as a suffix.

-GONGGONG: Term of address for a eunuch.

SHIZI: Title for the heir apparent of a feudal prince.

LAO-ZUZONG: Literally "old ancestor," an intimate and respectful term of address from a junior eunuch to a more senior eunuch.

PRONUNCIATION GUIDE

Mandarin Chinese is the official state language of mainland China, and pinyin is the official system of romanization in which it is written. As Mandarin is a tonal language, pinyin uses diacritical marks (e.g., ā, á, ǎ, à) to indicate these tonal inflections. Most words use one of four tones, though some are a neutral tone. Furthermore, regional variance can change the way native Chinese speakers pronounce the same word. For those reasons and more, please consider the guide below a simplified introduction to pronunciation of select character names and sounds from the world of *Ballad of Sword and Wine.*

More resources are available at sevenseasdanmei.com

NAMES

Qiāng Jìn Jiǔ

Qiāng: Q as in **ch**eese, iang as in **young**

Jìn as in **jean**

Jiǔ as in **geo**de

Shěn Zéchuān

Shěn: Sh as in **shh**, en as in reas**on**

Zé: Z as in **z**oom, e as in **uh**

Chuān: Chu as in **choo**se, an as in **un**derstand

Shěn Lánzhōu
Lan as in **lun**ge
Zhōu: Zh as in lun**ge**, ou as in **oh**

Xiāo Chíyě
Xiāo: Xi as in **ch**ic, ao as in **ou**ch
Chí: Chi as in **chi**rp
Ye as in **ye**s

Xiāo Cè'ān
Cè: C as in pan**ts,** e as in **uh**
an as in **un**derstand

GENERAL CONSONANTS

Some Mandarin Chinese consonants sound very similar, such as z/c/s and zh/ch/sh. Audio samples will provide the best opportunity to learn the difference between them.

X: somewhere between the **sh** in **sh**eep and **s** in **s**ilk
Q: a very aspirated **ch** as in **ch**arm
C: **ts** as in pan**ts**
Z: **z** as in **z**oom
S: **s** as in **s**ilk
CH: **ch** as in **ch**arm
ZH: **dg** as in do**dg**e
SH: **sh** as in **sh**ave
G: hard **g** as in **g**raphic

GENERAL VOWELS

The pronunciation of a vowel may depend on its preceding consonant. For example, the "i" in "shi" is distinct from the "i" in "di." Vowel pronunciation may also change depending on where the vowel appears in a word, for example the "i" in "shi" versus the "i" in "ting." Finally, compound vowels are often—though not always—pronounced as conjoined but separate vowels. You'll find a few of the trickier compounds below.

IU: as in **ewe**

IE: **ye** as in **yes**

UO: **war** as in **war**m

GLOSSARY

GLOSSARY

CONCUBINES AND THE IMPERIAL HAREM: In ancient China, it was common practice for a wealthy man to take women as concubines in addition to his wife. They were expected to live with him and bear him children. Generally speaking, a greater number of concubines correlated to higher social status; hence a wealthy merchant might have two or three concubines, while an emperor might have tens or even a hundred.

The imperial harem had its own ranking system. The exact details vary over the course of history, but can generally be divided into three overarching ranks: the empress, consorts, and concubines. The status of a prince or princess's mother is an important factor in their status in the imperial family, in addition to birth order and their own personal merits. Given the patrilineal rules of succession, the birth of a son could also elevate the mother's status, leading to fierce, oftentimes deadly, competition amongst ambitious members of the imperial harem.

CUT-SLEEVE: A slang term for a gay man, which comes from a tale about Emperor Ai's love for, and relationship with, a male court official in the Han dynasty. The emperor was called to the morning assembly, but his lover was asleep on his robe. Rather than wake him, the emperor cut off his own sleeve.

DUANWU FESTIVAL: Commonly known in English as the Dragon Boat Festival or Double Fifth festival, the Duanwu Festival occurs on the fifth day of the fifth month in the lunar calendar, and is celebrated by holding dragon boat races and eating sticky rice dumplings wrapped in bamboo leaves (粽子 / zongzi). In some parts of China, it's a common practice to hang up willow branches or Chinese mugwort on this day to ward off evil and sickness.

EASTERN PEARLS: Sourced from the northeastern regions of China, eastern pearls are freshwater pearls. They are milkier and more opaque in color than saltwater pearls, but more precious because they're rarer. In the Qing dynasty, they were worn only by royalty.

ERA NAME: A designation for all or part of the reigning years when a given emperor was on the throne. This title is determined by the emperor when they ascend the throne, or upon starting a new era mid-reign, and can often be used to refer to both the era and the emperor himself.

EUNUCHS: Courtiers castrated at a young age and bound to serve in the imperial palace. They occupied many roles within the palace, from simple attendants to highly regarded positions of power. In the Ming dynasty, the eunuchs were also part of Eastern Depot, a surveillance and tactical force created by the emperor to spy on officials and suppress political opposition.

GODPARENTAGE RELATIONSHIPS: Similar to the idea of "sworn brothers," godparentage relationships are nominal familial relationships entered into by non-blood-related parties for a variety of reasons. Entering into such a relationship meant that the godson acknowledged filial duties toward their godparent, who in turn took on a role of mentorship and patronage toward their godchild.

HONGMEN BANQUET: A banquet set up with the aim of murdering the guest. Refers to a famous episode in 206 BC when future Han emperor Liu Bang escaped an attempted murder by his rival, Xiangyu.

IMPERIAL EXAMINATION SYSTEM: The system of examinations in ancient China that qualified someone for official service. It was a supposedly meritocratic system that allowed students from all backgrounds to rise up in society as a countering force to the nobility, but the extent to which this was true varied across time.

The imperial examination system was split into various levels. In the Ming and Qing dynasties, these were the provincial exam, metropolitan exam, and the palace exam. The top scholars at each examination level were known as the Jieyuan, Huiyuan, and Zhuangyuan respectively, and a scholar who emerged top at all three levels was known as the Sanyuan, or Triple Yuan, scholar.

INCENSE TIME: A measure of time in ancient China, referring to how long it takes for a single incense stick to burn. Inexact by nature, an incense time is commonly assumed to be about thirty minutes, though it can be anywhere from five minutes to an hour.

KOWTOW: The kowtow (叩头 / "knock head") is an act of prostration where one kneels and bows low enough that their forehead touches the ground. A show of deep respect and reverence that can also be used to beg, plead, or show sincerity; in severe circumstances, it's common for the supplicant's forehead to end up bloody and bruised.

LAWFUL AND COMMON BIRTH HIERARCHY: Upper-class men in ancient China often took multiple wives. Only one would be the official wife, and her lawful sons would take precedence over the common sons of the concubines. Sons of lawful birth were prioritized in matters of inheritance. They also had higher social status and often received better treatment compared to the other common sons born to concubines or mistresses.

LONGYOU MERCHANTS: Historically, an influential group of merchants and businessmen. The Longyou Group (龙游商帮) was famous during the Ming and Qing dynasties for its operations in the jewelry, book-publishing, and paper-making industries.

MANDARIN SQUARES: Large embroidered badges worn by civil officials of the imperial court. Depending on their pattern, which might incorporate real or mythical animals, flowers, and other symbols, these badges could indicate either the rank of the wearer, the season, or the occasion on which the badge was worn. For example, a mandarin square with a double gourd was worn between the twenty-third day of the twelfth month and the New Year. Similarly, an emblem of tiger, mugwort, and five poisons (centipede, scorpion, toad, lizard, snake) was worn in celebration of the Duanwu Festival and Summer Solstice.

NEW YEAR AND SPRING FESTIVAL: The Lunar New Year, or Spring Festival, occurs on the first day of the first month of the lunar calendar. For the common people, this is an annual opportunity to gather with loved ones, indulge in meat that is normally too expensive for their tables, and put on new clothes.

OFFICIALS: Civil and military officials were classified in nine hierarchic grades, with grade one being the highest rank. Their salaries ranged according to their rank. The imperial examination was one path to becoming a court official, the other being referral by someone in a position of power, such as a noble, a eunuch, or another official.

QINGGONG: Literally "lightness technique," qinggong (轻功) refers to the martial arts skill of moving swiftly and lightly from one point to another, often so nimbly it looks like one is flying through the air. In wuxia and xianxia settings, characters use qinggong to leap great distances and heights.

TITLES OF NOBILITY: Titles of nobility were an important feature of the traditional social structure of Imperial China. While the conferral and organization of specific titles evolved over time, in *Ballad of Sword and Wine*, such titles can be either inherited or conferred by the emperor.

Significantly, conferred titles differ from imperial-born status. For example, an imperial prince like Li Jianheng is a bona fide royal prince with the surname Li (the surname of the founding Zhou emperor), whereas conferred princes like the Prince of Jianxing and Prince of Libei are titled and salaried officials of the imperial bureaucracy. Typically, these titles and lands conferred by the emperor can be inherited by their descendants—traditionally the eldest son of lawful birth—but do not place them in the line of succession for the throne.

WEIQI: Also known by its Japanese name, *go*, weiqi is the oldest known board game in human history. The board consists of a nineteen-by-nineteen grid upon which opponents play unmarked black and white stones as game pieces to claim territory.

YAMEN: An administrative office or department, or residence of a government official. For example, that of a local district magistrate or prefectural prefect. This is not the same as the Twenty-Four Yamen run by the eunuchs.

YELLOW REGISTER: In the Ming and Qing dynasties, households were classified and recorded into the huangce (黄册) or yellow registers according to their occupation. These records provided basic data for taxation and military recruitment. It was mainly divided into three categories: civilian, military, and trade households.